TRUST YOUR EYES

TRUST YOUR EYES

Linwood Barclay

**WINDSOR
PARAGON**

First published 2012
by Orion Books
This Large Print edition published 2013
by AudioGO Ltd
by arrangement with
The Orion Publishing Group

Hardcover   ISBN: 978 1 4713 5337 6
Softcover   ISBN: 978 1 4713 5338 3

British Library Cataloguing in Publication Data available

Printed and bound in Great Britain by
T J International Limited

For my brother

PROLOGUE

It was just by chance he turned down Orchard Street and saw the window when he did. It easily could have been a week from now, or a month, even a year. But it turned out that this was going to be the day.

Sure, he would have wandered down here eventually. Sooner or later, when he got to a new city, he hit every street. He always started out intending to be methodical about it — follow one street from beginning to end, then head over a block and backtrack on a parallel street, like doing the aisles in a grocery store — but then he'd get to a cross street and something would catch his eye, and all good intentions would be abandoned.

That was how it turned out when he got to Manhattan, even though, of all the cities he'd visited, it was the one that most lent itself to being explored in an orderly fashion, at least those parts of the city north of Fourteenth Street, which was laid out in that perfect grid of streets and avenues. South of that, once you got into the West Village and Greenwich Village and SoHo and Chinatown, well, it was chaos down there, but that didn't bother him. It certainly wasn't any worse than in London or Rome or Paris or even Boston's North End, and he'd loved exploring those cities.

He'd turned south onto Orchard from Delancey, but his actual starting point for this stroll had been Spring and Mulberry. He'd gone south to Grand, west to Crosby, north back to Prince, east to Elizabeth, south to Kenmare, then east, continuing along Delancey, then, when he got to Orchard, decided to hang a right.

It was a beautiful street. Not in the sense that there were gardens and fountains and lush trees lining the sidewalk. Not beautiful like, say, Vaci Street in Budapest, or the Avenue des Champs-Élysées in Paris, or Lombard Street in San Francisco, but it was a street rich in texture and steeped in history. Narrow, one-way, running north. Old brick tenement buildings, few more than five stories, many only three or four, dating back a century and a half. A street that represented so many different times in the city's history. The buildings, with their skeletal fire escapes clinging to the fronts, reflected the Italianate style popular in the mid-to-late nineteenth century, with arches above the windows, stone lintels projecting outward, ornate carved leaves in the trim work, but their ground floors housed everything from trendy cafés to designer dress shops. There were older, more conventional businesses, too. A uniform shop, a real estate agent, a hair salon, a gallery, a place that sold luggage. Many of the closed stores were shielded with drawn-down steel doors.

He meandered down the center of the street, not particularly worried about traffic. It wasn't a problem right now. He always found you got the sense of a place by walking down the middle of the road. It offered the best vantage point. You could look ahead or from side to side, or whirl around 360 degrees and see where you'd been. It was good to know your surroundings and your options, in case you had to make a fast move.

Because the building blocks of a city were his primary concern — its architecture, its layout, its infrastructure — he paid little attention to the people he came across in his travels. He didn't strike up conversations. He wasn't interested in saying so much as hello to that redheaded woman standing on the corner, smoking a cigarette. He didn't care what kind of fashion statement she was trying to make with her leather jacket, short skirt, and what looked like deliberately laddered black tights. He wasn't going to ask the athletic-looking woman in the black baseball cap who was darting across the street in front of him how she thought the Yankees were going to do this year. He never watched baseball, and cared nothing about it. And he was not about to ask why a dozen people with guidebooks sticking out of their pockets were listening to one woman in the center of the group, although he guessed she was a tour guide of some sort.

When he got to Broome Street he spotted an inviting-looking restaurant on the southeast corner with small white tables and yellow plastic chairs set up on the sidewalk. But there was no one sitting outside. The sign in the window read: "Come in and get warm." He went up close, peering through the glass at the people drinking coffee, working on laptops, reading newspapers.

Reflected in the restaurant's window was that car he'd been seeing throughout his travels. Nondescript sedan. Maybe a Civic. With the apparatus on the roof. He'd seen the car before. Many times. If he didn't know better, he'd think it was following him. He put it out of his mind and looked through the glass, into the restaurant.

He wished it were possible for him to go inside and have a latte or a cappuccino. He could almost smell the coffee. But he had to keep going. So much of the world to see and so little time. Tomorrow he had plans to be in Montreal, and, depending how much ground he covered there, maybe Madrid the day after.

But he would remember this place. The sign in the window, the tables and chairs outside. The other businesses on Orchard. The narrow alleyways between the buildings. Plus everything that he had seen on Spring and Mulberry and Grand and Crosby and Prince and Elizabeth and Kenmare and Delancey.

He would remember it all.

He was about a third of the way down the block from the Broome cross street when he made that upward glance.

That was really where the element of chance entered into it. It wasn't at all remarkable that he ended up on Orchard. It was the fact that he looked above the storefronts. He didn't always do that. He scoped out the businesses and read the signs in their windows, studied the people in the coffee shops, made a mental note of the numbers above the doors, but he didn't always cast his eyes above the first or second floors. Sometimes he forgot, and sometimes he was short of time. He might easily have gone down this street and never glanced upon that particular window of that particular tenement building.

Then again, he thought, chance might have had nothing to do with it. Maybe he was meant to see this window. Maybe, in some strange way, it was a test. To determine whether he was ready, even though he believed he was. But those who would make

11

use of his talents — they might need some convincing before taking him on.

The window was on the third floor, above a place that sold cigarettes and newspapers — there was that car again, reflected in the window — and a second shop specializing in women's scarves. It was divided into two panes. An air-conditioning unit stuck out from the sill, taking up half of the lower pane. Something white, above the air conditioner, had caught his eye.

At first, it looked like one of those white Styrofoam heads department stores and hair salons use to display wigs. He thought, *Isn't that funny, to put one of those in a window.* A bald, featureless white head keeping watch over Orchard Street. He supposed that in New York you could find just about anything in someone's window. If it had been his, he would have at least put a pair of sunglasses on it, to give the head some personality. A hint of whimsy. Although, he had to admit, people did not tend to think of him as whimsical.

But the more he looked at it, the less sure he was that it was a white foam head. The surface appeared more shimmery, slippery even. Perhaps plastic, like the bags the grocery stores used, or a dry cleaning bag, but not one of the clear ones.

He attempted to get a better look, zero in.

The thing was, this white, almost circular

object in the window still had the shape of a head. The plastic material strained against a protuberance that could only be a nose. It hugged tight across what appeared to be a brow near the top, a chin at the bottom. There was even a trace of mouth, the lips open as though gasping for air.

Or screaming.

It was, he thought, as though a white stocking had been pulled down over someone's head. But the material's sheen still made him think it was plastic.

That wasn't a very smart thing for someone to do. To put a plastic bag over their head. You could suffocate yourself doing something stupid like that.

A person would have to be pulling on the plastic bag, twisting it from behind, to make it conform so tightly to the contours of their face. But he didn't see this person's arms or hands doing anything like that.

Which made him wonder if someone else was doing it.

Oh. Oh, no.

Was that what he was witnessing? Someone putting a bag over another person's head? Cutting off their air supply? Smothering them? Could this account for the mouth that seemed to be struggling for air?

Who was this happening to? A man? A woman? And who was doing it to them?

Suddenly he was thinking about the boy in

13

the window. A different window. Many years ago.

But the person in this window, right now, didn't look like a boy, or a girl. This was an adult.

An adult whose life was coming to an end.

That certainly was how it looked to him.

He felt his heart begin to beat more quickly. He'd seen things before on his travels. Things that weren't right.

But they were minor compared to this. Never a murder.

That's what he was sure this was.

He didn't shout out. He didn't reach into his jacket for a cell phone to call 911. He didn't spring into the nearest shop and tell someone to call the police. He didn't charge into the building and race up two flights of stairs in a bid to stop what was happening behind this third-floor window.

All he did was reach out, tentatively, as though it were possible to touch the smothered face of this person on the third floor, to feel what was wrapped around his or her head, make some sort of assessment as to —

Knock knock.

Then, maybe then, he'd have a better idea what was actually happening to this person in —

Knock knock.

He'd been so transfixed by what was happening at the window that he did not, at first, realize someone was trying to get his attention. Someone was at the door.

He took his hand off the mouse, spun around in his padded computer chair, and said, "Yes?"

The door opened an inch. From the hallway, someone said, "Get your ass down for dinner, Thomas."

"What are we having?" he asked.

"Burgers. From the barbecue."

The man sitting in the computer chair said flatly, "Okay."

He spun around and resumed looking at the frozen image of the window on his oversized computer monitor. The blurry, white, wrapped head suspended there. A ghostly visage.

Had anyone seen this at the time? Had anyone looked up?

No one had seen the boy when he was in the window. No one had looked up. No one had helped him.

The man left the image on his screen so he could study it more closely when he came back up after dinner. Then he'd make a decision about what to do.

Two Weeks
Earlier

ONE

"Come on in, Ray."

Harry Peyton shook my hand and led me into his law office, pointing me toward the red leather chair opposite his desk. About the same age as my father, he looked years younger than Dad had. He was six feet, trim, with a head smooth as a melon. Baldness aged some guys, but not Harry. He was a long-distance runner, and his expensive suit fit him like a second skin. His desk was a testament to orderliness. A computer monitor, keyboard, one of the latest smartphones. And one legal file folder. The rest of the desk was as clean as a canvas before the first brushstroke.

"Again, I'm so sorry," Harry said. "There are a hundred things one could say about your dad, but Reverend Clayton summed it up nicely. Adam Kilbride was a good man."

I forced a smile. "Yeah, the minister did a pretty good job, considering he'd never met Dad. He wasn't much of a churchgoer. I

19

guess we were lucky to find anyone to preside. Thanks for coming to the service. It almost got us up to a dozen."

Eleven people showed up for the funeral, and that was counting the minister and myself. There was Harry, and three of Dad's coworkers from the company he'd worked for, including his onetime boss, Len Prentice, and Len's wife, Marie. Also there were a friend of Dad's who ran a hardware store in Promise Falls before the Home Depot opened up outside of town and put him out of business, Dad's younger brother Ted and his wife, Roberta, from Cleveland, and a woman named Hannah whose last name I never got who lived just down the road from Dad. And there was a woman Thomas and I knew from high school, Julie McGill, who worked for the local paper, the *Promise Falls Standard*, and had written the story about Dad's accident. She hadn't come to report on the funeral — how Dad died had made him a small news item, but he wasn't citizen of the year or head of the Rotary or anything. His service to the community was not newsworthy. Julie had come to pay her respects, simple as that.

The funeral home had a lot of egg salad sandwiches left over. They insisted I take some back to the house for my brother. I'd explained his absence by saying he wasn't feeling well, but no one, at least no one who knew my brother, believed it. I was tempted to pitch the sandwiches out the car window on the way home. Let the birds enjoy them, instead of my brother. But I didn't. I took them home, and they all got eaten.

"I'd hoped your brother might have come," Harry said. "It's been some time since I've seen him." At first I thought he meant to this meeting, which puzzled me, since my brother was not an executor. Then I realized Harry meant the funeral.

"Yeah, well, I gave it my best shot," I said. "He wasn't really sick."

"I figured."

"I tried to talk him into it, but it was pointless."

Peyton shook his head sympathetically. "Your father, he tried to do his best by him. Just like when your mother — Rose, God bless her — was still with us. How long's it been?"

"She passed away in 2005."

"After that, it must have been even more difficult for him."

"He was still with P&L then," I said. Prentice and Long, the printers. "I think, maybe, after he took that early retirement not long after that, it got tougher. Being there, all the time. It got to him, but he wasn't the kind of man to run away from something." I bit my lip. "Mom, she found ways not to let it bother her, she had a way of accepting things, but it

21

was tougher for Dad."

"Adam was a young man, really," Harry said. "Sixty-two, for Christ's sake. I was stunned when I heard."

"Yeah, well, me, too," I said. "I don't know how many times Mom told him, over the years, that cutting grass on that steep hill, on the lawn tractor, was dangerous. But he always insisted he knew what he was doing. Thing is, that part of the property, it's way back of the house — you can't see it from the road or any of the neighbors' places. The ground slopes almost forty-five degrees down to the creek. Dad would mow along there sideways, leaning his body into the hill so the tractor wouldn't tip over."

"How long do they think your father was out there before they found him, Ray?"

"Dad probably went out to cut the grass after lunch, and wasn't discovered until nearly six. When the tractor flipped over on top of him, the top edge of the steering wheel landed across his middle" — I pointed to my own stomach — "you know, his abdomen, and it crushed his insides."

"Jesus," Harry said. He touched his own stomach, imagining the pain my father must have felt for God knew how long.

I didn't have much to add to that.

"He was a year younger than me," Harry said, wincing. "We'd get together for a drink now and then. Back when Rose was alive, we'd play a round of golf every once in a while. But he didn't feel he could leave your brother on his own for the time it took to play eighteen holes."

"Dad wasn't very good at it, anyway," I said.

Harry smiled ruefully. "I'm not going to lie. Not a bad putter, but he couldn't drive worth a shit."

I laughed. "Yeah."

"But once Rose passed, your dad didn't even have time to hit a bucket of balls at the driving range."

"He spoke highly of you," I said. "You were always a friend first, and his lawyer second." They'd known each other at least twenty-five years, back to when Harry was going through a divorce and, after giving his house to his ex-wife, lived for a time above a shoe store here in downtown Promise Falls, in upstate New York. Harry used to joke that he had a lot of nerve, offering his services as a divorce attorney, after getting taken to the cleaners during his own.

Harry's phone emitted a single chime, indicating an e-mail had landed, but he didn't even glance at it.

"Last time I talked to Dad," I said, nodding at the phone, "he was thinking about getting one of those. He had a phone that would take pictures, but it was an old one, and it didn't take very good ones. And he wanted a phone that would be easy for sending e-mails."

"All this new high-tech stuff never scared Adam," Harry said, then clapped his hands together, signaling it was time to move on to why I was here. "You were saying, at the funeral, that you've still got the studio, in Burlington?" I lived across the state line, in Vermont.

"Yeah," I said.

"Work's good?"

"Not bad. The industry's changing."

"I saw one of your drawings — is that what you call them?"

"Sure," I said. "Illustrations. Caricatures."

"Saw one in the *New York Times Book Review* a few weeks back. I can always tell your style. The people all have really big noggins and the tiny bodies, looks like their heads would make 'em fall over. And they all have these rounded edges. I love how you shade their skin tones and everything. How do you do that?"

"Airbrush," I said.

"You do a lot of work for the *Times*?"

"Not as much as I used to. It's a lot easier to run a file pic than hire someone to do an illustration from scratch. Papers and magazines are cutting back. I'm doing more for Web sites these days."

"You design those things? Web sites?"

"No. I do artwork for them and hand it off to the Web site builders."

24

"I would have thought, doing stuff for magazines and newspapers in New York and Washington, you'd have to live there, but I guess these days, it doesn't much matter."

"Anything you can't scan and e-mail, you can FedEx," I said. When I said nothing else, Harry opened the file on his desk and studied the papers inside.

"Ray, I take it you've seen the will your father drew up," he said.

"Yes."

"He hadn't updated it in a long time. Made a couple of changes after your mother died. The thing is, I ran into him one day. He was sitting there in a booth at Kelly's having a coffee and he offered to buy me one. He was by himself, at a table by the window, staring out at the street, looking at the *Standard* but not really reading it. I'd see him in there every once in a while, like he just needed time alone, out of the house. Anyway, he waved me over and said he was thinking of amending it, his will, that is, that he might need to make some special provisions, but he never got around to it."

"I didn't know that," I said, "but I guess I'm not surprised. What with how things have been with my brother, I could see him wanting to give more to one than the other."

"I think, to be honest, if Adam had come in here wanting to make some changes, I might have tried talking him out of anything that

25

would have favored one child over the other. I'd have told him, the best thing to do is treat all your kids the same. Otherwise, that's going to lead to resentment after you're gone. Of course, it still would've been his decision. But while this existing will is fairly straightforward, there are things you're going to have to think about."

I was picturing my father, sitting in the diner, the rest of the booth unoccupied. He'd had plenty of time to himself in the house since Mom died, even if, technically speaking, he wasn't alone. He didn't have to leave the house for solitude. But I could understand his need to escape. Sometimes you needed to know that you were absolutely alone. You needed a change of scenery. It made me sad, thinking about it.

"So I guess the way it is now, then," I said, "is fifty-fifty. Once the estate is liquidated, half goes to me and half goes to my brother."

"Yes. Property, and investments."

"About a hundred thousand there," I said. "What he and Mom had managed to scrape together for retirement. They'd saved for years. They never spent anything on themselves. He could have made a hundred grand last him till the day he died." I caught myself. "If he'd lived another twenty or thirty years, I mean. And I gather there's a life insurance policy that's fairly small."

Harry Peyton nodded and leaned back in

his chair, lacing his fingers at the back of his head. He sucked in some air between his teeth. "You'll have to decide what to do about the house. You've every right to put it up for sale, split the proceeds with your brother. There's no mortgage on the place, and I'm guessing you could get three, four hundred thou for it."

"About that," I said. "There's nearly sixteen acres."

"Which, if you got that, would leave each of you with about a quarter million, give or take. That's not a bad chunk of change, all things considered. How old are you, Ray?"

"Thirty-seven."

"And your brother, he's two years younger, that right?"

"Yes."

Peyton nodded slowly. "Invested wisely, it might be enough to last him quite a few years, but he's still a young man. And he's got a while before he hits Social Security. He's not really employable, from what your dad told me."

I hesitated. "That's fair."

"For you, well, the money's a different thing. You could invest it, buy a bigger house for the time when you have — I know you're not married now, Ray, but someday, you meet someone, you have kids —"

"I know," I said. I'd come close to getting married, a couple of times, in my twenties, but it never happened. "I don't see any kids on the horizon."

"You never know." He waved his hand again. "None of my business, anyway, except in an unofficial capacity, because I think your dad hoped I'd look out for you boys, offer you guidance where I could." He laughed. "You're hardly boys anymore, of course. It's been a long time since that was the case."

"Appreciate it, Harry."

"The point I'm making, Ray, is for you it's a minor windfall, but you'd have made out fine without it. You make a good living, and if your work takes a downturn, you'll find something else, land on your feet. But for your brother, this inheritance is all he'll ever have. He might need the money from the house to keep him afloat, provided he can find a place, someplace suitable, where his rent's subsidized or something."

"I've been thinking about that," I said.

"What I'm wondering is, will you be able to get him out of the house? I mean, you know, not just for the afternoon, but permanently?"

I looked about the room, as though I might find the answer. "I don't know. It's not like he's — what's the word — agoraphobic? Dad managed to get him out, once in a while. Mostly for his doctor's appointments." I found it hard to say the word "psychiatrist," but Harry knew. "It's not getting him outside

28

that's the problem. It's prying him away from the keyboard. Whenever he and Dad went out, they both returned home pretty frazzled. Moving him out, settling him in someplace else, it's not something I look forward to."

Harry said, "Well, I'll get the ball rolling here. The great thing for you, being an executor, is there really isn't all that much to do, except to come in here the odd time and sign some papers. There'll be the occasional item I'll need your take on, and I'll have Alice give you a dingle. You might want to get the property appraised, tell you what it could go for." He ruffled through his papers. "I got all your numbers and e-mail address here I think."

"Yeah," I said.

"And you probably knew — your dad had sent me a copy of the policy for his files — that there was an accidental death provision in his life insurance."

"I didn't know that."

"Another fifty thousand. A little something else to go into the pot." Harry paused while I digested this news. "So, you're going to be hanging around for a while, then, before you head back to Burlington?"

"Until I sort things out."

We were done, at least for now. As Harry led me out of the office, he put his hand on my arm.

"Ray," he said tentatively, "do you think if

your brother had noticed how long it had been since your dad had been in the house, if he'd gone out looking for him a little sooner, it would have made any difference?"

I'd asked myself the same question. Dad, pinned to the ground just over the hill, probably several hours before my brother found him. There had to have been quite a racket when it happened. The tractor flipping over, the rotating blades roaring.

Did Dad scream? And if he had, would he have been heard over the noise of the mower? Would any of the sounds have carried up over the hill to the house?

My brother probably never heard a thing.

"I tell myself it wouldn't have made any difference," I said. "There's no point thinking otherwise."

Harry nodded understandingly. "I guess that's the best way to look at it. What's done is done. No turning back the clock." I wondered if Harry was going to offer up another cliché, but instead he said, "He's really off in his own little world, isn't he?"

"You don't know the half of it," I said.

Two

I got into the car and drove back to my father's house.

After Mom had died, I'd still thought of it for the longest time as my parents' place, even though Dad was living there without her. It took a year or so for me to move past that. With Dad dead less than a week, I knew it was going to take a while before I could think of it as anything but his place.

But it wasn't. Not anymore. It was mine.

And my brother's.

I'd never lived here. There was a guest room where I always slept when I came to visit, but there were no mementoes from my childhood here. No dresser drawer with stashes of *Playboy* and *Penthouse*, no model cars on the shelves, no posters on the walls. My parents had bought this place when I was twenty-one. I'd already moved out of our house on Stonywood Drive, in the heart of Promise Falls. My parents had hoped one of their sons would make something of himself, but put that dream on hold when I bailed on my university career in Albany and got a job at a Beekman Street art gallery in Saratoga Springs.

My parents were never farmers, but when they'd spotted this place, it fit the bill. First, it was out in the country, several hundred yards from the closest neighbor. They'd have their privacy. Some isolation. It reduced the likelihood of another incident.

Second, it was still a relatively short drive to work for Dad. But instead of driving into Promise Falls, through the downtown, and out the other side, he'd take the bypass they finished back in the late 1970s. Dad liked working for P&L. He didn't want to look for something closer to home.

Third, the house was charming, with its dormer windows and wraparound porch. Mom had loved to sit out there, three seasons out of the year. The place came with a barn, which Dad didn't have much need for, other than to store tools and park the lawn tractor. But they both loved the look of the structure, even if it wasn't storing hay every fall.

There was a lot of property, but my parents maintained only about two acres of it. Behind the house, the yard stretched out flat for about sixty feet, then sloped down and out of sight to a creek that wound its way to the river that flowed into the center of town and cascaded over Promise Falls.

I'd only been down to the creek once since I'd come home. A task awaited me there, when I finally felt up to it.

Some of the flat and treeless land, beyond where Dad maintained it, was rented to neighboring farm interests. For years, that had provided my parents with a secondary — if nominal — income. The closest woods were across the highway. When you turned in off the main road and started up the drive, the house and barn sat on the horizon like a couple of boxes on a flatcar. Mom always said she liked a long driveway because when she saw someone turn in — which was not, she'd have been the first to admit, often — it gave her plenty of time to steel herself.

"People don't usually come to your door with good news," she'd said on more than one occasion. It had certainly been her experience, most notably when she was a young girl, and officials of the U.S. government had come to inform her mother that her father would not be coming home from Korea.

I nosed the car close to the steps that led up to the porch, parking my four-wheel-drive Audi Q5 next to Dad's ten-year-old Chrysler minivan. He didn't think much of my German wheels. He questioned supporting the economies of nations we once fought. "I suppose," he'd said a few months ago, "when they start importing cars from North Viet-

33

nam, you'll buy one of those." Since he was so concerned, I offered to return for him his beloved Sony TV with a screen big enough that he could actually see the puck when watching the Stanley Cup playoffs.

"It being a Japanese set and all," I'd said.

"Touch that thing and I'll knock your block off," he'd said.

I took the porch steps two at a time, unlocked the front door — I hadn't needed to take a house key from Dad's ring; I'd always had one — and went into the kitchen. The clock on the wall said it was nearly four thirty. Time to start thinking about something for dinner.

I hunted around in the fridge to see what might be left in here from my father's final trip to the grocery store. He wasn't much of a cook, but knew the basics. He could boil water for pasta, or heat up an oven and throw a chicken in there. But for the days when he hadn't the energy for anything that fancy, he'd stuffed the freezer with hamburgers and fish sticks and french fries and enough frozen dinners to start a Stouffer's franchise.

I could make do with what was here for tonight, but tomorrow I was going to have to make a trip to the grocery store. The truth was, I wasn't much of a cook myself, and back in Burlington, found many nights I couldn't be bothered to make myself anything more ambitious than a bowl of Cheerios. I think, when you live alone, it's hard to get motivated to make a real meal, or eat it in a proper way. Many nights I'd eat dinner standing in the kitchen, watching the news on the TV, or I'd take my plate of microwaved lasagna up to my studio and eat while I worked.

I opened the refrigerator. There were six cans of Bud in there. My father liked his beer affordable and basic. Part of me felt funny, dipping into his last six-pack, but it didn't stop me from taking one out and cracking it.

"To you, Dad," I said, raising the can, then taking a seat at the kitchen table.

The place was almost as neat as I'd found it. Dad was meticulous, which made the upstairs hall all the more difficult for him to accept. I attributed his fastidiousness to his time in the Army. Drafted, he did his two years, most of it overseas in Vietnam. He never talked about it. "It's over," he'd say anytime it came up. He was more inclined to credit his habits to his work in printing, where precision and attention to detail were everything.

I sat there, drinking Dad's beer, working up the energy to defrost or nuke something. I cracked open another as I began pulling things out of the freezer. Given my unfamiliarity with this kitchen, I had to open several drawers to find place mats and cutlery and napkins.

When things were almost ready, I walked through the living room and rested my hand on the banister before heading upstairs. I cast my eye across the room: the checkered couch my parents brought here two decades ago from the house in Albany, the recliner my father always sat in to watch his Sony. The chipped coffee table they bought the same time as the couch.

While the furniture was dated, Dad didn't skimp on the technology. There was the TV itself, a thirty-six-inch flat screen with HD that he'd bought a year ago to watch football and hockey. He liked his sports, even if he had to enjoy them alone. There was a DVD player, and one of those gadgets that allowed him to order up movies from the Internet.

He watched those by himself.

The living room looked like a million other living rooms. Normal. Nothing extraordinary.

That changed as you got to the top of the stairs.

My parents had tried, without success, to keep my brother's obsession contained to his own room, but it was a losing battle. The hallway, which Mom had painted pale yellow years ago, was totally papered over, nearly every square inch covered up. Standing at the top of the stairs, looking down the second-floor hall that led to the three bedrooms and a bathroom, I thought of how a World War II underground war room might have looked, with oversized maps of enemy territories pinned to the walls of the bunker, military strategists waving their pointers, planning their invasions. But in a war room, there would have been more order to the map arrangement. Maps of Germany, the cities within its borders, would no doubt be collected together along one part of the wall. France would have been on another. Italy nearby.

It seemed unlikely that any war planner worth his salt would tape a map of Poland next to one of Hawaii. Or have a street guide of Paris overlapping a gas station highway map of Kansas. Pin a topographical map of Algeria next to satellite shots of Melbourne. Staple, right into the wall, a tattered National Geographic map of India next to one of Rio de Janeiro.

This tapestry, this crazy quilt of maps that obscured every bit of wall in the hallway — it was as if someone had put the world into a blender and turned it into wallpaper.

Red streaks from a Magic Marker ran from map to map, making obscure, seemingly irrelevant connections. There were written notations everywhere. Across a map of Portugal was scribbled "236 miles," for no apparent reason. Latitude and longitude numbers were jotted randomly up and down the hallway. Some destinations were adorned with photographs. A printout photo of the

Sydney Opera House was stuck with a short piece of green painter's tape to a map of Australia. A tattered shot of the Taj Mahal was stuck, with a glob of wadded gum, onto a map of India.

I don't know how Dad, on his own, tolerated it. When Mom was alive, she was a buffer. Told her husband to get out of the house, go to a sports bar and watch a game with Lenny Prentice, or one of the others from work. Or Harry Peyton. How did Dad handle it, walking down this hall each and every day, week after week, month after month, trying to pretend there was nothing on the walls but the pale yellow paint he'd helped his wife roll on there so long ago?

I went to the first bedroom door, which was, as usual, closed. I raised my hand to rap lightly on it, but just before I touched my knuckles to wood, I listened.

I could hear talking on the other side of the door. A conversation, but only one voice. I wasn't able to make out anything in particular.

I knocked.

"Yeah?" Thomas said.

I opened the door, wondering if maybe he'd been on the phone, but there was no receiver in his hand. I told him it was time for dinner, and he said he'd be right down.

THREE

"*Well, it sure is nice to hear from you.*"

"Thank you for taking my call."

"*I don't give my private line to just anyone. You're a very special prospect.*"

"I appreciate that, sir. I really do."

"*I got your latest e-mail message. Sounds like things are coming along very well.*"

"Yes, they are."

"*Good to hear.*"

"I'm still wondering . . . do you have any idea of the timing of the incident, sir?"

"*If only we did. It's like asking the exact moment when terrorists will hit next. We simply don't know. But we have to be prepared for when, and if, that moment comes.*"

"Of course."

"*And I know you'll be ready. You're going to be tremendously valuable to us. A wonderful resource.*"

"You can count on me, sir."

"*You do appreciate that there is risk in what you're doing?*"

"I know."

"Someone like you, there are forces hostile to our government that would be very glad to get their hands on you."

"I'm aware, sir."

"Good to know. Listen, I have to go. My wife gets back from a trip to the Mideast today."

"Really?"

"Yeah. She's got a lot on her plate, that's for sure."

"Is she sorry she didn't get to become president?"

"I'll tell ya, I don't think she's had a moment to think about it."

"I suppose that's true."

"Anyway, carry on."

"Thank you, thank you, Mr. President. It's — it's still proper to call you that, isn't it?"

"Of course. You retain the title, even when you no longer hold the office."

"I'll be in touch."

"I know you will."

FOUR

"Let's say you were staying at the Hotel Pont Royal and you wanted to get to the Louvre. How would you do that?" Thomas asked me. "Come on, this is a super-easy one."

"What?" I said. "What city are you talking about?"

He sighed and looked at me sadly across the kitchen table, as though I were a child who had disappointed him by not knowing how to count to five. We looked a lot alike, Thomas and I. Both around five-eleven, thinning black hair, but Thomas had a few pounds on me. I was the slender Vince Vaughn from *Swingers*, Thomas the meatier Vince Vaughn from *The Break-Up*. I was definitely healthier looking, but that had nothing do with physical build. When you hardly went outside and spent twenty-three hours a day in your bedroom — he managed to pack breakfast, lunch, and dinner in the kitchen into three twenty-minute interruptions — you developed a pasty, washed-out

41

complexion, an almost sickly pallor. He was probably suffering from a Vitamin D deficiency. He needed a week in Bermuda. And even though he'd never been there, he could probably name me all the hotels and tell me what streets they were on.

"I said *Louvre*. Doesn't that give you some idea where I'm talking about? Louvre, *Louvre*, think about it."

"Of course," I said. "Paris. You're talking about Paris."

He nodded encouragingly, almost frenetically. He'd already finished the frozen meatloaf dinner I'd heated up in the microwave even though I wasn't even halfway through my own and was unlikely to finish it. I'd have been happier with buttered foam core. He was sitting in the chair with his body twisted in the direction of the stairs, like he was getting ready to bolt back up there any second. "Right, so you want to get to the Louvre. Which way do you go?"

"I have no idea, Thomas," I said tiredly. "I know where the Louvre is. I've been to the Louvre. I spent six whole days there when I was twenty-seven. I lived in Paris for a month. I took an art course. But I have no idea where this hotel is you're talking about. I didn't stay in a hotel. I was in a hostel."

"The Pont Royal," he said.

I gave him a blank look, waiting.

"On the Rue de Montalembert," he said.

42

"Thomas, I have no fucking idea where —"

"It's just off the Rue du Bac. Come on. It's an old hotel, all gray stone, has a revolving door at the front that looks like it's made of walnut or something like that and right beside it there's a place that does X-rays or something, because it says mammography and radiology above the windows and above those are some apartments or something with some plants in the windows in clay pots and the building looks like it's eight stories and on the left side there's a very expensive-looking restaurant with a black awning thing and dark windows and it doesn't have any tables and chairs out front like most of the cafés in Paris and —"

All this from memory.

"I'm really tired, Thomas. I had to go in and talk to Harry Peyton today."

"The Louvre is like the simplest place to get to from there. You can almost *see* it when you come out of the hotel."

"Do you not want to hear what happened at the lawyer's?"

He waved his hands busily in front of me. "You go across the Rue de Montalembert and then across a triangle of sidewalk, and then you're on the Rue du Bac, and then you go right and you walk up that way and you cross the Rue de l'Université and you keep going and you cross the Rue de Verneuil — I'm not sure I'm pronouncing these right because I

43

never took French in high school — and there's this place on the corner that has all these really good-looking pastries in the window and bread too and then you cross the Rue de Lille but you keep on going and —"

"Mr. Peyton said the way Dad's will is set up, he left the house to both of us."

"— and if you look straight down the street you can actually see it. The Louvre, I mean. Even though it's on the other side of the river. You keep going and then you cross the Quai Anatole France on the left, and on the right it's the Quai Voltaire. I guess the road changes from one name to the other there and you shift a bit to the right but keep going over the bridge, which is the Pont Royal. I think *pont* means bridge. And when you get to the other side you're there. See how simple that was? You didn't have to do any twists or turns or anything. You just go out the door and turn and you're there. Let's do a harder one. Name a hotel in any other part of Paris and I'll tell you how to get there. Shortest route. Although, sometimes, there's a hundred different ways to get to the same place but it's still about the same distance. Like New York. Well, not like New York, because the streets are all over the place in Paris and not in square blocks, but you get what I mean, right?"

"Thomas, I need you to stop for a second,"

I said patiently.

He blinked at me a couple of times. "What is it?"

"We need to talk about Dad."

"Dad's dead," he said, again looking at me like I was short a few IQ points. Then, with something that looked like sorrow washing briefly over his face, he glanced out the window. "I found him. By the creek."

"I know."

"Dinner was late. I kept waiting for him to knock on the door and tell me that it was time to eat, and I was getting really hungry so I came down to see what was going on. I went all over the house first. I went down into the basement, thinking maybe he was fixing the furnace or something, but he wasn't there. The van was here so he had to be somewhere. When I couldn't find him in the house I went outside. I looked in the barn first."

I'd heard all this before.

"When I couldn't find him there I walked around and when I got to the top of the hill I saw him with the tractor on top of him."

"I know, Thomas."

"I pushed the tractor off him. It was really hard to do but I did. But Dad didn't get up. So I ran back up here and called 911. They came and they said he was dead."

"I know," I said again. "That must have been pretty awful for you."

45

"It's still down there."

The tractor. I had to bring it back up and put it away in the barn. It had been sitting out there at the bottom of the hill since the accident. I didn't know whether it would start. For all I knew, the gas had all drained out when the machine was upside down. There was a half-full gas can in the barn if I needed it.

"There are things that we have to get figured out," I said. "About what to do, now that Dad's, you know, passed away."

Thomas nodded, thinking. "I was wondering," he said, "whether it would be okay to put maps on the walls in his bedroom now. I'm running out of space. Because he and Mom said I couldn't put any on the first floor, or down the stairs, but his room is on the second floor so I was wondering what you thought about that since he's not sleeping in there anymore. And with Mom already gone, no one's sleeping in there."

That wasn't exactly true. I'd started off sleeping in the empty bedroom next to Thomas's, the one Mom had always kept ready for me when I came to visit, which was not that often. But last night I ended up moving down the hall into Dad's room because I could hear all the mouse-clicking through the wall and couldn't take it anymore. I'd gone in once to tell Thomas to shut it down but he'd ignored me, so I'd switched beds. I felt funny about it at first, slipping under the covers of my dead father's bed, but I got over it. I was tired, and I'm not much of a sentimentalist.

"You can't live in this house all alone," I said.

"I'm not alone. You're here."

"At some point I have to go back home."

"You are home. This is home."

"It's not *my* home, Thomas. I live in Burlington."

"Burlington, Vermont. Burlington, Massachusetts. Burlington, North Carolina. Burlington, New Jersey. Burlington, Washington. Burlington, Ontario, Ca—"

"Thomas."

"I didn't know if you knew how many other Burlingtons there are. You need to be specific. You need to say Burlington, Vermont, or people won't know where you really live."

"I figured you knew," I said. "Is that what you want me to do? Every time I tell you I have to go back to Burlington, do you want me to add 'Vermont,' Thomas?"

"Don't be angry with me," he said.

"I'm not angry with you. But we do need to talk about some things."

"Okay."

"When I go back to my own house, I'm going to be worried about leaving you here on your own."

Thomas shook his head, like there was

nothing to worry about. "I'll be fine."

"Dad did everything around here," I said. "He made the meals, he cleaned the house, he paid the bills, he went into town to get the groceries, he made sure the furnace was working and called the guy if there was something wrong with it. Anything else that broke, he fixed it. If the lights went off, he went down and flipped the breakers to get them back on. Do you know where the breaker panel is, Thomas?"

"The furnace works fine," he said.

"You don't have a driver's license," I said. "How are you going to get food into the house?"

"I'll have it delivered," he said.

"We're out in the middle of nowhere. And who's going to actually go to the grocery store and pick out the things you like?"

"You know what I like," Thomas said.

"But I won't be here."

"You can come back," he said. "Once a week, and get my food and pay the bills and see if the furnace is okay and then you can go back to Burlington." He paused. "Vermont."

"What about each day? Let's say you've got some food in the house. Are you going to be okay making your own meals?"

Thomas looked away.

I leaned in a little closer to him, reached out, and touched his arm. "Look at me," I said. He turned his head back reluctantly.

"Maybe," I said, "if you made some changes in your routine, maybe you could take on some of these responsibilities yourself."

"What do you mean?" he asked.

"Well, maybe you need to manage your time better."

He adopted a puzzled expression. "I manage my time very well."

I took my hand away and placed both palms down on the table. "Tell me about that."

"I do. I make very good use of my time."

"Describe your day for me."

"Which day? Like, a weekday, or the weekend?" He was stalling.

"Would you say your Monday-to-Friday routine is very different from your weekend routine?"

He thought on that. "I suppose not."

"Then any day would be fine. You pick."

Now he eyed me with suspicion. "Are you trying to make fun of me? Are you picking on me?"

"You said you use your time wisely, so tell me."

"Well," he said, "I get up around nine o'clock, and I have a shower, and then Dad makes me breakfast around nine thirty, and then I get to work."

"Work," I said. "Tell me about that."

"You know," he said.

"I just don't think I've heard you call it

work before. Tell me about that."

"I go to work after breakfast, and I take a break for lunch, and then I go back to work until it's dinnertime, and then I do some more work before I go to bed."

"And that's around, what, one, two, three in the morning?"

He nodded.

"Tell me about the work."

"Why are you doing this, Ray?"

"I guess I'm thinking if you spent a little less time on this work, as you call it, you'd be in a better position to look after yourself. Thomas, it's no secret you've got issues you've been dealing with for a very long time, and that they're ongoing, and I get that. Just like Dad and Mom did. And, compared to plenty of other people who have the same thing as you, who aren't able to shut out the voices or deal with other symptoms, you manage very well. You get up, you dress yourself, you and I can sit here and have a rational conversation about things."

"I know," Thomas said, somewhat indignantly. "I'm perfectly normal."

"But the amount of time you spend on your . . . work stands to interfere with your ability to look after this house on your own, or live here by yourself, and if you're not able to do that, then we're going to have to look at some other arrangement."

"What do you mean, another arrangement?"

I hesitated. "Living somewhere else. Maybe an apartment, in town. Or, and this is something I've only just started looking into, some sort of housing where you'd live with other people with similar issues, where there are staff who look after things you can't look after yourself."

"Why do you keep saying 'issues'? I don't have issues, Ray. I've had mental problems, which are very much under control. If you had arthritis, would you want me to say you had an issue with your bones?"

"I'm sorry. I was just . . ." I didn't know what to say.

"Is this place where I would live a hospital? For crazy people?"

"I never said you were crazy, Thomas."

"I don't want to live in a hospital. The food's terrible." He looked at my unfinished meatloaf. "Even worse than that. And I don't think a hospital room would have an Internet connection."

"Nobody's talking about a hospital. But maybe some kind of, I don't know, a kind of supervised house. You could probably do your own cooking. I could teach you how to do that."

"I can't leave," Thomas said matter-of-factly. "All my stuff is here. My work is here."

"Thomas, you spend all but an hour of your

51

waking day on the computer, wandering all over the world. Day after day, month after month. It's not healthy."

"It's only a more recent development," he said. "A few years ago, all I had was my maps and my atlases and my globe. There was no Whirl360. It's so much better now. I've been waiting my whole life for something like this."

"You've always been obsessed with maps, but —"

"*Interested.* I've always been *interested* in maps. I don't say you're obsessed with drawing silly pictures of people. I saw that one you did, of Obama, in the white coat with the stethoscope like he was a doctor, that ran in that magazine. I thought it made him look silly."

"That was the point," I said. "That was what the magazine wanted."

"Well, would you call that an obsession? I think it's just your job."

This wasn't supposed to be about me. "This new technology," I continued, "this Whirl360, has not been healthy for your *interest* in maps. You're wandering down the streets of cities all over the world, which I grant you can be an interesting thing to do, but, Thomas, *you're not doing anything else.*"

He looked down at the floor again.

"Are you hearing me? You don't go out. You don't see people. You don't read books or magazines. You don't even watch television.

You never come down and watch a movie."

"There's nothing good on," he said. "The movies are very poor. And they have so many mistakes in them. They'll say they're in New York, but you can tell from the background that it's Toronto or Vancouver or some other place."

"All you do is sit at the computer and click your way down street after street after street. Listen, you want to see the world? Pick a city. I'll take you to Tokyo. I'll take you to Mumbai. You want to see Rome? We'll go. We'll sit in some restaurant by the Trevi Fountain and you can order some pizza or pasta and finish it off with some gelato and it'll be the most fun you've ever had. You'll be able to see the actual city instead of some static image of it on a computer screen. You'll be able to touch these places, feel the bricks of Notre Dame under your fingertips, smell the Temple Street Night Market in Hong Kong, listen to karaoke in Tokyo. Pick a place and I'll take you."

Thomas looked blankly at me. "No, I wouldn't want to do that. I like it here just fine. I won't catch any diseases, or lose my luggage, or end up in a hotel with bedbugs, or get mugged or get sick in a place where I can't speak the language. And there's not time."

"What do you mean, not time?"

"There's not time to get every place in

person. I can get it done here faster, get the work done."

"Thomas, what *work*?"

"I can't tell you," he said. "I'll have to check and see if it's okay to tell you."

I let out a long sigh, ran my hand over the top of my head. I was exhausted. I decided to change the subject.

"You remember Julie McGill? From school?"

"Yes," Thomas said. "What about her?"

"She came to the funeral. She asked about you. Asked me to say hi."

Thomas looked at me, expectantly. "Are you going to say it?"

"What?" Then I got it. "*Hi.* If you'd come to the service, she could have said it to you herself." He didn't react to that. His refusal to attend was still a sore point with me. "Was she in your class?"

"No," he said. "She was a year ahead of me, and a year behind you." Thomas paused. "She lived at 34 Arbor Street, which is a two-story house with the door in the middle and windows on each side and three windows on the second floor and the house is painted green and there's a chimney on the right side and the mailbox has flowers stenciled on it. She was always nice to me. Is she still pretty?"

I nodded. "Yeah. Her hair's still black but it's short now."

"Does she still have a bod?" He asked this

54

without a hint of lasciviousness, like he wanted to know whether she was still driving a Subaru.

"I would say yes," I said. "Did you guys . . . did you have a thing?"

"A thing?" He really didn't know.

"Did you go out?"

"No," he said. I could have guessed. Thomas had never had a steady girlfriend, and had only gone on dates a handful of times that I could remember. His odd, inward nature didn't help, but I was never all that sure he cared about girls to begin with. Back when I was hiding skin mags under the mattress, Thomas was already amassing his huge map collection.

"But I liked her," Thomas said. "She rescued me."

I cocked my head, trying to recall. "That time, with the Landry twins?"

Thomas nodded. He'd been walking home from school when Skyler and Stan Landry, a couple of bullies with the combined IQ of a bucket of primer, had blocked his path and taunted him about how he talked to himself in class. They were starting to push him around when Julie McGill showed up.

"What'd she do?"

"She yelled at them to leave me alone. Stood between them and me. Called them cowards. And something else."

"What else?"

55

"Fuckheads."

I nodded. "Yeah, I remember."

"It was kind of embarrassing, a girl standing up for you," Thomas said. "But they'd have beat me up good if she hadn't come by. Is there going to be any dessert?"

"Huh? Uh, I don't know. I think I saw the end of a container of ice cream in the freezer there."

"Could you bring it up to me? I've been down here longer than I planned and I need to get back." He was already on his feet.

"Yeah, sure," I said.

"I saw something," Thomas said.

"What?"

"I saw something. On the computer. I think it would be okay for you to have a look at it. I don't think it would violate any security clearance or anything."

"What is it?"

"You should just take a look at it. It would take too long to explain."

"Can you give me a hint?" I asked.

And he said again, "You should take a look at it." He paused. "When you bring up the ice cream."

FIVE

I went up to Thomas's room five minutes later. There was a tub of vanilla in the freezer and I was just barely able to scrape out enough for one small serving, which was fine, because I didn't have much of an appetite.

I should have known better than to think I could reason things out with Thomas about how he spent his days. My parents had tried for years without success. I was a fool to think I could accomplish anything different. My brother was who he was. He'd always been this way and there was every reason to believe he always would.

The signs came early. At least some of them. The fascination with maps revealed itself when he was around six. At the time, my parents thought it was pretty cool. When guests came over they'd show off Thomas the way parents of a child piano prodigy would make him play something by Brahms. "Pick a country," Dad would say to visitors. "Any country."

My parents' friends, not really sure what it was Thomas did, would finally come up with one. "Argentina," they might say. And then Thomas, a pencil and notepad in hand, would sketch out the country. Add some dots for cities and label them. Write in the names of neighboring nations. Then he'd hand it over for perusal.

The thing was, our visitors generally didn't know Argentina from Arkansas, and didn't have a clue whether the map they'd been handed was accurate, so Dad would pull an atlas off the shelf, open it to Argentina, and say, "Look at that! Will ya look at that? Can you believe it? He even got the city of Mendoza in just the right spot. Kid's going to be a cartographer or something, I guarantee it."

If Thomas minded being offered up as a parlor trick, he never voiced an objection. At the time, he just seemed like a very gifted baby brother. Somewhat withdrawn, shy, but no indication that he was troubled in any serious way.

That would come soon enough.

My parents were proud as could be of him. Me, not so much. At least not on family vacations, when Mom would pack everyone's bag and Dad would load them into the trunk and we'd hit the road for Atlantic City or Florida or Boston. Mom had no sense of direction and had a terrible time reading the road maps the gas stations gave out, although she was a genius at folding them back up perfectly.

So Dad would read the map. When people today talk about the dangers of sending text messages while driving, I want to laugh. My father, had there been smartphones back then, could have tapped out Moby Dick while navigating the Buffalo bypass. He'd have Mom fold the map to a manageable size, drape it over the top of the steering wheel, and glance down every couple of seconds as we roamed across America.

Until Thomas got to be seven.

"I'll read the map, Dad," he offered.

Dad ignored him at first, but Thomas persisted. Finally Dad figured, what the hell, let the kid think he was being useful. But Thomas wasn't playing some game. He wasn't pretending to navigate, the way some children, long before they know how to read, will rhyme off words when they open the pages of a book.

Thomas only had to glance at it for a few seconds before he said something like, "Just stay on 90 for another ten miles, then get off and go east on 22."

"Let me have a look at that," Dad said, taking the map back and studying it over the steering wheel.

"I'll be damned," he said. "The kid's right."

Thomas was always right when it came to reading maps.

I'd try to snatch them from him, figuring

that, as the elder sibling, I should be the navigator. It tore me apart to see my father consulting my baby brother for assistance.

"Raymond!" my father would shout at me. "Leave your damn brother alone and let him do his job! He knows what he's doing."

I'd look at Mom, hoping for some sort of support. "You have things you're good at, *too*," she'd say to me. "But Thomas is really good at *this*."

"What am I good at?" I asked.

She had to think. "You're a really good drawer. Maybe you could draw some pictures of the places we visit on our trip. That would be fun."

How patronizing was that? We had a camera. What the hell purpose was served by my providing artistic renderings of the tourist attractions we visited? How was that supposed to help? Insulted, I reached into the case where I kept paper and pencils and safety scissors that I brought along to entertain myself on these trips and handed her an untouched sheet of black construction paper.

"That's the Carlsbad Caverns," I told her. We had been there the day before. "You can frame it when we get home."

There was a hint of things to come, where Thomas was concerned, during a summer trip to a lodge in southern Pennsylvania, about an hour and a half southeast of Pittsburgh, when I was eleven and Thomas was nine. It was a stately old resort built on the side of a mountain; looking back, the place puts me in mind of the Overlook Hotel from the Stephen King movie *The Shining,* but there wasn't blood flowing out of the elevators or a dead woman in a bathtub or some little kid pedaling a Big Wheel flat out down the hallways. There was mini-golf, and a pool, and bingo nights, and cookies and lemonade on the porch every afternoon at four. It was a fun week, but the most memorable part of the vacation was the drive home, when Dad decided to deviate from the route Thomas had prepared for him.

Thomas had spent several days — ignoring Mom's pleas that he come for a swim or play horseshoes — figuring out that we needed to take 99 north up through Altoona, and while we started out intending to go that way, Mom decided she wanted to go home by way of Harrisburg, just in case there was any good shopping there, and that meant going east on 76. It would take us quite a few miles out of our way.

"You can't do that!" Thomas said from the backseat once he got wind of this. "We have to take 99!"

"Your mother wants to go to Harrisburg, Thomas," Dad said. "It's not a big deal."

"I spent all week planning the route!" He was starting to cry.

"Why don't you start plotting out a different route home from Harrisburg?" Mom suggested. "That would be fun."

"No! We have to go the way the map says," Thomas insisted.

"Listen, son, we're just going to —"

"No!"

"Jesus, Ray? Get out some games or something and play with your brother. Where's the Mad Libs book?"

But now Thomas had undone his seat belt and gotten up on his knees on his seat, and was starting to bang his head against the window.

Dad said, "What the f—"

"Thomas!" Mom shouted.

I grabbed for him but he pushed me away. He kept banging his head against the window. A small smear of blood appeared on the glass.

Dad swung the car over onto the shoulder. Mom jumped out, nearly losing her footing on the gravel, and opened the back door. She wrapped her arms around my brother, pulling his bruised and bloodied head to her breast.

"It's okay," she said. "We're going to take 99. We're going to go home just the way you said."

I didn't like going into Thomas's room. Entering his domain made me uncomfortable in the same way the decorated hall did, only more so. Maps were stuck to the wall everywhere and scattered across the floor. The one set of bookshelves spilled over with various editions of atlases, old Auto Club TripTiks with the spiral binding (did anyone use those anymore?), large cardboard tubes with maps Thomas had ordered off the Internet, hundreds of printouts of maps he'd studied online. Satellite shots of cities I couldn't instantly recognize.

It was hard to find the single bed pushed up against one wall, it was so buried with paper. It was like vandals had gone on a rampage at the National Geographic headquarters. I wondered how many fire codes were being violated. Between this room and the map-plastered hall, all someone had to do was wander through with a lit candle and this place would go up in smoke in seconds.

I seriously had to think about that.

Thomas was seated at his computer. He had one keyboard and three flat-screen monitors arrayed in front of him, each showing a different browser. On the screens were three images of the same street — left, middle, and right-side views. At the top of each screen was the Web site address: whirl360.com.

I had to admit, it was a pretty amazing Web site. Ten years ago I couldn't have imagined anything like this.

Once you were there, you basically had the world at your fingertips. You picked a spot anywhere on the globe and initially viewed the location from above, either in a traditional map form, or in satellite mode, as though you were suspended in the sky. You could zero in right down to the roof vents on the sky-scrapers.

Cool enough.

But it got so much better.

You could click on a specific street, and see it. Really *see* it. Like you were standing there, right in the middle of it. With each click of the mouse you progressed several yards ahead. When you clicked and held, you could move to the left or right, or all the way around for a 360-degree view. If something in a store window or a restaurant caught your eye, you could zoom in on it. Read the daily special — "Liver and onions $5.99" — if you wanted.

It was the kind of site I found myself on occasionally. The year before, on a trip to Toronto, I'd visited a friend from my college days who lived just south of Queen Street in the Beach, a trendy neighborhood in the city's east end. In his e-mail, he told me to come by the house; then we'd head to an Italian restaurant that was only a short walk away.

I went on Whirl360, did the walk from his place up to Queen, then explored a couple of blocks in each direction. Only found two restaurants. I looked them up online, found the one billing itself as Italian, studied their online menu, and knew before I got there I was going to have the lobster ravioli.

So I could appreciate the fascination, understand how for someone like Thomas, the arrival of this kind of technology was a dream come true. Like a *Star Trek* fan waking up one morning to find out he was actually living on the USS *Enterprise*.

The street Thomas was currently fixated on was unknown to me. It was narrow, just enough room for one lane of traffic, with cars parallel parked down the right side. I was guessing maybe someplace in Europe.

I set the ice cream next to the phone. Thomas had his own line up here that our parents had put in back when Internet hookup was over the phone. Thomas spent so much time on the Net that our parents were missing calls and couldn't place any, so installing a second line meant Thomas could be on as long as he wanted. Now, with Wi-Fi in the house, Thomas didn't have much need for the phone, and about the only calls he got were from telemarketers.

He glanced at the ice cream and said, "No chocolate sauce?"

"We're out," I said. I hadn't actually looked. "Where's this?"

"Salem Street."

"Salem Street where?"

"Boston. In the North End."

"Oh, okay, yeah, of course. I thought you

65

were spending all your time lately in Paris."

"I get around," Thomas said. I didn't know whether he meant to be amusing, but I laughed. "You see anything weird?" he asked.

I looked. People, their faces blurred — that seemed to be a Whirl360 protocol, to blur faces that could be seen head-on, as well as license plates — were walking along the street. There were cars. Some street signs I couldn't make out.

"No," I said.

"See this silver SUV here?" He pointed. It was visible on the right screen, a profile shot.

"Yeah, I see it."

"Look what he's done. He's backed into this car, this blue one. You can just see where he's hit the blue car's headlight."

"Can you magnify it?" I asked.

Thomas clicked a couple of times. The image of the SUV's rear bumper and the blue car's front end got bigger, but blurrier.

"I think you might be right," I said.

"You can see it, right?"

"Yeah. So just at the moment the Whirl360 people were driving around with their picture car, they got a shot of this guy backing into the blue car. Son of a gun. They caught an accident in progress, and you just found it. That it?"

"I bet the SUV driver didn't even know he did it," Thomas said, spooning some ice cream into his mouth.

"Maybe not," I said. "I'm gonna watch some TV. Want to join me? We'll order up a movie or something. Something with authentic locations that won't annoy you."

"We need to report this," Thomas said. "The owner of the blue car needs to know who did this."

"Thomas, honestly. First of all, they blur all the license plates, so there's no way you could ever find out who owns the SUV, or the blue car. And second, this picture, this image of this street, has probably been up here for months, even a couple of years. I mean, you're talking about some minor damage that happened God knows how long ago. The blue car's owner got that fixed a year back, for all we know. He might not even *own* that car anymore. This is not some live stream, you know. These are snapshots in time."

Thomas didn't say anything.

"What?" I said. "Talk to me."

"It's not right to stand by and do nothing," he said.

"We're not — Jesus, it's not like you just saw the SUV run some guy down. This is exactly what I'm talking about, Thomas. You're spending too much time up here. You need to get out. Come down and watch a movie. Dad got this great TV. Wide screen, HD. It's going to waste down there."

"You go," he said. "I'll be down in a little while. You pick a movie and we'll watch it."

I went downstairs and turned on the television, then hit the right buttons on the collection of remotes so I could connect to a movie service.

I came across a film, only a couple of years old, made in New Zealand, called *The Map Reader*.

"Son of a bitch," I said. "Hey, Thomas! There's a movie here you'll love. About a kid who loves maps!"

"Sure thing," he said. "I'll be down in a minute."

He didn't come down. After waiting fifteen minutes, I turned off the TV without watching anything, went into the kitchen, and drank Dad's very last beer.

Six

Nine months earlier, Allison Fitch lifts her head an inch off the pillow on her pullout couch and looks at the digital clock readout on the DVD player on the other side of the small living room. Nearly noon. She tries to remember to close the blinds when she gets home from a late shift so the sun won't wake her in the morning, but unless you tape black paper to the entire window, or got some of those heavy curtains that block out everything, you really can't keep the rays out.

God, it's a sunny day out there today. She pulls the covers up over her head.

She's pretty sure she's alone right now in the apartment she shares with Courtney Walmers, who has the bedroom. Unless you found some place that was rent-controlled, there was no way you could live in this city by yourself, certainly not on what a waitress made. Courtney has an office job, down on Wall Street, so she's out of the apartment by eight. Allison usually starts her shift around five. Sometimes, if Courtney's able to sneak home from work early, they'll actually see each other for five minutes.

Allison hopes this isn't one of those days. Seeing Courtney is not something she looks forward to. She knows Courtney wants to have a *talk* with her — a real, *serious* talk — and it is a conversation Allison does not want to have. Because she knows exactly what it's about.

Money.

It's always about money. At least, that's all Courtney has wanted to talk about for the last couple of months. Ever since Allison hasn't been meeting her share of the rent, and other expenses, like the cable and Internet. Courtney is threatening to cancel the service altogether, although Allison is sure she'd never follow through. Courtney lives on Facebook when she's home. When she's at work, too, from what Allison gathers. Why that trading company hasn't fired her ass, Allison has no idea. At least when she goes to the bar, she *works*. She works her *ass* right off, that's what she does, waiting tables, dealing with asshole customers, taking abuse from the kitchen who can't get a single fucking order straight to save their lives.

Oh, she earns her money, Allison does. She just doesn't have enough of it. She's paid only half her share of the rent the last three months. Hasn't replaced anything in the fridge. Tells Courtney she'll pay her back when she can.

Courtney is all, *Yeah, well, I'll believe it when I see it.*

The bitch.

She makes way more money than Allison, and for what? Sitting on her butt in a nice cushy chair in front of a computer all day, doing trades, making money for other people. Allison doesn't even understand half of what it is her roommate does.

Things really escalated after Allison's call home a couple of months ago. Allison, talking to her mom back in Dayton, telling her the Big Apple wasn't quite everything she'd hoped it would be.

"Oh, sweetheart, you should come home," her mother said.

"Mom, I'm not coming back."

"Well, they need people at Target. There was a thing in the paper that they're hiring."

"I'm not coming back to Dayton to work in Target," Allison said.

"Have you met anyone?"

"Mom."

"I figured, you working in a restaurant, there'd be lots of opportunities to meet some young man."

"Please, Mom." Why does she always come around to this? Why the hell does her mom think she left Dayton in the first place? To get away from questions like this, that's why.

"You can't blame me for hoping my little girl will find a guy who'll make her happy. Your father and I were very happy, you know. We had a good life together. You're thirty-one, you know. You're not getting any younger."

She needed to throw her mother a bone. "I *have* met someone," Allison said. It helped that it was actually true. It's always easier to spin out a story when there's a grain of truth in it, especially when it's a story for her mother. She has met someone, and they've spent some time together. Some pretty *hot* times. The whole thing started with a single glance.

Sometimes two people looked at each other and they just *knew*.

Allison sensed her mother brightening on the other end of the line. "Who?" she asked excitedly. "Tell me all about him."

"It's too early," Allison said. "I'm just going to see how it plays out. If this is the one, I'll let you know. Okay? No third degree. Right now, I've got more serious things to worry about." Setting the hook.

"Like what?"

"Well, the customers, they're just not tipping the way they used to. And business is down. People are eating and drinking at home. And there was the whole thing with the chipped tooth."

72

"Chipped tooth? What are you talking about?"

"Didn't I tell you about that?" Of course she hadn't. She'd only just thought of it now. There was no chipped tooth.

"You never said a word. When did you chip your tooth? How'd that happen?"

"Okay, so, there's this girl I work with, her name is Elaine? And she's a total idiot. She's coming through the crowd with a full tray of drinks, right? And she's weaving in between these banker shitheads who —"

"Ally."

"Sorry. These banker numbnuts, and she raises her tray up just as I'm coming from the other direction, and the edge of it smacks right into my mouth and the drinks go all over the place and when I go into the ladies' room to look in the mirror I've got this little chip in my front tooth."

"Oh my God," Allison's mother said. "That's just awful."

"It wasn't huge, but every time I ran my tongue over it, it was like this sharp point, you know? So, anyway, I went to this dentist up on Madison and he fixed it and I swear, if you looked at it with a magnifying glass you'd never be able to tell."

Of that, Allison was certain.

"That must have cost you a *fortune*," her mother said.

"Yeah, well, it's not like the waitstaff have a

73

dental plan," she said, and laughed. "But don't worry about it. I'll manage somehow. Courtney'll understand, you know, if she has to wait a while for my share."

"Oh, honey, you can't do that to your roommate. That's just not fair. I'm getting out my checkbook right now."

She put a thousand dollars in the mail that day.

When the check arrived Allison immediately deposited it in her checking, bringing the balance to $1,421.87. Not enough to pay Courtney back everything Allison owed her, but at least she could make a start at it. But the longer Allison looked at the balance on her ATM slip, the less certain she was that she wanted to give any of that money to Courtney.

That "someone" she had mentioned to her mother was going to Barbados in two weeks, and had invited Allison to come along. Nothing had been said about paying her way, however, so Allison had said sorry, can't afford it.

All that had changed with the money to fix her chipped tooth.

So she booked a week in Barbados.

That's when the shit really hit the fan.

Courtney said, when she saw Allison packing her bags before grabbing a cab to JFK, "Are you kidding me? Tell me you're fucking kidding me. You're into me for more than two grand and somehow you've got enough for a vacation? You want to explain that to me?"

"It's not *my* money," Allison said. "My mom gave me the money for it."

Courtney said, "Excuse me?"

"I haven't saved up enough money from my job to pay you back yet. That's what I'm going to pay you with. *This* money, from my *mom*, for my *vacation*, is totally *separate*." It made perfect sense to Allison. Courtney could be so thick sometimes. Hard to believe she worked in the financial industry. You'd think she could get her head around it.

"I don't believe you," Courtney said. "I don't fucking *believe* you."

"Look, I really *need* this trip," Allison said. "How many places you been to in the last three years? Huh? Munich, for one. And then you went on that trip to Mexico. And what about London? You were there like five months ago. In all that time, where have I been?"

"What do my trips have to do with anything?"

"It's not fair that you're always getting to go someplace and I'm not. I can't believe how mean you are sometimes. I've gotta go. My flight leaves in like three hours."

Courtney must have sent her at least a hundred texts and e-mails while she was in Barbados. Ranting about what a selfish, self-centered, self-consumed bitch Allison was. It nearly ruined her holiday, her phone chirping and dinging all the time.

But it was still worth it.

When Allison returned, Courtney said she was going to kick her out, but Allison said she'd have to think twice about that, because both their names were on the lease. Allison put on a huge song and dance that she really, really, *really* was going to pay her back, that she was going to ask her mother for some money, that she was sure she could come up with a pretty good story, one that would touch her mother's heart, and there'd be a check in the mail within the week.

That was a week ago. There isn't likely to be a check in the mail today. She hasn't called her mother yet and asked her for money. Allison thinks it's too soon after the tooth story. She figures, if she can come up with an equally compelling tale, she'll try it on her mother in another week or so.

Maybe a bedbug story. Everyone's shitting their pants about bedbugs. She'll tell her mother she has them in her building, that she and Courtney must move to a hotel for a week while the pest control people come in and spray and kill the little bastards. And they're telling Allison, you have to throw out all your clothes, the bugs may be hiding in them, go buy yourself some new duds.

Allison's mother has already been e-mailing

76

her every news item she comes across about bedbugs. This story will play very nicely into her fears.

Her mother will send money. Allison is sure of it. She just has to keep herself from spending it on something else before she gives it to Courtney.

Allison's cell, sitting on the coffee table, rings.

She comes up from under the covers, guesses it will be Courtney, and damned if it isn't. She wants to ignore it, but Courtney will just keep trying her, so she reaches over to the table, grabs the phone, and puts it to her ear.

"Yeah," she says.

"It's been a week," Courtney says. "Did the money come from your mother?"

"Not yet. I mean, I haven't gone down to check the mail, but I don't think it's going to be here."

"Why would that be, Allison?"

"Okay, look, I haven't called her yet. I was trying to think of a good story for her, and I've finally got one, so I'm going to call her today. So, like, in three or four days, the money should be here."

"Honest to God, you are *such* a piece of work."

"I really mean it," she says. "I'm going to pay you everything I owe you."

"I don't care whether you're on the lease. If

77

you don't pay your share you're going to come home and find all your shit in the hall. I swear to God. I'm already looking around for another roommate."

"Jesus, what the hell kind of friend *are* you?"

"What kind of friend am *I*? What would you do if you were me?"

"Okay, look, if I haven't paid you by this time next week, you won't have to kick me out. I'll leave, and you can bring someone else in here."

"A week," Courtney says skeptically.

"I swear. Cross my heart and all that shit."

"I'm an idiot, a total fucking idiot," Courtney says and hangs up.

There's no sense trying to go back to sleep now. Allison sits up in bed, reaches for the remote on the coffee table, and clicks on the television. As NY1 comes on with the latest news roundup, she grabs her phone again to see whether she has any e-mails or Facebook messages.

She'll definitely call her mother this afternoon. First, though, she'll go online and read up on bedbugs so she has plenty of convincing details to work into her story. She thinks, in a way, her mother may even know she's being taken advantage of, but it's not nearly as unsettling as those times in the past when Allison disappeared. Just took off for a few months. At least, when Allison hits her up for

78

money, her mother knows where she is.

Allison glances from the phone to the TV and back again. Hears something about showers in the afternoon, clearing by evening.

She opens Safari on her phone and does a search for "bedbugs." Holy shit, only about a million stories. She narrows the search by adding the words "New York" and just about as many results come back.

Glances back at the TV. Someone has jumped onto the subway tracks on the Sixth Avenue line. Back to her phone. Thinks, maybe get the name of an actual bug-killing company that the landlord's hiring, give the story that extra ring of authenticity.

Looks back up at the TV. Is about to look away when she thinks she catches a glimpse of a face she recognizes.

WTF?

Her mouth drops open in stunned silence as a reporter standing on the sidewalk outside some downtown office building says, "Expected to be a formidable challenger to the incumbent governor, Morris Sawchuck, seen here with his wife, Bridget, is perceived as being much stronger on law and order issues, and has made no secret that he would like to see a return to more traditional values — it's a major plank in his campaign platform — although he has not said exactly how he could go about restoring them if he's elected governor. He's said to have some very powerful people working behind the scenes for him, including the former vice president of the United States. Back to you —"

She turns off the set and stares into space for a moment, trying to take it all in. She still has the image in her head, of the couple getting out of the back of a town car, waving to supporters, going into a building to give a speech or something.

"Sawchuck?" Allison whispers. "The guy's a goddamn politician?"

She puts both hands on her head, runs her fingers out through her shoulder-length black hair, and lets out a very long breath.

"Fuck me," she says to herself.

Allison is glad she hasn't already called her mother, because there may be another solution to her cash flow problem.

SEVEN

"You've got an appointment today with Dr. Grigorin," I said while Thomas poured some milk on his cereal. "Dad set it up a few weeks ago."

"I don't need to see her, Ray," he said, not looking at me.

"Well, I'd appreciate it if you'd go. I know Dad thought it was good for you to see her once in a while."

"I don't want to go," he said. "I have work to do."

"You can do it when you get back. I know you can leave this house if you have to. You'd just rather not."

"If I had a reason to go, I would go, Ray. But there isn't one."

I put my mug of coffee to my lips and took a drink. All Dad ever kept in the house was instant and it was pretty vile, but at least it had caffeine in it. I added a second spoonful of sugar. "There *is* a reason, Thomas. You, and I, have just been through something

81

pretty traumatic. We've lost our father. And as difficult as this is for me to get through, I suspect it's even more troubling for you. I mean, you guys lived under the same roof."

"He got mad at me a lot," Thomas said.

"Like when?"

"He was always telling me to do things I didn't want to do." He gave me a look. "Kind of like you right now."

"But Dad was never mean to you," I said. "Annoyed once in a while, maybe, but not mean."

"I guess," he said. "He didn't like me staying in my room all day. He wanted me to go out. He didn't understand how busy I am."

"It's not healthy," I said. "You need some air. Thomas, you have to know, in your heart, that there's a problem when you're so addicted to what you're doing that you don't even go to Dad's funeral."

"I had to go to Melbourne that day," Thomas said.

"Jesus, Thomas, you did not *have* to go to Melbourne that day. You did not *have* to go to Melbourne, or Moscow, or Munich, or fucking Montreal. You needed to go to our father's funeral." I knew I wasn't being fair, blaming Thomas for this. I knew he most likely couldn't help himself. As soon as I'd said the words, I regretted them. Getting angry with Thomas for not overcoming his obsession was like getting angry with a blind man for not seeing where he was going.

"I'm sorry," I said.

He didn't say anything. Neither of us did, for the better part of a minute.

I broke the silence. "I think it's important, right now, while I'm trying to sort out a few things, that you go see Dr. Grigorin. I'd also like to talk to her."

Thomas eyed me curiously. "Are you having some issues, too?"

"What?"

"I think, actually, that's a good idea. You should talk to her. She could help you."

I blinked. "Help me? Help me with what?"

"About your need to control other people. She might be able to give you something for that. She gives me something to help me with the voices. So she might be able to write you a prescription, too."

"Well, there's an idea," I said.

"You could go on your own," he suggested. "You can tell me what she had to say when you get back."

"We're going together."

He licked his lips, started opening and closing his fingers. His mouth was getting dry. Anxiety was setting in.

"The appointment's at eleven," I said.

"Eleven, eleven, eleven," he said, casting his eyes upward, like he was trying to remember what he'd written down in his datebook.

"I'm pretty sure you're free," I said. "We'll

need to leave here around ten thirty."

Thomas got out of his chair, took his bowl over to the sink, and rinsed it under the tap. He always left the cleanup to me, so I had an idea just how much he wanted to avoid me.

"Don't walk away, Thomas."

"I really have a lot to do," he said, starting to walk out of the kitchen. "You don't understand how important it is."

"You can fiddle around with the GPS in the car."

That stopped him. "You have a navigational system?"

"Built right into the dashboard," I said.

He looked at the closet by the front door, where his jacket was hanging. "We could go now."

"It's only eight thirty. We don't want to sit around waiting for the doctor for two hours."

He thought about that. "Okay, I'll be ready at ten thirty. But you have to promise to talk to the doctor about your behavior."

"I promise," I said.

After Thomas had gone up to his room, and I'd finished cleaning up the breakfast dishes, I decided it was time.

I headed out the back door, walked across the yard that was, a full week after it had last been cut, in need of a trim, then came to a stop where the ground sloped down to the creek.

It was, as I'd told Harry Peyton, a steep hill. The kind that, if you felt you had to cut the grass on it, you'd be best doing it with a weed trimmer, or maybe a hand mower. If it got away from you, the worst that could happen is it would bounce down the hill and end up in the water.

A lot of people, had they owned this place, would have been content to end landscaping duties at the hill's crest. Let the grass and weeds grow wild on the slope. But Dad liked the idea of a groomed yard that went right to the water. The creek didn't exactly make the Kilbride homestead a beach house, but Dad figured it was as close as he was ever going to come. So every week, spring, summer, and fall, Dad did the hill when he cut the grass on the rest of the property.

I remember Mom asking me, during one of our phone chats about a year before she died, to talk my father out of his practice of riding the mower on this hill, side to side, leaning into the slope to keep the machine from tipping over.

"He's going to get himself killed," she'd said.

"He knows what he's doing, Mom."

"Oh, you men," she'd said exasperatedly. "I tried to get Harry and Len to talk some sense into him and they said the same thing."

Turned out the men were wrong.

The tractor, with a green hood and fenders

and yellow seat, was sitting upright at the bottom of the hill. The hood was sitting askew over the engine and the tops of the back fenders were scuffed and scraped. The steering wheel was bent.

My understanding was, the tractor had rolled once and landed on Dad. When Thomas got there, it wasn't possible to roll the tractor back up the hill. It would have been too hard to go in that direction. So he'd given the tractor a shove downward. It had rolled a couple more times and landed on its wheels on level ground just before the creek.

It had been there ever since.

I walked carefully down the hill. It was easy to see where it had all happened. The grass was about three inches high going down the side of the hill, then jumped up to about five. At that point, the ground was torn up where the mower had dug in as it rolled.

I stood a moment, one foot ahead of the other for balance, looking down at the place where my father had taken his last breath. Where that last breath had been crushed out of him. I felt a lump forming in my throat. Then I went down the rest of the way to the machine.

I didn't know whether I'd be able to get it back to the barn. The accident might have damaged the engine. When it was flipped over, it was possible all the gas had drained out of the tank. The battery might very well be dead.

Tentatively, I swung a leg over and dropped my butt in the seat. It felt odd, sitting there, knowing I was the first person in this seat since my father. The key was still in the ignition, set to OFF. I went to raise the blade housing, which you put into the down position only when you are actually cutting grass, but it was already up.

I put the choke on full, slid the throttle all the way up, and turned the key.

The engine coughed a couple of times and black smoke puffed out of the exhaust. The damn thing roared to life. I brought the choke back down, eased off the throttle, pushed in the clutch, and dropped the machine into its lowest gear to get it back up the hill.

I held my breath the whole time I was making the climb.

Once I'd crested the hill I drove the tractor to the barn, parked it inside, slid the door shut behind me, and went back into the house.

Thomas was downstairs, all set to go, at ten. Wearing a blue plaid shirt, olive-colored pants, black shoes, white socks, and a windbreaker the color of a traffic cone.

"Where did you get that jacket?" I asked. "You get a job as a crossing guard?"

"No," he said blankly. "You know I wouldn't want a job like that. I don't like being around little kids."

"It was a bad joke. Where did you get that?"

"One time, Dad let me go to Walmart to buy some map books, and I saw it on sale. He got it for me."

"It's bright," I said.

"Are you ready to go?"

"We're a little ahead of schedule," I said.

"I think we should go."

"Okay." I grabbed my own, less fluorescent, sport coat and slipped it on.

We stepped out onto the porch and I locked the front door behind me. I thought Thomas might stand there a moment, to take it all in. There was a cool breeze, but the sun was shining. It was a beautiful day. But Thomas made a beeline for the Audi and yanked on the passenger door handle a couple of times.

"It's locked," he said.

"Give me a second." I dug the remote from my pocket, aimed, and pressed. Thomas got in, put on his seat belt, and watched me impatiently as I came around the car, got in, did up my own belt, and keyed the ignition. The dashboard screen that allowed the driver to monitor dozens of the vehicle's functions, including the GPS, came to life.

"Okay, how it works is —"

"I can figure it out," Thomas said. He started turning knobs, touching the screen. "So if I want to enter in an address —"

"You see that thing there? You just —"

"I got it. You put in the city first, right?" I watched him type in "McLean."

"What are you doing?" Dr. Grigorin's office was in Promise Falls.

"I want to see what directions it gives for McLean, Virginia," he said.

"Why the hell would we go to Virginia?" I asked. "That's hundreds of miles away. The doctor's ten minutes. Virginia would take us all day."

"I don't actually want to go there. I don't have an appointment or anything. I wanted to see if it would give us the best route." He studied the screen a moment longer, appeared to get frustrated, and said, "Fine, I'll enter in the coordinates for the doctor's office. It's 2654 Pennington, suite 304."

"You don't have to enter the suite number. We're not *mailing* her something. We're driving there."

Thomas stopped examining the system long enough to look at me. "Do you think I'm stupid?"

The question, coming from anyone else, would have been sarcastic, or confrontational. But Thomas's tone suggested he was really asking.

"No," I said. "I don't. I'm sorry if I came across that way."

"You think I dress stupid. I could tell. You were making fun of my coat. And now you think I'm too stupid to figure this out."

"No — I mean, okay, the coat is a bit bright. But I don't think you're stupid. You seem to be able to intuit these things almost instantly. Go ahead. Put in the doctor's address."

He entered it, waited a couple of seconds for the nav system to figure things out.

"*Proceed to the highlighted route,*" the car's computer said.

"That's Maria," I said, heading the car down the driveway.

"What?"

"That's what I call the lady in my dashboard. Maria."

"Oh," Thomas said. "Why Maria?"

"I don't know. She just strikes me as a Maria. Maybe she should be Gretchen or Heidi or something that sounds kind of German, but I like Maria."

He was studying the screen as I drove down the road and pulled onto the highway. He never took his eyes off the digital map. "We're just passing Miller's Lane," he said.

"You could look out the window and know that," I said. "Let me ask you something."

"About what?"

"About when you found Dad. You okay talking about that?"

"This red line," he said, pointing. "Is that the route the car wants us to take?"

"That's right. You mind my asking something about when you found Dad?"

90

"What do you want to know?"

"Either before or after you pushed the tractor off him, did you touch any of the controls on it?"

"What do you mean?"

"Like turn off the key, or lift up the blades?"

"No. I don't even know how to drive it. Dad never let me use it. This computer is wrong." He hadn't taken his eyes off the navigational screen the whole time we'd been talking.

"So you didn't touch anything," I said. "On the tractor."

"That's right."

"What about when the ambulance came, or the police. Did any of the paramedics touch it?"

"They only cared about Dad. And I never saw the police do anything with it, but I wasn't always there. Maybe later they came."

"But it hasn't been moved all week," I said. "It's been sitting down by the creek this whole time."

"Did you hear what I said?" Thomas asked.

"About what?"

"This thing is wrong." He was still staring at the screen.

"What do you mean, wrong?"

"The route. It's no good."

"*In three hundred yards, make a right turn.*"

"Maria's wrong," Thomas said.

"She is?"

91

"She's telling you the wrong way to go. There's a faster way to go."

"She does that sometimes. She tends to stick to the main roads. And some of the really new roads, she doesn't even know they're there. Don't worry about it. Think of Maria as an adviser. You can choose to take her advice, or not."

"Well, she shouldn't be giving advice if she doesn't know what she's doing." He started fiddling with the buttons. "How do you tell her she's making a mistake?"

"I don't know that —"

"In one hundred yards, make a right turn."

"No!" Thomas shouted at the screen. "If we go the way she's suggesting, she'll take us down Saratoga Street. I don't want to go down Saratoga Street."

"What difference does it make?"

"I don't want to go that way!" He was starting to sound frantic.

"Just tell me which way you want me to go," I said. "We can tell Maria to take a hike."

Thomas said he wanted to go downtown by way of Main, not Saratoga. I said okay, since it was about the same distance. I ignored Maria when, as we passed Saratoga, she implored me to turn around. When I kept driving in the same direction, she recalculated the route, but she kept wanting to send us back, eventually, to Saratoga Street.

"Shut up," Thomas told her.

Maria said, "*In three hundred yards, make a left turn.*"

"I don't believe this," Thomas said. He was becoming increasingly agitated. "Make her stop. Make her stop talking." He slapped his hand on top of the dashboard, the way my father used to deal with the TV years ago when the horizontal went wonky.

"Just cancel the route," I said. "That button there."

Thomas, who'd been so good at entering the data, became flustered when it came to undoing what he'd done.

"*Make a right turn.*"

"No! We're not doing it!" Thomas yelled at the dash.

I reached over, fiddled with the settings, and shut her down.

"It's over," I said. "I turned her off."

Thomas sat back in the leather seat and took a few deep breaths. Finally, he looked at me and said, "You should get rid of this car."

EIGHT

Once there was no more fun to be had with the car's GPS, Thomas became sullen and asked me to turn around and go home. But I stuck to my guns and said he had an appointment, and we had to keep it.

He sulked.

I took a seat in the waiting room while Thomas went in for his session with Dr. Grigorin. There was one other patient waiting to see her. A very thin woman, late twenties, with long, scraggly blond hair that she kept twisting around her index finger. She was studying a spot on the wall with great interest, like there was a spider there that only she could see.

I glanced at my watch, figured I had a bit of time, and stepped out into the hall. I took out my cell phone, looked up a number online, and tapped to connect.

"*Promise Falls Standard,*" a woman's recorded voice said. "If you know the extension, enter it now. To use the company directory, press 2."

I struggled through the process until an actual phone rang.

"Julie McGill."

"Julie, hi, this is Ray Kilbride."

"Oh, hi, Ray. How are things?"

"Things are, you know, they're okay. Listen, am I catching you at a bad time?"

"Just waiting on another call," Julie said, her words coming quickly. "I thought this was going to be the principal from Promise Falls High. Trying to get some details on a small explosion in their chemistry class."

"Jesus."

"No one got hurt. But they could have. What can I do for you?"

"I wanted, first of all, to thank you for coming to my dad's funeral. That was really good of you."

"No problem," she said.

"I wondered, if you had a second, if we could grab a coffee so I could ask you a couple of questions about my father. Since you did the piece for the paper."

"It was pretty short. Not much more than a digest item. I don't have a lot of detail."

I was picking up, from her tone, that she was worried her other call was going to come in. I was about to tell her to forget about it, apologize for taking up her time, when she said, "But sure. Why don't you come by around four? We'll grab a beer. Meet you out front of the paper."

"Yeah, sure, that would be —"

"Gotta go." She hung up.

As I stepped back into the waiting room, the doctor and Thomas were emerging from her office. Dr. Grigorin was saying, "Don't be such a stranger. You need to come see me more often. It's good that we stay connected."

Thomas pointed to me. "So you'll talk to him."

"I will."

"Tell him to stop telling me what to do."

"You got it."

Dr. Grigorin — her first name turned out to be Laura — had fiery red hair that would have fallen to her shoulders if she hadn't spun it up into a bun, and stood about five-four in her heels, which I guessed added at least three inches. She was a striking woman in her early sixties. Rather than wearing typical doctor garb, she wore a red blouse and a straight black skirt that came to just below her knees.

"Mr. Kilbride," she said to me. "Won't you come in."

"Ray," I said. "Call me Ray."

She told Thomas to take a seat in the waiting room while we spoke.

"I'm supposed to prescribe you something," she said, smiling and motioning for me to take a chair. Rather than sit behind her desk, she took a chair across from me and crossed her legs. They were nice legs.

"To keep my controlling nature in check," I said.

"That's right." I liked her smile. She had the tiniest gap between her front teeth. "How does he seem to you?" she asked.

"It's hard to tell. I know my father's death has to have affected him, but he's not showing it."

"I can tell he's upset, even though he keeps things bottled up," Dr. Grigorin said.

"Except with Maria," I said.

"Who's Maria?" she asked. I explained and she shook her head with amusement. "Your father was very concerned about how much time Thomas's preoccupation was taking up. Thomas said he's cutting back and watched a movie with you the other night."

"That's not true. It was all I could do to get him to leave the house to come here today. He didn't want to leave his *work*."

"Has he explained it to you?"

"I didn't know there was anything to explain," I said. "He likes to explore the world's cities online. It's his thing." I shook my head and grinned. "Although he did mention the other day that I needed a security clearance to see what he was up to."

Dr. Grigorin nodded. "Thomas said it would be okay if I told you what he's been doing."

97

I sat up slightly in my chair. "What do you mean, what he's been doing?"

"Thomas believes he's working for the CIA. Consulting for them."

"I'm sorry. The what? The Central Intelligence Agency?"

"That's right."

"Working how? What's he doing — what does he *think* he's doing for them?"

"It's somewhat complicated, and not everything fits together quite right, not unlike dreams where you have different elements bumping up against one another. First of all, Thomas believes there's going to be a cataclysmic event, some kind of digital, electronic implosion or explosion. I'm not sure which. Perhaps a global computer glitch, or even something orchestrated by some foreign power — an ingenious computer virus — that will cripple this country's intelligence-gathering ability."

"Oh, man."

She continued. "When this happens, the first thing that will go down will be online maps. They'll all vanish instantly. Poof, gone. All the people in the intelligence community who depend on those will be scrambling, because they've been under orders from on high to save paper costs —" She must have noticed my eyebrows going up and she smiled. "Really, paper costs. Budget cuts are even hitting delusions now." She looked a bit sheepish, like maybe she shouldn't have made the joke. "Anyway, the point is, the government no longer has any hard copies."

My shock was giving way to fascination. Knowing Thomas as I did, it all made sense, in a bizarre kind of way.

"And when that happens," Laura continued, "who do you suppose the CIA is going to be turning to?"

"Let me guess."

She nodded. "He'll be able to draw for them, from memory, all the street plans of all the major cities in the world. He's got them all up here." She tapped her temple with her index finger. She wore red nail polish.

"But hang on," I said. "There'd still be old maps around. On paper, in libraries, in people's homes. Millions of school atlases, for crying out loud."

"Now you're being logical," Laura Grigorin chastised me. "The way your brother visualizes this apocalyptic event, those resources have already been destroyed. Libraries everywhere got rid of them and went digital. Every household has put their old maps out with the newspapers in the recycling and now relies solely on the computer. That's why this is going to be such a catastrophe. It'll be a world without maps, and the only person who will know how to reproduce them will be Thomas. And not just maps, but how each and every street in the world looks. Every storefront, every front yard, every intersection."

I shook my head in wonderment. "So he's getting ready for if and when this happens."

"Not if," she said. "It's coming. That's why he's spending every moment in his room traveling the world, memorizing as many cities as he can before this event. I had a patient — this was several years ago — who worked at a paper in Buffalo, and every night when he went home he took all the various editions of that day's paper with him because he was convinced that one day the entire newspaper would burn down, and he'd be the only one with a complete record of the paper's history — at least for the period that he was there."

"Unbelievable."

"His house, every hallway, every room, every surface, was filled with newspaper. He had to squeeze his way through stacks of newsprint to get anywhere."

"Sounds like one of those hoarders shows," I said.

"The interesting thing is," Laura said, "the newspaper *did* burn down."

My jaw dropped. "You're kidding."

She shook her head. "And they found the gas can that started it in the patient's house."

I was stunned, briefly, and then laughed. "You're not suggesting Thomas is going to arrange a global map-destroying virus, are you? Because I think that's a bit beyond him."

"I only mention the other story to show you that your brother's obsession, while unusual, is not entirely unique. Just different in its shadings."

"My God," I said. Something occurred to me. "McLean."

"What?"

"Isn't that where the CIA has its headquarters? Thomas wanted to program a route into my car's GPS system to get there, then thought better of it. Maybe because I didn't yet have clearance." I laughed. "I guess, now that he's letting you tell me all this, I have it now."

"Your brother trusts you. That's a plus. People with schizophrenia often lose trust in those closest to them. They're fearful of everyone." She took a breath. "Now, I started off telling you there were different elements to this."

"Okay."

"In the meantime, before this map-destroying incident happens, Thomas believes the CIA may call on him for other help. For example, let's say they have an agent in jeopardy in, I don't know, Caracas or someplace. The bad guys have found him and he's on the run, and he doesn't know which way to turn. The CIA will put in a call to Thomas, ask him for an escape route. He'll be able to give them one, faster than they could get it on a computer."

I ran my palm from my forehead to the back of my neck. "He just might be able to do it, too."

"Thomas mentions escape routes quite often, about being able to help people who are trapped, cornered in some way."

I shook my head slowly, trying to imagine being in his head.

Grigorin continued, "And governments might also want him for help in disasters. Natural or otherwise. Think about all the tornadoes we've been having lately, or the earthquakes in Christchurch, in Haiti, the tsunami in Japan. Entire communities wiped out, vanished. Or, God forbid, another 9/11 kind of event. Rescuers could call Thomas, tell him that they're at such and such a corner, and he could tell them what was there, what they should be looking for."

"Anything else?"

Grigorin smiled sadly. "That about covers it."

I rested my palms atop my thighs. "So where does this leave us?"

"I'm not sure. I understand, as a result of your father's death, there may be a need to change Thomas's living arrangements."

I discussed my concerns about his living in the house alone.

"Your concerns are valid," she said. "He should be living in town, in an environment where he can be checked in on. Not in a repressive kind of way, just someone watching out for him. I can recommend a place you might want to take a look at."

"Do you think he'd go?"

She leaned back in her chair and crossed her arms. "I think, if you introduce him to the idea gradually, he might. He'd be able to keep his computer. He could still maintain his . . . hobby. But it's important you get him out of the house more. Take him on a picnic. A movie. The grocery store. To the mall. The more he's out of his bedroom, the more comfortable he becomes, the easier it will be to move him into a new environment. I take it you don't want to move back to your father's house and look after your brother full-time."

"I don't . . . I don't want you to think I don't care about him."

She shook her head. "Not at all. In fact, I'm not sure that would be the best thing for him. We need him to be more independent. Your father meant well, but he allowed Thomas to become totally dependent on him. He did everything for him. In many ways, he enabled your brother's obsession by freeing him of all responsibilities."

"I think Dad figured it was just easier to do everything himself," I said. "Do you think Thomas is worse? Since Dad died?"

"I don't know. I asked him if he still hears the voices — often associated with schizophrenia — and he says occasionally. He talks to former president Bill Clinton, who's acting as his liaison with the CIA. Thomas's medication keeps the voices to little more than a whisper, and I don't want to up his dose. He does take his medication every day, yes? You've seen him? Olanzapine?"

"Yes."

"A higher dosage would make Thomas sluggish. It could also cause some dizziness, weight gain, dry mouth, a number of things he wouldn't like. What we're looking for is a good balance. With your support, we can continue to manage the situation adequately."

"Yesterday, he got all worked up because he'd seen what he thought was some minor traffic mishap in Boston. He wanted me to do something about it, try to get in touch with some anonymous driver who had his headlight broken probably months ago."

"You need to be patient," she said. "It's easy to become discouraged. I think, considering everything, Thomas is doing well. He has his troubles, some of which he won't talk to me about, but —"

"Like what troubles? What's he not talking about?"

"Well, if he'd talk about them I'd know," she said. "I know there's something, from his childhood, that haunts him, but he's never opened up about it."

I thought about that infamous car trip,

where Thomas bloodied his head against the window. I told her the story, wondering whether she'd heard it.

"I have," she said, so that wasn't it.

She moved on. "The good thing is, Thomas thinks the world of you. He's brought me clippings of your illustrations to show me."

"I didn't know that," I said.

"I think he's always been envious of your talent, of being able to take a picture that's in your head and put it on paper."

"It's what he does with maps," I said.

"You have similar gifts, but they manifest themselves in different ways," Laura Grigorin said.

"Did you talk to my father when he came in with Thomas?"

"Yes," she said.

"How did he seem to you?"

"What are you asking?"

"I don't know, exactly. When I was talking to Harry Peyton, the lawyer handling the estate, who was also a friend of Dad's, I got the idea Dad might have been depressed."

"I can't offer an opinion as to whether he was clinically depressed," she said. "I never treated him. But he did seem . . . *weary.* I think the strain of looking after your brother, alone, was wearing on him."

"He had an accidental death insurance policy," I said. "That, along with the some other things, would be enough to set Thomas up for a while, at least."

Dr. Grigorin's green eyes were piercing. "Are you suggesting something, Ray?"

I just shook my head. "I don't know." I waved my hand. "Let's forget about it."

"How about you?" she asked. "How are *you* doing?"

"Me?" The question took me by surprise. "I'm fine."

Our time was up. I stood. "Oh," she said. "I almost forgot. I'm supposed to give you something to deal with your bossiness."

She reached into her desk and came out with an opaque prescription container filled with oversized pills in several different, brilliant colors.

"What are these?" I asked as she put them into my hand.

"M&M's," she said.

NINE

Stunned after recognizing her new lover on television, Allison Fitch fires up her laptop to do some research.

"Son of a bitch," she keeps whispering under her breath.

While Morris Sawchuck has his eye on the governor's mansion, he already wields plenty of power as the state's attorney general. ("Son of a bitch," she says again.) He's fifty-seven and Bridget is his third wife. He married her three years ago, and it's still a subject of gossip among the chattering classes, what with her being twenty-one years younger, and quite a looker, too. There's talk about the fact they take separate vacations, but Allison already knows that.

Sawchuck met his first wife, Katherine Wolcott, while attending Harvard. They married shortly after he got his BA, and she worked as a legal secretary to support him while he went on to Harvard Law. Five years later, he divorced her for Geraldine Kennedy (no relation to *those* Kennedys, or at least not close enough to spark invitations to the family compound at Hyannis Port, as one of the stories Allison finds suggests).

Sawchuck didn't divorce Geraldine. She committed suicide, in 2001. Sits in her BMW with the garage door closed and the engine running and lets the carbon monoxide do its thing. She had, the stories said, been in and out of the hospital and diagnosed manic depressive. There's one quote attributed to Katherine, which she denies ever making: "I don't know why I didn't do that. God knows, when I was married to the cheatin' son of a bitch, I sure thought about it."

There were stories. And puzzlement. Katherine was beautiful, and Geraldine had been a stunner as well. Why was it always the guys with gorgeous wives who ended up looking for something else?

Sawchuck never dignified the rumors with a response. He settled into an appropriate period of mourning, threw himself into his work as a prosecutor. He garnered a lot of attention, going after crooked union bosses, Russian mobsters, a gang of child pornographers. Of the last, Sawchuck reportedly said if he could find a way to get them strung up by their nuts in Times Square, he'd do it. Scored him points, although, according to one pundit, it would lose him the child pornographer vote.

Several death threats were made against him. He reportedly now carries a concealed weapon whenever he is out.

A couple of years after Geraldine's death, he was spotted occasionally with a number of different, and very attractive, women. He got his picture in the papers at play openings, fund-raisers, political functions, usually with someone different on his arm each time. Some talking heads expressed concern that his eye for the ladies might, at some point, prove a political liability. Everyone admired a player, to a point, but players had too many secrets that could rise to the surface and embarrass them later. Like that old Italian president with his harem of strippers, although that guy, man, he made philandering an Olympic sport. Those same pundits said that before Sawchuck pursued his ambitions for higher office, he'd have to settle down, or at least appear to.

And then came Bridget.

A onetime fashion model with jet black hair who stands five-ten in her stocking feet — she has a passing resemblance to Allison herself — she works for a prestigious public relations firm with offices in SoHo, London, Paris, and Hong Kong. She had organized an event to raise funds to build a kids' baseball diamond in an underprivileged area — a favorite cause of the attorney general's — and they appeared to hit it off from the get-go. A whirlwind courtship — as they say — followed, and before some kid who doesn't have enough money for breakfast can run to first base, the two are engaged. Three months later, they're married.

Sawchuck, Allison's research finds, has powerful friends from across the political spectrum, but the majority of them are on the right. He knows two former vice presidents, one Republican, one Democrat, well enough to have them to dinner at his home whenever they're in town.

Oh, and there's something else that's of particular interest to Allison. The dude is loaded.

Estimated worth falls into the "holy shit" category. Most of it inherited. You don't make that kind of money working for the state, unless you are very, *very* dirty, and there's nothing to suggest Morris Sawchuck is, even if his closest friend and adviser, Howard Talliman (nickname: Howard the Taliban) has been known to cut a few corners here and there. Morris's father, Graham, had been a big-time real estate developer and owned a couple of dozen skyscrapers in Manhattan. Sawchuck inherited the business when his father died, which is now run at arm's length to avoid any allegations of conflict of interest. Sawchuck doesn't mind having property and more money than anyone like Allison can even imagine, but what he really craves is attention and influence and the high profile, and he's found the best way to get it is through the relentless pursuit of those who break the law. Everybody loves a crusader.

Allison jumps from Web page to Web page, finding more information about how much money Sawchuck has. Millions, for sure, if not billions.

It's enough to make one's head spin.

Looks like she might be able to get what she needs to pay back Courtney, and buy herself a new pair of Manolo Blahniks, too. Girl always needs new shoes.

She paces the apartment for the better part of an hour, practicing what she's going to say. She doesn't want it to sound like out-and-out blackmail. What she's really looking for is a loan. Except, unlike most loans, this would be one she gets to pay back on the installment plan. Payments stretched out over, say, the next couple of thousand years. So, okay, maybe it's more like a gift she's seeking. But is that such a big deal? All that money, how big a deal can it be to throw a few thousand her way? And Allison can return the favor. No doubt about it. Allison knows just the right way to show gratitude. And not by putting her mouth in some special place to make someone happy.

She can show gratitude by keeping that

mouth shut. That's her way of saying thank you.

She can decide not to go to the *Daily News* or the *Times* or the *Post*. Or one of those TV shows, like *Dateline*.

Won't that be a nice thing not to do?

Because something like this, coming out, well, that's not going to help Mr. I-Want-to-Be-Governor one little bit.

Maybe she's not even going to have to get to that point. She won't have to mention the newspapers or the TV shows. Maybe she'll have a check in her hands seconds after she says the words "I know who you are."

Allison picks up her cell, starts to enter in the number she was given, then stops. Her heart is pounding. Making up stories to get money out of her mother, that's one thing.

This is something else again.

This is what happens when a girl leaves Dayton for the big city.

"Hello?"

"It's me. It's Allison."

"What — Allison?"

"Yeah, Allison. Remember me?"

"Of course I — look, I really can't talk now."

"We need to get together."

"This isn't a good time."

"I saw you on the news."

"You — what?"

"I had no idea. No idea at all who you are. How'd you forget to mention something like that? First, that you're married, and second, that —"

"Look, Allison, I'll try to give you a call in a week or two. There's a lot going on right now. If you saw the news, you know things are starting to heat up in the campaign and . . . and . . . there are other problems. A possible investigation of —"

"You remember where we first hooked up?"

"Yes, of course."

"Be there at three. Before it gets busy, and you can still make it to Lincoln Center or Broadway or whatever thousand-dollar-a-plate dinner you have to go to tonight."

"I can't meet with you. We can't — I'm really sorry but we can't be seen together."

"Three o'clock."

"Jesus, what the hell is this about?"

"Well, I can put your mind at ease about one thing. I'm not pregnant."

By half past two, Allison's at a Gramercy Park bar, around the corner from that place where O. Henry wrote "The Gift of the Magi." Manages to get the same booth they shared on their first date. Date? Was it really a *date*? Doesn't "date" imply some kind of adherence to social convention? "Clandestine meeting," maybe? What's that old-fashioned word, again? "Tryst?"

She orders herself a gin and tonic, keeps an eye on the door. She's still rehearsing what she's going to say, although she wonders why she's bothering. Despite all the time she spent practicing her lines before making the call to set up this meeting, once the ringing stopped and the cell was answered, she started saying the first thing that came into her head. Winging it. Including that line about being pregnant, which, she has to admit, was pretty goddamn funny.

At three o'clock, right on the dot, someone walks through the door, sees Allison in the booth.

It's not Morris Sawchuck.

It's his wife, Bridget.

She doesn't look like the Bridget Sawchuck Allison saw on the news. She has her hair wrapped up in a red and black scarf Allison is guessing is Hermès. She's wearing sunglasses that cover up half her face.

But it's her, all right. The attorney general's hot little wife. Strutting in on her three-inch heels, hands tucked into the pockets of her trench. Turning a few heads as she walks past the bar. But not getting recognized. She'd turn heads whether you recognized her or not.

Bridget Sawchuck walks straight to the booth where Allison's sitting, slides onto the leather seat across from her.

"You look like a freaking spy," Allison says,

grinning.

"I only have a few minutes," Bridget Sawchuck says. "Why the urgent meeting?"

"Like I said to you on the phone, we've got some things to talk about."

TEN

"I don't want you think I'm the sort of person who gets caught up in titles, but what will mine be?"

"Gosh, I don't know. I must admit, I haven't really put my mind to it. Do you have any ideas?"

"Assistant director. Not of the entire agency. But of the division I work for."

"What about Assistant Director, Mapology."

"Mapology?"

"That was just off the top of my head. I'll come up with something better. And we need to talk about an office."

"I won't need an office, Mr. President. I'll work from home. I like working from home. My brother is living with me now, and my computer is here."

"Yes, but don't forget, once the catastrophe hits, you may be reduced to paper and pencil, or pen. This virus, or whatever it is, will render computers obsolete. You're going to need lots of big tables, lots of flat space to lay out the

maps you draw for us."

"I could put them on the kitchen table, and the living room floor."

"Is your brother going to be okay with that?"

"I hope so. He's like our father. Always trying to get me to do things I don't want to do. My dad, he made me very angry sometimes. Have I mentioned that?"

"Yes."

"I feel bad about what happened to him."

"He never understood the importance of your work. What about your brother? Is he getting in the way of your progress?"

"No. I told my doctor about him, and she gave him some pills. I told the doctor she could tell him about what I was doing."

"Do you think that was wise?"

"He's my brother. I'd told my father, too. And besides, if you need me for an emergency, like, right away, he's going to have to know what I'm doing. There could be another earthquake, or a tsunami."

"If you think it's okay to tell him, then fine."

"And you're sure you don't mind my communicating with you directly? I've always admired you. At first I was dealing with CIA director Goldsmith, but then he had to resign after all that trouble, and then, as of course you know, he killed himself, and so I thought it just made sense to talk to you."

"I don't mind at all."

"That's good, B—. Oh, you know what I

almost did? I almost called you Bill."

"*Hell, that's okay. That's what everybody calls me. We're becoming good friends, aren't we?*"

"Yes. Yes, we are. I'll send you another e-mail report later today. Take care."

ELEVEN

Dad didn't worry about leaving Thomas on his own, and neither did I. While my brother had a number of odd notions and peculiar habits, there was nothing to suggest he was a threat to anyone, or himself. He'd never exhibited any suicidal tendencies, nor had he ever attacked anyone. My father would leave Thomas when he drove into Promise Falls to buy groceries or run other errands. And, as Harry had pointed out, to sit in the diner, order a cup of coffee, and stare out the window.

I'd left Thomas home during Dad's funeral when he refused to attend. While that had really pissed me off, I wasn't worried that he'd get into any trouble while I was gone. The one apparent benefit of spending all his time in his room, going on his virtual tours, was that he didn't get into any mischief. What could happen to him staring at those screens all day, with the possible exceptions of eyestrain or repetitive stress injury to his mouse-clicking wrist?

So I didn't have any qualms, later that afternoon, telling Thomas I was going to be out for a while. "I'll bring back dinner."

"KFC," he said, his back to me as he advanced up some street in Bolivia or Belgium or who knew the hell where.

"I can't eat that stuff," I said. "I was thinking I'd grab a couple of subs."

"No black olives," he said, his eyes never leaving the screen.

I had the Audi parked in the *Promise Falls Standard* lot fifteen minutes later, a couple of minutes after four. I was afraid I'd be keeping Julie McGill waiting in the lobby, but she wasn't there when I went in. I'd have asked the person at reception to let her know I was there if there'd been anyone at reception, but there was only a phone on the desk inviting me to dial an extension, a list of them taped to the desk beside it.

I was looking up her name when I heard a series of speedy clicks on a set of nearby stairs.

"Hey," Julie said. "I see you've met the receptionist."

She said the closest place to grab a beer was Grundy's, a place that was new since I'd left for Burlington. Which still meant it could be more than a decade and a half old. She was dressed in black boots, jeans, a men's white dress shirt with button-down collar, and a well-worn black leather jacket. An oversized black purse that looked like it could hold little more than a jackhammer and half a dozen cinder blocks was hanging from one shoulder, making her walk slightly lopsided. Her black hair had half a dozen gray streaks that did not appear to have been put there on purpose.

We grabbed a booth and Julie's purse made a thunking sound as she dropped it next to her.

"I carry around a lot of shit," she said. She held up a hand to the waitress, caught her eye, and smiled. "Hey, Bee, my usual and something for the lady."

Bee looked at me. "I'll have whatever she's having," I said.

As the waitress walked away Julie said, "Again, sorry about your dad. But it's good to see you. Long time." She smiled.

"Yeah," I said. There was something in Julie's voice that suggested we had some kind of history.

Her face broke into a grin. "You don't remember."

I opened my mouth, but nothing came out. I smiled and said, "I was going to try to bluff my way through something but thought better of it. You look like someone who'd be hard to put one over on."

"Sadie Hawkins dance. You were six months from graduating. I was a year behind you.

You got asked by Ann Paltrow, had been drinking before the dance, were pretty hammered by the time you got there. She got mad and ditched you, at which point you started putting the moves on me. Turns out I'd downed a few Buds myself and before you knew it we're in the back of your dad's car making out for an hour. Tell me you've forgotten that."

I smiled, swallowed. "I have forgotten that."

"Then I guess you've also forgotten that I left town a few months after that, and nine and a half months later —"

"Jesus."

She smiled, patted my hand. "I'm just messing with you. About the last part, anyway. I mean, I did leave town, but I just had to get out of this place. I never felt like I fit in around here. You always seemed a bit out of place, too, but you got along okay because — hope you don't mind my saying this — you were kind of a Goody Two-shoes."

"I suppose," I conceded. "And you . . . not so much."

She smiled. "I had my moments."

"There was a while there, I remember, during exams, someone kept calling the fire department, saying the school was on fire, or there was a bomb. Word was, that was you."

She went stone-faced. "I have no idea who would do such a thing. That's totally irresponsible." She paused. "But I can certainly understand how someone who wasn't fully prepared to take a difficult test might feel she had no choice but to resort to extreme measures." Another pause. "And it was only twice."

"Shit, so it was you."

"Fifth," Julie said. "But it was one more reason to get out of town."

"Yeah, I didn't hang in all that much longer."

"And now we're both back," she said as the waitress delivered two Coronas. "At least you've got an excuse. A death in the family."

"What's yours?"

"I traveled around, got jobs at several small-town papers. No one cared all that much back then whether you had a journalism degree, which I did not. By the time I applied for a job at the *Los Angeles Times* I had plenty of experience. And then they started downsizing, and I was out of a job. Every other paper was cutting back, too, but as it turned out, tough as times are, the *Standard* newsroom had openings. One woman got herself fired, and there was this other guy, Harwood — God, the problems that guy had — left town to start his life over again someplace else, good luck with that. So I came back. The paper has no money, it's a real shit show run by a bunch of fuckheads, but it pays a tenth of the bills till I find something else. And believe me, I'm looking."

I laughed.

"What?"

"Your word for the folks you work for. Thomas says that's what you called the Landry brothers."

Now it was her turn to try to remember. "God, *those* two. Dumber than shoes. I called them fuckheads?"

"When they were picking on Thomas. You stepped in, chased them off. I know it's probably a little late to say thank you, but thank you."

"God, I'd forgotten about that." She grabbed the Corona by the neck and took a very long drink, rested her back against the seat. "You know they're both dead?"

"Seriously?"

"Both drunk, pulled over to the side of the road in a pickup. One was around back, dropping something over the tailgate. Other one backed over him, not knowing he was there, heard the bump, got out to see what was wrong but forgot to put the truck in park, started running after it, tripped and got caught under the back wheel. I'm just sorry it happened before I got here. Would love to have written the story." She looked at me and made an apologetic face. "Sorry. Wasn't thinking there. You wanted to talk to me because of the story I wrote about your dad."

I shook my head, warding off her apology. "That's okay. I read the story. I wondered if there was anything more you knew about it."

"Not really."

"Do you know whether there was any kind of investigation afterward?"

"Yup. The usual. Death-by-misadventure kind of thing. The facts were pretty straight-forward. There was no inquest. I wrote a short follow-up piece but it didn't have any surprises so it never even made the paper. I know, when it's something that happens to you, it's a big deal, the details matter. But for the *Standard*, it was a one-day story, and only about two inches at that. It kind of jumped out at me on the day's police logs because I knew who Adam Kilbride was, that he was Thomas's and your dad."

"I shouldn't have troubled you with this."

"It's okay," Julie said. "These things, I mean, you know, they're hard. Look, is there anything I can do for you, for Thomas?"

"No, it's — yeah, I mean, drop in sometime. I know Thomas would be happy to see you. He's — I guess you know he's kind of differ-ent."

"He always was," Julie said.

"I think now he's even more so," I said.

Julie smiled. "He always had this thing about maps. He still into those?"

"Yes."

I worked on my Corona. Julie had nearly

125

finished hers. "You were a bit weird yourself, you know. Always drawing things. You weren't exactly a jock."

"I threw the javelin," I said defensively. It was true. It was about the only sport, if it can be called that, I ever went out for. And I was damn good at it. That, and playing darts in our basement rec room.

"The javelin," Julie said. "Really. One of the big full-body-contact events. I see the drawing thing paid off for you, though. Your illustrations made the *L.A. Times* every now and then. They're good."

"Thanks."

"You get married along the way?"

"No. Came close a couple of times. You?"

"Lived a few months with a guy who does that relaxation music, you know, like they play when you're getting a massage? With birds chirping and brooks babbling in the background? Mellows you out? He had that effect on me. I nearly slipped into a coma half a dozen times with him. Then there was a thing with an NBA coach, a reality TV producer, and a guy who raised iguanas." She paused reflectively. "I've had a knack for attracting people outside the boundaries of normalcy. But hey, that's California. Maybe it's good to be back here."

Out of nowhere, I had a flashback.

"Purple," I said.

"What?"

I pointed my index finger at her, waved it about in a general way. "Your underwear. It was purple."

Julie smiled. "I was hurt there for a bit, thinking I failed to make an impression."

TWELVE

The next day, at breakfast, I said to Thomas, "I liked Dr. Grigorin."

"She's okay," he said, grabbing a banana from the bowl. "What kind of pills did she give you?"

I shrugged. "Who knows what the hell all these drugs are called."

He peeled the banana down to the halfway point. "Did she tell you?"

"Tell me what?"

"What I'm doing. I told her you could know about it."

"She told me."

"I thought it was time for you to know what I'm working on."

"Why didn't you just tell me yourself?"

He bit into the banana. "I figured, coming from her, you'd believe it. Because she's a doctor."

"You think Dr. Grigorin believes it?" I asked him. "What it is you're doing? Memorizing maps and street plans so you can help secret agents on the run? And that one day, there won't be any maps at all and you'll have all the information stored up here?" I tapped my index finger just above my temple.

He put the banana down and rested his palms on the kitchen table. "If she didn't believe it, why would she ask so many questions about it? If she didn't believe it, she'd dismiss it out of hand." Disappointment washed over his face. "I guess you don't believe in what I'm doing. I was wrong, thinking Dr. Grigorin could convince you."

"Think about it, Thomas. You're just some guy, living in a house outside Promise Falls in upstate New York. You've never worked in law enforcement or for any kind of government agency. You don't have a degree in whatever one gets a degree in if they're an expert in maps and —"

"Cartographer."

"What?"

"A person who's an expert at making and studying maps is a cartographer. But you can't really get a degree in cartography. You'd probably get a degree in geography and apply what you'd learned while acquiring that degree when you began working as a cartographer."

He'd thrown me off my game for a moment there, but it didn't take me long to get back on track. "Okay, so, you don't have a geography degree, and you've never worked as a cartographer."

"That is correct," Thomas said, nodding.

"So what you believe is, you, with no actual qualifications and no connections to the powers that be, have attracted the attention of the Central Intelligence Agency, this multi-billion-dollar organization with operatives all over the world, and they want you to be their map guy."

Thomas nodded. "I know. It's amazing, isn't it?"

"That it is," I said.

"But I have a good memory. So I've been chosen."

I leaned back in my chair and said, "*You* are the chosen one."

"Now you're mocking me again," he said.

"I'm not — okay, I suppose it sounds like I am. What I'm trying to do, Thomas, is point out to you how totally absurd this is. Dr. Grigorin even told me that you've been in touch with former president Clinton."

The night before, standing at Thomas's partially open door, I'd watched him carry on a conversation with someone who wasn't there. The phone was on the hook, and he wasn't on the keyboard or looking at the monitor. I'd heard him say, "I almost called you Bill."

"That's right," Thomas said. "But you can still call him Mr. President. Former presidents are still called that."

130

"I know."

"I don't want to talk about this anymore," Thomas said. "Those pills the doctor gave you aren't working. I thought they'd make you more tolerant and understanding. But you're just like Dad."

He left his unfinished banana on the table, got up, went back up to his room, and slammed the door.

We needed food in the house. I couldn't keep going out for subs and pizza. I was loading up on frozen foods at Price Chopper when I ran into Len Prentice and his wife, Marie. Len and my father had maintained a friendship after Dad left the printing company. Normally of pasty white complexion, he looked as though he'd gotten some sun lately, although he'd lightened up slightly since the funeral. Marie, however, was pale and washed out. She'd had health problems as long as I'd known her. I couldn't remember what, exactly, but thought it had something to do with chronic fatigue syndrome. Always tired. I'd known the two of them — admittedly, not well — for the better part of three decades. They had a son, Matthew, who was about my age, and whom I'd hung out with some when I was in my teens. He was an accountant now in Syracuse, married, with three kids.

"Hey, Ray," said Len, who was pushing the cart. Marie had been trailing along behind him. "How're you and Thomas doing?"

Before I could answer, Marie said, "Ray. Good to see you."

"Hi," I said to both of them. "We're good. Managing. Just getting in some provisions."

"It was a lovely service," Marie said earnestly. Dad had always referred to her as "Mary Sunshine," although not to her face. Despite her health problems, she was perpetually cheery. The minister could have dropped his pants and waved his dick around and she'd still have commented on how nice the flowers were before anything else.

"Yes," I said. "Thanks again for coming." I looked at Len and smiled. "I meant to ask you the other day whether you fell asleep under a sunlamp."

Marie patted my arm playfully. "Oh, you. Len got back from a vacation a couple of weeks ago."

"Where'd you go?" I asked. "Florida?"

Len shook his head, like it didn't really matter, but said, "Thailand."

Marie said, "Tell him how beautiful it was."

"Oh, it was that. Absolutely stunning. The water, it's this coral blue color unlike anything you've ever seen. Have you been there, Ray?"

"Never," I said. "But I've heard people say it's wonderful. You didn't go, Marie?"

She sighed. "I just don't have the energy for travel. Not to go that far. I don't mind packing up and spending a week at a lodge

132

you can drive to in a couple of hours, but all that walking through airports, lining up at customs, having to take your shoes off and put them back on again. It's too much for me. But just because I'm not up to gallivanting around the globe doesn't mean Len shouldn't head off with others who feel more up to traveling than I do."

"Ray," Len said, "I've been meaning to come out and see you before you go back to Burlington."

"Not sure when that will be," I said. "I need to get Thomas sorted out first. I have to decide what to do about the house. Thomas can't live there on his own."

"Oh mercy, no," Marie said. "The boy needs looking after."

I felt my back go up, but didn't show it. She was right, that Thomas needed some looking after. But he was a man. Not a boy. He didn't deserve to be treated as though he were a child. And then I felt a pang of guilt, wondering if I'd been too hard on him, the way I'd been challenging him about his mission.

"Yeah, he does," I said. "But I'm going to see if I can make him a little more self-sufficient."

It was something I'd been thinking about. Just because Thomas believed in things that were not real didn't mean he couldn't make a contribution in the real world. I wanted to get him making his own meals, and helping out around the house. Maybe, if I started giving him responsibilities, it would keep him out of his room for longer intervals. Involve him, if not in the outside world, in the operations of the household.

"Well, we should let you go," Len said. "Good to see you."

"I keep meaning to drop by with a casserole for you boys," Marie said. "Or maybe you'd like to come over for dinner?"

"That's very kind," I said. "I'll talk to Thomas about that." *Fat chance*, I thought, although dinner out with people he knew might be worth a try. A baby step out of the house. We'd already managed a trip to the psychiatrist without a major incident, so long as you didn't count Thomas's quarrels with Maria.

"Thomas still memorizing maps for when the big computer virus hits?" Len asked, a hint of a smile in the corner of his mouth.

I was caught off guard. "You know about that?"

"Your dad told me. I guess he needed to talk to somebody about it."

Slowly, I nodded. Marie said, "Len, don't bring that up. It's none of your business."

"It was. Adam told me," he snapped at her, and Marie blinked. To me, he said, "Your dad was feeling the burden of it all, you know?"

So everyone seemed to be telling me.

■ ■ ■ ■

I tapped on Thomas's door and opened it far enough to stick my head in. "I'm back."

Thomas, clicking away on his mouse, traveling with his back to me, said, "Okay."

"And you're making dinner."

That got him to turn around. "What?"

"I thought I'd let you make dinner tonight."

"I never make dinner."

"Then all the more reason to start. I got some frozen stuff. It'll be simple."

"Why aren't you making dinner? Dad always made dinner."

"I've got a job, too," I said. "You've got yours, and I've got mine. I've got calls to make, and I may have to bring back some of my stuff from Burlington —"

"Vermont."

"Right, from Burlington, Vermont, so I can work here while we sort things out."

"Sort things out," Thomas said quietly.

"That's right. I'll walk you through it. How to put the oven on, all that stuff. But you'll need to come down around five."

I treasured Thomas's shell-shocked expression as I closed the door.

Almost on cue, my cell rang. It was my agent, Jeremy Chandler, who'd been fielding job inquiries for me for the last ten years.

"I've got three jobs here for you but it's not

like the Sistine Chapel is asking you to paint a ceiling and you've got forty years to do it. These are magazines and one Web site, Ray, with deadlines. Looming deadlines. If you can't do the work, I need to know now so I can farm these jobs out to other artists who, while not nearly as gifted as yourself, are clearly much hungrier."

"I told you, I'm at my father's place."

"Oh shit, yeah, I forgot. He died, right?"

"Yes, that's exactly what he did."

"So, the funeral and all that stuff, is that over?"

"Yes."

"Then you'll be back in your studio when, exactly?"

"I have some stuff to deal with, Jeremy. I might have to set up a makeshift studio here temporarily."

"Good idea. Otherwise, I'll have to get Tarlington for these illustrations."

"Oh, God," I said. "The guy paints with his feet. His Obamas look like Bill Cosby. Every black guy he does looks like Bill Cosby."

"Look, if you can't take the job, you don't get to criticize. Did I tell you, I heard from Vachon's people?"

"Jesus." Carlo Vachon, a noted Brooklyn crime family boss, was facing a slew of possible indictments on everything from murder to unpaid parking tickets. I'd been commissioned by a New York magazine to do a drawing of him in which I'd exaggerated all his physical features, particularly his girth, as he held a gun to the Statue of Liberty. In my version, she had both her arms in the air.

I was breaking out in an instant sweat. "Is there a hit out on me?"

"No, no, nothing like that. Apparently he loved the illustration and he wants to buy the original. The thing is with these mob guys, they love the attention, even when it's not exactly positive."

"You have the original?"

"I do."

"Send it. No charge," I said.

"Done. But that's not even why I called."

"What is it?"

"There's a new site about to start up. It's got backing from some very big people, and they want to take on HuffPo, but they want something different, and I said to them, what about an animated political cartoon, kind of like those ones on *The New Yorker* Web site. Ten seconds long, but the animation is actually kept to a minimum. You create movement by panning across the image and —"

"I get how it could be done," I said. "You mentioned me?"

"I didn't even have to. They came to me. This woman who's setting it up, her name's Kathleen Ford. Got financial backing like you wouldn't believe. Lots of media money. She wants to have a sit-down with you ASAP."

"Okay, but right now I —"

There was a knock at the front door. A solid, purposeful, somebody-means-business kind of knock. I hadn't heard a car pull up, but Jeremy did tend to talk as though he was trying to drown out a 747, even when there wasn't one in the vicinity.

"Someone's here," I said.

"Ray, this is *huge.* You've got to meet with this woman. It's major bucks."

"I'll get back to you."

I left the phone on the kitchen table and went to the door.

There were two of them standing there on the porch, a black sedan parked behind my Audi, blocking it in, I supposed, should I decide to make a run for it. A man and a woman, both in their forties, both dressed in shades of gray. Both in suits, although his came with a narrow, businesslike tie.

"Mr. Kilbride?" the woman asked.

"Yes?"

"I'm Agent Parker, and this is Agent Driscoll."

"Huh?"

"FBI," she said sternly.

138

THIRTEEN

Bridget Sawchuck believes that if she's going to have to discuss her situation with her husband's closest friend and chief adviser, Howard Talliman, it better be in a public place. Maybe he'll be able to resist the temptation to throttle her if there are witnesses, although she isn't one hundred percent sure that will save her. She invites him to lunch at the Union Square Café, booking a table for one o'clock.

Talliman has been Morris Sawchuck's best friend since God was a boy. They went to Harvard together, got drunk together, practiced law together, vacationed together, probably even got laid together on a joint trip to Japan a couple of years after Geraldine died. Howard, very early on, began working behind the scenes on political campaigns — Republican, Democrat, didn't matter. Only winning mattered. If a hockey player could be traded from the Rangers to the Bruins, then slam his former teammates into the boards, Talliman could formulate strategy for any party that was willing to pay his price. He's never wanted to be the candidate. He is short and paunchy, and says he has the sex appeal of a garden gnome, but he knows how to play the political game from behind the bench and turn others into winners.

"You can take this as far as you want to go," Howard told Morris more than a decade ago. "The only thing that limits you is your own ambition. If you've got enough of it, it'll take you right to the top. But you have to build in increments. A tough prosecutor, then an attorney general — you start drawing a line and see where it takes you. It takes you right to the fucking top, that's where it takes you."

Howard Talliman mixes the Kool-Aid, and Morris drinks it.

All the hard work is paying off. Big time. Morris is surely headed to the governor's mansion, and who knows where the hell he'll go after that?

As proud as Howard is of shaping his best friend into a political star, it was finding him a new, beautiful young wife to stand at his side during victory speeches that really puffs him up. He'd encountered Bridget at the PR firm he had hired on behalf of another client, a circuit court judge who'd found himself with his nuts in a vise after his son was arrested for running a meth lab out of the judge's summer place in New Hampshire. The moment Howard saw her he knew she'd look perfect standing next to Morris at every campaign stop across the state of New York. She was sexy in a Michelle Obama–Jackie O kind of way. Statuesque, long neck, nice figure but not too busty. Poise to spare.

Howard, Bridget realizes now, maneuvered Morris and her together without their even knowing it at the time. He brought her in to organize that kids' baseball diamond fund-raiser, which put Bridget and Morris together at the same place at the same time. Howard made the introductions, whispered into each of their ears that the one was interested in the other.

Machiavelli with a little Cupid's arrow, that's what Howard was.

But there was something there. Within a week, Bridget found herself sprawled across the backseat of Sawchuck's limo, belts un-buckling, snaps unsnapping, a would-be governor's head between her legs.

A lot of fun, even if Bridget has not always been, strictly speaking, *exclusively* hetero-sexual. But what the hell. Once she found out the kind of life she was looking at, hook-ing up with someone like Morris Sawchuck, she figured she could play on just the one team forever.

Didn't turn out to be the case, but that realization didn't dawn on her until after she and Morris were married.

Not that Allison was her first time falling off the hetero wagon. But she was the first one Bridget had slipped away with for a few days. She didn't consider it serious, and Allison didn't appear to, either. Bridget hadn't used her real name — made sure Allison never saw her passport — and stuck with the oversized sunglasses and sun hat whenever they were out and about. The truth was, even though people spotted her husband in public and sometimes even asked for his autograph, very few recognized her when she was on her own. Sure, men noticed her, and women, too, for any number of reasons. But people didn't look her up and down because of who she was, only because of what she was: gorgeous.

And now Bridget's in trouble.

She glances at the café menu, and when she looks up, there he is.

"Bridget," he says, bending down and giving her an air kiss on the cheek. "You look delicious, as always. Good enough to eat with a spoon."

"And you look wonderful."

"Oh please. When I was coming past the bar I heard someone whisper that they just saw Danny DeVito."

Bridget laughs awkwardly as Howard settles into his chair across from her. She can see it in his face. He knows something is up. He wouldn't be where he is now without being

142

able to read people.

Although he never read her right. Not when he met her. If he had, well, they wouldn't be where they are now, would they?

"We're going to need drinks, I suspect," he says. "What will you have?"

"Uh, white wine spritzer," she says.

Howard's eyebrows go up. "Things can't be *that* bad, then, can they? A spritzer? That's the kind of drink you turn to when your *Times* shows up at the door fifteen minutes late." He turns in his chair and catches the attention of a passing waiter. "The lady will have a white wine spritzer. Scotch neat for me. So, what's on your mind, Bridget? I figure you didn't bring me here to start an affair. I honestly don't think I could squeeze one into my schedule." Howard has never been married, and if he has any kind of love life — other than his love for political chicanery — no one is aware of it.

But then, everyone has secrets.

Bridget swallows. "You know I would never do anything to intentionally cause trouble for Morris."

"Oh my," Howard says.

"I would never want to embarrass him. Never."

Howard studies her. "Well, let's see . . ." He looks her over, like he's trying to guess how much Morris spent on her diamond earrings. If he'd guessed twenty grand, he'd have

143

been right, but that wasn't what he was thinking about. It was what kind of trouble Bridget had gotten herself into.

"It's money, or it's sex," he said. "Or it's both. There's really nothing else. No matter what you've done, it'll come back to one or both of those."

"It's both," she says.

"I see," Howard says. "Just how bad is it?"

Bridget looks down into her lap, then back to Howard. "Bad." She collects herself. "I'm being blackmailed, Howard."

"So, there's the money part. And the leverage your blackmailer has over you, that will be the sex part. Unless, of course, I have this all totally wrong, and you've gone and killed someone."

"I haven't killed anyone," she says.

"Well," Howard says, as the drinks are placed in front of them, "there's a cause for celebration. Although, I've seen people bounce back from murder convictions." He takes a sip of his scotch and watches the waiter retreat. There is a part of him, Bridget suspects, that's probably actually enjoying this, because Howard thrives on problems. But if he is enjoying this, she doesn't think it will last for long.

He asks, "And there aren't pictures out there of you having sex with a goat or anything, are there?"

"No."

"Well, anything else should be a breeze to deal with by comparison. Out with it."

"I had an affair," Bridget says.

Howard nods wisely, as though he has been expecting this. "We're talking about something recent, something that has transpired since you and Morris engaged in the bonds of holy matrimony."

"Yes."

"Is it over? This affair?"

"Yes."

"Do I know him?"

Bridget pauses. "No."

Howard cocks his head slightly. "That was a troubling hesitation, Bridget. It means I may know him, and you're lying, or you're responding truthfully in a deliberately obtuse way. Let me see if I can discern which it is." His eyes bored into her. "I think it's the latter."

Bridget says nothing. Howard is, if you can take a step back, which is rather difficult for Bridget at this moment, amazing to watch.

He keeps his eyes on her another moment, then asks, "Who is she?"

He really is something. "Her name's Allison Fitch."

Howard's eyelids flutter rapidly. It's what he does when he's searching through his mental database. "You are right. I don't know her." He drinks more of his scotch. "You know, Bridget, you might have mentioned,

145

after I arranged for you and Morris to connect, and I quietly asked you whether there was anything compromising in your history, that you were a muff diver."

Bridget sits rigidly in her chair and says nothing.

"Did you make it known to this Allison Fitch that you were the wife of a prospective governor, the state's current attorney general?"

"No. I gave her another name altogether. But she saw me on television, on the news, at a function with Morris, and there wasn't much to put together after that." Bridget gives him the *Reader's Digest* version of the story. Where they'd met, how many times they'd seen each other, the time they'd gone away together.

Howard smiles humorlessly. "I mentioned pictures of you with a goat a moment ago. What about with this woman? Are there any photos? Hidden camera, that kind of thing? A goat, now that I think of it, might be less politically damaging."

Bridget's gaze narrows. "Are you worried about their blackmail potential, or did you just want me to get you a copy?"

"So they exist?"

"I don't think so. Allison never mentioned it. I don't see why she would have filmed me. She didn't know, at the time, who my husband was."

146

"Then what proof has she? One possible strategy is to ride the thing out. It'd be ugly, but we stonewall, deny, suggest that your husband's opponents choreographed the entire episode. In the meantime, we dig into her past, find something good on her that destroys her credibility, and believe me, we will find something even if we have to make it up, and after the press has some fun with it for a while, everyone gets bored and we continue on as though it never happened. In fact, without any proof, I make some calls and a police investigation is initiated and before you know it she's up on an extortion charge. Handle it like that talk show host, what's-his-name with the teeth, who was getting blackmailed by the guy who said if he didn't pay up he'd tell the world he'd been sleeping with half his staff. Brought in the cops, set up a sting, the bozo did time. Difference with you is, you'll stick to the line that you don't know this woman. Maybe you bumped into her someplace, on vacation, at some function, but you have no idea who she is. By the time we're done with her no one will believe her if she says it's raining in the middle of a Katrina."

"There are texts," Bridget says.

"Say again?"

"No pictures, but there are texts. Between us. Phone records, and texts."

"And what do these texts say, Bridget? What

147

is their nature?"

"They're . . . I guess the word would be salacious."

"And would you be the author of any of these salacious texts, or are they all written by Ms. Fitch?"

"Fifty-fifty, I'd say."

Howard runs his tongue over his teeth. "How much is she looking for, and what does she intend to do should you not meet her demands?"

"One hundred thousand. Or she goes public, to whoever'll pay the most for the story."

"I see. Not very imaginative, is she?"

"I'm sorry?"

"If I were her I would have asked for at least a million. And how do we know she won't take the money and sell her story, anyway?"

"She said she wouldn't do that," Bridget says.

Howard leans back in his chair and opens his arms. "Ahh, well then, nothing to worry about."

"I know what you're thinking. That she'll come back again and again, always asking for money."

"I think that's very likely, Bridget. Perhaps, with the right degree of persuasion, she can be happy with one reasonable sum. And then she agrees to go away, and we never hear from her again."

Bridget sighs. "I knew you'd know how to handle this. You're just so . . . so cool and collected about these things."

"It's all about putting out fires, my dear. We want to douse this one before it consumes an entire forest, that's all."

"Howard, I don't want Morris to know about this. I mean, Morris and I have been very frank with each other about our . . . idiosyncrasies, but he doesn't have any idea that I've seen someone else since we were married. You're not going to tell him, are you?"

He shakes his head and reaches out to touch her hand. "What purpose would that serve? I love you both too much to do that. You have a beautiful future ahead of you if you learn to control your . . . impulses."

"It was a slip," she says. "It's never going to happen again."

"Of course not," he says, still patting her hand, "because I will not — repeat, not — allow anyone to get in the way of Morris's destiny, and that includes you. So if there is a repeat of this kind of behavior, then I will personally strangle you with your own brassiere, chop you into bits, feed you to the Central Park squirrels, and find a way to pin the whole thing on your husband's opponent. Is that clear?"

Bridget nods. "Perfectly."

FOURTEEN

"We'd like to come in and speak with you," FBI Agent Parker said. She wasn't asking.

"What's this about?"

"We'll discuss it with you inside."

I asked to see their IDs, which they both flashed at me, then motioned for the two of them to enter the house. I gestured toward the living room couch and chairs, but they chose to stand. I did the same.

"We need to see some identification," Driscoll said.

"Do I need a lawyer or something?"

"We'd just like to establish exactly who we're talking with," Parker said.

Not knowing whether I should cooperate or not, but fearing the consequences of being disagreeable, I reached around for my wallet and dug out my driver's license. Parker took it in her hand.

"You're Mr. Kilbride," she said.

"That's right."

"*Ray* Kilbride."

"Yes."

"You ever go by any other names?" she asked. There was an accusing tone in her voice, as though she suspected me of having a raft of aliases.

"No. Of course not."

"What do you do, Mr. Kilbride?"

"I'm an artist. An illustrator."

"And just what kind of things do you illustrate?" Agent Parker asked. Her tone suggested she was probably thinking porno comics.

"My work's appeared in newspapers, magazines, Web sites. I had something in the *Times Book Review* the other week."

"So, if you do work for a Web site, I guess you do a lot of your work on the computer."

"Sure," I said.

"And you live out here and do that?"

"I don't live here. I live in Burlington."

Agent Driscoll stepped in. "Then whose house is this?"

"It's my father's." I cleared my throat. "It *was* my father's."

"What's that mean?" Agent Parker snapped.

"It means he's dead," I snapped back, looking her right in the eye. I'd thought that might put her in her place, however briefly, but it didn't faze her.

"What happened to your father?"

"He died in an accident out back of the house a few days ago. A lawn tractor rolled on him and killed him. His name was Adam Kilbride."

Agent Driscoll said, "Did your father have a computer?"

I shook my head, still wondering what the hell this was about. It should have bit me by now. "What? Yes, he did. A laptop."

Agent Parker had her notebook out. "What day did your father die?"

"Friday, May fourth."

She nudged her partner with her elbow, showed her notebook to him. "Messages that day, and since."

Now I was getting it.

"You're Ray, and your father was Adam," Agent Parker said. "Is there a Thomas Kilbride who resides here?"

"Yes."

"And what would his relationship be to you?"

"He's my brother."

"Is he here now?" Driscoll asked.

"Yes," I said again. "He's upstairs." I was already ill at ease, but my discomfort had now multiplied exponentially. What the hell had Thomas done to bring the FBI down on us? And how was he going to react when he learned that they were here to see him? "My brother stays in his room most of the day. I don't know what you want with him, but he's absolutely harmless."

"What's he doing in his room?" Parker asked.

"He's on his computer."

"He's on it a lot, is he?" she asked.

"Look, my brother has certain psychiatric issues. He prefers to spend a lot of time on his own."

"What sort of psychiatric issues?" Driscoll asked.

"Nothing that anyone else needs to worry about," I said. "He's got his problems, but he never bothers anyone. He's very . . . docile, basically."

"But he likes to send e-mails," Parker said.

This wasn't getting any better. "What kind of e-mails?"

"Do you monitor your brother's communications?" Driscoll asked.

"What? No. I don't. I'm not even *aware* of his communications. I told you he keeps to himself."

"Are you aware that Thomas Kilbride has been e-mailing the Central Intelligence Agency on a regular basis?"

"Oh, Jesus," I said.

"And that many of these messages have been addressed to former president Bill Clinton?"

I felt my insides liquefying. "Please tell me these were not threatening messages. That you're not here to arrest him or anything."

The two glanced at each other, exchanging

some unspoken decision, and Parker said, "No, not threatening. But . . . concerning. You want to call him down or shall we go upstairs and get him?"

I hung my head and shook it. "Wait here."

I went upstairs, opened Thomas's door without knocking.

"It's too soon for me to start dinner," he said. "Leave me alone."

"I need you to come downstairs, Thomas," I said.

"What is it?"

"You have visitors."

I expected him to ask who, but instead he just said, "Oh." He stood from the chair, and as he was heading for the hall I grabbed him gently by the arm.

"They're government people," I warned him.

That stopped him. It took a second to register, and then he nodded quickly a couple of times, as though he'd been expecting this to happen sooner or later. "Oh," he said. "That's great."

"Thomas, it's not great. What the hell kind of messages have you been sending to the CIA?"

"Progress reports," he said, and slipped past me for the stairs. Once he hit the living room, he went straight for them, the woman agent first, then Driscoll, shaking hands.

"I'm Thomas Kilbride," he said. "It's a

154

pleasure to meet you. The president never said anything about you dropping by for a visit."

"The president," Agent Parker said.

"Well, former president," Thomas said. "But Mr. Clinton said you can still call him that. But I hardly need to tell you this if he's the one who sent you."

"Why would he have sent us?" Driscoll asked, stone faced.

For the first time, Thomas looked concerned. "Aren't you from the CIA?"

"No," Parker said. "Agent Driscoll and I are from the FBI."

Thomas was unable to hide his disappointment. "FBI?" he said. "I thought you'd be from the CIA." He reminded me of a kid who opens up a Christmas present he thinks is a video game, and it turns out to be socks. "They're the ones I've been in touch with."

"Actually," Parker said, "they contacted us. We're helping them out today."

"Is this about where I'll do my work? Because I'd like to be able to work from home. I don't want to go to Washington. Tell them, Ray. I like it here."

"Mr. Kilbride," Driscoll said, "why don't we all have a seat." The agents took the two chairs, and Thomas and I sat on the couch on the other side of the coffee table from them.

"Don't get the wrong idea," Thomas said.

"I didn't mean to offend you. The FBI does a good job, too. But I was expecting the CIA."

"Well, we all work together," Driscoll said. "All on the same side, right?"

I was detecting the slightest change in tone from him. Less edge. Now that they had met Thomas, they could see — I hoped — that he did not present a threat.

"You've been writing to the CIA about a computer virus that's coming," Parker said. Maybe Driscoll had lost his tone, but not Parker.

"Well," Thomas began, "I've already explained this in my messages to the CIA, and President Clinton and I have talked about it."

Just recently, I thought.

Thomas continued, "But I don't mind going over it again. I don't actually have any inside information on the virus. It's speculation on my part. I don't even know if it will *be* a virus. It might be a solar flare, or a kind of nuclear explosion. It could even be caused by a meteor hitting the earth. That kind of thing can be very cataclysmic."

"Uh-huh," Parker said. "So, whatever it is, what is it you think it's going to do?"

"Wipe out all the GPS systems and maps that are stored on computers. All gone, just like that." He snapped his fingers, but he was never very good at that, and the action hardly made a sound. Thomas then explained his role in helping the country through this catastrophe; how he was memorizing the streets of all the major cities in the world. "And, as you know, I'm at the ready, should any agents of the U.S. government be on the run in a metropolitan area anywhere in the world, to offer guidance. Street locations, alleys, that kind of thing."

"Uh-huh," Parker said. "Thomas, you wouldn't be trying to write some kind of virus yourself that would cripple the computer systems of the U.S. government, would you?"

"No," he said, not the slightest bit offended. "I'm not really that good with computers. I mean, I'm *on* mine a lot." He looked my way, perhaps expecting me to weigh in with a critical comment. "I know how to turn them on and do e-mail and how to use Whirl360 to get around, but that's about it. I don't know how to take them apart. When my computer needs to be fixed my dad takes it to a shop in town." He paused. "But not anymore. My dad died."

"We heard about that," Driscoll said. "Sorry."

"I found him," Thomas said. "The tractor killed him." He said this almost formally, as though he wanted our guests to be very clear about what had happened.

"So your brother said," Driscoll said.

"And what is it you want from the CIA, Thomas?" Parker asked.

157

Thomas sat up a little straighter. "I don't want anything *from* them. It's what I have to give. I'm offering my services. You should already know this if you've seen the e-mails. When all the computer maps crash, I'll be able to assist the government."

"And just how will you be able to do that?" she asked.

Thomas looked at me, as if to say, *Are these people thick or what?*

He sighed. "Because I have them in my head. All the maps. All the streets. What everything looks like." He made a *tsk* noise with his tongue to signal his irritation. "When all the computers fail I'll be able to draw the maps, or be a guide, if needed. Although, to be honest, I would prefer to work from home. I like it here. I could give directions to someone, anywhere in the world, over the phone, even if I was still here."

"Of course," Parker said. "So you're telling me you can remember what all the streets are like in lots of different cities just by looking at them online?"

Thomas nodded.

Parker's tongue pushed her cheek out. "Okay. You ever been to Georgetown, Thomas?"

"Georgetown, Texas? Or Georgetown, Kentucky? Or Georgetown, Ontario? Or Georgetown, Delaware? Or —"

"Georgetown, in Washington, D.C."

158

Thomas nodded, like he should have guessed that in the first place, given that these were FBI people. "No, but actually, I've never been to any of them, anyway."

"So let's say I'm in Georgetown, and I'd like to buy a book, and —"

Thomas squeezed his eyes shut for a moment, and opened them. "There's a Barnes & Noble bookstore, on M Street, NW, at Thomas Jefferson Street. And if you're hungry, there's a Vietnamese restaurant right across the street, although I don't know if it's any good or not. I've never even eaten Vietnamese food. Is it like Chinese food? I like Chinese food."

Agent Parker, for the first time, looked as though she'd been thrown off her game a second. She glanced at her partner, her eyes saying, *What the fuck?*

"I know the government is trying to save money these days, so it's important you know that I'm not looking for any big salary," my brother said. "Just enough to cover any of my expenses. I don't have an extravagant lifestyle. I'm offering my services because I think it's a good thing to do, as a citizen."

"Thomas, Agent Driscoll and I would like to see where you work."

"Sure," he said.

I felt a few more of my internal organs turn to water as I followed everyone else up the stairs. When they got to the second floor, the

159

agents stopped and took in the wall of maps. It didn't even occur to Thomas to point them out as he opened the door to his bedroom.

"This is my workstation," he said. "And I sleep here, too."

"Christ on a cracker," Driscoll muttered under his breath, taking in the room.

"What's this?" Parker asked, pointing to the three monitors. One of them showed an office building with the letters CIBC running across the windows. It looked like a financial institution. The second and third were the same street, one looking up, the other down.

"Yonge Street, Toronto," Thomas said. "It runs north and south, starting at Lake Ontario, at Queen's Quay Boulevard. I started at the southern end and I've gotten up to Bloor. It's a very long street, so instead of going all the way up, I'll start wandering the east-west streets."

"So how much time do you spend doing this?" Parker asked.

"I sleep from around one at night to nine in the morning, and I take meal breaks, and I have a shower every morning, but all the other times I'm working. I had to see my psychiatrist yesterday so I lost some time there, but tell them at the CIA not to worry. I'll make it up. And I'm losing some time now, but this is work-related so I guess it's okay."

I saw the agents exchange looks when

160

Thomas said "psychiatrist." Parker said, "Show us what you do."

"Okay." Thomas sat in his chair and put his right hand on the mouse, then moved the cursor around the street on the center monitor. "I keep clicking and I move up the street, and then I hold the button down and I can move around three hundred and sixty degrees like this and see all the stores and the businesses but you usually can't see the people clearly and the license plates on the cars and trucks are blurred but everything else is really clear."

"Can you open up your e-mail program, Thomas?" Parker asked.

"Okay."

He clicked on the postage stamp at the bottom of the screen and up came his e-mails. His in-box — and I couldn't recall seeing an in-box like this before — was empty.

"You delete all your mail right away?" Driscoll asked.

"I don't get any," Thomas said. "I don't have any regular friends that write to me. Sometimes, I get junk. Like to" — he craned his neck around and looked at Agent Parker and blushed — "you know, make your, you know, thing bigger or something. I delete those immediately."

I was thinking maybe I should raise an objection, that if they wanted to snoop around in my brother's e-mails, they should have a warrant. But then I worried that would raise a red flag for them. It was my hope that once they saw what Thomas was up to, how innocent his pursuit was, whatever it was that worried them about him would evaporate.

"Show us what's in your deleted file," Driscoll said. Evidently he needed convincing.

"I always forget to empty this," Thomas said. "There."

The folder was, as Thomas had said, filled with junk e-mails of the penis enlargement variety.

"And now the folder with sent messages," Parker said.

Thomas did a click with the mouse and there it was. The sent file. The messages filled the screen from top to bottom. Hundreds and hundreds of messages. Written by Thomas Kilbride.

All of them — every last one — directed to the same address.

The e-mail address of the Central Intelligence Agency.

"Oh my God," I said.

"I like to keep everyone apprised of what I'm doing," Thomas said.

FIFTEEN

I was stunned. Agents Parker and Driscoll, not so much. After all, this was why they were here. Seeing as how these e-mails had been sent to the CIA, I figured they'd seen them already.

But despite that, Driscoll asked, "Why don't we open a couple of those e-mails at random."

"How about this one?" Thomas asked, pointing, and Driscoll nodded. He clicked on one that, like all the others, had been directed to the general inquiries e-mail address of the CIA, which I was guessing was available on the Internet to anyone. Thomas had typed "whirl360update" into the subject line.

It read:

Dear Former President Clinton: Today I went through all the streets of Lisbon and tomorrow I am going to start San Diego. Sincerely, Thomas Kilbride.

"Next one," Driscoll said.

Dear Former President Clinton: Los Angeles is going to take a lot longer than I had anticipated but you have to expect that of cities that are sprawling in nature. San Francisco was easier because it is contained by the mountains. I hope everything is going well with you. Sincerely, Thomas Kilbride.

"Let's do one more," Agent Driscoll said. Thomas clicked and opened this:

Dear Former President Clinton: I'm sure you have lots of connections with all government agencies, not just the CIA, so I would urge you to have them start checking into what this catastrophic event is that is coming. It makes sense to do it now because once it happens, it will be a lot harder to deal with. Because computers will be affected, I want to give you a phone number where you can reach me, and my address. Just call and tell me what you need a map of and I will get right to work on it. Sincerely, Thomas Kilbride.

The contact details followed. I had been wondering, up to now, whether the FBI had tracked the messages to this house through an IP address or something, but clearly that kind of high-tech investigative legwork had not been necessary.

"Thomas," Agent Parker said, "have you ever been in trouble?"

He poked his tongue into his cheek before answering. "What kind of trouble?"

I wondered if this was what it felt like when your car plunged into the water.

"I don't know, Thomas. Trouble with the police?"

"No, I've never been in any trouble with the police."

"What about in 1997?" Driscoll asked.

Oh, no.

"What about 1997?" Thomas asked.

"There wasn't an incident then? Something that involved the police?"

Thomas looked at me. I spoke up. "That was nothing. I can't believe you're dredging that up. The police never laid a charge."

"Would you like to tell us about it, Thomas?" Parker asked.

"Ray," Thomas said softly, "could you tell them? Some of it, I don't remember."

"When we . . . when Thomas and my parents lived downtown — I'd just moved away around that time — there was a misunderstanding with the neighbors."

Parker and Driscoll waited.

"Thomas had found the original survey maps for our house, you know, the kind you get when you buy or sell a property. The maps show exactly where the house is situated on the property. And the maps showed

165

the houses on either side of us, and across the street."

"They were wrong," Thomas said.

I looked at him and smiled. "Yeah, Thomas didn't think the survey maps were accurate, so he wanted to check them, make a map of our property and the neighbors'. So he got a fifty-foot tape measure and —"

"I still have it," Thomas said. "Do you want to see it?"

Parker said, "No, that's okay."

"He got this tape measure and started measuring everything. How far the houses were from the sidewalk, from one another, how big they were. He didn't tell anyone he was going to do this. He just started doing it. And the thing is, he was right. Some of the survey measurements were off, ever so slightly. Which would have been kind of satisfying, if Thomas hadn't ended up being discovered outside the first-floor bedroom window of our neighbors to the south —"

"The Hitchens," Thomas offered.

"That's right. This was at the time that Mrs. Hitchens was getting dressed."

"Hmm," said Parker.

"She was naked," Thomas said matter-of-factly. "That window was exactly twenty-eight feet, nine inches from the sidewalk. The survey had it as twenty-eight feet, eleven inches."

"Mrs. Hitchens got pretty upset, called the

166

police. My parents managed to persuade her, and the police, that Thomas's actions were entirely innocent, but after that, the neighbors were never quite the same with my brother. It became very awkward for my parents. That was when they decided to move out here."

"The survey for *this* property is dead on," Thomas said.

Parker and Driscoll exchanged looks again. I'd lost count of how many times they'd done this. Parker said to Thomas, "Why don't you get back to work and we'll let your brother show us out."

"Okay," he said, turning back to his mouse and keyboard.

When the three of us got back downstairs, I asked Parker, "What now?"

She said, "We'll make our report. This visit was a threat assessment, Mr. Kilbride. I don't believe Agent Driscoll sees one, and I would have to concur. The U.S. government hears, on a daily basis, from a great many," and here she paused to choose her words carefully, "individuals whose interpretations of the world around them are somewhat unique. Ninety-nine percent of them present no discernible threat — they're harmless — but we spend a lot of time tracking down the one percent that do."

I felt I'd been holding my breath for an hour. I took what she had to say as good news, but my stress level was off the scale.

167

On top of that, I was furious with Thomas. I knew I had to make certain allowances for him, but bringing the FBI to our door? The blood coursing through my veins was electrically charged.

Parker continued, "Your brother needs to find some other hobbies. If he keeps communicating with government agencies with his tales of a computer infrastructure meltdown, you're going to be visited again. If not by us, then someone else."

"I hear you."

"It's a different world than twenty years ago," she said. "No one takes these things lightly. Look at what happened in Tucson. Thomas mentioned a psychiatrist. He sees someone regularly?"

"Yes."

She had out her notebook again. "Name?"

I didn't want to give it to her, but how long would it have taken her to find out on her own? Five minutes? Ten, tops? I had to put my faith in Laura Grigorin to either paint Thomas in a good light, or simply tell these two to get lost.

I gave Parker the name.

"Good day, Mr. Kilbride," she said.

Driscoll nodded but said nothing. I watched the two of them go down the porch steps and get back into their government-issued wheels.

I wasn't proud of what I did next.

SIXTEEN

Howard Talliman understands why Bridget Sawchuck wanted to tell him the details of her dilemma in a public place. Not only did it keep his reaction in check; there was nothing at all suspicious about the two of them being seen together. It's perfectly natural for Howard to meet his best friend's wife for lunch. He is as much an adviser to her as he is to Morris.

But Howard does not want to meet Allison Fitch where they can be seen together. He does not want anyone to know about this meeting.

So he books a suite for the day at the Roosevelt at Madison and Forty-fifth. He wants a room with a separate living area, thinking Allison might find it slightly unnerving being in a small space with a man she's never met before, a king-sized bed the most dominant piece of furniture in the room. As though beckoning them. He instructs Bridget to contact Allison and invite her to the hotel for

169

two in the afternoon to discuss the woman's proposal. What Allison does not know is that Howard will be taking the meeting.

He orders coffee for two from room service with instructions that it be delivered ten minutes before Allison's scheduled arrival. He doesn't know whether she is inclined to punctuality, but is guessing that when one hundred thousand dollars is at stake, that's a pretty good reason to be on time.

The china cups and saucers are set out on the coffee table, the silver spoons and white linen napkins in place next to them, when there is a soft rapping at the door at one minute before two. Howard gets up from the couch where he has been sitting casually with one leg over his knee. He opens the door a foot.

Allison's mouth drops open. "I'm sorry. I've knocked on the wrong —"

"Ms. Fitch, a pleasure to meet you," he says, opening the door wide and sweeping his arm inward. "You're right on time."

She hesitates, then steps into the room.

"Where's Bridget?" she asks.

"I will be representing Bridget's interests here today," he says.

"Who the hell are you?"

"My name is Howard Talliman." He doesn't see the point in using some sort of alias. If this woman has been researching Bridget and Morris online — as he is sure she has — then

170

she will certainly have come across his name and photo at some point. "I am a friend of the family."

"Oh yeah, I know who you are," she says. "You're like . . . you're his campaign manager or something like that."

"Won't you sit down? I've ordered coffee."

Allison's eyes take in the room as she moves toward the couch. "Where's the bed?" she asked. "I mean, not that — I've never seen a hotel room that didn't have a bed in it."

Howard points to a closed door. "The bedroom is in there."

Allison is impressed. "A hotel room where the bedroom is separate?"

"Yes."

"May I see?" She tips her head at the closed bedroom door.

"Be my guest."

She opens the bedroom door and whistles. "Wow." She comes back to the couch and sits down. "What's a room like this run you for the day?"

"That's not really what we're here to discuss, is it?" he says.

"I'm just saying, if Bridget can afford a room like this just so you and me can have a chat, maybe I'm aiming too low."

Howard has already thought her demand for one hundred thousand dollars lacks ambition, but he chooses not to say that. He picks up the silver coffeepot by the handle and says,

"May I pour you a cup?"

"Yeah, sure."

Steam rises from the coffee as it streams into the cups. Allison adds cream and sugar to hers, while Howard takes his black. He leans back comfortably in his chair, saucer in one hand and cup in the other.

"So, Ms. Fitch, you've certainly stirred things up, haven't you?"

"Yeah, well, I don't know what exactly Bridget has told you."

"She's told me enough. That you two became friends, very special friends, that you spent some time away together in Barbados, and that you subsequently learned that she is married to Morris Sawchuck."

"Yeah, that's pretty much it." She sips the coffee, makes a face, spoons in more sugar, and stirs.

"And once having learned this, you saw an opportunity."

Allison Fitch blushes. "I don't know if you'd call it that."

"What would you call it?"

"I guess . . . I guess I would call it doing Bridget a favor."

Howard's bushy eyebrows soar briefly. "Explain that to me."

"Well, I figured she wouldn't want it getting out that the two of us, you know, that we had had a thing, and I was offering her a way to make sure that didn't happen."

Howard nods. "I see. You're a very kind-hearted person, aren't you? Just how were you hoping to ensure that this information did not become public?"

Her eyes narrow. "You're a pretty smug son of a bitch, aren't you?"

"I am many things, Ms. Fitch."

"Look, you already know the answer. I told her I've been having kind of a cash flow problem lately, and that if she could help me out, I'd make sure nothing came out about her, something that could ruin her husband's chances of being governor or president or head of the glee club or whatever it is he wants to be when he grows up. I mean, news of his wife sleeping with someone other than him would be bad enough, but with another *woman*? All those supporters of his who when they aren't spending five hundred bucks a plate at some fund-raising dinner for him are spending millions to fight same-sex marriage, they're going to just love that. I mean, come on, what's a hundred grand for her and her husband? That's like, what? Lunch money? A little trip to Gucci or Louis Vuitton? That's nothing for them. I could have asked for a lot more."

Howard Talliman smiles. "How do you know the police aren't listening in on this conversation in the other room? How do you know they're not about to bust in here and arrest you for extortion and blackmail?"

173

Allison tenses up. He can see it in her eyes that, for a second there, she's actually expecting it to happen. But then her muscles appear to relax.

"I don't think you'd do that. Because then it would all come out. That the governor's wife had been having a lesbian affair."

"You think you could survive that kind of publicity?"

"Sure."

"How do you think your mother in Dayton would handle it?"

That gets her. You can almost hear her make a cartoon *gulp*. Knows he's done his homework. But she composes herself again. "I think Mom's been suspecting it for years."

"You've not come out to her."

"No. But this would save me the trouble of a painful sit-down, I guess. The real question is, could Bridget and her husband survive it?"

"They'd simply deny it," Howard says. "Your word against hers. She's married to an attorney general and you, my dear, are a barmaid."

"A barmaid with proof."

He's been waiting to see whether she'll play this card. The text messages. The phone records.

"Proof," he says. "And what proof would that be?"

"We had a lot of conversations. The kinds

174

that there's a record of."

"Your phone."

She nods.

"Let me see. Prove it to me," he says.

Allison shakes her head. "Do I look stupid?" He does not answer. "Like I'm going to give it to you."

"If you want the one hundred thousand, you will have to produce your phone at the time of delivery so that I can be certain those messages have been expunged."

Allison appears to be thinking about this point, like she doesn't want to lose her leverage.

"I suppose that's okay," she says.

Howard puts his cup and saucer on the table and clears his throat. "And what assurances does Bridget have that you won't come back and ask her for more money?"

"You'll just have to take my word on that," Allison says, and there's a trace of an impish grin.

"Yes, I suppose I'll just have to do that," Howard says. He slaps the tops of his knees. "Well, thanks so much for dropping by. We'll be in touch."

Makes it sound like an audition.

"Don't you have my money?"

"Not at the moment," Howard says, standing. "Perhaps you were expecting Bridget to bring it today, but I wanted to get a sense of the situation first. It will take time to get that kind of money together. I'm assuming you weren't expecting me to write you a check."

Embarrassment washes over her face as she stands. "No, of course not. But, is it *all* going to be *cash*?"

"I think we'd agree it's better that there be no record of this transaction," he says.

"God, what will I do with all that cash?"

"I would suggest you rent yourself a safe-deposit box. And then draw from it as your needs dictate."

There's a sparkle in her eye. He can see she's already picturing all that money, wondering just how big a pile a hundred thousand dollars is.

"Okay, okay, I can do that. Where do you get these box things?"

Howard sighs. "I would try a bank."

"You'll get in touch when you have the money?"

"Absolutely."

Howard is thinking ahead, wondering what kind of damage there will be if this gets out. Suppose she does go to the press? Howard is confident, as he has told Bridget, that they'll be able to find enough on this woman to discredit her. They will ruin her in the public eye. It could be a tough go, no doubt about it. But then again, Bridget is not the one running for office. If this scandal is to end up destroying her, so be it. Morris can probably survive it, even if it means cutting Bridget loose. The whole thing could conceivably garner the man some sympathy, once the hoopla dies down. Extramarital affairs, stains on blue dresses, hanky-panky with hotel maids — there was no end of things politicians seemed able to bounce back from.

But paying her the hundred grand — how will that look if it gets out? Howard's mind races. He thinks there's a way to spin it. He'll take the blame, say he did it to spare his friend and his wife pain and embarrassment. Resign as Sawchuck's adviser if he has to, at least publicly, and continue to manage things from behind the scenes.

Still, it will be a mess if it gets out. While survivable, it'll set back the timetable a bit. They've already had to put things on hold because of that other matter, wondering whether the proverbial shit is going to hit the fan, but as each day passes, things look more promising. And as for this woman, maybe, just maybe, once she has her money, she'll really go away.

The things you had to do.

And then Allison Fitch says, "Just don't try anything funny. Because, you know, I know stuff."

Howard blinks. "I'm sorry?"

She's on her feet now, heading for the door. "Now that I know who Bridget is, who she's married to, you think back, stuff you saw, stuff you overheard, it all starts to come together."

Howard feels a chill. "What, exactly, are you talking about?"

The last thing she says as she goes into the hall is, "You just come up with the hundred grand and you won't have to worry about it."

Howard stares at the door as it closes.

He is going to have to have another chat with Bridget. And before that, he would put in a call to Lewis. Whenever things looked as though they were going to escalate, he talked to Lewis.

SEVENTEEN

When I walked into his room, Thomas, staring at the screen with his back to me, said, "I thought they were nice, but they should have sent the CIA."

I came up around the side of his map-and-computer-cluttered desk and crouched down, then reached over to where the power strip went into the wall outlet. I yanked it out. The soft whirring of the computer stopped instantly with a barely audible *pop.*

Thomas screamed, "Hey!"

Then I reached over another few inches, where the phone line went into the jack, and pulled that out as well. Thomas stared, dumbstruck, at the suddenly black monitors.

"Turn them on!" he shouted. "Turn them back on!"

I shouted back, louder, "What the fuck were you thinking? Can you tell me that? What in the goddamn hell were you thinking? Getting in touch with the CIA? Sending them e-mails? Are you crazy?"

Even as I said it, I knew it was wrong. But I couldn't stop myself.

"Jesus, I can't believe it. The FBI! The goddamn FBI at our door! You're lucky they didn't arrest you, Thomas. Or both of us! At the very least, I'm amazed they didn't walk out of here with your computer. Thank God you didn't actually threaten anyone. Do you have any idea what the world is like today? You start sending e-mails to government agencies, telling them some cataclysmic event is on the horizon? Have you any *idea* how many alarm bells that sets off?"

"Plug it back in, Ray!" He was out of the chair now, dropping to his knees, scrambling for the cord that led out of the power strip.

I grabbed him by the shoulders and pulled him away. "No! This is it, Thomas! I've had it! Enough!"

But Thomas scrambled ahead, crablike, getting himself under the table. I grabbed hold of his legs and dragged him out.

"I hate you!" he shouted. There were tears streaming down his red, angry cheeks.

"You're done with this!" I said. "Done! You're getting out of this room and going outside! You're going to start living like a normal person!"

"Leave me alone leave me alone leave me alone," he whimpered. I'd dragged him to the middle of his room, both of us sprawled out on the floor. The bare hardwood had

180

made it easy to move him, but several maps and printouts had bunched up under him in the process. He grabbed one of the crumpled papers caught under his thigh, opened it, and tried to flatten it out on the top of his leg.

"Look what you've done!" he said.

I grabbed the map from his hands, crumpled it into a ball, and tossed it across the room.

"No!" he said.

I knew this was wrong. Yelling at Thomas, pulling the plug on his computer, and, maybe worst of all, treating one of his precious maps like a used paper towel. I'd lost control of the situation, and I'd lost control of myself. Losing my father, coming back here, trying to figure out what to do with the house and Thomas, and now a couple of federal agents at the door — I'd snapped. But there was no excuse for coming down on Thomas this hard.

So maybe I shouldn't have been surprised when Thomas snapped, too.

He came at me like he'd been shot out of a cannon. He lunged, reaching out and grabbing me around the neck. I toppled over onto my back and he landed on top of me, our legs tangling, his hands still clutching at my throat.

"You're just like Dad!" he cried. His eyes were wide and manic. Choking, I grabbed his wrists but couldn't break his grasp.

181

"Thomas!" I croaked. "Let . . . go!"

I reached up, grabbed his left ear with my right hand, and yanked.

Thomas yelped and released me. I rolled and squirmed out from under him. Pulling his ear seemed to have had the effect of stunning him. He looked at the chaos around us, then at me, and shook his head.

"No no no," he said, and instead of turning any further anger on me, began to hit himself. He was driving the heels of his hands, alternating left and right, into his forehead. Hard.

"Thomas!" I said. "Stop it!"

I tried to get my arms around his, but they were like pistons. He was pounding his head hard enough that it sounded like wood hitting wood. I threw myself on him, pinning him to make him stop.

He made unintelligible grunting noises of frustration.

"It's okay!" I said. "Thomas, stop!" I kept my weight on him, hoping that by restricting his movements I'd calm him.

"It's okay," I said again. "I'm sorry."

Like a switch had been flipped, he stopped. His forehead was red and beginning to bruise. Between the battering he'd given himself and his red and swollen eyes, he looked as though he had just lost a bar fight.

He was crying.

I felt myself becoming overwhelmed. My throat felt thick, my breathing quickened.

Now I was crying, too.

"Thomas, I'm sorry," I said. "I'm sorry. I'm going to get off you, okay?"

"Okay," he said.

"I'm getting up. Promise me you won't hit yourself anymore, okay?"

"I won't."

"Okay, that's good. We're good." I eased him up into a sitting position, ran my hand on his back.

He glanced over at the power strip. "I'm going to plug it back in," he said.

"I'll get it, let me." I crawled over, shoved the plug into the outlet. The computer tower started to hum. Before Thomas could get up I said to him, "But we need to establish some rules, okay? Before you start exploring again."

He nodded slowly.

"First thing we have to do is get an ice pack on your head. You okay with that?"

He considered my offer. "Okay," he said.

I extended a hand, and was relieved when he took it. I noticed his hands were bruised, too. "Jesus, you really made a mess of yourself."

He looked at me. "How is your neck?"

It hurt. "Fine," I said.

"I'm sorry I tried to kill you," he said.

"You weren't trying to kill me. You were just angry. I was an asshole."

He nodded. "Yeah. A fuckhead."

He sat at the kitchen table while I found a

soft ice pack in the freezer. Dad was always suffering from some kind of strain or pulled muscle and there were enough packs in there to cool a Dairy Queen. "Hold this on your head," I said, handing Thomas one.

I pulled over a chair so I could put an arm around his shoulder.

"I shouldn't have done that," I said.

"No," Thomas said.

"I kind of lost it."

"Have you been taking your medication?" he asked.

I hadn't had a single M&M since returning from Dr. Grigorin's. "No, I guess I forgot to take them."

"You run into problems when you don't take your medication," he said.

I kept my arm around him. "There's no excuse for what I did. I know . . . I know you're the way you are, and screaming at you, that's not going to make things any different."

"What are the rules?" he asked.

"I just . . . I just want you to check with me first before you send any e-mails, or make any phone calls. But you can still wander all the cities you want for as long as you want. Is that a deal?"

He thought about it, still holding the freezer bag to his head. "I don't know."

"Thomas, not everyone in the government understands that you're trying to help them.

They don't understand that you're a good guy. I want to make sure there aren't any misunderstandings. It's not just you who could get in trouble. It's me, too."

"I guess," he said. He took the bag from his head. "It's really cold."

"Try to keep it there. It'll keep the swelling down."

"Okay," he said.

"I've never seen you get that angry," I said. "I mean, I had it coming, but I didn't know you had it in you."

As Thomas held the cold bag to his head, his eyes were shielded.

"I'm going to go back to work now," he said, slipping out from under my arm and heading for the stairs, leaving the bag on the table.

His back to me, he said, "Am I still making dinner tonight?"

I had forgotten. "No," I said. "Don't worry about it."

EIGHTEEN

Bridget is coming out of the building on Thirty-fifth Street where the PR firm she works for is headquartered when she sees him waiting there for her.

He grabs her firmly by the elbow and starts leading her down the sidewalk.

"Howard!" she says, glancing down at his hand. "Let go of my arm. You're hurting me."

Howard Talliman says nothing. He swiftly moves her along, Bridget struggling to maintain her balance on her heels. He steers her into the lobby of a building, the first place he's spotted where he can talk to her without anyone else listening in.

"What does she know?" Howard asks once they are inside. He has moved Bridget up against a marble wall and still not released his grip on her.

"Howard, what the hell —"

"She says she heard things." He is hissing, almost snakelike.

"What? What are you talking about?"

186

"I met with her. When she was leaving, she said she heard things."

"Heard what? What did she say she heard?"

"She didn't say. But she intimated that it was something damaging. Things you'd said, things that made sense once she knew who you are."

"Howard, I swear —"

"Did you talk to Morris while you were in Barbados?"

"Of course. We talk all the time."

"You talked to him when you were with Allison Fitch?"

"Yes, yes, I'm sure I did. Howard, I can't feel my hand. You're cutting off the circulation."

He releases his grip but is still only inches from her, his face pressed up to hers. "Was she present when you had those conversations?"

"No, I mean, she might have been in the other room. I talked to him when I was in the bathroom, or maybe when Allison was. I talked to him by the pool one day, when she went off to get us drinks."

"So she might have heard any of them. She could have been behind you, or on the other side of a door," Howard says.

"Okay, I suppose it's possible, but even if she did, we didn't — I'm sure I never said anything that —"

"You know about Morris's situation,"

187

Howard says grimly.

"He doesn't tell me everything."

"But you *know*."

"I know what they're looking into, okay. How could I not know? Morris is going out of his mind about it, thinking sooner or later it's going to come out, that Goldsmith will implicate him."

So she did know.

Howard had never been able to persuade Morris not to discuss political liabilities with his wife. He'd clearly told her how Barton Goldsmith, the CIA director, had involved Sawchuck in his plan to cut deals with a handful of terrorism suspects. Goldsmith argued he was doing it to protect the people of the United States, but it turned out the people of the United States didn't quite see it that way after the *New York Times* did an exposé on how Goldsmith had leaned on various prosecutors and law enforcement agencies across the country to allow certain terror suspects to walk in return for information.

Like those two nut jobs who were about to set off a bomb in a Florida theme park when they were nabbed. The moment he was notified of the arrests, Goldsmith was leaning on Florida's highest-ranking law enforcement officials to hold the two men until his people arrived. Goldsmith's intelligence experts said something much bigger was coming, and those clowns in Florida agreed to tell everything they knew in return for a couple of air tickets back to Yemen. (The U.S. government even paid their airfare home, the *Times* noted, a fact that rankled almost as much as the prospect of the devastation they nearly caused.)

Goldsmith credited the deal with thwarting another underwear/shoe-type bomber before he boarded a Washington-bound plane in Paris. But the *Times* story could find no definitive link between the two events. It suggested Goldsmith was inflating the value of the intel he'd received from the two theme park terrorists to justify sending them home.

Goldsmith was pilloried. He resigned. Florida's attorney general followed.

What the *Times* didn't know was that Florida was not the first such incident.

A Saudi illegal with al Qaeda sympathies had tried to set off a Ford F-150 filled with explosives around the corner from the Guggenheim. He'd parked it in the middle of the night and set it to go off at nine in the morning. But a woman looking out her brownstone window wondered why he kept checking something in the truck's cargo bed, and called the police. A tactical team arrived and disabled the device before the bagel carts had set up for business. The truck was traced to its owner, the man arrested. Goldsmith was in the loop from the beginning, scooped the suspect, found out he had a bunch of similar-minded friends he was willing to roll on, all in return for a trip home.

Goldsmith called Morris.

Morris balked at first. He'd prosecute the son of a bitch. Told Goldsmith he wasn't interested in making deals with terrorists. Goldsmith said, "You know, terror suspects aren't the only people we have a lot of background intel on, if you get my meaning."

There wasn't an ambitious politician alive who didn't have secrets he hoped were buried forever. Morris Sawchuck could only have guessed what Goldsmith might have had on him. Knowledge, perhaps, of one or more dirty tricks Howard had performed on his behalf. Campaign donations that hadn't gone through channels. Maybe even something about Bridget's sexual history. Or even his own.

Sawchuck allowed himself to be overruled.

The bomber went home.

When the *Times* story broke, Howard and Morris waited for the other shoe to drop. The *Times* would keep digging and find out Morris had caved. They could see the headlines: "New York AG Allows Guggenheim Bomber to Skip Country."

It would have finished him.

No one who let terrorists go free got to the governor's mansion, let alone the White House. Morris would have been lucky to serve on the board of a community college after this got out.

It is all this, Howard fears, that Allison Fitch has heard Bridget talking about on the phone with Morris.

"Jesus Christ, Bridget, how stupid are you?" Howard shakes his head. "How stupid is Morris?"

"He never talked about anything specific. Everything was in general terms. Just that he's worried. That he hopes all this will blow over soon."

"That's the thing, Bridget. We think it's all going to blow over soon. There's a very good chance this will all go away." His voice is very low. "But not if you start blabbing about it on the phone, where some blackmailing lesbo bimbo can hear you."

"Howard, really, she's bluffing. She never heard anything. I'm sure of it."

He turns, takes two steps away from her, turns and looks at her again. He approaches and says, "The blackmail thing — I could see us getting out from under that. But if this woman really heard something, she's got information that trumps some girl-on-girl action. She's got dynamite. You understand what I'm saying, Bridget? She has dynamite. She has a goddamn nuclear weapon."

"Howard, honestly, I'm sure, even if she heard every word I said, she never heard anything that would —"

"Enough," he says. "Enough." He shakes his head slowly, thinking. He points a finger at her and says, "Not one word to Morris. Not one single word."

Then, abruptly, he leaves her there, striding out of the lobby to the sidewalk and heading east.

Bridget braces herself against the wall, tries to regain her composure. Howard doesn't have to worry that she'll tell Morris. He scares her far more than her husband does.

NINETEEN

"The FBI sent some people to talk to me, Mr. President."

"*Yes, of course, that makes sense.*"

"Did you send them?"

"*It's standard procedure.*"

"Okay. Because they weren't friendly. They asked if I'd ever been in trouble."

"*What did you say?*"

"They knew about the time that I saw Mrs. Hitchens naked. But they didn't know about the other thing."

"*And you didn't tell them.*"

"No. And I think they meant the kind of trouble where I was the one who did the bad thing. But it wasn't my fault. I don't like to talk about it. Dad wanted to talk about it just before he died, wanted me to talk about it. It was very confusing, because for years and years he wouldn't let me talk about it, to anyone. And I never did. Not even Dr. Grigorin knows."

"*I know.*"

"It's safe, telling you."

"*What about your brother? Should you tell him?*"

"No. No, I don't think so."

TWENTY

Driving home, Michael Lambton wants some.

He can go home and get it — just shake Vera so that she wakes up enough to roll onto her back — but that's not really what he has in mind. This is a celebration, after all. If you're going to celebrate, do you really want the same piece of ass you can get any day of the week?

And this is definitely a cause for celebration. He's pulled it off. At least, it sure as hell looks as though he's pulled it off. The vote's this coming Sunday, and all indications are the dumb bastards are going to approve it. Narrowly, probably, but they're going to ratify a contract that gives them a zero pay increase, a clawback in benefits, and no job security clauses. But they still have jobs, and they don't want them moving to Mexico or China or Taiwan or any of those goddamn places.

They want to keep making automotive parts — door panels and dashboards and steering

195

wheel assemblies — and shipping them off to GM and Toyota and Honda and Ford plants, not just here in the good ol' USA but overseas, too. They've seen what's been happening across this country, for years now, where the jobs are going. And when these jobs leave, are they ever coming back? Not fucking likely.

That is what Lambton tells them when he presents the company's offer. He calls it "piss poor." He calls it "a motherfucking insult." He calls it "a punch to the gut of each and every hardworking man and woman in this plant."

He calls it all those things. He also calls it "our best hope of keeping our jobs."

"Let's face it, folks. These sons of bitches can close up shop and be set up in Asswipe, South Korea, before you've even gotten home from the evening shift, cracked open a beer, and put on Leno. Do I like this contract? I *hate* this contract. And I'm here to tell you tonight, as your union leader, that on Sunday I am going to be voting for this piece of shit contract. You know why? Because I'm a realist. Because I got mouths to feed, and I know you do, too. Because I got a mortgage to pay, and I know you do, too. Because I got kids to send to school, and I know you do, too. Because I got people who depend on me, each and every day, and I know you do, too."

There's grumbling in the union hall, but it isn't as bad as Lambton fears it will be. There was a time when they'd have been throwing chairs at him. But that was then, when there was still a Pontiac and an Oldsmobile division. Before Hummer and Saturn got sold off. Before Chrysler nearly went tits up. This is now. It's a whole new ball game. And even though there are signs things are coming back, that the big car companies are going to be buying parts from this particular manufacturing plant for the foreseeable future, people are still nervous. They don't want to derail this recovery. They want to keep their homes.

They know, in their hearts, that Michael Lambton is right. They don't like hearing what he has to say, but they know he's a no-bullshit kind of guy. They know Michael Lambton is looking out for them. They know Michael Lambton is a straight shooter.

They know shit.

Weeks ago, the company bosses have him in for a little chat in the boardroom. Three of them on one side of a long, mahogany table, Lambton on the other.

They slide some paperwork across the table to him and the company president says: "You are going to sell our offer to your people. You can bad-mouth it all you want. You can tell them they deserve better. You can tell them the company is forcing them to eat shit and smile as they swallow and say, 'May I have some more, sir?' But in the end, you're going to sell this offer, because it's the best they're going to get in the current climate. Tell them that if they're happy for someone named Juan or Felipe or Dong Hung Low to make these parts, then vote to reject. But if they want their jobs, they'll take this contract."

Michael Lambton calmly pushes back his chair, stands, unzips his jeans, and sends a stream of urine across the mahogany tabletop, thoroughly soaking the contract in the process.

The company people, seated on the other side of the table, push their chairs back a little as the puddle of piss spreads.

Lambton tucks his penis back into his pants, zips up, and says, "That's what I think of your offer. The economy's coming back. GM's having a good year; so's Chrysler. The bailout worked. You guys are making money and you can afford to continue to give my workers a decent wage; don't even think about any takeaways." He smiled. "Are we done here?"

The president turns to the man next to him and says, "Get some paper towels and blot that up."

The man can't believe what he's being asked to do, but he does it. When the mess is cleaned up, the president places a leather satchel on the table.

"It's half a million," he says. "You can count it if you want. All you have to do is get your people to vote for this contract."

Lambton takes a moment to consider this new bargaining tactic. He says, "That does change things."

It would not be the first time he's done bad things for money. He is a practical man.

"Half now, half after the vote, assuming it goes the way it's supposed to," the company president says.

Now, leaving the union meeting, he's certain he'll be getting the other quarter mil. In a few days, the members of the local will mark their ballots. Michael Lambton has been doing this kind of thing a long time, has addressed a lot of crowds, and can read a mood. All the votes he's been through, he's never called one wrong.

They'll go for it. They'll hold their noses when they vote, but they'll go for it.

Driving home from the meeting, sitting in the power, heated, leather captain's chair of his SUV, thinking about all that money he has coming his way, he has some major wood going on.

He thinks, briefly, about hitting a bar, maybe lucking into somebody. But that can be a hit-or-miss play. He may end up paying for it, and he can damn well afford it, but feels that's beneath him. He considers himself a good-looking guy. Maybe a bit heavy around the middle, but Tony Soprano had a gut, too, and it didn't stop him from getting some strange whenever he wanted it.

He's heading down the two-lane highway, hitting the wipers every ten seconds or so to clear some light drizzle coming down, when he sees a car pulled over onto the shoulder about a hundred yards up ahead.

Some Japanese import wagon, the back door swung open. The way Lambton figures it, in some ways, it's the Japs' fault he's taken the money, that he's compromised his principles. It's the Japs who nearly killed North American auto manufacturing. The Germans, too. Two former enemies, getting their revenge at last. Lambton, taking that money, keeping his guys working, it's the Japs and Krauts who've forced his hand. Because when you really thought about it, they —

Hold the phone, what's this?

Some chick's trying to wrestle a spare tire out of the back. He can only see her from behind, but he likes what he sees. Blond hair to the shoulders, black jacket, blue jeans, over-the-knee leather boots. Slim. Could use a little more meat on her bones for Lambton's liking, but not bad.

She has the floor panel in the hatch propped open and the tire halfway out.

Lambton slows as he cruises past, scoping her out through the misted passenger window. She glances over and he can see she's probably late thirties. Nice face.

Pull over and help, or not?

He doesn't have to think long. He noses

200

over onto the shoulder just ahead of her car, kills the engine, and takes out the key. He's got his hand on the door when his cell rings.

"Shit."

He reaches into his jacket, looks at the number. It's no one he knows. But he hears from a lot of people, some who like to use different phones all the time. Ones that are hard to trace. Michael Lambton knows how important that can be.

But he doesn't want to talk to anyone right now. He's got to tend to a damsel in distress. He slips the phone back into his jacket.

Lambton doesn't see another car coming either way on this stretch of road. *Not much traffic out here*, he thinks. Something could happen to someone out here, no one would ever know.

Don't let your mind go there, he says to himself. Then, *Okay, maybe just for a minute or so.*

He pulls his long jacket around the front of him, buttons it. Not just to keep dry against the drizzle. He doesn't want to scare this chick from the get-go by showing off the growing bulge in the front of his pants.

"Trouble?" he shouts.

Figures, help her out, change her tire, then see if she wants to grab a coffee somewhere. He'll be all wet by that time. She'll feel sorry for him, indebted. It'll be hard for her to say no. Maybe she'll suggest he come back to her place, dry off.

The woman peers out from behind her car.

"Oh my God, thanks for stopping!" she says. "I think I ran over a nail or something!"

"You call Triple A?" he asks, hoping she'll say no. Doesn't want some tow truck driver crowding in on his action.

"I'm just kicking myself, right? I get those notices in the mail, telling me I should join, but then throw the things away. Total idiot, right?"

He's around the back of the car now, getting a good look at her. Five-nine, maybe 140 pounds, high cheekbones. Small tits, but you couldn't have everything. Looked European or something. Long legs, jeans fitting her good and tight like leggings, tucked into her boots. Leather gloves. Something athletic about her. The way she holds herself.

"You should join," he tells her, then worries she'll suggest he call using his own membership. He's only a couple of feet from her now. Doesn't want to crowd her, frighten her. She looks wary. Like, *I'm glad you stopped, but please don't start waving it at me, okay?*

"I guess I'm lucky you were going by," she says.

"What's your name?"

"Nicole."

"I'm Frank," he says. Why use his real name on what is clearly not the beginning of a long relationship?

"You want to sit in my car while I do this?"

"Oh, that's okay," Nicole said.

Lambton's cell rings again but he ignores it.

"Is there anything I can do?" Nicole asks. "Like, hold a flashlight or something?"

"You got one? I got one in the truck."

She takes out her own cell phone from inside her jacket pocket, which Michael thinks is interesting, since most women keep them in their purse. "I've got this app. I can turn the phone into a flashlight."

"You don't want to get that all wet," he says. He has a grip on the tire and is leveraging it over the back bumper, getting ready to drop it to the ground.

"Which tire's flat, anyway?" he asks. It occurs to him, at that moment, that he hasn't noticed the car listing to one side or settling on any one corner.

"Front passenger," Nicole says.

As he peers around to the front of the car, Nicole bends down, like she's giving a tug on one of her knee-high boots.

"Nicole, that tire doesn't look flat to —"

The ice pick, swift and noiseless, feels hot going into his right side, just above his waist. In the second it takes him to register the pain, Nicole has withdrawn it, the pick red and glistening, and thrust it into him once again, this time higher, between his ribs.

Nicole withdraws again, then drives the ice pick in a third time.

Hard.

Michael Lambton gasps and falls to the wet gravel. He tries to speak but all that emerges from between his lips is blood.

Nicole kneels down and says to him, "Your people, they wanted me to tell you, they know you sold them out. They know about the double-cross. They know you fucked them over."

Then, just to be sure, she runs the ice pick into him a fourth time, piercing his heart.

She stands and turns her face up to the rain. It feels good. Cleansing.

She rolls Michael Lambton down into the ditch and slips the spare tire back into the hold below the hatchback floor. Once she's behind the wheel and heading off down the two-lane blacktop, her own phone rings.

"Yes."

"It's me." No hello, no introduction. But she recognizes the man's voice. It's Lewis.

"Hey," she says.

"I'm calling about your availability. I mean, it's not like you're exclusive with Victor any-more."

"Kind of busy right now," she says.

"I may have something for you."

"I'm north of the border. About to take some time off."

"But if I had something for you, could you

204

take it on? It'd be worth your while."

"What do you mean, if?"

"I have to make the case to my boss. I think he'll go for it. I'll know very soon."

She thinks. She really wants some time off, but then again, she hates to turn down work.

"What's the job?"

"Some chick works in a bar," he says. "Piece of cake."

"Sounds like a job anyone could do," Nicole says.

"We need some distance on this one, too."

"Let me know when you've talked to your boss."

She ends the call.

There's something about his voice. It reminds her, just a little, of her father's, although she hasn't actually spoken with him for many years. The miserable son of a bitch.

But he's always in her head, dear old Dad.

She can still hear him saying, "Jesus Christ, *silver*? We came all the way to Australia so you could win *silver*? You know what they say? If you win bronze at the Olympics, you're just happy to go home with a medal. But when you win silver, when you come within a hair of winning gold, it eats you up for the rest of your life. It's like being the second guy who walked on the moon. Who remembers him?"

She can still remember the slap she got when she said, "Buzz Aldrin."

TWENTY-ONE

The following morning, it was as though it had never happened.

Thomas came down for breakfast like it was any other day. Even though I hadn't stopped feeling guilty about how I'd handled things after the visit from the FBI, Thomas was going about things the way he always did, which is to say, he stayed in his room and traveled the world.

So many things about him puzzled me. I wished I could get inside his head. He'd always been a mystery to me, even when we were kids. There was this bubble around him, something that kept me from getting through, and him from reaching out. I'd always wondered, why him and not me? Why was he the one to be — is afflicted the right word? — with psychiatric problems, and not me? How fair was that? Did God look down at my parents and think, "I'll give them one with a good head on his shoulders, and the other — I'll have a bit of fun with him."

206

There was no shortage of theories about why Thomas was schizophrenic. When we were kids, bad parenting — or, more specifically, bad mothering — was often blamed, which didn't go over well with our mom, who was a patient, loving woman. A nurturing woman, she'd have been more likely to mitigate the effects of someone's mental distress rather than exacerbate it. Over time, other theories came to the fore. It was genetic. Environmental. A chemical imbalance in the brain. Stress. A childhood trauma. Processed foods. A combination of all of those things.

Or maybe something else entirely.

The bottom line was, no one really knew anything. I could no more explain why Thomas was the way he was than I could explain why I was the way I was. And Thomas, while troubled, was also tremendously gifted. His ability to remember all the things he saw while on Whirl360 was beyond my ability to comprehend. I asked him once if he'd be happier without this so-called gift, and he threw it right back at me. Would I be happier if I had no artistic ability? What I judged to be his curse, he saw as his talent. This was what made him different. This was what made him proud. His obsession was his source of pleasure. And when you thought about it, wasn't that true of all talented people?

I just didn't know.

What I did know was that my parents did everything they could to help Thomas, and loved him unreservedly. They took him to doctors. They took him to specialists. They met with all his teachers. They never stopped worrying about him. Often, as the older brother, I was drawn into that circle of anxiety. Once — I think I was fifteen at the time — Thomas had been missing for hours. He'd often get on his bike and wander Promise Falls, mapping it, learning every square inch of it. He'd return, his notebook filled with street plans, detailed right down to the placement of the stop signs and fire hydrants.

This particular day, he hadn't returned home in time for dinner. That wasn't like Thomas.

"Go see if you can find him," Mom said.

I hopped on my bike and headed downtown. It struck me that that was where I'd find him. The crisscross of streets was more intricate downtown, and offered more entertainment value for someone with Thomas's interests. I couldn't find him.

But I found his bike.

It was tucked in an alley off Saratoga, between a barbershop and the Promise Falls Bakery, which made the best lemon tarts in the history of the universe. I thought maybe Thomas had gone in there for one, but the lady behind the counter had not seen him.

I went up the street and back, checking into every business, asking if anyone had seen my brother. At one point, I stood on the sidewalk out front of a shoe store, overcame my fear of drawing attention to myself, and shouted: "Thomas!"

When I went back to where I'd found his bike, it was gone.

I pedaled home furiously, getting there about ten minutes after he'd returned. Thomas was particularly sullen, never saying a word through dinner. But that night, I heard him in the basement, arguing with our father, or, more accurately, Dad speaking angrily to him. I figured Thomas was getting chewed out for going AWOL, but when I asked him about it later, he said it was nothing.

Whatever he'd been up to that day never came up again.

I was sitting at the kitchen table, pondering these and other weighty issues and watching Thomas eat his cereal, when I said, "Instead of making dinner, I have something else for you to do."

He looked up from his bowl. "What?" He sounded alarmed.

"The house. It needs a cleaning."

He scanned the kitchen and out to the living room. "It looks good to me."

"It needs a vacuuming. A lot of stuff gets walked in here. I'll clean the bathrooms, you vacuum the house."

"Dad always did the cleaning," he said. When I said nothing, he added, "He just always did it. I've never used the vacuum."

"Do you agree that the house needs to be cleaned?" I asked.

Slow to answer. Finally, "I guess."

"Well, if Dad's no longer here, how do you think we should solve that problem? It's the two of us living here, at least for now, and I want to include you in the problem solving around here."

"I suppose," he said thoughtfully, "you could do it."

"I'm already doing the grocery shopping. And I've been making the meals. And dealing with the lawyer. And, Thomas, I have a job. I'm either going to have to nip back to Burlington —"

He started to say it, but I held up my finger as a warning and stopped him.

"I'm either going to have to nip back to Burlington, or I'm going to have to work here. Either way, I have things to do."

"Me, too," he said.

"That's true. I figured, if I have to cut into my work time to get errands done, then it's only fair that you should, too."

Thomas's eyes darted about nervously. "I don't know where the vacuum is."

210

I pointed to the closet near the back door. "It's right in there."

"When did you want me to do this for you?" he asked.

"You have to understand, Thomas, that you're not doing this for *me*. This is something for the household. Pitching in, sharing chores, we do that for each other, and for ourselves. You get where I'm coming from?"

"Yes. I guess so. So when do you want me to do this?"

I raised my hands. "What about now? You get it out of the way, you've got the rest of your day free. That's all I'm going to ask you to do today."

"How many rooms do I have to do?"

"All of them," I said.

"The basement?"

"Okay, skip the basement."

"What about the stairs?"

"Yes, the stairs." His shoulders slumped, already feeling the weight of the assignment. "Go haul out the vacuum, I'll show you the basics."

He pushed back his chair, went to the closet, and dragged out the machine with all the grace and familiarity of a yak handling a set of golf clubs.

"How do you plug it in?" he asked. "The plug only comes out an inch. It won't reach the wall."

"Press your foot on that pad there — no,

right next to that — and then you can pull out the cord. Keep pulling until it won't come out any more." I stood up. "Let me show you a few things."

I gave him a brief lesson. How to turn it on and off, when to use the power head, and what the various attachments were for. "This is for carpet," I said, "and this is for bare wood floors."

"What about tile?" he asked.

"Same as a bare wood floor. Just keep going over the whole floor. Nothing to it."

I might have looked like Thomas did had someone dropped me into the cockpit of the space shuttle. At my urging, he flipped the switch and the machine roared to life. I shouted, "I've got some mail and stuff to deal with, so I'll leave you be."

I'd come back to Promise Falls in such a rush that I hadn't packed a laptop; I was using the e-mail program on my cell, and any correspondence that required a reply of more than a few words was a pain to type out on the phone's keypad. Plus, I knew I had a few bills that needed to be paid, which I could do online.

Dad had a laptop, the second he'd owned. "This one is lighter, faster," he'd said to me in a message a few months ago. He'd started reading newspapers online, but still bought a print one every day. He said it was for the local ads, but it was really about the ritual of getting into the car and driving down to the store to buy one. It was his daily morning adventure. He always got a coffee, too, and was still home in time to make Thomas breakfast.

He kept the computer on the kitchen counter. I took it out with me onto the porch. The wireless signal worked out there, and I wanted to get away from the noise of the vacuum. I took in Thomas's technique as I walked past. He was stooped over as he wandered the floor, like he was actually hunting for the dust he had to suck up. He evidently believed the power head needed to rest atop each section of carpet for several seconds to do its job. At this rate, he wasn't going to get up to his room until noon.

I sat in one of the wicker chairs, opened up the computer, and hit the power button. I probably could have used a sweater out there, but it wasn't cool enough to make me want to go back inside and find one.

I entered the password to get into my e-mail program. Some junk, a couple of notes from Jeremy Chandler, a message from an editor at the *Washington Post* praising my last illustration, which depicted Congress as a sandbox full of children.

Inside, it sounded like the vacuum had just sucked up a squirrel. Thomas had undoubtedly caught the carpet fringe. He'd figure it out.

I found the Web site for the *Promise Falls Standard*. I couldn't find a specific e-mail address for Julie, but under Contact Us it said you could reach a reporter by typing in their first initial followed by last name and then @pfstandard.com.

So I was able to write Julie:

Thanks for the beer, and making the time to talk. It was nice to see you again. Like I said, if you're driving by, pop in and say hi to Thomas.

I hit "send."

She'd been on my mind since our meeting at Grundy's, and I was hoping she'd take me up on the invitation. I hadn't spent much time with her, but it was long enough to realize she was easy to talk to. You could speak plainly to her, no bullshit. And I didn't have many people to talk to these days. I really couldn't talk to Thomas. I mean, could I? When all he really cared about was getting back to his Whirl360? He was more concerned with assisting the CIA with a nonexistent global catastrophe than he was with helping me figure out what to do with the house and him.

I sighed and opened up Safari. I wanted to look into the residence Laura Grigorin had suggested might be a good place for Thomas. I went up to the corner of the screen to enter some key words into Google.

As soon as I began to type, a list of previous searches popped up onto the screen. These would have been the things Dad was looking up the last time he used this computer. Before he died.

I glanced at the list. It was short. Three items.

smartphones
depression
child prostitution

I stared at the list a long time. Felt the world getting ready to open up and swallow me whole.

The door opened. "I think the vacuum's broken," Thomas said.

Twenty-Two

Howard Talliman is sitting on a bench in Central Park, just north of the Arsenal, south of Sixty-fifth, waiting for Lewis Blocker.

For years, Howard has employed the former New York police officer. It started as the occasional freelance job, but that meant there might be times when Howard needed Lewis when he was busy doing work for someone else. That didn't work for Howard. So he put Lewis on an annual salary, twice what he'd made as a cop, so he could be confident that whenever Lewis's skills were required, he would be available.

Howard needs Lewis right now more than he ever has before. He's never had a crisis quite like this one.

Howard looks south, sees Lewis. The man is just under six feet, and if he had any hair on the top of his head he'd probably top out at six-one. Thick neck, broad shoulders, a bit soft in the middle. But that's just padding over the six-pack. Howard knows that if he drove his fist into Lewis's gut with everything he had, the guy wouldn't move, and Howard would end up with a broken wrist. His eyes are small and penetrating, flanking a nose that's bent slightly to the left. He'd had it broken years ago and chose not to get it fixed. It let people know he'd been hurt, and survived, and didn't have any qualms about getting hurt again.

Lewis Blocker nods at Howard and sits down next to him.

"Well?" Howard asks.

"You could give her the hundred grand," he says, "but that won't be the end of your problem."

"Go on."

"I asked around," he says. Howard does not have to ask Lewis whether he has been discreet. That's what Howard pays him to be. Lewis knows how to find things out without drawing attention to himself.

"Allison Fitch owes money. She bounces checks. She borrows money and doesn't pay it back. She hasn't been paying her share of the rent and her roommate wants to kill her. When she gets money, instead of paying back the people she owes it to, she blows it on herself."

"Okay."

"I think, if you give her that money, it'll blow her mind. She'll go through it like shit through a goose. You ask me, that hundred grand will actually put her in deeper debt. She'll get her own place, she'll lease a flashy car, she'll open a charge account at Bloomie's. The hundred grand'll be gone, and she'll be on the hook for another hundred in no time."

Howard nods thoughtfully. "So she'll be back."

"No question. And the way she's going to spend that money, it's going to attract attention. A lot of attention. People are going to wonder where she came into this fortune. Some people, they shake you down and they're smart about it. Tuck the money away, save it for a rainy day, that kind of thing. But those kinds of people, they're in the minority. You find someone who's sensible with money, they're not typically into blackmail. You know?"

"I get it," Howard says. "What if — I can't believe I'm suggesting this — we gave her more money, from the outset, but made it clear there'll never be any more. *Ever.*"

Lewis looks disapprovingly at him.

"Okay, I know, dumb idea," Howard says. "Maybe, what we do is give her the hundred, but you have a word with her. You can be very persuasive. You scare the shit out of her, make her understand that if she flashes the money around, draws attention to herself, or comes back for more, it might not be in her interest."

"Hurt her," Lewis says. "A little."

Howard can't look the ex-cop in the eye. He's watching a Filipino nanny corral three small Upper East Side children, all clad in Burberry, as they head in the direction of the zoo.

"That's your call, Lewis," Howard says. "You're the expert."

"Yeah," he says. "That's why I think you should hear me out on what I think you need to do. Because, you know, we haven't even addressed your other problem."

Howard looks at him. "About what she might know."

Lewis nods.

"I spoke to Bridget," Howard says. "She thinks it's *possible* Fitch might have overheard one of her phone conversations with Morris. And it's *possible* they may have discussed his problem."

"But she doesn't know for sure."

Howard shakes his head. "No."

"But it's not the sort of thing you want to leave to chance."

Howard rubs his hands together. "Maybe, if you had a chat with her, you could determine what she knows and what she doesn't."

Lewis looks down at his feet. A couple of pigeons are pecking at some specks of popcorn near the toe of his left shoe. He kicks suddenly, catching one of the pigeons in the head. The bird staggers off like it's had too much to drink.

"I don't think that's a good idea, Howard. If she doesn't actually know anything, we'll be telling her we've got more to hide than the fact that Bridget swings both ways. Gives her even more leverage."

"Jesus," Howard says under his breath. "What a fucking mess. And honest to God, Lewis, how the hell did you miss this about Bridget?"

His eyes narrow. "Maybe because you didn't ask me to do anything but a superficial check. Finances, criminal record, unpaid parking tickets. She came out smelling like a rose, there. She was so perfect for Morris you didn't want to dig too deep and run the risk of fucking it up."

Howard sighs because he knows this is true. But he can't stop himself from adding, "Well, you should have done it on your own initiative. You should have done what you knew was most prudent."

"Interesting you should say that," Lewis says.

"What?"

"I'm going to recommend what I think you need to do about Allison Fitch."

Howard looks wary. "What?"

"You have to make it so she won't be a recurring problem."

"How the hell do we do that?"

Lewis says nothing, waits for Howard to

figure it out.

Once he has, his face blanches. "Oh no, you can't be serious."

Again, Lewis says nothing.

"Jesus Christ," Howard whispers under his breath. "No, that's not — look, I've done some things in my time. Things I had to do. But, Lewis, we don't kill people."

Lewis gives a measured nod. "It wouldn't be us, Howard."

"What?"

"It wouldn't be us. It wouldn't be you, and it wouldn't be me. It wouldn't be connected to us."

Howard's mouth is very dry. "Then . . ."

"I've already had a preliminary discussion with someone about our situation," Lewis says calmly. "I know her work, and she can do this for us."

"Oh, Lewis, Jesus." Howard takes a deep breath, lets it out slowly. Then, abruptly, he turns and says, "Her?"

Lewis nods.

Howard shakes his head. "I don't know. I just don't know."

"You have to ask yourself how long you want this problem to continue. If you're prepared to endure it indefinitely, for this woman to keep coming back for more, for her to blab to her friends how she came into this money, to run the risk that she knows something that could be very damaging to

Morris, then go ahead and give her the hundred thousand now."

Howard puts his head in his hands for a few seconds, then sits up straight, stares ahead, and says, "Do what you have to do."

TWENTY-THREE

"The vacuum sucked up the edge," Thomas said as I came into the house, leaving Dad's laptop on the porch chair. He pointed. The power head appeared to have digested half of a carpet runner that ran between the front door and the kitchen. The machine turned itself off when it jammed.

"Thomas, just pull the carpet back out of it."

"With my hand?"

"Yes."

"What if it comes back on and sucks off my fingers?"

"It's not going to —"

The phone rang.

"Goddamn," I said. I picked up. "Yeah?"

"Is this Ray Kilbride?" A woman's voice.

"Yes."

"Ray, it's Alice, at Harry Peyton's office? We were wondering if you had a moment to pop in and sign a few papers related to the processing of your father's estate."

"Uh, yeah, sure," I said, trying to collect my thoughts. "Of course. When does Harry want me to come in?"

"Well, it's actually pretty quiet here right now. This may not be a convenient time, but if you had a chance —"

"Fine. I'll be there in a few minutes."

I hung up. When I turned around, I nearly bumped into Thomas, who'd been standing only a foot away, awaiting instructions, the disabled vacuum behind him.

"What's going on?" he asked.

"I have to go to the lawyer's office and sign some papers."

"I'm going to go back to work," Thomas said, his eyes darting upward. "I'm way behind."

"Fine. I'll sort out the vacuum later. I'll be back in a bit."

Driving into town, I couldn't stop thinking about why my father would be scouring the Internet for information on child prostitution. The first two search items I could get my head around. He'd been talking about getting a new phone, one that could connect to the Net and take pictures and do any number of other things. And, based on the snippets I had heard lately from Harry and Len, maybe Dad was depressed. He could well have been diagnosing himself.

But child prostitution?

224

All the places my mind took me were places I did not want to go.

I tried to think of some logical reasons why Dad would be doing such a search. There had to be some.

Think.

Okay. So maybe he'd seen something on television, some news program, about the sexual exploitation of children. He was so appalled by what he'd seen, he wanted to learn more. And the reason for that would be . . . ? Maybe he wanted to make a donation to a charity that was working to free children around the world from this kind of servitude.

Did that sound like my father? Did he have a history of seeking out organizations to give his money to?

No.

He was a good man. There was no question about that. When people needed help, he was there. I could remember, when I was a child, our neighbors' house — not the Hitchens, but the people on the other side — catching on fire. The fire department got there before the house was destroyed, but there was considerable damage to the kitchen. They had no insurance, couldn't afford to hire someone to rebuild, and opted to do the work themselves. The only problem was, while they had the determination, they lacked the skills. And while Dad had never worked as a plumber or carpenter, he was a pretty good do-ityourselfer, having learned those things from his own father. For a month, whenever he had time, Dad worked on that kitchen.

So Dad liked to help, but in a hands-on kind of way. He'd donate time and energy, but he wasn't a guy who picked up the phone and divulged his credit card number for some humanitarian organization.

So that nixed *that* reason for researching child prostitution.

Maybe he'd heard that it was a problem in the upper New York State area, and wanted to make sure it wasn't becoming a problem in Promise Falls. *That* seemed even *more* unlikely.

So what other reason?

The one I couldn't bring myself to consider was that Dad was *interested* in the subject.

When I got back to the house, I'd check the history of Web sites Dad's search had led him to. Maybe those sites, whatever they turned out to be, would shed light on my father's motivations.

I'd heard stories over the years, people discovering things about their parents after they'd died. A mother who'd had a child she'd given up for adoption before she married. A father who'd been having an affair with his secretary. A mother who'd for years kept hidden her pill addiction. A father who'd led a dual life, with a separate, secret family in another part of the country.

Any one of those discoveries would be shocking, but they'd be nothing compared to learning your father was a pervert.

Which I did not know to be true. Which I simply could not believe.

There was one other possibility.

Dad never looked up child prostitution in the first place.

Someone else had been using Dad's laptop.

"You okay, Ray?" Harry Peyton asked as I pulled my chair close to the edge of his desk to sign a few documents.

"Yeah, sure," I said.

"You look stressed out."

I scribbled my signature in the places he was pointing. "I'm fine."

"You don't need to be worried about things. All the paperwork's going through without a hitch."

"That's good to hear."

"How about things at the house? How's Thomas?"

I put the pen down and leaned back in my chair. "How's Thomas," I repeated, looking down. "There's a question."

"Ray, what's on your mind?"

"Harry," I said, "you're sort of my lawyer, too, aren't you?"

"Ray, of course."

"I mean, I know you were Dad's lawyer, and you're handling all this estate stuff, but

227

are you my lawyer, too, about other things?"

"Yes," he said. "I'm your lawyer. You can talk to me."

I started to speak, and then didn't know where to begin. Not with Dad and what I'd found on his laptop. But that discovery was not the only thing that had happened in the last twenty-four hours to leave me shaken.

"The FBI paid us a visit," I said.

"They what? Jesus Christ, Ray, you should have called me. Did they have a warrant?"

"They just showed me their IDs."

"Good Lord."

I told him all of it. How they came in, asked questions of Thomas and me. Finding out Thomas had sent all those e-mails to the CIA, addressed to Bill Clinton. How I'd heard him having an imaginary conversation with the former president.

Harry placed his palms on the table. "Unbelievable. You've got a lot on your plate, Ray."

"There's something else I wanted to bounce off you," I said.

"What?"

"About Dad."

"Go on."

"Did Dad ever . . . did you ever get a sense of what Dad's private life was like?"

"What do you mean, private life? Are you talking about his sex life?"

"I guess," I said.

228

Harry shrugged. "I don't know. You mean, since your mother passed away?"

Not really, but I said, "Sure."

"I don't honestly know. I can't see him bringing anyone to the house, and Adam never left the home for extended periods of time because of your brother. He sure wouldn't have gone anywhere overnight. But then again, if he had met someone, he could have gotten together with her during the day, when he didn't have any qualms about leaving your brother for a few hours."

"You ever see him with anyone? Did he ever talk about seeing anyone?"

Harry shook his head. "No. But you know, a man his age, there's every reason to think he'd be, you know, sexually active. Do you mind my asking why this is an issue, Ray? Are you thinking there's going to be some woman coming out of the woodwork, saying she's got some sort of claim on the estate?"

"No, no, it's okay," I said. "You know what? Forget I even asked. It's nothing."

Maybe that was what I should have done. Forgotten about it. Pretended I never saw those two words on my father's computer.

But before I let this go, I was going to see what Web pages that search led him to. I didn't want to know, but I had to know.

When I got home, Thomas was where I expected him to be. Dad's laptop was sitting on the kitchen table, closed. Thomas must have brought it in from the porch and turned it off.

I opened the lid, hit the button, waited the half minute or so it took for the computer to power up. Then I opened the Web browser.

I went to the search field and typed in a single letter to bring up the previous searches.

There was nothing there.

Nothing about smartphones, depression, or child prostitution.

"What the hell?" I said under my breath.

I moved the cursor up to History and clicked. It was empty. The list of all the Web sites that had been visited with this machine had been erased.

TWENTY-FOUR

Many nights, even after all these years, she dreams of being on the bars.

It's 2000. The Sydney Olympics. Nicole is fifteen. Performing her routine on the uneven bars before thousands of spectators, hundreds of cameras, her fellow artistic gymnastics team members, her coach. She feels the chalk on her hands, then leaps for the lower bar, grasping it firmly, feeling the pull on her arms, spinning around it twice before having enough momentum to propel herself to the higher bar, and then she is off, rotating, the stadium, the people, flying past her field of vision, except she's not seeing them. They're not out there now. There are no spectators, no cameras, no fellow team members, no coach. There is only Nicole, and these two bars. There is nothing else in the entire universe for the next minute, which seems so much longer than a minute. When she is dreaming, this minute can go on for hours. She is soaring. Flying like a bird. Weightless.

231

There's nothing like it, no way to describe it. She thinks about how impossible it must be for someone who has walked on the surface of the moon to describe the experience. She is not walking on the moon, but when she is on the bars, the high she feels, can it really be all that different? Olga knows. Nadia knows. There is no way to put it into words. There are the bars, and then there is everything else.

The nights she does not dream about the bars, she dreams about the kills.

They are, in their own way, equally graceful. Swooping in on one's prey as noiselessly and as swiftly as moving from the upper bar to the lower. No wasted effort. No superfluous moves. In their own way, a thing of beauty.

A perfect execution.

Whether her dreams are of uneven bar routines or assassinations, they are always gold medal performances. Never a silver. Never a bronze. Sometimes, her dreams meld. As she comes off the high bar, doing her final maneuver, preparing for her dismount, her hands now free, she sees in them a dagger. As her body, an instrument in its own right, descends, so, too, does the dagger.

Woe be to anyone who waits below.

She is on Orchard Street.

Nicole has the address. She has been briefed. She has a picture. Tall, with long,

232

dark hair. The target will be there. Allison Fitch. She shares an apartment with a friend, but the friend works days. Allison works in a bar at night, so she sleeps through the day.

Nicole doesn't know who this Allison Fitch is, or what she has done. She doesn't know who, exactly, wants this woman dispatched, but given that it is Lewis who has engaged her, she can guess that this woman presents a threat to someone very important. Fitch has something on someone, and it may be in her phone. Nicole has been told to make sure she recovers it.

But none of this really matters to Nicole. It's a job.

She pulls her black baseball cap down low on her forehead as she crosses Orchard. She feels in her pocket for the plastic bag. It's a strong one. Even if the woman claws at it with her fingernails, it will not tear. Nicole does not use guns. She does not like guns. She does not like the noise they make. She doesn't have to do much self-analysis to figure out why. From the moment she started out in track and field, she hated the starter's pistol. Muscles tensed, breath held, waiting for it to go off. It was those last milliseconds, before the gun exploded, that she'd always hated the most.

She doesn't like them now, even when they are equipped with a silencer. A gun is heavy, difficult to conceal. And it makes so little use of the body. Anybody can use one. Nicole likes physical involvement. Suffocation involves strength. So does thrusting with an ice pick. But today she will use a simple plastic bag.

No one has ever been arrested for carrying a plastic bag, although she is carrying other devices that would definitely interest the police if they were to stop her for any reason. She stands at the entrance to the building, and before entering glances up and down the street.

Nicole sees no police cars, nothing to worry her. A block away, there is a car, with some odd contraption strapped to its roof, stuck in traffic, but it is of no concern to her.

Nicole steps into the lobby of the building, studies the directory of names and buzzers. She presses several at once, careful not to buzz the one for Allison Fitch. A few seconds later, a voice crackles from the speaker. "Hello?"

But another, less cautious tenant has actually hit the button to buzz someone in. Nicole opens the door and enters the building, then waits for a couple of minutes. She doesn't want anyone opening their apartment door to see who was hitting the buzzer. They'll peer out, see no one, then go back inside.

This is a building without elevators. She climbs the two long flights of stairs and is relieved to encounter no one. However, even if she does, she knows that anything anyone might remember about her, other than that she is a white woman in her twenties, will be wrong. The brim of her cap, as well as the sunglasses, shields much of her face. Her hair is black this afternoon, but it will be blond tonight.

She determines, once she is in the hallway, that the apartment overlooking Orchard is the one at the very end of the hall. She approaches the door to apartment 305, but before going to the trouble of picking the lock, she tries turning the doorknob with her gloved hand, in case it is unlocked.

No joy. It's locked. She reaches into the inside pocket of her windbreaker and finds the tool she carries for just such an occasion. As locks go, this looks like a simple one. If there's a chain on the inside, that will slow her down for maybe another thirty seconds. She has several rubber bands in her pocket. All you have to do is tie the band to the chain, then loop the end of it over the knob. Then, as you close the door, the chain is pulled from the slot.

Practiced it a million times. Now, she can do it with her eyes closed.

The door opens.

The chain is not in place.

She opens the door a fraction of an inch and listens. She can see a sliver of kitchen, and beyond that, a small living room. A fold-out couch has been left open, the covers askew. Two people share this apartment. If the target is not using the pullout, she must be in the bedroom. Nicole is guessing that room is to the left of the living room.

In one smooth motion, Nicole opens the door, steps in, and closes it behind her, all without sound.

Now that she's in the apartment, she stands frozen, listening. A window must be open, because the sounds of the street are distinct. That's a good thing. Although she moves stealthily, a bit of background noise can't hurt.

Nicole listens for another person. Snoring, soft breathing. A shower running.

A heart beating.

She hears nothing, yet senses a presence. She takes a couple of steps toward the living room, waiting for a glimpse of the door into the bedroom.

She edges past a kitchen table set with two chairs that scream IKEA. A monthly calendar printout, with Allison Fitch's bar shifts penciled on it, is held to the fridge by a magnet in the shape of a cat.

Jesus, she thinks. *Don't let there be a cat in here.* She does not sense one. She doesn't smell one. There is no bowl on the floor. But the kitchen is in some disarray. The sink is full of dishes. A half-full cup of coffee sits on the table.

Nicole can see the bedroom door, and into the room. It's a typically small New York apartment bedroom. Eight by ten, maybe. Just enough room for the unmade double bed. A window on the far wall. Raised.

There she is.

Not in the bed, but standing at the window, her back to Nicole. Dark hair hanging to her shoulders. Her hands resting on top of the air-conditioning unit. Looking down at the street. She is dressed. Dark blue skirt, white blouse. The way she's standing, she's probably in heels, but Nicole is unable to see below her knee; the bed is in the way.

There's only twelve feet between them.

She's measuring the distance in her head. Not enough time to run around the bed. Have to go over it. Start at a run, leap, left foot hits the bed, right foot lands on the other side. She'll be on her in half a second. Got her Nikes on.

And she notices, right there, near the foot of the bed, a purse. Most likely where she will find the cell phone. Nicole reaches into her pocket and quietly draws out the white plastic bag. Waves it lightly to open it up.

In a second, she leaps onto the bed, uses it as a springboard to get to the far side. By the time her prey realizes she's not alone, it's too late. Nicole has the bag over her head.

She lets out a muffled scream, but then,

237

just as Nicole knew she would, she's clawing at the bag, trying to rip it from her face. But Nicole has twirled her wrist around several times, drawing the bag so tight it is a second skin.

The woman, in her final gasping seconds, collapses onto the air conditioner as the car with the unusual contraption on its roof drives past. She rests there for a second, then drops to the floor.

Nicole, kneeling, keeps the bag tight around the woman's head for a good minute, just to be sure. Then, once she is certain the woman is dead, she removes the bag, wads it into a tight ball, and returns it to her jacket pocket.

Next, the phone.

She grabs the purse that's resting on the bed, unzips it, and finds the phone almost immediately, tucked into a pouch in the side. She slips it in her pocket with the bag.

Then she gets out her own phone, unlocks it, presses twice.

"Done. Cleanup set to go?" This is a job where the client doesn't want a body left behind. Nicole is good at what she does, but removals are not her area of expertise.

"Yes." Lewis.

She ends the call without another word, puts her own phone away. A golden performance. No falls. No marks lost for poor form or empty swings. No fumbling on the dismount. No cause for deductions whatsoever, in her own humble opinion.

No roaring crowd, either, but you can't have everything.

She stands, takes one last look at the dead woman, and is getting ready to leave when she hears the apartment door opening.

It's too soon for the cleanup crew to be here.

Twenty-Five

I rapped on Thomas's door to tell him that dinner was nearly ready.

"What are we having?" he asked.

"Burgers on the barbecue," I told him.

When dinner was over, and the dishes put in the sink, I put my hand on his arm so he wouldn't jump up from the table and head back upstairs.

"I really have to go," he said.

"I need to talk to you about something." I took my hand off him but felt I might have to grab him again to keep him here.

"What do you want to talk about?"

"You brought Dad's laptop in off the porch."

He nodded. "Someone might have taken it."

"What did you do with it?"

"I put it in the kitchen."

"I mean, did you do anything on the laptop?"

He nodded. "I turned it off. The battery

240

might have been dead by the time you got home if you'd left it on."

"Did you do anything else with it?"

"Like what?"

"Did you do anything with the history?"

"I erased it," Thomas said.

"You did."

He nodded.

"Why did you do that?"

"I always do that," he said. "Before I turn off a computer I always erase the history. Every night when I go to bed I erase the history on my computer. It's like, I don't know, brushing my teeth or something. It's like the computer is all clean for the next morning."

I felt very tired.

"Okay, so that's what you do with your computer. Why did you do it with Dad's?"

"Because you left me to deal with it."

"Did you always erase the history on Dad's laptop?"

"No. Because Dad would shut it down himself. Can I go now? There's something really important on my screen."

"It can wait. When you erased the history, did you look at it first?"

Thomas shook his head. "Why would I do that?"

"Thomas," I said very firmly, "I want you to answer me honestly here. This is very important."

"Okay."

241

"Do you ever use Dad's laptop?"

He shook his head emphatically. "No, never. I have my own computer."

"Did Dad ever lend his computer to anyone? Or did anyone ever come here and use it?"

"I don't think so. Can I go now?"

"Just a second."

"I already lost time this morning vacuuming."

"Thomas, please. If no one has used that computer since Dad died, why was there still some history on it when I used it this morning? Why hadn't you erased it?"

"Because when Dad used it, he turned it off himself. I'd tell him to erase the history, but he didn't worry about it like I do."

I rested my back against my chair. "Okay. Thanks."

"So I can go?"

"Yeah, you can go."

But instead of getting up and going back to his room, he stayed in his chair, like now he had something to ask me.

"What is it?" I asked him.

"I know you're still mad about when the FBI people came to the door. And I haven't sent any e-mails to the CIA or to President Clinton since then."

"Good to know."

"But what if I saw something I really needed to tell them about?"

242

"Like what?"

"If I saw something I thought the CIA really should know about, like a crime, would it be okay if I sent them just one little e-mail?"

"Thomas, I don't care if you saw someone putting a nuclear bomb on a school bus. You are not calling the CIA."

I could see the frustration on his face. "Thomas, what is it? Another fender bender or something?"

"No, something bigger."

"Because when you got all worked up about that before, that just wasn't important."

"It's not like that."

"So what is it?"

"It's about a window."

"A window."

"That's right."

"Someone broke a window and you want to report it to the CIA?"

He shook his head. "It's about something that's happening in a window. Sometimes things happen in windows."

"Thomas, look, whatever it is, just don't worry about it."

Abruptly, he pushed back his chair and stood. "Fine." He marched toward the stairs.

"Thomas, do not send a message to the CIA. I swear to God."

He kept moving. When he was at the bottom of the stairs I shouted, "Thomas! Jesus, are you listening?"

He stopped, his hand on the railing. "You're the one who isn't listening, Ray. I'm trying to talk to you. I'm trying to do what you asked. You don't want me to call the CIA so I ask you what I should do about what's happening in the window and you don't listen."

"Okay, okay. You want me to have a look?"

"Yes," he said.

"Fine. I'll have a look."

I followed him up the stairs and was going to enter his room when he suggested I get an extra chair so I didn't have to lean over his shoulder the whole time. Which meant this was going to take a while.

There was a plastic folding chair tucked into a closet in Dad's bedroom. I grabbed it, returned to Thomas's room, and opened it up next to him in his computer chair. Thomas had waved his mouse to bring the monitors back to life.

"So where the hell are we tonight?" I asked.

"This is Orchard Street."

"And Orchard Street is where?"

"In New York. In Lower Manhattan."

"Okeydoke," I said. "Show me what you've got."

Thomas pointed, his finger half an inch from the screen. He was pointing to a window, one of several perfectly arranged windows on the side of what appeared to be a five-story structure. An old tenement building, probably dating from the late 1800s, although early New York architecture was not something I knew a lot about.

"You see that window?" he said. "On the third floor?"

I looked. There was a white blob in the window's lower half. "Yeah, I see it."

"What do you think that is?"

"Beats me."

"I'm going to zoom in on it," Thomas said. He clicked twice on the image. That had the effect of making it larger, but slightly less distinct. But it was starting to look like something.

"Now what do you think it is?" my brother asked me.

"It kind of looks like . . . it looks like a head," I answered. "But with something wrapped around it."

"Yeah," Thomas said. "You look here and you can see the shape of the nose and the mouth, and there's the chin, and up here's the forehead. It's a face."

"I think you're right, Thomas. It's a face."

"What do you make of it?"

"I don't really know what to make of it. It looks like someone with a bag over their face."

Thomas nodded. "Yes. But because you can see all the person's features so well, the bag has to be on really tight."

"I guess," I said. "Maybe it's a mask or something."

"But there are no holes for the eyes, or the

245

mouth, or the nose. If that's a mask, how is the person supposed to breathe?"

"Can you zoom in on it any more? Can you get closer?"

"I could make it bigger, but it starts to get blurry. This is as good a picture as I can get out of it."

I stared at the image, not sure what to make of it. "I don't know, Thomas. It is what it is. Someone goofing around with a bag on his head. People do dumb shit. Maybe someone knew the Whirl360 car was coming and thought they'd do something silly for the camera when it went by."

"On the third floor? If you wanted to do something silly, wouldn't you stand on the sidewalk?"

"Maybe. I don't know."

"I don't think this person is goofing around," he said.

"Okay, so you tell me what you believe is happening here."

"I think this person is being killed," Thomas said. "This is a murder."

"Sure it is. Come on, Thomas."

"This person is being smothered."

I turned from looking at the screen to stare at my brother. "That's what you think."

"Yes."

"And just what the hell do you want me to do?" I asked.

"I want you to check it out," Thomas said.

"Check it out," I repeated.

"Yup. I want you to go there."

"You want me to go to New York and check out this window," I said. "I don't think so."

"Well then, I guess I'll have to make some calls," Thomas said, "and I'm sorry, but I'm going to have no choice but to e-mail the CIA and ask them to look into it."

"Thomas, listen very carefully to me. First of all, you are not making any calls to the CIA or Homeland Security or the Promise Falls Fire Department, for that matter. And as far as my going into the city to look at this stupid window, that's not happening."

I went downstairs.

A few minutes later, as I was making myself comfortable on the couch, wondering what there might be to watch on Dad's big flat screen, Thomas came down the stairs.

He said nothing to me, didn't even look in my direction. He went to the closet by the front door, opened it, and grabbed a jacket. He slipped his arms into it and was zipping it up when I asked, "Where you off to?"

"New York," he said.

"Really."

"Yes."

"Where in New York?"

"I'm going to look at that window."

"How you getting there?"

"I'm going to walk." He paused. "I know the way."

"That's going to take a while," I said.

"It's 192.3 miles," he said. "If I walk twenty miles a day, I'll be there in —"

"Oh, for Christ's sake," I said.

TWENTY-SIX

If the traffic's not bad, you can drive from Promise Falls to New York in about three and a half hours. But that's a big *if* certainly where the latter part of the drive is concerned. You can be clipping along just great, the Manhattan skyline looking close enough that you could stick your hand out the window and touch it. Then some idiot in a delivery van cuts off a cabbie, sets off a chain reaction crash, and you're bumper to bumper for two hours.

So I opted for the train. The plan was to catch it early in the morning, do what I'd promised to do, and catch one home the same day, so I wouldn't be leaving Thomas alone overnight. Maybe, another time, I would have trusted him to be on his own from one day to the next, but ever since the FBI incident, I didn't like to let him out of my sight for any longer than I had to.

He'd promised he wouldn't do anything that would upset me while I was gone, so long as I kept my part of the bargain.

If Thomas wanted to think I was making this trip into New York just for him, he was welcome to. But the moment he started pushing for me to go into the city, I thought of the woman Jeremy wanted me to meet. This was something I really needed to deal with. It meant future money for me, and from the sound of it, quite a bit. As soon as I left Thomas's room I called Jeremy and asked whether he could set something up for the following day, and he said he'd get back to me. An hour later he reported that while Kathleen Ford already had a luncheon engagement, she could meet us for a drink afterward at the Tribeca Grand Hotel.

I said I'd be there.

Jeremy said we should grab lunch beforehand, and we arranged to meet at the Waverly Restaurant, on Sixth Avenue between Waverly Place and Eighth Street, which would be handy enough to get to the hotel, and to run my little errand for Thomas.

When I told Thomas where I was having lunch, he closed his eyes and said, "At Avenue of the Americas, or Sixth Avenue, as I believe it is more commonly called, and Waverly Place. There's a neon sign hanging over the door, 'Waverly' in green letters and 'Restaurant' in red, right across the avenue from a Duane Reade drugstore, and to the south, across Waverly Place, there's a store that sells vitamins. The 't' in 'Restaurant,' the first one, isn't lighting up when you look at the sign if you're coming down Waverly from the west."

I was up before the sun, drove into Albany, caught the train at Rensselaer, and managed to get some more sleep during the two-and-a-half-hour trip. While I was awake, looking out the window at the scenery flying by, I had time to think about whether agreeing to go by the Orchard Street address, where Thomas had seen the smothered head in the window, was a stupid thing to do — whether it would just encourage him.

But if it kept Thomas from sending another message to a federal agency and attracting any more unwanted attention, it was a smart thing to do. Short of straitjacketing him, there really wasn't any way to keep Thomas from getting in touch with the outside world. I wasn't about to unplug his computer again, and even if I'd been willing to deal with the fallout from doing so, Thomas could always pick up the phone and just call someone. He could write a goddamn letter and put it in the mail. And while Thomas chose to stay in the house, I didn't want him to feel as though he was some kind of prisoner whose access to others was strictly controlled.

The problem with giving in to Thomas on this particular occasion was, what if he saw something else, in another window, in another city, tomorrow, and that city just happened to be Istanbul? Would he expect me to check that out, too?

I figured I'd deal with Thomas on a case-by-case basis. If he did come across something else on one of his virtual travels that he wanted me to investigate, I'd be able to point out that the last time I'd indulged him it had cost me an entire day, not to mention a train ticket. Whether that would persuade my brother to let something go was anyone's guess.

I'd been able to dissuade him from doing anything rash when he'd gotten himself in a lather about that possible minor traffic mishap in Boston. So it was possible to discourage him from pursuing frivolous matters. But there was something about this covered face in the window that had gotten to him.

"People don't look up enough," he said to me.

Once on the train, I was grateful for the time to myself, to think. My thoughts kept returning to my father. Perhaps I was making too much of those two words he'd entered into the search field.

He saw something on child prostitution on the news.

He was appalled.

He decided to learn more.

End of story.

I chided myself for allowing my mind to go places it should never have gone.

I'd left home with a printout of the scene in the window, and took it out of my pocket as the train ran down alongside the Hudson. I had to admit, there was something intriguing about the image. I wasn't inclined to buy Thomas's theory that the passing Whirl360 camera car, while on its mission to video all the streets in Manhattan, had caught an actual murder in progress. That was pretty far-fetched. But the longer I looked at the image, I had to concede Thomas's interpretation was not entirely off the wall. It did kind of look like a person being suffocated, as though someone had come up behind and slipped a bag over his or her head and drawn it tight.

But I also knew it could be any number of other things. For example, it looked like one of those white Styrofoam heads that are used to display wigs. Maybe one was sitting on top of that A/C unit. Or someone, at the moment the image was snapped, passed by the window with one.

It was a very grainy image.

Before embarking on this mission, I suggested to Thomas we do some online research. Thomas was very good at what he did on the computer, but when it came to searching the Net for specific information, I was better. So I got Dad's history-cleared laptop and entered into the search field "Orchard Street New York" and then, before hitting the button to start the search, added the word "murder."

My goal here, honestly, was to take the wind out of Thomas's sails. If our search produced no stories about people being suffocated in windows, I hoped Thomas would mellow out a bit.

And there were no stories about people being suffocated in windows. But some interesting items were returned. I was led to a *New York Times* site listing all stories that ever mentioned Orchard Street. I read up on a few folks who had died there, and not from natural causes. In May 2003, a man had been run down by someone driving a Mercedes-Benz convertible who'd fled the scene. In the mid-nineties, bad blood between the two owners of a handbag store prompted the son of one of them to hire a hit man to kill the other. Police made an arrest before the murder could take place. Seven years ago, a young banking executive was shot in the chest on Orchard Street between Grand and Broome. Police were investigating competing theories; was the banker shot by someone he knew, or a total stranger?

All of these events had happened before Whirl360 was even in existence. While we didn't know when the picture of the head in the window was taken, we could safely assume it had been within the last two or three years. There had been nothing in that time about any suspicious deaths on Orchard, at least none that involved someone dying by having a bag put over his or her head. The only story that even remotely caught my interest was a short news item about a thirty-one-year-old waitress named Allison Fitch of Orchard Street (no specific address given) who was reported missing the last week of the previous August. The story had run the first week of September, but I didn't see any follow-ups, so it seemed likely the matter had resolved itself. Thousands of people went missing every single day across the United States, and within a few hours pretty much all of them reappeared. The stats were there if you wanted to look them up.

I got off the train at Penn Station and headed first down to Canal Street, to Pearl Paint, the huge artist supply store. I lost myself wandering around its several floors for nearly two hours and ended up buying a dozen Paasche airbrush needles and a couple of air caps, as well as a box of fine-point black Sharpie pens, and another box with broad tips. I already had plenty of these back in Burlington, but you could never have too many Sharpies.

Then I grabbed a cab and got dropped off out front of the Waverly. Before going in, I had to see how well Thomas, who had never been here in person, had described it.

There was the vitamin shop, the Duane Reade across the street. He even got the burned-out letter in the sign right.

He was pretty goddamn amazing, no doubt about it.

Jeremy was already in a booth by the front window, looking at the menu with a cup of coffee in front of him, when I came through the door. I slipped in opposite him.

"You won't believe who I urinated next to," he said. Jeremy always tried to impress with stories of his brushes with celebrity.

"I can't imagine," I said.

"Philip Seymour Hoffman," he said. "In the men's room at those theaters up by Lincoln Center."

"Please tell me you didn't strike up a conversation."

He had not. I pointed to the old black-and-white framed photos of celebrities that adorned the walls.

"Pee next to any of them?"

"They're all dead," Jeremy said.

I ordered coffee and a grilled cheese with bacon. Jeremy got scrambled eggs and home fries, served right in the skillet. We talked about the declining state of the newspaper and magazine industry and the growth of sites like The Huffington Post, and how this new opportunity was coming at just the right time.

Jeremy said Kathleen Ford wanted one animated drawing a week and was willing to pay fifteen hundred dollars for each one. That might sound like a lot, but it actually meant dozens of drawings to make it work. "I'll bet there's a program or something that'd make it easier," he said.

I knew of a couple that would make the job much less labor intensive. Once I had an idea, I could probably knock one off in a couple of days, which would still leave me time for other freelance jobs.

Jeremy grabbed the bill when it came and then we caught a cab to the hotel. Ford was fifteen minutes late, but she looked like a woman who never had to apologize for her tardiness. People would be grateful to see her whenever she showed up. Five-ten, slim, mid-fifties, brilliant blond hair, and if I could have seen the tags on her clothes and accessories I'm guessing they would have read Chanel, Gucci, Hermès, and Diane Von Whatserface. She was instantly captivating, said she was a huge fan of my illustrations, once we had *repaired* — there's a word I'd never thought to use in that context before — to the bar, talked almost nonstop about all the important New Yorkers she knew who were going to be contributors to her new Web site, including Donald Trump, who, by the way, she knew very well but still couldn't figure out how he did what he did with his hair, and not once did she ask me any questions except how my father was doing, whom she had heard was not well. Then, just as she whisked off to her next engagement, she said I had the job. The site was to be up and running in three months.

I accepted.

Once she was gone, Jeremy said it felt as though a tornado had just whipped through. Jeremy and I agreed that we'd be talking soon, and I left. Outside the hotel, I hailed a cab.

"Houston and Orchard," I said. As the driver headed in that direction, I leaned back on the black vinyl seat. That was definitely unlike any other job interview I had had before.

I laughed quietly to myself, then turned my thoughts to what the hell I was going to do next. I thought back to the exchange I'd had with Thomas the night before.

"And when I get to this address on Orchard Street," I'd said, "what exactly am I supposed to do? I mean, it's not likely this head is going to still be in the window after all this time."

"I don't know," Thomas said. "You'll think of something."

TWENTY-SEVEN

Howard Talliman had not been sleeping well.

Howard Talliman had not been sleeping well for nine months. He hadn't had a good night's rest since the end of August.

He'd lost weight, too. Sixteen pounds. He'd come in two notches on his belt. If it weren't for the bags under his eyes and his gray pallor, he'd look pretty good, or at least as good as a guy who's shaped something like a garden gnome can ever look.

Talliman's appearance and his short temper, brought about by too little sleep, were sources of embarrassment to him. They sent a signal that something was troubling him, and Howard did not want anyone to think he was worried.

It was not in Howard's nature to worry. Howard made other people worry. It was not in Howard's nature to feel anxious. He made others feel anxious.

It was tough, these days, keeping up appearances.

"You look terrible," Morris Sawchuck had been telling him. "Have you been to a doctor, Howard?"

"I'm fine," Howard insisted. "You're the one I worry about, Morris. You've always been my number one concern."

Howard normally thrived on pressure. It was his oxygen. Any election campaign he'd ever worked, it didn't matter how grim things looked, how far his candidate was behind. He never gave up. He never broke a sweat, even as those around him were saying it was all over. He assessed problems, and solved them. One time, on a city councilman's reelection bid, the primary challenger was a woman touting her considerable experience as a community volunteer. She'd put in hundreds more hours helping the poor and disadvantaged than Talliman's self-serving son of a bitch ever had.

"We have to find a way," Talliman said, "to make her volunteerism a negative."

To which everyone on the campaign went, "Huh?"

Talliman said if John Kerry's service in Vietnam could be used against him, anything was possible. Go after the woman's strength, and find a way to undermine it. Talliman put Lewis Blocker on it. He found evidence that could be used to prop up the suggestion that the woman's commitment to helping others had been at the expense of her children and

260

husband. Her teenage son had been picked up for coke possession, although the case never went to court. Her husband spent a lot of time in neighborhood bars and never saw a waitress's butt he didn't want to pinch. Talliman made sure the press found out, even though he never passed on the information directly. If these stories weren't proof the woman was turning a blind eye to the home front, what was? With only a couple of weeks left in the campaign, Talliman flooded the district with flyers depicting his candidate as a strong family man, implying that his opponent cared more about strangers than her own family.

No one cared if a man put his career ahead of his family. But a woman?

It was slimy and underhanded and a misrepresentation of the truth. Worked, too. "Positively Rovian," his admirers, and detractors, called it after the woman lost by more than three thousand votes.

It was around then that Howard put Lewis Blocker on permanent payroll.

It couldn't have come at a better time for Lewis, who needed the money. He'd left the police before qualifying for a pension. He and several other officers had been called to a hostage-taking. A man was holed up in an apartment, threatening to kill his family. Shots were fired from inside the unit. Then the door flew open and someone charged out.

261

Lewis, positioned down the hall, fired.

Too bad it was the shooter's sixteen-year-old son trying to make a run for it.

No charges were filed, but Lewis Blocker's career as a cop was finished that day.

Sometimes, Howard Talliman mused, things happened for a reason. If a young man had to die so Lewis Blocker could help advance the political careers of great men, well, who was Howard to argue with God's plan?

But surely, Howard thought, God couldn't have wanted things to go the way they had back in August.

The action he'd approved back then, the wheels he had allowed Lewis Blocker to set in motion, with the intention of protecting Morris Sawchuck, had the potential to destroy them all.

Sawchuck was more than a close friend to Howard. He was Talliman's ticket to the Big Show. Once Sawchuck was governor of New York, it was only a matter of time, Howard knew, before he moved up the ladder from there. Sawchuck had the personality, the showmanship — even the most perfect set of *teeth* — to make it to the White House.

Howard had believed that Bridget's lesbian affair with Allison Fitch, and — even more critically — what that woman might know about Morris's political problems, could derail all that. He'd trusted Lewis's instincts about what needed to be done. He'd also

262

trusted Lewis's instincts about who was best suited to get it done.

Not that Howard hadn't expected there to be some fallout once the job had been executed, as it were. When a young woman is murdered, or goes missing, it's likely to draw some attention.

There was one story in the *Times*. Police were trying to track down Allison Fitch's whereabouts when she failed to show up for work. The article reported that she was originally from Dayton, and there was a line from her mother, who said she had not heard from her.

The *New York Post* ran something as well, deep inside, just before Sports. And it made NY1 one day. Her smiling face on screen for no more than five seconds.

After that, not so much. A missing person in Manhattan was not news for long. Some girl from Ohio doesn't come to work one day? Big deal. So maybe she couldn't hack it in the big city and went home. Unless someone stumbled upon a body, a missing person was barely going to make it through a single news cycle.

No one had stumbled upon a body.

Ordinarily, a body being stumbled upon would have put Howard Talliman at ease. Because even if the rest of the world did not know what had happened to Allison Fitch, *he* would know what had happened to Allison Fitch.

But he did not.

Lewis didn't know, either.

No one had known for quite some time.

Shortly after Nicole had been sent to do the job, Lewis placed a call to Howard.

"I heard from her. There's a problem."

"What sort of problem?"

Lewis had explained that normally, Allison Fitch, who worked nights, would be home throughout the day, asleep, while her roommate, this Courtney Walmers woman who worked regular hours, would not.

At which point Howard Talliman had started to get a very bad feeling.

But on this particular day, Lewis had explained, there was an unforeseen development.

"The woman in the apartment was not Allison Fitch. The wrong target was taken out."

Howard, sitting in his office, had struggled to remain calm. But Jesus, the roommate? Dead? Someone who'd never posed a threat in the first place? Someone he didn't even know? Sure, Howard had caused collateral damage in the past. His political shenanigans had destroyed more than his opponents' reputations. He'd seen defeated candidates lose their homes to pay off campaign debts. They left their wives, or their wives left them. One became an alcoholic, drove his car into

264

a bridge abutment, and never walked again.

But nothing like this. No one had ever died.

And as unexpected, and bad, as this news was, Howard had still wondered whether this woman Lewis had hired, once she'd realized her mistake, had still managed to get the original job done. What about the intended target?

"What about Fitch?" he had asked Lewis.

"Gone," Lewis had said. "She walked in on it. Saw what happened. Took off like a bat out of hell."

In the intervening months, Allison Fitch remained missing. Probably scared shitless, terrified to show herself.

As long as she was out there, somewhere, she was a ticking bomb, just waiting to go off.

Back when Howard had taken that original call from Lewis, he'd exploded with muted rage and sheer terror.

"Jesus Christ, this is one colossal fuckup."

And Lewis had said, "It gets worse."

TWENTY-EIGHT

I thought Thomas's confidence in me might have been misplaced. He'd seemed so certain I'd return from Manhattan with The Mystery of the Head in the Window all solved. I really wasn't all that keen about heading down to Orchard Street.

I mean, once I was able to see, with my own eyes, the window in question, what was I supposed to do? My hope was that the head would still be there, that it was, in fact, one of those Styrofoam heads used for wig displays, and that seeing it in person would confirm all this.

As I walked south on Orchard, having jumped out of the cab on East Houston, out front of Ray's Pizza, a couple of doors west of Katz's Delicatessen, I worried the head would not be there, at which point I'd have no idea what to do.

Turn around and go home, most likely.

This part of the city wasn't quite the Village, or SoHo, but it had a charm of its own.

These old tenement buildings were rich in architectural detail and history. I started off in the two-hundred block, walking past a gift shop and a diner and some buildings that were being extensively renovated. At Stanton I caught a whiff of pizza from Rosario's.

I continued to stroll south on the west side, past a luggage store that had a display of suitcases that covered half the sidewalk, then by several clothing stores and a guitar shop. None of these storefronts looked like the streetscape in the picture that was folded and tucked into my jacket pocket. I took it out for another quick look and realized that the building Thomas had zeroed in on was in the sixties. It turned out I'd bailed out of my cab too far north. I'd have to cross Delancey before I was down in the right neighborhood.

So I kept on walking.

A couple of minutes later, I thought I was in the general area. Below the third-floor window I was looking for was supposed to be a store that specialized in scarves, and beside it, a smoke shop selling newspapers. The entrance to the apartments was a lobby door between the two businesses. I was to find it on the west side of the street.

I figured it would be easier to scope out the building from the east side. That would give me a better view.

And then, suddenly, there it was.

The window.

I looked again at the image Thomas had printed out for me, just to be sure. Studied the arrangements of neighboring windows, where the fire escape came down, the store-front below.

I'd found it.

There was no white head in the window above the air conditioner.

Nuts.

Aside from the air conditioner, there was nothing to look at. Not so much as a flower-pot. The window was shut, and the glass, with no curtain behind it, looked black, reflecting the building across the street.

I got out my phone, set it to camera, and took a shot of the building, centering it on the window.

So, I'd come all the way to New York, found my way here, to the scene of the — what, exactly? — and taken a snapshot that I could show to Thomas to prove I had honored his request.

What an amazing accomplishment.

Would this picture be enough to satisfy him? Doubtful. I had to admit, if I were him, I'd find my effort somewhat half-hearted.

I supposed it wouldn't kill me to go up there, knock on a door, say hello to whoever lived there. Maybe, if I had a peek into the apartment, that Styrofoam head I was so desperate to see would be sitting on a kitchen table or something.

Another case cracked by Ray Kilbride, illustrator by day, crime fighter by night. Except, okay, it was still daytime.

I studied the window so I'd have a chance of figuring out which apartment it was once I was inside the building, then crossed the street. I entered the lobby, which was really nothing more than an alcove with mailboxes and a directory. I tried the inside door and found it locked. No surprise there.

Judging by the directory, there appeared to be five apartments on the third floor, the last names indicated with thin strips of shiny black tape from one of those Dymo press-and-punch label-making guns. I remember Dad had one of those when we were kids and I labeled everything in my room. "Bookshelf." "Bed." "Door." "Window."

The tape strips all looked weathered with age, some were starting to peel off, and the one for apartment 305 was half missing, reading "ch/Walmers." Kazinski was in 304, Goldberg in 303, Reynolds in 302, and Michaels in 301. I took out my phone and snapped a picture, in case I needed to remember any of them later. I also took a shot of a note posted next to the directory, with a number for rental inquiries.

What to do, what to do.

As I pondered this, a man in his twenties came charging out the door, heading for the street. Without even thinking about it, I reached out and grabbed the handle before the door could close.

I climbed two flights of stairs. When I was on the third floor, I took a second to get my bearings so I could figure out which apartment was most likely the one that faced the street above the scarves store.

I settled on 305.

There were a number of ways I could play this. I could knock on the door, and assuming someone answered, say, "So, listen, how are you, my name is Ray Kilbride, and my brother, Thomas, who's a bit, well, you know, was surfing the Net and happened to notice someone being smothered in your window. Does that ring a bell? Because I don't know about you, but that's the sort of thing I'd remember."

Perhaps there was a better approach.

I could take the printout from my jacket, show it to whoever came to the door, and just say, "We saw your place on Whirl360, and noticed this in your window, and if you don't mind my asking, what the hell is it?"

Also, not so hot. But of the two, I preferred it.

Maybe there was some kind of cover story I could come up with. I'm an illustrator, I'd say. I had a Pearl Paint bag in my hand, after all. I could say I'd been commissioned to illustrate a *Times* article on lower Manhattan architecture, and was looking up your street online, came upon this image, and had to know, what is that, anyway?

Pathetic.

What I'd do was this. I'd knock on the door and show whoever answered the printout and just ask.

Maybe they'd tell me. If they had questions, I'd do my best to answer. I'd be honest. I'd tell them I had a brother who was obsessed with Whirl360, and every once in a while he saw something online he had to know more about.

God.

With the printout in my left hand, I knocked on the door with my right, still holding the Pearl Paint bag with it. The bag swung up against the door as I knocked.

When no one came after three seconds, I tried again.

And waited.

I debated whether to knock a third time. Maybe someone was sleeping. Did I really want to wake them up over this?

I was about to do it anyway when a door down the hall opened. 303, I thought it was. I turned and saw a heavyset woman, hair in curlers, looking at me through black, heavy-framed glasses. Half her body was in the hall, the other half still in her apartment, but her face leaned out so I could see all of it.

"No one lives there," she said.

"I'm sorry?"

271

"No one lives there. The girls are gone."

"Oh, okay, I didn't know."

"Been gone for months," she said. "Landlord hasn't rented it out."

"Okay," I said again, nodding. "Thanks."

She stepped back into her apartment and closed the door.

So that was that.

I turned left as I walked out the front of the building, heading north up Orchard, thinking about what I would tell Thomas when I got home. Not much, really. I gave it a shot, but the place was empty.

What the hell else could I do?

I was sitting on the train, looking out at the passing Hudson, when, out of nowhere, something that had been troubling me for some time at an unconscious level came bubbling up to the surface: *Why was the blade housing up, and the ignition in the OFF position, on Dad's lawn tractor?*

TWENTY-NINE

Thomas knew he was going to have to make his own breakfast and lunch. Ray had told him it was going to be his responsibility. Ray had said if he was going to have to get up before the crack of dawn to grab a train into Manhattan to go on this cockamamie adventure (Thomas was pretty sure that was the word he'd used), then the least Thomas could do was feed himself.

"Okay," Thomas said. "What do we have?"

"There's bread and jam and peanut butter and tuna. Look around. Open the cupboards and help yourself."

"If I make tuna, where's the can opener?"

"Thomas, look at me."

"Yes, Ray?"

"Use your head. If you can't find something, look for it."

"Okay."

Ray didn't seem very eager to check out that window on Orchard Street, but Thomas was pleased he'd agreed to it. He wasn't sure

he'd have sent another message to the CIA
outlining his concerns about the face with
the bag over it — he wanted to keep his
relationship with the agency on a professional
level. If the government got the idea he was
going to involve them in every suspicious act
he'd observed on Whirl360, they might be
less inclined to use his services when The Big
Thing happened, whatever The Big Thing
turned out to be.

Regardless, Thomas was feeling more confident with each passing week that he was
ready for it. At the end of every day, when he
finally closed down Whirl360, erased his
computer's history, turned out the light, and
lay his head on his pillow, he put himself to
sleep by walking through a city he'd recently
gotten to know. The night before, with his
eyes closed, he had wandered San Francisco.
He was going down Hyde, turning right onto
the downhill corkscrew stretch of Lombard,
the Coit Tower off in the distance. Or walking straight along Hyde, where it starts to
slope down, off in the distance there, that has
to be Alcatraz. Then crossing Chestnut, the
buildings giving way to not much of anything
on the left, something called the Russian Hill
Open Space. And if he kept going this way
on Hyde, pretty soon he'd be . . .

Asleep.

Ray poked his head into his room sometime
around five, waking him. "I'm off," he said.

"Don't get into any trouble."

"I won't," Thomas mumbled into his pillow.

The sun was coming through the window when he finally got up. He turned on his computer and set up Whirl360 before he went into the bathroom, had a quick shower, and got dressed.

In the kitchen he stood a moment, staring at the cupboards, contemplating his course of action. He was pretty sure the cereal was in that cupboard next to the fridge. He opened it tentatively, as though expecting a rat to jump out, but there was the box of Cheerios he was hoping to find.

The milk was in the fridge. Of course he knew *that*, he thought. He got a bowl, poured cereal into it, added milk, ate it all up, and returned to his room, leaving the dirty dish on the table and the cereal and container of milk on the counter. This wasn't neglectfulness on his part. While Ray had made it clear he was responsible for feeding himself, he had said nothing about cleaning up. Thomas figured Ray would want to do that when he got home, just to make sure it was done the way he liked. That was how it had been with their father. Adam Kilbride wanted to be in charge of cleanup. He never let Thomas do the dishes. Which was why Thomas wasn't up to speed on such things as loading the dishwasher, operating the vacuum cleaner, doing laundry, scrubbing the floors, or dusting. The one chore Thomas had thought might be fun was cutting the grass, but his father wouldn't let him operate the lawn tractor. But now, even if Ray let him, he'd never want to drive that tractor.

After breakfast, he continued his exploration of San Francisco. Went through the Mission, Sunset, and Richmond districts and Haight-Ashbury, and strolled over the Golden Gate Bridge. Took quite a few mouse clicks to make that crossing. He became so absorbed with that part of the trip he almost forgot he was responsible for his own lunch.

He returned to the kitchen just before one. A tuna sandwich seemed like more than he wanted to take on because he'd have to use the can opener, and even when his father opened tuna he used to swear when the lid finally popped off and tuna oil spilled all over the place. So Thomas found the peanut butter and some bread and was in the middle of making himself a sandwich when there was a knock at the door.

For a second, he didn't do anything, because it was always someone else who opened the door, but then he realized he was the only one there, so he set down the knife slathered with peanut butter and went to see who it was.

"Hello, Thomas."

It was Len Prentice, or as Adam Kilbride

often called his former boss, Lenny.

"Oh, hi, Mr. Prentice."

Thomas could see the man's car a few steps away from the porch, but there was no one else in it. He had come out to the Kilbride house alone. He stood like he was expecting to be invited in, but Thomas didn't want to do that. He had never liked Len Prentice.

"Your brother around?" he asked.

"He's in New York City today," Thomas said.

"What's he doing there?"

"He's checking to see whether somebody was murdered by having a bag put over their head."

That stopped Len for a second. "Huh," he said. Then, "You really are crazy, aren't you, Thomas? Can I come in?"

He hesitated, then said, "I guess it's okay."

"I was driving by and thought I'd pop in and see how you boys were getting along."

Thomas didn't say anything. Len Prentice hadn't actually asked him a question.

"Got a beer or anything?" he asked.

Thomas said, honestly, "I don't know."

"Never mind. I'll have a look." Len crossed through the living room to the kitchen, opened up the fridge, and found what he was looking for.

"So whattya been doing to keep yourself busy, Thomas?" he asked, twisting off the cap and taking a swig.

277

"I work on the computer."

He nodded knowingly. "Oh yeah, right. Pretty much all the time, right?"

"I have stuff to do."

"What did you say Ray was doing again?"

"He's in New York."

"Yeah, yeah, but the other part? What's he doing?"

"He's meeting a friend about work, and he's trying to find out what happened to the person in the window."

Len drank more of his beer. "Is this the person who had a bag put over his head?"

Thomas nodded.

"Your dad used to talk to me," Len said. "I wasn't just his boss, you know. He and I, we were friends. And he said you were always finding pictures of things on the Internet that got you all riled up. Used to tell me he considered unplugging you from the Net, but letting you sit on the computer all day was really the only thing that gave him any peace."

Thomas wanted Len Prentice to leave so he could finish making his peanut butter sandwich and take it upstairs with him.

"It was Marie suggested I drop by. She thinks it would be a nice thing if you and your brother came over to the house for dinner."

"I'd have to talk to Ray," Thomas said. He didn't want to go, but didn't feel comfortable saying that. He would get Ray to tell them they couldn't go.

"Your dad used to say he just didn't know why you're the way you are. Happy to be cooped up in this house all the time, sitting on your computer all day. Never going out except maybe to see your psychiatrist. What's her name? Gargantuan?"

"Grigorin."

"The thing I can't believe is, you wouldn't even go to your own dad's funeral. Was your little computer fixation so great you couldn't even do that for him?"

Thomas blinked. "Why are you saying these things to me, Mr. Prentice?"

"I don't know. Just making conversation, really. I guess I'm a simple man, Thomas. I don't know a lot of psychiatric mumbo jumbo. I thought I knew what this schizo thing is you have, that it means you have a split personality, but your dad told me that was a common misconception, that it's not like that at all. What I don't get is, if you know you've got a problem, why don't you do something about it?"

"I don't have a problem," Thomas said.

Len chuckled. "A son doesn't go to his own father's funeral service? That, to my way of thinking, is a problem."

"I had things to do," he said. "And . . ."

"And what, Thomas?"

"And there would be people there I didn't want to see."

"Who'd that be? You talking about me, Thomas? Haven't I always been nice to you?"

Thomas shook his head. "I have to make my lunch. I'm making a peanut butter sandwich."

"I've got an idea," Len Prentice said. "Why don't I take you out for lunch?"

"What?"

"I mean, why don't I take *you* out of the *house* in a *car* and we'll go get something to eat?"

"I already started making the sandwich." He pointed to the kitchen counter.

"So what? You can eat it later for an afternoon snack. I'll take you for a drive. It would do you good to get out of the house."

"No."

Len set his beer down and said, "I insist."

"I don't want to go."

Len closed the distance between them. "I think that's where your dad made his mistake. He always let you get your way. He needed to be more forceful, introduce you to new experiences. We could go into Promise Falls, hit the McDonald's or get a slice. We could even go back to our place, have Marie make you something."

Thomas took a step back.

"You know, from what I hear, you're going to have to get used to being out of this house. What about when your brother sells this place?"

"I don't know for sure he's going to do that."

"You don't think he's going to leave you here on your own, do you? That's not exactly a terrific idea."

Thomas said, "Maybe he'll decide to live here. We could live together." But even as he said it, Thomas wasn't sure this was what he wanted. He loved his brother, but he could be difficult. Like their father, he was critical. Picking at him all the time about things he couldn't do anything about.

"Well, whatever happens, I'm sure it'll work out for the best," Len said. "Now, you want to grab a jacket or something? I don't know about you, but I could go for some KFC. You like KFC?"

Thomas did like KFC, but his brother wouldn't get it for him. Their father brought it home sometimes. But he did not want to go anywhere with Len Prentice. He felt himself becoming increasingly anxious, like there were bugs crawling around just under his skin. His breathing quickened, became more shallow. He might have been willing to go out, briefly, with some people, people he liked and trusted, but he did not like or trust Len Prentice.

And his father never really had, either. They'd had a friendship. They'd get together once in a while and watch a game, or grab a beer. But whenever Adam Kilbride returned home from spending time with Len, he'd say, "Jesus, but that guy can really suck the life out of you."

Len reached out and grabbed Thomas by the arm. Not rough, but firm. "Let's go, pardner. Let's have some fun."

Thomas wrenched his arm free. He put more into it than he needed to, and his hand flew up accidentally and slapped Len across the cheek.

Len stopped, rubbed the side of his face, and said, "Well, Thomas, I sure wish you hadn't gone and done that."

THIRTY

Truth be told, Lewis Blocker wasn't sleeping all that well, either.

Allison Fitch was out there, somewhere, and not knowing where she was, or what she might do, had Lewis worried for all the same reasons it did Howard Talliman. If, and when, she decided to walk into a police station and tell everything she knew, it was all over for them. All over for Howard, all over for Morris, and all over for Lewis Blocker.

Everything he and Howard had done to try to tie up the loose ends on this colossal fuckup, as Howard so aptly called it, would unravel the moment Allison Fitch decided to come out of hiding. Once she'd told the authorities about the murder, confessed to her blackmail attempt, and revealed her meeting with Howard, the shit would hit the proverbial fan.

They had to make sure that did not happen.

Several steps were being taken in that direction. First, Lewis had Nicole watching Fitch's mother in Ohio. He figured, sooner or later, the girl would attempt to get in touch with her. What daughter in trouble didn't want to talk to her mom? What daughter wouldn't be wracked with guilt while her mother despaired over what had happened to her? Wouldn't she, eventually, feel she had to allay her mother's fears?

Lewis had decidedly mixed feelings about keeping Nicole on this project after the way she'd screwed up. His earlier confidence in her had been immeasurably shaken, and his initial impulse had been to make Nicole pay the ultimate price for her mistake. But right now, he needed all the help he could get, and Nicole, feeling her neck, had said she would help, indefinitely, to make things right. So he would use her until this mess was resolved.

Lewis also wanted to maintain surveillance, of a sort, on the Fitch apartment. Although he thought it highly unlikely the woman herself would return to the unit, he believed it was possible someone who knew her might show up at some point. Maybe just a friend dropping by to say hi. Or, and this was the eventuality Lewis most hoped for, someone Allison had been in touch with and instructed to go to her old place to see what was going on.

Either way, such a visitor might provide a clue to Allison Fitch's current whereabouts.

Lewis couldn't post someone in the hallway 24-7. Too obvious. And even though he'd spoken to the landlord, in the guise of a relative of one of the former tenants, and arranged to make sure the rent was paid every month for the foreseeable future, Lewis didn't have the manpower to have someone in the apartment at all hours in case a visitor showed up. He stayed there himself for the first month, and the only person who came knocking was a guy distributing takeout menus for an Italian place down the street.

But he couldn't shake the idea that a person of interest might, someday, show up. And when that person did, he wanted to have a look at who it was.

Which was why he installed the camera.

A pinhole affair, motion-activated, mounted behind the door, with an excellent view of the hallway. Whenever a person came to within a few feet of the apartment, it came on. At the end of every day, Lewis reviewed any images, which were automatically sent to his computer.

There was almost always something. Usually, it was the super, vacuuming the hall. One day, a pizza delivery guy at the wrong door. Lewis watched as he got out his cell phone, called his dispatcher, and sorted it out.

Lewis got a little hungry, watching that one.

On Halloween, some kids got into the

building and went door to door, looking for candy. Two girls, one dressed as Lady Gaga, the other as an alien from another world — actually, he wasn't sure which was which — struck out at apartment 305.

Every day, something. But nothing of value.

Lewis was thinking it was time to abandon this idea, take out the camera, stop paying on the apartment.

And then the guy with the Pearl Paint bag shows up.

Lewis sat at the desk in the study of his Lower East Side apartment, looking at the oversized monitor of his computer. Studying. The man knocked three times with the hand holding the bag from the art store. Lewis, in his investigation of Allison Fitch, before and after her disappearance, had never seen him before. Had no idea who he was, or whether this visit was in any way significant.

Was the guy selling something? Was he at the wrong apartment? Was he, in fact, someone who knew one of the two previous tenants, and had stopped by for a visit? If he'd known the two people who'd lived here, wouldn't he, possibly, have shouted into the door? Something like, "Hey, anybody home?" How had he gotten into the building? Did he have a key? Did someone heading out of the building allow him access, or had he buzzed a bunch of people at random until one of them was dumb enough to buzz back?

Did it matter? Was this visitor important at all?

Then Lewis caught a look at the piece of paper in his other hand.

What was that? It had flashed twice past the lens very quickly. Lewis played the short bit of footage several times but was unable to make it out.

So he paused the video, and then used the cursor to inch it along, ever so slowly, until he got to a place where the piece of paper was marginally visible.

It appeared to be a standard piece of eight-and-a-half-by-eleven paper. The kind you put into your printer. There was a square, color image in the upper left quadrant of the page. It looked like a grouping of windows, although it was hard to tell for sure.

At the top of the page, some printing. Impossible to read on the monitor. But there was a logo of some kind in the upper left corner, multicolored. Lewis wasn't sure, but he thought he recognized it. It led off with a stylized W, and there appeared to be three numbers at the tail end.

Lewis was pretty sure he knew what it was. The Whirl360 logo. For that Web site that allowed you to look at the actual streets of cities all over the world. He used it now and then. Like everyone else did at some point, he'd looked to see whether the house he'd grown up in was online. He'd keyed in the address of his Denver home, and sure enough, there it was.

If this was, as he suspected, the logo for Whirl360, then it made sense that the image on the page had been printed off that Web site.

Lewis magnified the blurry image as far as the computer would allow. It did appear to be a series of windows, like the ones on the old tenement buildings in the neighborhood where Allison Fitch's apartment was. But it was impossible to see anything with any clarity.

Well, Lewis reasoned, if this guy could find the image online, then he could do it, too.

He opened up a browser, went to the Whirl360 site, and entered "Orchard Street, New York City." And almost instantly, he was there, clicking his way down the street. When he got to the block where Fitch lived, he dragged the mouse across the screen, allowing himself to whirl around Orchard, looking from north to south and back again.

Maybe this guy who'd banged on the door was some kind of architecture student. Or someone from the city's building department. Who the hell knew?

He positioned the image so he was looking directly at Fitch's building, moved the mouse to the top of it, clicked, held, and dragged down, which had the effect of craning one's neck upward to see the building's upper stories.

"What?" he said under his breath. "What . . . is . . . that?"

He was focused on one particular window. He clicked to magnify the image.

"Holy shit," he whispered.

They met again on the same Central Park bench. Lewis Blocker handed Howard Talliman a sheet of paper, folded once.

"What's this?" Talliman asked.

"Something I printed off the Net. Just look at it."

Talliman unfolded the sheet and looked at it, puzzled. "I have no idea what this is." Howard had never been to the Orchard Street address.

"That window, that's the apartment. What you're holding there, that's a printout from the Internet."

Howard touched his index finger to the head in the window. "Lewis, is this what I think it is?"

"Yes."

Howard handed the page back to Lewis, who tucked it into his jacket. "I still don't understand."

"You familiar with Whirl360?" Lewis asked.

"I don't live in a cave, Lewis."

"That was printed right off the site. That picture, as we speak, is online. Anyone in the

289

world with a computer who happens to explore Orchard Street and angles right there can see that. What had to have happened is, one of those Whirl360 cars with the panoramic cameras was going along Orchard Street at the same time that Nicole was doing her thing at the window."

Howard, starting to grasp the enormity of it, blurted, "Dear God. How the hell did you discover this? You just found it?"

"No," Lewis said. "It was brought to my attention."

"What? How?"

"Someone came to the apartment. A man, I'd say late thirties, early forties. Knocked on the door. The camera activated."

"Okay."

Lewis patted his jacket where the printout was resting. "He had a sheet, just like this, in his hand."

Howard's mouth was open. He put a hand to his forehead. "Who was he?"

"I don't know."

"What was he doing with that? How would he have that?"

"I don't know."

"What the hell *do* you know, Lewis?"

He remained unruffled. "I know that we have a couple of problems, Howard. The first is this man. Who is he? Why does he have that printout? How did he discover it online? Did he happen upon it, or did he know it was already there? Is he acting alone, or on someone else's behalf? Does he know what that image represents? Is he with the police? Why was he knocking on Fitch's apartment door with it in his hand? What did he want? Who was he looking for?"

"Jesus," Howard said. He paused a moment, then looked at Lewis. "What's the second problem?"

"The image," he said. "It's still up there. On that Web site. Just waiting for someone else to find it."

THIRTY-ONE

It was nearly ten when I turned down the driveway. What struck me first was how dark the house looked.

The front porch light, the one at the side of the house, and the one on the barn door are all on timers, so they were on. But there was no light emanating from behind the windows. The living room was in darkness. Same for the second floor. Not even a bluish computer haze from Thomas's room. It seemed un-likely, but maybe he'd gone to bed early.

The front door was locked. I let myself in, turned on some lights, then stopped and listened. No sounds. Not that Thomas was ordinarily noisy. Whirl360 had no audio.

"Thomas?" I called out softly, thinking he might be asleep. I didn't want to wake him. I had expected him to be waiting up for me, eager to know what I'd learned. Not much, as it turned out, but he didn't know that yet.

I could see through to the kitchen. "Shit," I said under my breath.

Dirty dishes littered the table. Not just from breakfast, but lunch, too. Dinner I wasn't too sure about. I put my hand on the half-full container of milk left sitting out. Room temperature. I gave it a sniff.

"Jeesh," I said, and upended it in the sink. Then I noticed the peanut-butter-smeared knife stuck to the counter next to the open jar.

I mounted the stairs to the second floor and knocked on Thomas's door ever so quietly. When there was no response, I eased it open.

I didn't need to turn on a light to see whether he was in his bed. Moonlight streaming through the window illuminated the covers. The bed was empty. At that point, I flicked on the light.

The computer tower was still humming but the screen had gone to black from disuse. It was Thomas's routine to shut everything down when he was done for the day.

I stepped out into the hall, traveled a few steps down to the bathroom. The door was open. I hit the light.

No sign of him there.

"Thomas!" I called out, no longer worried about making too much noise. "Thomas! I'm home!"

Unease washed over me. I never should have gone into Manhattan and left him for an entire day. He'd gotten into some kind of trouble, but what, exactly? I hoped to God the FBI hadn't returned and taken him away.

I returned to the first floor, made my way to the door to the basement that was off the kitchen. "Thomas?"

No reply, but I descended the steps, anyway. Using light from the kitchen to reach the bottom, I then pulled the chain to turn on a bare bulb fixture. This room was used mostly for storage, and there were innumerable boxes of things my parents had stored over the years. An awful lot of stuff to have to go through. I walked around the room, peeked behind the furnace. Thomas was not down here.

I went out the kitchen door and took a few steps into the yard. The air was cool, the landscape lit softly by the moon. There wasn't a cloud in the sky, and if I'd ever studied astronomy I might have been able to pick out some constellations other than the Big Dipper.

"Thomas!" I shouted, then, under my breath, said, "Goddamn."

I wondered whether I should call the police. I decided to do more searching first. Starting with the barn. I sprinted across the yard and slid open the broad, towering door. Once inside, I found the large electrical box screwed into a vertical beam and turned on the lights.

There wasn't much in here, aside from the lawn tractor that had killed our father.

"Thomas! Damn it, if you're hiding from me —"

I cut myself off, knowing how unlike Thomas it would be to play hide-and-seek. Displays of playfulness were rare from him. Once I'd stopped shouting, I listened. There was the nightly chorus of crickets, the kind of noise that's always there, but that you really don't notice. Not far from me, there was rustling in the bits of leftover straw that had been there for several decades, back to the time when this building was actually owned by a farmer.

A mouse scurried along, looking for safety.

I took a few steps into the structure, running my hand along the cracked hood of the tractor as I passed it. I wished, at this moment, that Thomas owned a cell phone. I would have tried calling him.

Struggling to think where he might be, I wondered whether he'd gone down to the creek, to where he'd found Dad. I killed the barn lights and ran to the crest of the hill behind the house. "You down there, Thomas?"

Nothing.

Who was there to call, other than the police? Thomas had no friends. It wasn't like he'd gone to a sleepover.

This wasn't like him.

I went back inside, decided I couldn't wait any longer, and called the Promise Falls police. I told them my brother was missing.

"Sir, we'll have an officer out to your place as soon as possible," said the female dispatcher, "but in the meantime, I need you to provide a description of your brother. First of all, how old is he?"

I had to stop and think. "Thirty-five? He's a couple of years younger than me."

"And when did he go missing?"

"I don't know. I was out for the day and I just got home and he's not here."

"Uh, well, hang on a second, Mr. Kilbride. This is a grown man of thirty-five you're talking about? And for all you know he might have stepped out just before you returned? Maybe he went to the store or something, or for a drive."

"No, it's not like that. He doesn't leave the house."

"Maybe he finally got tired of being cooped up."

This was going to take too long to explain. "Thomas is a psychiatric patient. Okay, not a patient, exactly, but he does see a psychiatrist on a regular basis, and this is not normal for him, to leave, to not be here."

"You left a psychiatric patient on his own, Mr. Kilbride?"

"Jesus, it's not — could you just send someone out and I'll try to explain it to them?"

"We'll send a car around, sir. But —"

"I have to go," I said.

I didn't want to spend my time arguing with the dispatcher the whole time I waited for a cop to show up.

Even after I called the police, my unease was evolving into panic. I went out to the porch, looking out to the road and to the left where, about a hundred yards away, our closest neighbor lived. A woman who'd been on her own since her husband died several years ago. I didn't see anything else I could do right now aside from waking her up.

That was when a car started slowing along the highway, coming from the direction of town. About two car lengths from the end of our driveway, it edged off the pavement, tires crunching on gravel.

The car turned and started approaching the house. I came down the porch steps, worried that this was not someone bringing Thomas home, but someone bringing me bad news about him.

With the headlights shining directly at me, I couldn't make out the car or tell whether anyone was in it beside the driver. It pulled up just behind and on the other side of mine, so that when the passenger door opened, I could see Thomas getting out, but not the person behind the wheel.

"Thomas! Where the hell have you been?"

He was holding something in his hand, about half the size of a clipboard. I realized it was one of those high-tech tablets that allowed you to do a hundred things, including surf the Web. He didn't look the slightest bit concerned about the worry he'd caused me. "I went out to get something to eat. KFC. This thing is way better than the GPS in your car. What did you find out in New York? I want to hear everything. Come into the house because it's cold outside."

He strolled right past me, went up the steps into the house.

I heard the driver's door open and close. Seconds later, someone appeared, looked at me, and smiled.

"Hey," Julie said. "Your brother's something else. We had a great time. And this thing about somebody's head in a bag? Man, that's some kind of story."

THIRTY-TWO

Before saying a word to either Thomas or Julie, I took out my cell and called the police back and told them my brother was home safe. Then I said to Julie, "What's going on?"

"You said drop by. I dropped by. You were out. Thomas was home. He was puzzling over what to do about dinner so I asked him if he wanted to go out and grab a bite and he said sure. You asking me in for a drink or am I gonna have to drive home sober?"

"What did you find out?" Thomas shouted. He'd come back out and was standing on the porch with the tablet in his hand.

"Give me a second here," I said to him. "I'll be right in." To Julie, I said, "Where'd he get the thing?"

"I'm letting him borrow it," she said. "I showed him how he could look up maps on it anywhere. Doesn't have to be sitting at his desk all the time."

"I want to get one of these, Ray," Thomas said. "Can you get me one of these?"

"Thomas," I said, aggravation creeping into my voice, "I'll be in, in a minute."

Thomas went back into the house.

"He's right," Julie said.

"About what?"

"The way you talk to him," Julie said. "He said you're mean to him."

"I am not — he said that?"

Julie nodded, and said offhandedly, "That's what he tells me."

"I'm not mean to him. I'm trying to do my best."

She smiled. "I'm sure you are."

"You're patronizing me."

Her smile broadened. "Yeah, I guess. Listen, I suppose I'll just head back and —"

"No, come on in," I said. "You can fill me in on what a terrible brother I am."

"How much time do you have?"

As we were going up the steps, I said, "I'm surprised you got him to leave the house. He hates leaving the house."

"Letting him play with the gadget helped. That, and offering to get him some KFC."

"That would do it," I said as we walked inside.

Thomas could be heard clicking away upstairs. He called down, "Come upstairs!"

"I better deal with this," I said. "You wanna come up?" She nodded. "I kind of need to prepare you for what it looks like up here."

"Thomas already showed me," Julie said.

300

"No big deal. My brother used to have naked women all over his wall. I'll take maps."

I looked at her for a second and shook my head. "Okay."

"Well?" Thomas said as we came into his room, his eyes on the center monitor, advancing forward through some metropolis somewhere.

"If we're going to talk about this, you have to stop and look at me," I said.

"That's just what he was talking about," Julie whispered to me. "You talk to him like he's a kid."

I shot her a look as Thomas lifted his hand from the mouse and did a quarter circle on his computer chair. "So what happened?"

I cleared my throat. "Okay, so I went to Orchard Street, and I found the address. Here." I took out my phone, opened the camera app, and handed it to him. "There's a picture of the place."

Thomas studied the tiny image, then compared it to a printout similar to the one he had given me before I'd gone to Manhattan.

He nodded. "That's the window. The brick patterns all match up."

"And as you can see," I said, "there's no head in the window."

"You say that like it proves something," Thomas said.

"I'm just pointing it out, that's all."

"If someone had a car accident at the end

301

of our driveway six months ago, and you took a picture of it, taking another picture at the end of our driveway today wouldn't prove that the accident never happened."

"He's got ya there," Julie said.

I ignored her. "I know, Thomas. I'm just telling you what I saw."

"What else did you do?"

"I did go up to the apartment," I said. "Knocked on the door."

Thomas studied me. "Then what?"

"No answer. The place is empty."

"Empty?"

"Apparently. A woman down the hall told me. No one's lived there for months."

"Did you ask her if anyone had been killed in the apartment?"

"No, I did not ask her if anyone had been killed in the apartment. I'm guessing that's the kind of thing she might have mentioned."

"Not if she did it," Thomas said.

"She didn't look like a murderer to me. She said the girls or whatever had moved out a long time ago."

"And the apartment has been empty ever since?" he asked.

I shrugged. "I guess."

"Isn't that kind of weird?"

"What do you mean?"

"I've heard that apartments are in very short supply in New York City," he said. "Why would someone let an apartment sit empty all that time?"

"I don't know, Thomas."

"What did the landlord say when you asked him?"

"What?"

Thomas still had my phone, and had swiped his thumb across the screen to see the next picture. "What's this?"

"Oh, that's the directory, in the lobby."

"Is that the landlord's number?"

"Yes, it is."

"So you talked to him?"

"No, I did not talk to him."

"Why didn't you talk to the landlord? He would probably know if someone had been killed in one of his apartments."

"Thomas, look, I got you some pictures, I knocked on the door, there was no one there, I don't know what else I could have done."

Julie made a little snorting noise.

"What?" I said.

She asked, "How hard would it have been to talk to the super? Or some of the other neighbors?"

"And this involves you how?"

She smiled. "You were already there. In the city, in the building. You might have knocked on a couple more doors, make it worth the trip."

I glared at her.

"Yeah," Thomas agreed, looking at me with disapproval. "Why did you even bother? I should have gone myself last night."

"Yeah, well, you still wouldn't be there for another week," I said.

"But at least when I got there, I'd have found out something. This is just like before, when there was someone in trouble in a window."

"What?" I asked.

"This wasn't much of an investigation. It's certainly not up to the standards of the Central Intelligence Agency. I hate to think what they'd have to say about it."

"Yeah," said Julie.

"Okay," I said, raising my hands in defeat. "Next time, you can leave the house and get on the train and go to New York and be Archie Goodwin and I'll be the one who sits in the house while you go around and gather clues. I'll just tend to my orchids."

"Archie? Orchids?"

"Thomas, I did what I could. Honestly. There's nothing at all online about anyone being killed at that address. No news stories. Whatever you saw, it's pretty clear it was nothing. The best thing to do now would be to let this go." I took the printout from my pocket, crumpled it, and tossed it into the trash. Thomas studied the paper ball as it bounced into the receptacle, then looked back at me.

"That's a bit dickish," Julie said.

I gave her another look, then sighed. Maybe

she was right, but it had been a long day, and I was exhausted.

I was expecting Thomas to agree with Julie, but what he said next came out of left field.

"I don't like Mr. Prentice."

I blinked. "What?" I allowed my brain two seconds to switch gears and asked, "Why don't you like Mr. Prentice?"

"He wants me to do stuff I don't want to do."

"Thomas, what are we talking about here?"

"He wanted to take me out for lunch and I didn't want to go."

"Today? He came by here?"

My brother nodded. "He grabbed me to make me go and then I hit him."

I took a step forward and put a hand on his shoulder. "Jesus, Thomas, you hit Len Prentice?"

Thomas nodded. "Only a little." He stood up out of the computer chair so he could demonstrate. He took my hand and put it on my arm. "He grabbed me like that and then I pulled away and then I hit his face." He did it in slow motion, touching my cheek with the back of his hand.

"You hit Len Prentice in the face."

"I don't like him. I've never liked him."

"Thomas, you can't go around hitting people."

"I told you, he grabbed my arm first. I didn't hit him hard. He didn't bleed or cry

305

or anything."

"What did he do then?"

"He left."

I sighed. I was never going to be able to leave Thomas alone again. At least not for an entire day. Before I could sell this house and go back to Burlington, I was going to have to get Thomas settled in a place where he'd be supervised. The other thing that alarmed me was that, within a very short time, Thomas had gotten physical. Twice. He'd tackled me. And now he'd struck Len Prentice. In his defense, both times he'd been provoked.

"Thomas," I said, "it's not like you to lose your temper. This isn't like you."

"I know," he said, settling back into this chair and looking at the monitors. "Usually I'm good."

Thomas started clicking on the mouse and said nothing more.

I felt Julie's hand on my back. "Come on," she said softly. "I think we could both use that drink."

THIRTY-THREE

"Who's Len Prentice?" Julie asked as I handed her a beer from the fridge.

I told her, and said she might remember him from the funeral. When I described him, she did. "Thomas has never liked him," I said.

"What the hell was he doing here trying to drag your brother out for lunch?"

"I don't know. Thing with Len is, he doesn't quite grasp the concept that some people are different. He figures if Thomas hears voices he should just put in earplugs, and his ailing wife should be more energetic so she can travel with him. You know. 'Walk it off.' "

"Yeah, I know the type."

"Maybe I should call Len. See if he's upset. It's too late now. Maybe in the morning. Honest to God."

We stood there in the kitchen, leaning up against the counter, sipping our beers, not saying anything for a few seconds.

Finally, I said, "Thank you for being so nice to him, taking him out for dinner, letting him use your iPad."

"You see, that's what he's talking about," Julie said.

"I'm sorry?"

"You're thanking me for spending time with him. Like I was babysitting, or looking after your cat."

"I never meant —"

"Thomas is a nice man," Julie said. "A decent, well-meaning guy. Yeah, he's got some issues. He's slightly out of the ordinary. I mean, he told me how he got you to go to New York looking for this head-in-a-bag person, which I have to admit is kind of out there. Sorry about calling you dickish, by the way." Her smile suggested she wasn't sorry at all. "Did you really go into the city just to do that?"

"I had a meeting about a job."

"How'd that go?"

"Not bad."

"You moving there?"

"No, it's the kind of work I can do from my studio."

She nodded. "Anyway, thing about your brother is, there's more to him than just this map stuff. That's what I was going to say."

I had no comment.

"Did you know he dreams about your dad every night?"

I turned my head. "He told you that?"

"Yeah."

He'd never told me. "I'm sure he misses him," I said.

"He said, when he's wandering all these different cities in his sleep, he keeps seeing your dad sitting in cafés and restaurants."

That made me sad.

"And you remember Margaret Tursky?" Julie asked.

I had to think. "Yeah, I do. Red hair? Braces?"

"Thomas had a real thing for her."

I looked at her skeptically. "I don't think so."

"It's true. He told me. He was eating a drumstick at the time."

"He and I, we don't really talk about stuff like that. We kind of deal with more immediate issues. There's kind of a lot going on around here, Julie, since our dad passed away."

She turned, leaning her hip into the counter, and said, "Look, I know I'm speaking out of turn here, that's it's none of my business. There's just more to Thomas than meets the eye. Reminds me of my aunt. She's gone now, bless her, but she was in a wheelchair for a while, and whenever I took her out, like to a restaurant or whatever, people would ask me what she wanted. 'Would your aunt like to start with a drink? Would your aunt like an appetizer?' Assholes. 'Ask her,' I'd say. Just 'cause she couldn't walk didn't mean she was deaf. It's like that with Thomas. Just because he's got a few screws loose, and I say that with respect, there's still a lot of other shit going on." She reached out and poked me in the chest. "And you're not mean."

"But he said I was."

She nodded. "He did. But after that, he said you're just trying to do the right thing. Ray, he loves you, he really does. I didn't mean to give you the gears."

"No, you're right," I said. "I guess . . . I guess all I tend to see when I look at him is his, you know, handicap, although he doesn't see it that way. I don't always look at the entire person."

She took a step closer and gave me a friendly punch in the shoulder. "Maybe this is why I do what I do. I like to try to see all sides, to see the whole picture. I'm not claiming to be all holier than thou or anything. You're just really close to the situation, and like you say, you've got a lot on your plate. Don't beat yourself up about it."

"He must trust you, to tell you those things," I said.

"Maybe it's just that nobody asked," Julie said. "When we were having our chicken, I got talking to him about high school. And speaking of chicken." She touched her lower belly. "I don't think that stuff totally agreed with me." She drank down the rest of her beer. "That'll help."

"Let me just try again and say thanks, without it meaning anything derogatory about anyone."

She smiled and nodded. "You are welcome." She took another step, closing the distance between us, went up on her toes, and gave me a peck on the cheek. "All is forgiven."

I set my beer on the counter and took hold of Julie's arm. I leaned in to kiss her, and not on the cheek, and she was showing no signs of trying to stop me from doing this, when Thomas started shouting from upstairs.

"Ray!"

I let go of Julie and moved back as I heard Thomas coming down the stairs. He said, "I called the landlord." I recalled that he'd lingered on that picture on my phone of the tenement building's directory. He'd memorized the number.

Thomas continued, "He had some interesting things to say, which you would have found out if you'd taken the time to ask."

Julie started heading for the door. "G'night, guys," she said.

THIRTY-FOUR

There were times when Nicole wondered how she'd gotten here.

Not *exactly* here, in Ohio, in this Dayton apartment across the street from Allison Fitch's mother's residence. She'd gotten here by car.

But hold on — that really *was* what she was pondering. How was it that someone who'd beat all the odds to make it to the Olympic Games, who had returned home from Sydney with a silver medal hanging from her neck — how could it be that that same person could be sitting here now, surrounded by electronic eavesdropping equipment, waiting for a break so she could find Allison Fitch and kill her?

How did that talented young athlete, who'd performed her routine on the uneven bars for thousands of spectators in the stadium and millions more on television around the planet, end up killing people for a living?

Well, you had to do *something*, right?

Anyone else might have returned from the Games with their head held high. Okay, so maybe you didn't win gold, but bringing back a silver medal, doesn't that say you came pretty damn close?

"Close only counts in horseshoes," her father had always liked to say.

And it was true what they said, that winning silver, it was worse than coming in third and taking the bronze. You won bronze and you thought, *Okay, I'm coming home with a medal, and that's pretty fucking awesome, and the great thing is, I don't have to beat myself up over coming so close to winning.* But when you came in second, when the gap between your score and the winning one came down to inexplicable differences of interpretation by the judges, you drove yourself mad. The "what-ifs" made you crazy. What if your landing had been just a bit steadier? What if you'd held your head up a little straighter? Was it because you didn't smile? Did they just not like the look of you?

Was there anything you could have done to win gold?

You lay awake at night, wondering.

"Close only counts in horseshoes."

The bastard.

And her coach wasn't much better. The two of them, those two impossible-to-please men, had put all their hopes and dreams on her. She'd been a fool to ever think she was doing it for herself. Turned out she was doing it for them. She just might have been proud of herself for winning silver, but not them.

"Look at the endorsement deals you've lost," they told her. "Millions of dollars, thrown away. The life you could have had."

Her father didn't talk to her all the way home. Pretty long flight, Sydney to L.A., then the connecting trip to New York, the limo ride back to Montclair.

She started doing poorly in school. Went from being an A student to getting Cs, and worse. Her father wanted to know what the hell was wrong with her. Did she take a stupid pill in Australia? Was it something in the water?

Nicole — of course, that wasn't her name then — knew what the problem was. She could never make the man happy, so why bother? Maybe, if her mother hadn't died from cancer when Nicole was twelve, things might have been different. That woman, she had a life as a successful real estate agent. She didn't have to live through her daughter, unlike her dad, whose greatest achievement in life was being assistant manager at a Payless Shoes outlet.

She didn't just let her grades slip. She partied. She slept around. She did drugs. Let her once perfectly toned body get out of shape. When she was eighteen, she met up with a man thirty years older than her who

314

didn't actually run a meth lab, but worked for someone who did.

His name was Chester — honest to God, like from an old Western — and he had one of those RV things, a Winnebago, and he used to load that thing up with product. Maybe Chester was the perfect name for him, given that the RV was like a modern covered wagon. Meth was stuffed everywhere. In the fridge, under the beds, in the actual walls of the RV. Because you couldn't send meth by FedEx or Purolator and you couldn't take it on a plane, if you wanted to get it from one part of the country to the other you had to damn well take it there yourself. And because Chester's boss was linked into a major distributor based in Las Vegas, it meant making plenty of trips to Nevada.

But driving an RV cross-country all by yourself, that could look kind of suspicious, so Chester hired Nicole to tag along with him. If he ever got pulled over by police, and if they asked, he'd tell them she was his daughter, and he was taking her out west to be with her mother. Plus, Chester got her to help out. She made meals in the RV kitchen while they made good time on the interstates. She'd take the wheel while he had a nap. Only time they ever had to stop was to fill the tank.

Sometimes, Chester would have Nicole meet his needs in ways that didn't involve getting him a drink or making him a sandwich or cutting him up an apple. She didn't like it, but he always threw an extra hundred her way when she helped him ease his "interstate tensions."

This business of making men happy, it never ended.

They made the trip from New Jersey to Vegas a dozen times. Always pulling the RV into the same warehouse on the outskirts of Vegas, making the exchange with the same people. Looked like they were all trying out as extras in a *Scarface* sequel, but nice enough. They'd all have a drink when the exchange was made. They liked Nicole, and loved to tease Chester about how he passed the time driving all those thousands of miles, back and forth across the country, with that hot young thing riding along with him. Chester would give them a nod and a wink, doing nothing to make them think otherwise.

She kind of hated him for that.

It was the thirteenth trip where things went off the rails.

Nicole knew something was up the moment the warehouse door began retracting. Usually, first thing they'd see would be the *Scarface* guys' Escalade sitting in there, back hatch open, the boys leaning up against the grill. But instead of the Escalade, there was a Ford Explorer. No one outside the car, but two inside.

"I don't like this," Nicole said, standing behind Chester, looking through the massive front window like it was a movie screen.

"Don't worry about it," he said. "I got a call couple hours back, while you were sleeping. They said they'd have someone else receiving today."

"They say why?"

"They're gonna tell me their troubles? Don't worry about it."

Nicole took a few steps back into the kitchen, slipped open a drawer, grabbed something. Chester pulled the RV up alongside the Explorer, killed the engine, got out of his oversized captain's chair, and opened up the side door.

The two men from the Explorer were out now, waiting near the door of the RV for Chester to hop out.

The *Scarface* guys tried a little too hard to look tough, but they were always well dressed. Nice suits, shined shoes, hair combed back all in place, a few too many gold rings, the high-end sunglasses that were a total cliché. But they looked like guys who worked for someone who cared about appearances. Who didn't want his employees going out looking anything less than professional.

But these guys, from the Explorer, they looked to Nicole liked they'd just come in from milking the cows. Jeans, plaid shirts, boots. Weren't those cowboy hats she'd seen on the dash of their car? One had dirty blond hair; the other one didn't have any hair at all. But he was too young to have gone bald. Had to have shaved it to look like that. Some kind of skinhead who held his Nazi meetings in a barn.

"Hey, fellas," Chester said, getting to within a couple feet of them. "Don't believe we've met before."

The blond one reached behind his back with his right hand, pulled out a gun that had been tucked into his jeans, and shot Chester through the head.

Made a hell of a noise in that big empty warehouse.

The second he started reaching for the gun, Nicole knew what was coming. And she knew she'd have to go for him first. The bald one hadn't gone for a weapon. It didn't mean he didn't have one, but the fact was, he didn't have one in his hand, so she had to go for the one who did.

Nicole had been standing behind and to the side of Chester when the gun went off. Just as well she wasn't standing directly behind him, given that the bullet went clear through his head and out the other side.

Chester hadn't even hit the ground before she had the knife out of her back pocket. The one she used to cut Chester's apples. A four-inch blade, solid handle. Very sharp. All she'd been able to tuck into her jean pocket was the blade. The handle was sticking up, easy to grab.

Something happened in that moment. It was like she was back in Sydney. Suddenly, her body knew instinctively how to move, how to spring, how to measure distances.

And there wasn't that much distance to cover.

Clearly, Blondie wasn't expecting Nicole to attack. Who knew what he was expecting. Maybe he was thinking, because she was a girl, she'd just stand there and scream like some dumb chick in a fucking movie. Maybe he thought she'd try to run. Maybe he thought she'd just stand there while he shot her in the head, too.

But he clearly never considered that she'd come at him. Or that she'd have a knife. Or that she'd have it buried in his neck before he had a chance to train the gun on her.

The knife went in fast and hard. Blondie made a noise that sounded like he was choking on a pigeon. He didn't even try to turn the gun on her. He dropped it almost immediately, and then he went down to the cement, too.

The bald guy jumped back when the blood spurted. Nicole figured it wouldn't be long before he pulled a gun, if he had one. When he turned and started running for the Explorer, she guessed he didn't.

But maybe there was one in the car.

She could have reached down and grabbed Blondie's gun, but she knew, almost instinctively, that it was not her weapon of choice.

She bolted after him, caught up just as he had the door to the car open and was half inside. She threw all her weight against the door, slamming it against him, smashing his head up against the pillar.

He was seeing stars when she ran the knife into his side. She opened the door, allowing him to slide to the cement.

She dropped on top of him, plunged the knife into him a second time to let him know she was serious.

"Who do you work for?" she asked.

"Jesus," he said. "I'm fucking dying."

"Tell me who you work for and I'll get you an ambulance."

"Higgins," he gasped.

Then she slit his throat.

They found the *Scarface* boys' Escalade in the middle of the desert. They'd all been shot in the head, the SUV set ablaze.

Their boss, a man named Victor Trent, offered Nicole a job. He was impressed, and grateful, not only that she had killed the two men who'd murdered his employees, but that she'd had the presence of mind to get the name "Higgins" out of them before finishing them off.

If he'd known her a little longer, and she'd

had a bit more experience, he'd have had her take care of Higgins herself. But he had one of his longtime employees do that. Higgins met his maker in the desert, too, but no one ever found him. Nor did anyone ever find the two men Nicole had killed in the warehouse.

Victor took Nicole into his inner circle. She had, he quickly determined, abilities that far exceeded other girls — and most boys — her age. She had control. She had discipline. She had a willingness to learn.

And he was happy to teach her.

Before long, Nicole was Victor's go-to girl when he had a problem that needed to be taken care of. Among Victor's circle of associates, her reputation grew. There was always work for a woman like Nicole.

She never told him who she used to be, and he never asked. One time, in 2004, he brought her into his office to give her an assignment, and the Athens summer Games were playing on the television. Victor told her how much he loved the Olympics, how he watched as much of them as he could, while Nicole stood there, watching Carly Patterson on the uneven bars. He had no idea, and that was for the best.

She spent five years working for him and was paid well. At one point, Victor introduced her to a former NYPD officer by the name of Lewis Blocker. Victor had hired Lewis do some surveillance work for him, and in addition wanted him to teach Nicole the craft. She learned a great deal from him.

Finally, Nicole reached a point where she did not want to work solely for Victor Trent anymore. She was indebted to him in many ways, but she believed that theirs had grown into a mutually beneficial relationship. She had eliminated many problems for him, and now she wanted the freedom to eliminate them for others, as well.

Nicole invited him for dinner at Picasso in the Bellagio. Told him what a wonderful mentor he had been to her, how much she'd valued his friendship and guidance these last few years. Worked up to it as gently as she could, finally telling him that she wanted to go it alone. It didn't mean she wouldn't still work for him, but she would be a free agent from now on.

"I need this," she said. "For myself. This is what I have to do. And I'd never be in a position to do this without your support and guidance."

"You fucking ungrateful bitch," he said, and left without finishing his Maine lobster salad with apple-champagne vinaigrette.

When you got down to it, men, they were really all the same.

And she'd done pretty well on her own, until now.

Nicole didn't know anyone in her line of

work have something go this wrong. Not that hired killers got together that often and compared notes. But you heard things. There was a grapevine. There were people out there whose work you knew. Some were good at it, some not so much. Sometimes, they made mistakes. It happened in any line of work.

But Nicole's mistake, even she had to admit it was up there.

It was bad enough she'd killed the wrong person. That alone would have pissed off any client. But to have the intended target then show up, see what had happened, and get away?

Not the sort of thing you put on your résumé.

Sure, there were other killers out there who'd screwed things up. Sadistic sex killers who convicted themselves by recording their crimes on video. Husbands who were so dumb they turned to the Yellow Pages to find hit men to take care of their wives. Wives with the same thing in mind for their husbands, who didn't know the contract killers they were conspiring with were actually under-cover cops. Desperate businessmen who torched their operations, taking a few lives in the process, and put their gas-soaked sneakers back in their bedroom closet.

These people got caught, and went to jail. Why? Because they were *amateurs*. Ending lives was not their day job. They were accountants or stockbrokers or car salesmen or dentists.

They might be professionals in their own world, but they were not professional killers.

Nicole was supposed to be a professional. This was her day job. She took it seriously. She had no particular ax to grind with her targets. She didn't know them. It wasn't personal. She wasn't ruled by jealousy or greed or sexual obsession. Those were the qualities that tripped you up, that blinded you to your mistakes. Nicole wasn't in this line of work because she took pleasure in ending someone's life, although there was the satisfaction of a job done well. If she could be said to actually enjoy any of her assignments, it was when the subjects were male. She always imagined them to be her coach. Or her father. Or Victor.

Having screwed up a job, she had an obligation to make it right. All anybody had in this life was their reputation, and she wanted to do what she could to restore hers. Besides, they were expecting it of her.

Too bad it was taking so much longer than anticipated.

Nicole had been monitoring Allison Fitch's mother's residence for months now. She'd gotten into it within days of Allison's disappearance, while Doris Fitch was out meeting with Dayton police to discuss what progress was being made in New York to find her daughter. Nicole had used that time to plant a listening device on Doris Fitch's phone, and another within the apartment itself, and to install a program on the women's computer that would allow Nicole to monitor it from her own laptop. She'd spoken to Lewis when she ran into a couple of technical hitches and he guided her through it. Nicole was able to read Doris Fitch's e-mails, anything she wrote on her Word program, even look at all the entries she made on her computer banking program, should Doris make some large, out-of-the-ordinary cash withdrawals. Nicole figured it was only a matter of time before the daughter got in touch.

Not that this system was foolproof. Allison could conceivably approach a third party to relay a message to her mother. But, if and when such a message was delivered, there'd likely be a change in Doris's routine. She'd book an airline ticket, for example.

Nicole remained hopeful Allison would, at some point, make contact. The former bar employee was probably afraid to do so, with good reason. She'd figure they'd be watching her mother. But Allison might also be hoping these same people would let down their guard after all this time, maybe even think she was dead.

Which was why Nicole had to wait her out. She just hoped it wouldn't be too much longer. She hadn't made a dime in months.

She was dipping into her reserves.

Maybe it was time for a career change. Get out of this line of work before her luck ran out, if it hadn't already. She had a bad feeling about Lewis — that maybe, when this was over, he was going to settle up with her for her mistake.

She'd have to be ready.

Waiting for Allison, Nicole had plenty of time to contemplate her situation.

Doris Fitch lived in a low-rise apartment complex in the Northridge area of Dayton, close to 75. Nicole had found a vacant apartment across the street that allowed her a view not only of the Fitch apartment, but the lot where she parked her car, a black Nissan Versa.

It wasn't possible to sit here by the window and watch the woman's place twenty-four hours a day, seven days a week. Nicole needed provisions. She needed sleep. But she'd covered herself in this area. The surveillance equipment was voice activated. The moment it was engaged, the recording equipment began. If the Versa moved, a tiny beacon would alert Nicole.

Still, it was prudent to stay close. She worried that the second she took her eyes off the apartment a cab with Allison Fitch in it would stop out front.

Nicole's cell rang.

"Yeah?"

"Hey," Lewis said.

"Yeah," Nicole said.

"Something's come up," he said.

"I'm occupied."

"You have to go to Chicago."

The way this son of a bitch was talking to her lately. She didn't like it.

"Can't," she said.

"Not up for debate. It's as important as what you're waiting on now."

"What's in Chicago?"

"You got your laptop in front of you?"

"Hang on. Okay, go ahead."

"Go to the Whirl360 site. You know it?"

"Yeah."

"Go to New York. Orchard Street. I'm guessing you know the address."

Nicole thought, *Huh*? She opened a browser, went to the site, entered the relevant address. It took a few seconds for the images of the street to load.

"Okay, so I'm on the street," she said. "What's the deal?"

"Pan up."

Nicole clicked and dragged her finger down across the laptop's track pad, altering the perspective on the image as the focal point moved from street level to the building's third floor. To the apartment she had been in one time.

She saw the window.

She clicked to blow up the image.

"Tell me I'm not seeing this," she said.

She never even thought about flying. She could drive to Chicago in four hours. Take I-70 West, skirt the north side of Indianapolis, grab I-65 all the way to Gary, then follow I-90 the rest of the way.

She hoped that if Allison Fitch decided to visit her mother over the next day, she'd make it an extended visit.

Lewis had given Nicole a name: Kyle Billings. Thirty-two years old. Had worked for Whirl360, at their Chicago head office, for three years. According to the information Nicole had, Kyle was responsible for, among other things, overseeing the program that deleted selected portions of the streetscapes when they were posted online. Vehicle license plates, people's faces. It was supposed to happen automatically, and Kyle Billings was the lead person entrusted to make sure it did. He'd devised the program.

Nicole needed Kyle to go back into that program and delete an image on Orchard Street before anyone else found it. How the hell had Lewis been tipped to this, she wanted to know. Some guy had shown up at the door, a Whirl360 printout in hand. Lewis was on it, trying to figure out who the guy was.

What a clusterfuck.

First, killing the wrong person.

328

Then Allison Fitch getting away.

Now this.

Focus.

Wasn't that what she'd done in Sydney? Focused? Concentrated on the task at hand. Put everything else out of her head. No crowd. No television cameras. No commentators.

Just her and the bars.

That was what she had to do now. Think about what must be accomplished *today*. Not what she had to do tomorrow. Or the next day. Or the day after that.

Today.

What she had to do today was find Kyle Billings, and use all her powers of persuasion to get him to go into the Whirl360 database of streetscapes, erase that image in that third-floor window, and purge it from the database forever.

She knew Kyle Billings would do exactly what she wanted.

Kyle Billings had a wife.

THIRTY-FIVE

"Thomas?"

"Yes?"

"It's Bill Clinton."

"It is?"

"That's right."

"Oh, hi. It's good to hear from you."

"How are things going?"

"They are going very well. I'm memorizing more streets every day. Have you been getting my updates?"

"Of course, of course. You're doing very well. Just terrific work. Everyone's amazed by what you can do."

"Thank you so much."

"But, Thomas, there is something I'm a little worried about."

"Yes?"

"I understand the FBI came to see you the other day."

"That's right. Remember we talked about this? I think they were just making sure I was staying on task, you know?"

"Sure, sure. But you have to be very careful these days, Thomas, about who you talk to. FBI, CIA, even the Promise Falls police. Even people who are close to you."

"What do you mean?"

"Just be very prudent about what you tell anyone. Never reveal anything very personal. For example, your father just passed away, and I understand that you might find that upsetting, but you need to present a strong front, or you might be perceived as being weak. This would be true for any traumatic incidents in your life. You keep them to yourself, and you move forward. Do you understand?"

"I believe so."

"That's good. And you also need to cover your tracks. Like erase your computer history —"

"I already do that."

"And your call history, too."

"Sure. I do all that, Bill."

"I can't begin to tell you how proud I am of you, Thomas. Everyone at the agency is very impressed."

"I won't let you down. Since I have you on the line, I wanted to tell you about something. When I was memorizing the streets of New York, I saw —"

"Thomas, I have to go. Maybe next time, okay?"

"Okay, Bill. Okay. Good-bye."

THIRTY-SIX

Thomas wouldn't tell me anything about his chat with the landlord after Julie left. He said he was too annoyed with me. He went back up to his room and closed the door. I could hear him in there, chatting with one of our former presidents.

So the following morning when he came down to the kitchen, rather than beg him for details, I asked nothing. Except for what kind of cereal he wanted.

Halfway through the bowl, as I was pouring myself a second cup of coffee, Thomas said, "Don't you want to know about my conversation?"

"Who with?" I asked, figuring he meant Bill Clinton.

"With the landlord. Mr. Papadapolous."

"If you want to tell me. You didn't last night, so it's up to you."

"I think I woke him up," Thomas said. "He seemed very angry. And I had some trouble understanding him. He had some kind of accent."

"I'd bet Greek."

"Why?" Thomas asked.

"Never mind. Carry on with your story."

"I told him who I was, and that I am a consultant to the Central Intelligence Agency."

I put down my coffee. "Jesus, Thomas, no."

"I didn't want to lie. And I think identifying myself that way made him more agreeable to answering my questions."

I figured it was only a matter of time before the FBI returned. They might have overlooked Thomas bombarding the CIA with e-mails, but telling people he was working on behalf of a federal agency? This could only get worse.

"I asked him who had lived there before," Thomas said.

"Go on."

"Two women."

"That's what the woman down the hall said," I reminded him.

"I asked if they were sisters, or a mother and daughter, or just friends, and he said they were roommates, but not very good friends, because sometimes one of them didn't always pay her rent on time and the other one had to come up with the extra money."

I nodded. "Good questioning."

"He said their names were Courtney

and . . . the other one I think he said was Olsen but it was hard to tell with his accent."

"That's a first name and a last name."

" 'Olsen' was a first name. I have the last names. I wrote them down. He said as far as he knew Olsen still hasn't been found."

I perked up. "Hasn't been found? What do you mean, hasn't been found?"

"That's what he said. And I asked what he meant and he said the CIA must be pretty stupid if it didn't already know all about that and I had to explain to him that the CIA has many branches and is a very large organization and —"

"So what did he tell you?"

"He said Olsen disappeared. And I asked him who was living in the apartment now, and he said nobody."

"That's what I said."

"But," Thomas said, holding up a finger, like he was Sherlock Holmes or something, "the apartment is being rented."

"Who's renting it?"

"Mr. Blocker," Thomas said.

"Who's that?"

"The man who's renting the apartment."

"I know, but who *is* he?"

"I don't know," Thomas said. "Why would someone rent an apartment but not use it?"

"Lots of reasons. Maybe he doesn't live in New York but has to come in all the time on business."

Thomas was dubious. "That seems very wasteful."

"People who have money don't worry about being wasteful," I said. "It's just easier for them to have a place instead of renting a hotel room every time they come into town."

That was a hard concept for Thomas to get his head around. "I don't know. But what I do think is, it's probably the Olsen woman who's in the window. She got killed, and that's why no one has seen her."

"I see. And why was she killed?"

He thought a moment. "So Mr. Blocker could have her apartment when he came into Manhattan."

I laughed. "Is that what you think this is about? Someone needed an apartment so they killed to get one?"

"I've heard that rental accommodation is hard to come by in New York," Thomas said, dead serious.

"I was in the building. I don't think those apartments are worth killing for." I placed my palms on the table. "Look, Thomas, let's take a moment to review. All we know is, two women used to live there, and now they don't, and your landlord friend says Mr. Blocker now pays the rent on it but doesn't actually live there."

"The landlord's not my friend. I don't even know him."

"Okay. But that little bit of information

doesn't add up to a murder."

"Except one of the women is missing."

"According to the landlord, who is not exactly a detective for the New York Police Department. Maybe the woman's been found, but no one's bothered to tell this guy."

"That's a good idea," Thomas said.

"What's a good idea?"

"Calling the New York Police Department."

"I didn't say that was a good idea. I just said that the landlord might not be your best source for information."

"Then we should go to the best source."

"I don't know if that's such a good idea."

"Well, then, I can send an e-mail and ask the CIA to get in touch with them."

Now, that was definitely not a good idea.

"Okay," I said. "Leave this with me. I'll put in a call to the New York police. Ask them about this missing woman, see if she turned up."

"And tell them to go online, check out Orchard Street on Whirl360, and tell them to look at the face in the window."

"Sure," I said.

Thomas went back to eating his cereal. In my head, I breathed a huge sigh of relief. We were *done* with this. More done than Thomas realized. The odds of my picking up the phone to talk to the NYPD were about as good as anyone at the NYPD paying any attention to me if I actually made the call.

336

I could imagine how a New York detective would react when I told him my brother — the one now on file with the FBI for sending updates on his street memorization project to a former president — believed he'd seen a murder on the Internet.

Oh yeah, that was a call I wanted to make.

I said to Thomas, "Let me ask you something."

"Go ahead," he said, a drop of milk running down his chin.

"When this big meltdown happens, when all the online maps go kaplooey, what do you think is actually going to cause it?"

He put down his spoon and dabbed his chin with a paper napkin.

"I think the most likely cause will be an alien attack," he said matter-of-factly. "The attack will most likely come from beyond our own solar system, although I think it's possible it could be launched from either Venus or Mars. Once the aliens disable our mapping systems, it'll be easier for them to make their landings undetected."

A sad, hopeless feeling enveloped me.

"Gotcha," Thomas said, never even cracking a smile. "You should see your face."

I told Thomas I was driving into town and would be back in an hour or so.

Clicking away, he said, "Uh-huh."

"I'd like you to make lunch today," I said.

337

"For both of us. And I'll do dinner."

He stopped and spun around in his chair. "Do I clean up, too?"

"Yes. Hey, Julie was saying, back in high school, you kind of had a thing for Margaret Tursky. That true?"

"I don't see where that's any of your business."

I gave it a shot.

"Catch ya later," I said. He nodded and returned to work. I didn't think I'd be gone long enough for him to get into any mischief, but you could never know for sure.

I pulled into the driveway of a single-story ranch on Ridgeway Drive and rang the bell. It was Marie Prentice who answered.

"Why, Ray, what a surprise!" she said, holding open the screen door. She shouted back into the house: "Len! Ray's here! Ray, did you bring your brother? Is he in the car?"

"I came alone, Marie," I said, stepping into their house.

"Oh, that's such a shame!" she said, slightly out of breath, but still managing to ooze enthusiasm with every syllable. "It would have been *so* nice to see him."

Marie collected small ceramic figurines of forest creatures that adorned nearly every surface in the house. The slender table in the front hall was littered with deer and raccoons and squirrels and chipmunks, none of them to scale with one another, at least I hoped

338

not, or else there were chipmunks out there somewhere capable of eating Bambi for lunch.

Peering into the living room I could see more of the menagerie. Len had carved out a small piece of territory on the coffee table for his remotes, but otherwise the animals had taken over. Marie also fancied herself a painter, and the walls were decorated with her own portraits of owls and moose and bunnies.

"Len!" she screamed again.

A door in the hallway just off the living room opened and Len emerged from the basement. I was willing to bet he spent a lot of time down there. I knew he had a workshop, that he made furniture.

"Ray dropped by!" Marie said. "Isn't that nice?"

Len cracked a nervous smile. "Hey there," he said. "You on your own?"

"Yeah," I said.

"Would you like some coffee?" Marie asked. "I was just about to start a fresh pot."

"That's okay," I said. "I just wanted to have a word with Len for a second."

"Why don't you come downstairs and I'll show you what I've been working on," he said, giving me a look that told me he knew why I was there, and that he didn't want to talk about it in front of his wife.

"Sure," I said.

339

"You positive you won't have something?" Marie asked, following us to the basement door.

"We're good, Marie," Len said, holding out his arm for me to precede him down the steps. He closed the door behind him as he followed me.

"Nice workshop," I said. It looked as though Len had, in this well-illuminated room, every tool a master craftsman might need: jigsaw, drill press, lathe, a large worktable, a Shop-Vac, and a wall adorned with hand tools of every description. On the far side of the room, a broad set of stairs led up to a pair of angled, swinging doors. So that was how he'd get the furniture out. There wasn't a speck of sawdust on the floor, which made sense, since I didn't see any project under way. No chair legs or dresser drawers or cabinet doors lying about, waiting to be made into something whole.

"I try to keep it nice," Len said.

"So what are you working on?" I asked. "This place looks too pristine to actually build anything."

"I don't have any projects on the go," Len said. "I figured you'd want to talk privately."

"Thomas told me there was an incident yesterday," I said. "I came over to find out more. I understand Thomas struck you."

Len reached up and touched his cheek. "Yeah, well."

340

"I'm sorry. Thomas shouldn't have done that."

"I guess he can't help it," Len said. "Being crazy and all."

"He's not crazy," I said. "He has a mental illness. You know that."

"Come on, Ray. That's just a nice way to say he's nuttier than a fruitcake."

I felt something tingle at the back of my neck. "What happened, exactly? When you came out to the house."

"I dropped by, just to see how you boys were doing, that's the kind of thing your dad would have wanted me to do, and you weren't there, just Thomas. He said you were in New York?"

"And what happened?"

"I tried to do something nice, that's what happened."

"I don't understand why Thomas would get angry if that's what you were trying to do."

"I just wanted to get him —"

"Everything okay down there?" Marie called. She had opened the door.

"We're fine, damn it!" Len barked.

The door closed.

Len cleared his throat and continued. "I offered to take him out for lunch."

"You know Thomas doesn't like to leave the house much." I didn't add that he especially wouldn't have liked leaving it to go out with Len.

"Yeah, yeah, I know that, but I thought it would do him some good. He can't stay cooped up in there all the time. It's just not healthy. Used to drive your dad batty."

"So when did Thomas hit you?"

Len shrugged tiredly. "I guess I was kind of pressing the point. Trying to talk him into coming out. I took hold of his arm, thought I could nudge him along, you know? He yanked his arm back and he caught me on the side of the face. If Thomas said it was anything more than that, if he said I hurt him or anything, that's totally not true. That's one of his flights of imagination, that's what that is."

"He never said anything like that," I said.

He nodded with satisfaction. "That's good. Because crazy people can say all kinds of shit that's just not true, you know what I mean? He thinks a former president is his friend, for Christ's sake."

I kept my voice level, and firm. "Len, I suspect you meant well, and I know you were my father's friend for a very long time, and I mean no disrespect, but I won't have you calling Thomas crazy. He's a good, gentle, decent person. I'm not going to try to argue that he's not a bit unusual. I get that. But you've no right to call him names. And if he doesn't want to take you up on your offer to go to lunch, you need to respect that the way you would if you were asking anyone else." I took

342

a breath.

As I turned for the stairs, Len said, "He's not so gentle, you know."

"What?"

"Your dad told me. Thomas could get real angry. Tried to push your dad down the stairs one time. Oh, he made all kinds of excuses for your brother's behavior, but if you want my honest opinion, he ought to be locked up in a loony bin."

THIRTY-SEVEN

"I don't know why you had to wear that red dress to the party last night," Kyle Billings said to his wife, Rochelle. "I told you, even before we left, that you should put on something else."

"You know I like that dress," she said. "I like how it makes me feel."

"What? Like a slut? Is that how you want to feel?"

"Fuck you," she said, and stormed out of their en suite bathroom — Jacuzzi, shower built for two, double sinks, bidet, the whole nine yards — into the bedroom with the curved windows that looked out onto the tree-lined street, and straight into her walk-in closet.

There was one for her, and a walk-in for him, and there was more square feet for either one of them than in the basement apartment in Chicago's South Side where Kyle had lived ten years ago. Mice and mold, and almost every night, the tenants on the floor above screaming at each other about everything from too little butter on the toast to his staying out late drinking with his friends.

Now Kyle didn't have to listen to the neighbors fighting, nor did the neighbors have to listen to him and Rochelle. They had a refurbished multimillion-dollar place on Forest Avenue in Oak Park, right next door to an honest-to-God Frank Lloyd Wright house, one of several on the street. Kyle Billings believed it was only a matter of time before one of the Wright-designed houses went on the market and he'd be able to snatch it up. That, finally, might impress the hell out of his father, who didn't seem to give a shit that Kyle had become a multimillionaire before he was thirty through his Whirl360 wizardry, but worshipped at the altar of Frank Lloyd Wright, America's greatest architect, living or dead. "Why'd you buy this house, and not that one?" Kyle's father had said, pointing to the closest Wright house. "I thought you were doing well."

Asshole.

Kyle Billings followed his wife into her closet. "You know when you dress that way you're just going to draw attention to yourself. You were getting everybody's motor running. All the guys there — their tongues were practically on the floor. Every one of them was fucking you with his eyes."

She spun around, stood there barefoot in her jean shorts and red tee, and placed her hands defiantly on her hips. "I could start wearing a burka if you'd like. That the look you want me to go for?"

"Jesus," Kyle said. He knew, deep down, he was an idiot to be bitching about this. Face it, what the hell attracted him to Rochelle Billings — Kesterman before she married him — in the first place, when he saw her at the software trade show in San Francisco five years ago, prancing about onstage in her stilettos, drawing more eyes to herself than to the finer points of some just-had-to-have-it phone app?

She was as stunning now as she was then, with her black ass-length hair, long legs, and small but perky breasts that looked you right in the eyes. Her skin, the color of coffee with cream, gave her an exotic touch. He'd had to meet her right away. Found her behind the curtain after her performance, invited her for a drink, worked into the conversation his success, the 911 Turbo, the Chicago condo he had, at that time, overlooking Lake Michigan. How this new thing he was in on, that would let people explore cities all over the world from the comfort of their computer chair, was going to make him richer than God.

Rochelle liked that part.

Five months later, they were married.

Kyle knew if she could turn his head, she

was going to give other guys whiplash, too. He was okay with it for a while. Seeing men give her the eye, then they'd exchange glances with him and he'd give them the smile, the one that said, *Yeah, you can look all you want, dickwad, but I'm the one who gets to ride this at night.*

And what a ride.

The sex was something else. Rochelle was inventive in bed, and not the least bit selfish. As if that weren't enough, she was astonishingly flexible. Back in high school, and into college, she had been a competitive gymnast. She'd given that up, but still worked out four days a week, and was as limber as ever.

Kyle knew he was lucky. Any man would kill to have her.

But his reaction to his wife's good looks had changed over time. Pride was giving way to jealousy and uncertainty. If she could have anyone, how much longer would she want him? He had money. They had this house. They went to Europe two or three times a year, stayed in the best hotels. He'd spent two hundred grand on that Mercedes with the gull-wing doors for her.

Trouble was, he wasn't the only one with money. If that was all she wanted, there were plenty of overnight millionaires in his line of work. Did she love him for *him*? Or for the life he provided her?

She'd never shown signs that it was any-

347

thing but the former. And yet, that wasn't enough for him to stop torturing himself. To wonder if maybe she wasn't enjoying flaunting it just a little too much. So now he wanted her to dial it down a notch, tone down the hot stuff. Wear a skirt that was short, okay, but not one that was hiked so high it flashed the Brazilian when she took a tumble off the Christian Louboutins.

"You're making me crazy, you know," she said, flinging clothes, ninety percent of them black, across the rod. "Maybe I dressed that way to get your motor running, not anybody else's. You ever thought of that? Where the hell are those pants?"

"You're sending off signals," he told her. "And even if you don't mean to be, believe me, other guys are picking them up."

She took a hanger off the rack, inspected the pants, put them back. "Shit, where are they?"

"Are you listening to me?"

Rochelle stopped and glared at him. "No, I am not. Because you're losing your fucking mind." She squeezed past him and out of the closet. She went to her bedside table to pick up a cell phone, and said, "I need some space, away from you. I'll be out on the patio if you decide you want to tell me you're sorry about being a total jerk-off."

He plopped down onto the edge of the bed as she walked out of the bedroom. Still couldn't take his eyes off her ass. That was the one bonus when she got mad at him; he got to watch her walk away.

"Stupid," he said, and he wasn't talking about his wife. "Fucking stupid." He knew, in his heart, that possessiveness would produce the exact opposite result of what he wanted. He'd seen it with some of his friends. The harder they tried to keep a woman, the more she tried to get away.

He sat there for ten minutes, then twenty, wondering whether to go find her and apologize, or just walk out the front door, get in his Ferrari, and drive around for a couple of hours. No, maybe go out in the car, but buy some flowers, or something a lot better. Hit the Magnificent Mile, come home with something expensive and sparkly. Around ten grand. Accidentally leave the receipt someplace where she'd find it.

He'd waited a good three quarters of an hour when he decided he was ready to swallow his pride, tell her he was sorry, tell her if she wanted to dress that way, fine, but she had to know that —

His cell went *glink*! Not a phone call, but an incoming text. He got off the bed and grabbed the phone and was greeted with a picture under the name "Rochelle."

Rochelle had texted a photo to him.

A very strange photo.

It was a picture of a woman — not only

was Kyle pretty sure it was a woman; he was pretty sure it was his wife, judging by the red T-shirt and jean shorts — but it was difficult to be sure, what with the plastic bag that was wrapped tightly about her head. Her chin, lips, nose, eyebrows — they were a relief map of her facial features.

And while the picture didn't show her entire body, he could just make out her arms, and something silvery on them. Was that tape? Holding her into a chair? Not a patio chair, because this shot was not taken outside. Wasn't that one of the chairs from the basement?

"What the hell?" he said.

What kind of crazy game was this?

"Rochelle!" he shouted.

As he started heading for the stairs, the phone made another noise in his hand. Not a text, but an actual call.

Again, from Rochelle's cell.

"Hey," he said. "What the hell was that picture you —"

"Mr. Billings."

"Huh?" A woman's voice, but it didn't sound like Rochelle.

"Mr. Billings, you need to stop and listen."

"Rochelle?"

"This is not Rochelle. And you need to listen very carefully."

He was halfway down the stairs when he stopped.

"Your wife can still breathe, just," the woman said. "But if I tighten the bag any further, it will cut off all her oxygen."

"Who the hell is this? What the fuck is going on? I'm coming down —"

"If you come down here, she will die. Are you listening, Kyle? She will die."

He stopped at the base of the stairs, not far from the front door. "Who is this? What do you want?"

"You must listen, Kyle," the woman said calmly. "You must. Or Rochelle will die."

"Jesus Christ," he said, and he felt his legs weakening. He clutched the banister with his free hand.

"Everything is going to be fine so long as you listen and do exactly what you're told."

"I have money," he said quickly. "I can get you money." And then he thought, *Shit, it's Sunday.* But he could find a way. He knew there'd be a way. When you had the kind of money he had, the bank was open whenever you wanted it to be open.

"This isn't about money," the woman said.

"What, then? The cars? You want the cars? Take them. But please, please don't hurt Rochelle. Just tell me what you want me to do."

"I don't want anything of yours. I want you to do something for me. First, the ground rules: You will not call the police. You will not inform anyone in any way about what is transpiring. If you do anything to alert anyone to what's going on, your wife will run out of air and she will die."

"I get it. I get it. What is it you want? What is it you want me to do?"

"You're going to find for me another picture very similar to the one you got a minute ago. And then you're going to get rid of it."

Then Nicole got specific.

"Don't normally see you here on a Sunday, Mr. Billings," the security guard at the Whirl360 front desk said as Kyle strode across the lobby.

"Hi, Bob," Kyle said. "Just popping in for a second."

Bob hit a button, and overlapping Plexiglas panels retracted to allow Billings to pass through. A few yards beyond that, Kyle hit the elevator button. As the doors parted and he stepped into the empty box, he touched his finger to the Bluetooth device clipped over his ear.

"Let me talk to Rochelle," Kyle said.

The voice in his ear said, "One second. Say hello."

"Kyle?" His wife sounded like she was several feet away from her captor, as though the woman had held the cell phone up to the air.

"There," she said. "You've heard her. She's just fine. Took the bag off her head so she could breathe a bit more easily. And that thing with Bob, that was very good. You sounded very natural. You're doing just fine."

"Okay, the door's about to open."

"That's fine," Nicole said. "I'm here if you need me."

Kyle entered the main office space of Whirl360. It wasn't like other companies here. Sure, there were dozens upon dozens of workstations throughout the open-plan environment, but few firms ringed the work area with pool tables and foosball and video games. When Whirl360 employees needed a break, they pushed themselves away from their monitors and played a few rounds of virtual golf, battled space aliens, watched some 3-D television. And when they felt recharged, they went back to work.

The office was quiet today. Only a handful of employees were seated at their terminals, entering in new images from Whirl360 cars that were photographing city streets around the globe every second of every minute of every hour of the day.

"Hey, Kyle."

"What's happening, Kyle."

"How's it going, Kyle."

Everyone felt they needed to say hello.

He gave each of them a nod, found the computer station where he always worked. No individual offices here. Everyone, no matter where they were placed on the corporate food chain, worked here in the main room.

Kyle wished he could have done what he had to do from home, met the hostage taker's demands immediately. But Whirl360 had one of the most hacker-proof systems on the planet. Access from beyond the building was impossible.

"I'm at my desk," Kyle said quietly enough that no one in the office could hear.

"Excellent," Nicole said. "We're fine here."

"I do this thing for you, we never hear from you again," he whispered.

"That's right. You erase the image, you wipe it from the system like it was never there, and we're good."

"I've got your word on that," Kyle said.

"Of course," Nicole said.

"Okay, I'm in." A flurry of keystrokes. "New York . . . Orchard Street . . . This shouldn't take long."

Nicole took the phone away from her ear, rested her hand on her thigh. If Kyle had anything to say to her, she'd hear it. She was feeling optimistic. She could tell he wanted this to be done as quickly as possible, that he wanted to please her. He wasn't going to fuck this up.

"Is he doing it?" Rochelle asked. Just as Nicole had said, the bag was off Rochelle's head now, but she remained bound with duct tape to the leather Eames chair in the Billings home's expansive basement. There was everything down here. Billiards table. A bar. Sixty-inch 3-D TV. An elaborate Lionel train set with mountains and buildings and bridges that had to be ten by twenty feet, for Christ's sake.

"He's doing just fine," Nicole said, sitting across from Rochelle in a matching leather chair. She was wearing another ball cap with visor plus a pair of sunglasses to make her face less identifiable. Her hands had been in latex gloves since she'd been in the house. The alarm system hadn't been a problem. Nicole knew how to deal with these things.

"He'll do what you say," Rochelle said. "He will."

"I'm counting on it."

"We'll never say anything to anyone," Rochelle said. "Promise me you won't hurt him."

"I don't think there's any need for that," Nicole said. She could hear something coming from the phone, grabbed it and put it to her ear.

"I'm getting some coffee, Kyle. Want anything?" A coworker's voice.

"No, no, I'm good," Billings said.

"You know that Jag I was telling you about? Okay, so we took it out for a test drive yesterday and it drove nice, you know, and it had everything on it, but it was red, and to my way of thinking, an XKE back in the sixties, that would look great in red, but today, I

355

think red kind of screams at ya. Hey, did you go to that thing at the Hyatt last night?"

Nicole said, "Get rid of him."

Billings said. "Yeah, we did. Got home kind of late."

"That was the homeless thing, right?"

"Yeah. They raised a lot of money."

"What's that you got on your screen there?"

"Nothing, just . . . doing a test on the fudging. Seeing why sometimes not all plates or faces get totally blurred. A lot of it has to do with the angle. If the software isn't sure what it is, it's not going to fudge it."

"Do I have to tell you again?" Nicole said.

"Listen, nice chattin', but I got a lot to get done here, but thanks for dropping by."

"Take it easy."

"You bet."

"Is he gone?" Nicole asked.

"Yeah," Kyle whispered. "I'm good."

Nicole breathed a small sigh of relief. She noticed that Rochelle was looking at her closely. She'd caught her doing that a couple of times.

"What?" Nicole said, putting the phone down on her thigh again, this time facedown.

"It's none of my business what you're doing, or why. I don't care," Rochelle said. "Doesn't matter to me at all."

"Good."

"That's why I want you to know you don't have to worry when I tell you this. But I just,

I just want you to know."

What was that look Rochelle was giving her? Nicole had seen it before, but not for a very, very long time. The good feeling she'd been having about how things were going was slipping away.

"All I wanted to say," Rochelle continued, "is that I thought you were amazing."

"I'm sorry?" Nicole said.

"At Sydney," she said. "I watched every minute of the Olympics. But *especially* the gymnastics."

"Really," Nicole said.

"The minute I saw you, even with the glasses on, there was something — I think it was your chin, the way you hold it. Just before you'd make your first jump onto the lower bar, there was this thing you did with your chin. This kind of determined way you set it."

"No one's ever pointed that out to me before," Nicole said. "But, now that I think about it, I know what you mean."

"I took gymnastics all through high school and even into college, but I was never as good as you. Not even close. I was your biggest fan." Rochelle forced an admiring smile despite her predicament. "Like I said, I don't know how you got from there to here, to what you're doing now, but I'm sure there's reasons for the way things turn out. Everybody's life takes a different path, right?"

"That's true," Nicole said.

"What I really wanted to say was, you were robbed," Rochelle said.

Nicole suddenly felt very . . . what was it? Sad. She felt sad. Sad about what had happened to her in Sydney, all that had happened to her since. Thinking about how her life might have been different, had she won the gold. Where she might be now. Not here, not in this basement in Chicago.

And there was something else she felt. *Touched.*

"Thank you," Nicole said, and meant it. "Thank you for saying that. That's sort of how I felt, but you don't say it out loud, because then everyone thinks you're a sore loser or something."

"Oh, you showed a lot of class," Rochelle said. "You held your head up high when they gave you the silver on the podium there. But you know what?"

"What?" Nicole asked.

"I could tell. I could tell, looking at you, that your heart was broken."

Nicole tapped at the bridge of her sunglasses. Didn't want Rochelle to see her eyes.

"Well, it was a very emotional moment," Nicole said, feeling emotional right now.

"I bet, if they did an investigation, I bet they'd find out that the judges took some kind of bribe. The Russian ones, maybe. Or the French."

"I don't know about that," Nicole said. "There was never any suggestion of that."

"Well," Rochelle said emphatically, "that's what I think. Although I guess it would be hard, after all these years, to get them to look into something like that."

"I think you're right. What's done is done," Nicole said. "No one has ever really said anything like this to me before."

"I hope you don't mind."

"No, it's okay."

"I used to do searches of you online, wondering what happened to you. But there haven't been any stories in years."

"No," Nicole said. "I left that life behind. I left . . . it all behind."

"I did read stuff about how much everyone expected of you, the pressure that got put on you."

Nicole smiled, to think that anyone still remembered. "My coach, he was furious with me. And my own father, he wouldn't talk to me. He disowned me after that." Nicole paused. "I guess he was living out his dream through me and I blew it for him."

"You're kidding," Rochelle said. "That's horrible."

"Well," Nicole said.

"The whole reason I'm telling you this is, I know it might seem kind of stupid, but you were a real inspiration to me then. I had a picture of you taped to my bedroom wall."

359

"My picture?"

"I still have it. Not on my wall anymore. But I save stuff. I have it tucked away somewhere, with lots of clippings about you. I figured you'd want to know, because there's no way I'd ever say anything that would cause trouble for the great Annabel Kristoff."

It had been her name then.

Nicole's smile was not a happy one. "It's been a long time since anyone called me that." She swallowed to clear the lump that was forming in her throat, then turned over the phone and put it to her ear.

Kyle was in midwhisper. "— there? Are you there? Hello?"

"I'm here," Nicole said, putting the phone to her ear.

"It's done."

"The image is gone?"

"Yes. The head's been blurred out, and now the window just looks dark."

"Are there any previous versions that can still be accessed?"

"No. They're wiped. The database is clean."

"That's excellent." Nicole smiled at Rochelle, who was smiling back and tearing up a little. "Okay, Kyle, I guess we're done. Thank you for this. You'll find Rochelle in the basement when you get home."

"Is she okay?"

"She's fine. Rochelle, say hello." Nicole held out the phone.

360

"Hi, honey! I love you! I'm so sorry about this morning."

"You, too, babe. I've been such an asshole. Everything's going to be okay."

Nicole pulled back the phone. "Okay, Kyle. Good-bye."

She ended the call, and tossed the phone, which was Rochelle's, onto the carpet. And then she just sat there, looking at the floor, resting her elbows on her knees.

Thinking.

"What?" Rochelle asked. "Aren't you going to go? He did what you want, didn't he?"

"He did," Nicole said. "He did."

Still have to do it, she told herself. *Even if she is a fan.*

Nicole picked up the plastic bag that had been on the woman's head earlier.

"What are you doing with that?" Rochelle asked.

It took much longer than she would have liked. The woman fought her hard, harder than most. She thrashed her head violently back and forth for as long as she could before the air ran out. Long enough for a single tear to drop onto the outside of the bag.

When it was finally done, Nicole settled back into her chair and waited for Kyle Billings to come home.

THIRTY-EIGHT

Len Prentice's attitude, and comments, had left me shaken.

Calling Thomas crazy, saying he should be committed to a "loony bin," had made me furious, but his revelation that Thomas had tried to push our father down the stairs had left me deeply troubled. Was it as bad as it sounded? Had it really happened? Dad had never mentioned anything like this to me, but that didn't mean the incident never occurred. It wasn't in my father's nature to burden his family with his problems. About ten years ago, when he noticed a lump on his testicle, he never said a word to Mom. He went to the doctor, had it checked out. When the tests came back, it turned out he was fine, and the lump receded on its own. It was only some time later, when Mom was feeling ill, that the doctor they shared happened to ask her how Adam was doing.

She gave him shit. She told me all about it, hoping I'd give him shit, too. I didn't. That was the way Dad was, and I knew there wasn't any changing him. Whatever problems he'd had sharing a house with Thomas he had kept from me. He'd probably worried that if he had told me, I'd have felt obliged to help him out — something I'd like to think I would have done — but he wouldn't have wanted that. He'd have seen Thomas as his responsibility, not mine. I had my own life to lead, he'd have reasoned.

But he must have felt the need to unload on someone, someone who wouldn't feel they had to step in and actually help him with his situation. Len had been a sympathetic ear for my father, although there was nothing about his attitude that suggested sympathy to me. He was a simpleminded, judgmental asshole, as far as I could tell.

I wanted to ask Thomas about this, but was my brother a reliable witness to his own actions?

Driving away from the Prentice house, I felt myself getting swallowed into some kind of vortex. I'd come to Promise Falls from Burlington to deal with my father's estate, set my brother up someplace, and get rid of the house, and really hadn't made a dent in any of it. I kept finding myself sidetracked. Strange and unsettling words on Dad's laptop. Thomas's preoccupation with that goddamn face in the window. An unfortunate encounter between Thomas and Len Prentice, and apparently another, between Thomas and our father.

There was this other thing niggling away at my brain. The lawn tractor. The key in the OFF position. The blade housing raised, which indicated Dad had stopped mowing the lawn. But the job wasn't finished, so why had he raised the blades?

It made me wonder whether he'd been interrupted. Was it possible someone had come down the side of the hill to talk to him? It was almost impossible to carry on a conversation with the tractor running, so Dad would have turned off the ignition. And if he thought this interruption was going to be an extended one, he'd have brought up the blades.

Was that what happened? Had someone stopped to chat? It wasn't the best place for a conversation. It was a precarious spot, given how steep the slope was. Dad, sitting on the tractor, would have had to continually lean into the hill to keep the machine from tipping. Sitting straight up in the seat might have been all the leverage that was needed to topple the damn thing.

Which, in the end, was what happened.

But if the tractor rolled, and killed him, when it was already stopped, and if the reason Dad had come to a stop was because someone had wanted to talk to him, then who the hell was that person, and why hadn't they called for help right away?

Thomas had been the one who finally dialed 911. After he'd found Dad, already dead, pinned by the machine.

Unless . . .

Unless Thomas was the one Dad had stopped for. To have that conversation. If it had turned into a heated argument, a simple shove would have been all Dad needed to go tumbling, taking the machine with him.

No.

That was unthinkable. My thoughts were running wild again, even worse than when I'd found "child prostitution" in the search field of Dad's laptop. My mind was going places it had no business going.

It was stress, I told myself. The stress of losing my father, of having to take responsibility for Thomas — it was taking a toll.

I hadn't even taken time to grieve. When had I had a chance? From the moment I'd arrived at my father's house, I'd been thrown right into it. Making funeral arrangements, meeting with Harry Peyton, looking after Thomas, taking him to see Laura Grigorin.

Only now was I realizing how adrift I felt without Dad, without his guidance and steady hand.

"I miss you," I found myself saying aloud, my hands gripped on the steering wheel. "I need you."

I steered the car over to the shoulder, stopped, put it in park, and rested my forehead on the top of the steering wheel for a moment.

I hadn't cried once since getting the phone call from the Promise Falls police about my father's death. Now it was taking everything I had to keep the lid on. Maybe I was more like my father than I'd realized. I kept things bottled up, didn't share my problems with others.

I loved my father. And I felt lost without him here beside me.

I got out my phone. A few seconds later, someone said, "*Standard*. Julie McGill here."

"Why don't you come out to the house for dinner tonight?"

"Is this George Clooney?"

"Yes."

"Sure."

When I walked into the kitchen I saw a tuna sandwich sitting on a plate on my side of the table. There was a napkin folded at the side, and an opened bottle of beer that was now warm to the touch.

"Son of a bitch," I said to myself. "He made my lunch." I knew I'd asked him to, but I guess my expectations had been low. I felt bad.

I knocked on Thomas's door and stepped in.

"Thanks for making me a sandwich," I said.

"No problem," he said, his back to me.

"Where are you?" I asked.

"London," he said.

"How is it?"

"Old," Thomas said.

"Did you eat? I hope you weren't waiting for me."

"I ate. And I put my plate and my glass and the bowl I mixed up the tuna and mayonnaise in into the dishwasher."

"Thanks, man. We're going to have a guest for dinner."

"Who?"

"Julie."

"Okay."

I sat on the edge of the bed, which put me at a ninety-degree angle to him as he stared at the screen.

Thomas said, "Let's say you come out of the Opera House on Bow Street in Covent Garden and you want to get to Trafalgar Square. Do you turn right and walk down to the Strand, or left and go up to —"

"Thomas, stop. I need to talk to you."

"Just tell me which way you think."

"Left."

"Wrong. The faster way would be to go right, down to the Strand, then right and keep on going." He turned and looked at me. "You can't miss it."

"Can you stop for a second?"

Thomas nodded.

"I want to ask you a few things. Things

367

about Dad."

"What?"

"Okay, first, the day Dad died, did you go out and talk to him when he was cutting grass on the side of the hill?"

Thomas cocked his head to one side. "I was going to. I was looking for him."

"You didn't go out, even to give him a phone message or anything? Something that made him turn off the machine and lift up the blades?"

"No," he said again. "The only time I went out was to find him because I was hungry."

"And he was trapped under the tractor."

He nodded.

"The two of you, you got along pretty well most of the time, didn't you?"

"Sometimes he got angry with me," Thomas said. "You've asked me about this before."

"Did you — I don't know how to ask this without it sounding like I'm accusing you of something."

Thomas showed no concern. "What is it?"

"Did you try to push Dad down the stairs?"

"Did Dad tell you about that?"

Would it be better if he thought our father had told me, or to admit I'd learned this from Len Prentice?

I sidestepped. "Is it true?"

Thomas nodded. "Yes. Sort of."

"What happened? When was this?"

"About a month ago."

"Tell me about it."

"He wanted to talk about something that happened a long time ago," Thomas said, glancing back at the London street scene on his monitor.

"What? Something that happened to Dad?"

"No. Something that happened to me."

"To you? What happened to you?"

"I'm not supposed to talk about it. Dad told me not to." He paused. "At the time. He told me I wasn't ever to talk about it or he'd get really angry with me."

"Jesus, Thomas, what are you talking about here? When was this?"

"When I was thirteen."

"Dad did something to you when you were thirteen that he told you never to talk about?"

My brother hesitated. "Not . . . no, not exactly."

"Thomas, look, whatever happened, it was a long time ago, and Dad's gone. If there's something you need to tell me, then you can do it."

"There's nothing I want to tell you. President Clinton says I'm not supposed to talk about this stuff. It makes me look weak. And I'm just on my way to Trafalgar Square."

"Okay, but, Thomas, can we just go back to the thing that happened a month ago. What was that about?"

"Dad wanted to talk about the thing that happened when I was thirteen."

369

"Had you ever talked about it all these years?"

Thomas shook his head. "No."

"But out of the blue, Dad wanted to talk about it again?" I was grasping here, trying to figure out what the hell Thomas was talking about, what this thing was that had happened twenty-two years ago.

"Yes."

"Why?'

"He said maybe he was wrong, maybe he'd done a bad thing, and that he was sorry about it. Dad was following me up the stairs, saying he wanted to talk to me about it, but I didn't want to talk about it. I'd tried really, really hard not to think about it for all those years and so I stopped and turned around and said I didn't want to talk about it and that if he didn't want to listen to me when I was thirteen why did he want to listen to me now and I put my hand out to stop him from following me and I didn't push hard but he tripped on the stair and he fell a little bit."

"Fell a little bit?"

Thomas nodded.

"Could you explain that?"

"We were on the fourth step going up, so he didn't fall very far. He landed flat on his back."

"Jesus, Thomas. What did you do?"

"I said I was sorry, and I helped him get into the chair and I got him one of his ice packs. I was sad that he fell."

"Did he go to the hospital? Or the doctor?"

"No. He took some extra-strength Advils."

"He must have been furious with you."

Thomas shook his head in the negative. "No. He said it was okay. He said he understood. He said I was entitled to be mad, and if I didn't forgive him, he'd live with that. And the pills started to work, and he started to feel better, but it hurt for about a week."

Len must have noticed my father was in pain and asked what he'd done to himself. Maybe Dad had related what happened, but not made a big deal about it. Len had said Dad made excuses for Thomas, which seemed to match the version of the tale my brother was telling me.

But what was Dad sorry about? And why didn't Thomas want to talk about it? What did my dad think he wouldn't want to forgive him for?

I said, "There's something, some incident, Dr. Grigorin said you won't talk about. Is it this? This thing Dad was apologizing for?"

Thomas nodded without hesitation.

"You need to tell me," I implored. "I need to know."

"No you don't. It doesn't matter. He's not going to hurt me again."

"Dad? Dad can't hurt you anymore?"

Thomas shook his head. I didn't know whether he was saying no, or dismissing me.

"Dad would have believed me if you'd looked up at the window," he said, but when I asked him to explain, he walked away.

At dinner, it struck me that Julie was not digging into her fish sticks with much enthusiasm, although the same could not be said about her jam jar glass filled with pinot grigio.

"Sorry," I said. "When I went to the store the other day I kind of loaded up on stuff that would be easy to throw together."

"No, it's great," Julie said. "You'll have to give me the recipe."

Thomas said, "You just take the fish sticks box out of the freezer, put them on a metal tray, and put them in the oven. And then you put a glop of tartar sauce on them from the jar. Isn't that right, Ray?"

"Yes, Thomas," I said. "That's pretty much it."

"I could make this," he said, nodding proudly to himself. Unlike Julie, he'd wolfed down the fish sticks and the french fries, which had also come out of a bag from the freezer.

"Really, it's great," Julie said. She looked across the table at me and said, "You've been kind of quiet."

"I guess I've got a few things on my mind."

"Like calling the police?" Thomas asked.

"What?"

"You said you were going to call the police in New York."

"I haven't done that yet," I said. "I'll get right on that tomorrow."

If Thomas suspected I was being anything less than sincere, he didn't show it. He got up from the table, took his plate to the sink and rinsed it off, and said he was going up to his room.

"Let me clean up," Julie said.

"Just leave it," I said. "Come on." We took our jam jar glasses of wine into the living room and sat down on the couch.

"You're not going to call the police, are you?" she asked. I had filled her in, briefly, on my trip to New York, Thomas's call to the landlord, and my pledge to get in touch with the NYPD.

I shook my head. "No."

Julie kicked off her shoes and curled her legs up on the couch. "I guess I get that."

"You guess?"

"Yeah. I mean, it would be hard to explain, and hard to get anyone to listen to you. A blurry white head in a window. What the hell is that, anyway? I love Thomas, I do, but after what you told me about the FBI coming to visit, maybe keeping a low profile is a smart thing." She knocked back the rest of her wine. "More?"

I nodded.

She hopped off the couch, opened another

373

bottle, and brought it back. She refilled her glass and mine.

"There was something in your voice when you called me this afternoon," Julie said. "You sounded kind of, I don't know, shaky."

I let the wine surround my tongue a few seconds before answering. "I was having a moment of self-pity, I guess. Thinking about my dad, about Thomas. It was all getting me down at the moment. Look, I don't want to burden you with all this shit."

"It's okay," she said. No one spoke for a few seconds. Then, "I remember you in school, how you were always drawing things. Sometimes I'd see you, sitting on the floor in the hall, leaning up against your locker, a hundred kids shuffling around you and yelling and goofing around and slamming their lockers, and you'd be sketching something in your book, totally oblivious to everything that was going on around you. I'm like, always looking around at what's going on, but there you were, in your own world, doing your thing."

"Yeah," I said. "I guess."

"I think you and Thomas are more alike than you might think. He's wrapped up in his world, but I can picture you, back in Burlington, up in your studio all by yourself, just you and your airbrush or your pencil or your CAD program, letting out some image, some picture that's been trapped in your head, setting it free." She had some more wine. "I think I'm starting to feel this a little."

I was, too, but not so much that my mind wasn't still racing. "I keep thinking about how Dad died. The key in the OFF position, the blades —"

Julie put a finger on my lips. "Shh," she said. "What was it you told Thomas? Let it go. Let it all go, just for a while."

Julie put our glasses on the coffee table and snuggled in closer to me. I slipped my arms around her and placed my mouth on hers. This went on for a while until Julie said, "This ain't high school anymore. We don't have to stay on the couch."

"Upstairs," I said.

"I was thinking my place," she said, clearly a reference to Thomas clicking away upstairs.

"He won't be coming out of his room. Sometime around midnight, or later, he'll hit the bathroom and brush his teeth and pack it in. We're not going to see him before that."

So we slipped upstairs. I steered Julie into the bedroom at the end of the hall, and over to the queen-sized bed my father had slept in, alone — so far as I knew — since my mother's passing.

"Isn't this your dad's room?" Julie asked.

"This is where I've been sleeping. Would you like to go out to the car, like last time?"

She gave me a look. "No, this'll do."

I barely had the door closed when Julie

started unbuttoning my shirt. I slid my hands under her sweater and felt her warm skin under my palms. My mouth was on hers as we moved to the bed. Julie pushed me onto my back and straddled me, reaching down and unbuckling my belt.

"I know some excellent stress reduction techniques," she said, swinging her legs back off me so she could slide off my jeans and boxers. She tossed them onto the floor, got back on top, crossed her arms to the opposite sides, and whisked her top off in one swift motion, exposing a lacy, purple bra. She gave her head a shake to get her hair back into place.

"Purple?" I said. "Is that the same —"

"Oh please. I was a skinny, 110-pound school brat."

"Just asking."

She reached behind her back in that way women can that makes you think their elbows are going to snap, and unhooked and tossed her bra in the direction of my jeans.

"Come here," I said. She leaned over, allowing her nipples to brush lightly across my chest.

"*Ray!*"

Julie sat bolt upright. "Jesus!" she said under her breath.

My heart went off like a trip-hammer. "Fuck," I whispered.

I could hear Thomas's door open. "Ray!

Come here! Ray?" I'd never heard him call for me this way before.

I went to call out, then stopped myself. I didn't want to bring him in here. Julie half-naked. Me entirely so.

"Where are you?" he called. I heard the guest bedroom door open. "Ray? Are you in Dad's room?"

Julie looked at me, wide-eyed. She whispered, "You have to do something."

"Thomas! Give me a sec—"

The door flung open. Thomas walked straight in. Didn't even look at Julie as she hopped off me and grabbed the bedspread to cover herself. As she did so, she exposed me, and my current state, completely.

"Ray!" he shouted. "It's gone!"

"Thomas, for Christ's sake, can you see —"

"It's gone! The head's gone."

"What?" I said, swinging my legs off the bed and reaching down for my boxers. "What are you talking about?"

"You have to see this!" he said. He exited the room and ran back down the hall to his own.

I followed him, wearing nothing but my underwear. Julie had struggled back into her top, not bothering with her bra, and came along after me.

As I went into Thomas's room I saw that he had all his monitors focused on the window on Orchard Street. It sure looked

377

like the same window, except this time there was nothing in the frame. It was black. No more bag-wrapped head.

"What the hell?" I said.

Thomas stood there, pointing. "Where did it go? What happened to it?"

I stammered, "They must, they, I guess, they must have updated it. Taken pictures of the street again."

"No!" he said. "Everything else is exactly the same! The same people on the street. The same cars! Everything's the same except the head is gone!"

I dropped myself into Thomas's chair and looked at the screen. "Son of a bitch," I said.

Thomas grabbed a sheet of paper off the table and handed it to me. A printout of the original image, like the one he'd sent with me to New York. "It's exactly the same, right?"

I studied the printout. "It's the same, Thomas, it's the same."

Julie sidled up next to Thomas, then took the printout from me and studied it, not saying anything.

"Why, Ray?" Thomas asked. "Why is it gone? Why is it gone, right after you went into the city to check it out?"

I was shaking my head. I couldn't make any sense of it. In the last twenty-four hours, someone had gone into this site and wiped out the image. Since I had been down there.

Since I'd knocked on the door and had a few words with the neighbor.

I felt a chill. And not just because I was sitting there with almost no clothes on.

Julie touched my brother gently on the arm. "Okay, you know what, Thomas? Start from the beginning. Tell me all about what you've seen, and what you think it means."

THIRTY-NINE

Lewis Blocker called Howard Talliman Monday morning.

"It's done."

Howard said, "Hold on." He put the cell phone on the granite counter in the kitchen of his Upper East Side brownstone and supported himself on the countertop with both hands. He hadn't slept in days and he felt like his body was shaking all the time, like he was walking around in a world with nonstop low-level earth tremors.

This was the call he was waiting for, and now that he'd received it, he had to steady himself, take a few breaths. He picked up the cell again and said, "I'm here."

"Go to your computer."

Howard hauled himself up onto one of the barstools and opened the laptop on the raised stretch of counter. He entered the Whirl360 address into the Web browser and found his way to that Orchard Street window.

The head was gone.

"Lewis," he said.

"I'm here."

"I looked. It's gone."

"Yeah. She got it done."

Howard was pleased, but he wasn't about to shower any accolades on the woman who'd screwed this thing up from the get-go. "Any complications?"

"Some."

"Any that could blow back and hurt us?"

"No."

"Okay. Where are we on the other matters?"

"She's gone back to Dayton to babysit the mother. Still waiting. And I'm still looking for our visitor."

"It's nice to have a little bit of good news for once," Howard said. "But we're still deep in the woods."

"Yes." Lewis paused. "I'll keep you posted."

Howard ended the call, slid the phone across the counter, and put his head into his hands. God, he needed a drink and it was only eight. He needed his strength. He had an appointment with Morris Sawchuck this morning.

The man was becoming increasingly restless. He wanted to reactivate his campaign plans. Announce formally, after delaying for nine months, that he would be seeking the office of the governor of the State of New York.

It had made sense, back in August, for Morris to put his ambitions on hold. One very personal reason that had become very public, and another — his complicity in the CIA director's deal with terrorists — that he'd prayed would never become public at all.

And a third reason he knew nothing about.

Oblivious, Morris believed there was no longer a reason to put his career on the back burner. Enough time had passed. Had he known a woman named Allison Fitch was still out there — and that she could destroy him — he might well have felt differently.

Every day, Howard Talliman lived with the fear the woman would surface. He checked Web sites on his phone before he was even out of bed. He grabbed the TV remote, turned on CNN in his bedroom, flipped back and forth between it and the *Today* show. Imagined Wolf Blitzer saying, "And now, in a CNN exclusive, we talk to a woman who's come out of hiding to accuse Morris Sawchuck and the people around him of trying to have her killed. Not only is she accusing the New York attorney general of attempted murder, but of being complicit in the disgraced former CIA director's plan not to pursue charges against —"

That was when Howard imagined turning off the TV, getting his hands on a gun, and blowing his brains out.

Not unlike what Barton Goldsmith ultimately decided to do.

While Howard and Morris fretted that the attorney general's involvement in the CIA director's deal with terrorists would become known, Goldsmith was feeling the pressure as well. He was going to be called to testify before a congressional committee. Everything was going to come out.

So Barton Goldsmith rose early one morning, walked into the backyard of his Georgetown home, stood among the beautiful flowers in his garden, put the barrel of a pistol in his mouth, and pulled the trigger.

God bless him, Howard thought. Morris, as was his nature, was circumspect. "A terrible thing," he said in an interview. "Such a loss." Inside, Howard believed, Morris had to be dancing a jig.

So with Goldsmith out of the picture, Morris felt that threat had been neutralized. But Howard knew a bigger one remained. If Fitch surfaced, and talked, everything would start spilling out. Howard didn't know what, exactly, Fitch had heard, or thought she'd heard, Bridget saying on her cell phone during that Barbados vacation. But she'd intimated she knew something.

Sooner or later, Fitch would overcome her fear of the authorities. When an attorney general, or at least those working on his behalf, orders a hit on you, it's bound to make you hesitant about going to the police. But one day, Howard believed, she'd screw up her courage.

Howard could not allow Morris to move forward with his plans while that remained a possibility. The trick was keeping the man in check without telling him why he needed to hold off.

Howard could not tell him the truth.

Howard could *never* tell him the truth.

He was sitting at his desk when the phone buzzed. It was his secretary, Agatha. "He's here," she said. She hadn't even finished that short sentence before the door opened and in strode The Man himself.

Howard was up and around his desk, hand extended. "Hey," he said. Morris returned the handshake with a firm grip. He walked over to the bar Howard kept in the corner of his office and poured two scotches.

"I had a very interesting conversation this morning," Morris said, handing one to Howard.

"Who with?" Howard said.

"Bridget."

"Is that a fact," Howard said, settling himself into a chair as Morris did the same. "What did you talk about?"

Morris grinned. "A lot of things. We talk all the time, you know."

"I'm sure you do."

"But today, it was kind of special. She told me it was time."

Howard drank. "Did she?"

Morris nodded. "She told me to follow my dream. She said to go for it. She said I'd waited long enough. She told me she didn't want me waiting any more because of her."

"Well."

"Because, honestly, she's been the only reason I've still been waiting, Howard. This thing with Goldsmith, it's over. When's the last time you saw the *Times* do a story on it? The man's secrets died with him."

"Other people know. Other people in the agency."

"They won't talk, Howard. They've closed ranks. It's over."

"We can't ever be certain of that."

"So what are you saying? That we never move forward? That we never get back on the horse?"

"I'm not saying that, Morris. But we still need to proceed with caution. We can't lose sight of our long-term objectives. Morris, you can make it all the way. You know that, don't you? You can get there, right to Pennsylvania Avenue. I know it. I have faith. But it can't happen if we take the short view. We have to make our decisions with the future in mind."

Morris knocked back his drink, set the glass on the table between them, and looked down into his lap. He went very quiet.

"Morris? Are you okay?"

"Bridget said something else," he said.

"Morris, do you really think —"

"She said she forgives me." He raised his head and looked at Howard. "That's what she said. She forgives me."

"Well, that's good, Morris, but I don't see how that relates —"

"Do you know what that meant to me? Do you have any idea the guilt I've been feeling?"

"Of course I do. God knows, we've been over it. And I've told you, you don't have anything to feel guilty about. You weren't the only one who didn't see the signs. None of us did. Some people, they keep their troubles to themselves, buried deep inside."

"I still can't get my head around it. I asked her, you know."

Howard swallowed. "You asked Bridget."

"I did. I asked her, when she appeared to me, I asked her why. Why didn't she just talk to me? We could have worked it out. You know what she said to me?"

Howard closed his eyes. He didn't know how much more of this he could take. "What did she say, Morris?"

"She said not to blame myself."

"Well, that's terrific. That really is."

Morris gave his friend a sharp look. "Don't be flip about this, Howard. I don't appreciate it."

"I'm sorry. Really, I am. But, Morris, we can't move forward based on what Bridget tells you. I'm dealing with the real world.

With the press, and federal investigators, a scandal that could still bite us in the ass."

Morris seemed not to be listening. "It's just, when you compare what Bridget is saying now, to what she told you on the phone — it's very different. She told you I was sucking the life out of her. Wasn't that what she told you?"

"You have to consider her state of mind at the time."

"What if, at that moment, she was thinking as clearly as she ever had?"

"Jesus Christ, Morris!" Howard exploded. "Enough."

Morris sat back in his chair as though he'd been shoved.

"You can't keep doing this to yourself. You have to stop. You have to move on."

"Haven't you been listening, Howard? That's exactly what I want to do, what Bridget wants. You're the one holding me back."

"And you should thank God I am," he snapped back. "While you're having chats with ghosts, I'm dealing with political realities." He was on his feet, pointing a finger at Morris. "And you need to wait. You get back into this too soon, those goddamn pundits, you know what they're going to say? That you got over her pretty fast, that's what they'll say. You'll look insensitive."

Morris looked away. "Two wives," he said.

"What?"

"It would be hard enough for a man to have one wife kill herself. But two? What does that say about a man? What does that say about *me*? First Geraldine kills herself in the garage. And then Bridget." He looked imploringly at Howard. "Just what kind of monster am I?"

"You see?" Howard said. "This just proves that you're not ready to get back into the game. You still need time to heal. Morris, trust me. I'm your friend. And I'm telling you this, as your friend, that this is not the time."

Yeah, I'm some friend, Howard thought. *I sent someone to kill your blackmailer, and ended up killing your wife instead.*

Sometimes Bridget spoke to Howard, too, but she was far less forgiving.

FORTY

It is August.

Allison Fitch has worked her usual shift, and would normally be sleeping now, this time of day, but she is up early. She's had a phone call, and now she has an errand to run. She's dressed, ready to go out. She has to run downstairs to the scarf store. She had managed, the week before, against all odds, to get them to accept a personal check for $123.76 for two silk scarves. "I live on the block, practically above your shop," she'd told them. "I'm in here all the time," she'd said. She'd shown them her ID, a driver's license. Gave them her cell phone number. The girl on the cash register was new and finally relented.

Check bounced.

The manager has called. Three times. Most recently, fifteen minutes ago. Told Allison that if she isn't there with $123.76 in cash in the next hour, she's going to call the police and tell them Allison Fitch has defrauded them.

389

As it turns out, Allison has more than five hundred dollars in cash in her purse. A bunch of dickheaded traders from a prominent Wall Street firm had a party at the bar last night. They'd made some kind of killing in the market and were celebrating. Throwing money around. Tipping big. And, earlier in the day, Allison had gone to the ATM and taken out a couple of hundred. With all that cash, she figures she could go on a shopping spree when she gets up the next day. A warm-up before the *really* big money comes. She figures Howard Talliman will be in touch anytime now to set up a meeting, where he'll hand over the cash in exchange for her silence.

Boy, she thinks, the expression on his face when she let him believe she'd heard Bridget having some kind of top secret chat with her husband. Guy looked like he'd just eaten a rat sandwich. She'd just figured it stood to reason a man like Morris Sawchuck had secrets, and that he might discuss them with his wife.

Suppose she'd heard some of them?

Hilarious thing is, she never heard a goddamn thing. But now she's more sure than ever that she's going to get that one hundred grand. Pretending to hear the call was just the icing on the lesbo-affair cake she needed to seal the deal.

So she figures, what the hell, she'll pay off

that bitch for the scarves, then come home, go back to bed.

She is slipping on her jacket, throwing the strap of her purse over her shoulder when she gets a buzz from the lobby.

Allison hits the button. "Yeah?"

"It's me. We need to talk."

Shit. *Bridget.*

Allison lets her in and half a minute later Bridget is at her apartment door.

"Hey," Allison says, closing the door as the woman comes into the kitchen.

"What did you tell him?"

"What?"

"What did you tell Howard? What did you tell him you heard?"

Allison holds up a hand. "Look, we met, we came to an arrangement, and everything's okay, so don't worry about it."

"What did you hear?"

"I'm not getting into this with you. And listen, if anyone's got a bone to pick, it's me. You should have been up front with me. You should have told me who you really were."

"Allison, listen to me. You're making a mistake, pushing Howard too far."

"We got along fine. Everything's cool."

"Whatever he's agreed to give you, you have to promise him you'll never, ever, hit him up for more. He'll do anything to protect my husband. If you're smart, you'll call it all off. You'll tell him you don't want any money, that he doesn't need to buy your silence, that you'll never say a word about us to anyone, that you never heard any —"

"Look, this is fun and all, but I really have to go. I've got to run downstairs and deal with this bitch who says I owe her money. I'll be, like, five minutes. Stay here, make yourself at home, whatever, we'll talk when I get back."

"You have to believe me," Bridget says. "You're in over your head."

"Fine, fine, we'll talk about it when I get back." Allison slides her purse strap higher onto her shoulder and heads out into the hall, pulling the door closed behind her.

Bridget stands briefly in the kitchen, then, feeling restless, moves farther into the apartment. She walks into the living room area, where the pullout couch Allison sleeps on is extended, the covers a mess. She reaches for a *Cosmopolitan* on the coffee table, looks at the cover featuring Ashley Greene and the headline "60 Sex Tips," notices the issue is months old. She drops it back onto the table.

Bridget goes to the living room window, gazes down the street, looks at the traffic. There's a car down there with something funny on top of it. A small car, a Civic maybe, with a short pole fixed to the roof with brackets, and something mechanical-looking on the end of it.

Bridget steps away from the window, still

restless. She wanders into the bedroom, casts her eye upon this second unmade bed. She walks around it to the bedroom window and stands there, listens to the muffled sounds of the city through the pane of glass, feeling anxious. She berates herself, for at least the hundredth time, for allowing herself to get into a compromising relationship. For putting everything at risk. Herself. Her husband. His future.

I'm such a fool, she thinks. *Such an idiot. I have everything and I'm throwing it away. Need to control my impulses. There's that weird car again. What is that on —*

Hears something behind her. Starts to turn.

Everything goes white.

She cannot breathe.

Nicole is finished. She has retrieved the cell phone from the target's purse. She is preparing to leave when she hears the door open. It's too soon for the cleanup crew. She has only just made the call.

The roommate. It must be the roommate. She's supposed to be at work. She's come back to the apartment during the day.

Shit shit shit.

From the kitchen, a woman calls out, "Bridget?"

Bridget?

Nicole's briefing for this job included two names: the target, Allison Fitch, and Court-

393

ney Walmers, the woman with whom she shares this Orchard Street apartment.

If the woman Nicole has just killed is Bridget, then the person entering the apartment could be the target. Or it could still be Walmers.

Doesn't much matter. It could be goddamn Britney Spears, for all Nicole cares. It's a complication she must deal with.

Nicole intends to move around the bed, flatten herself up against the wall before the woman comes into the bedroom. But before she can make the move, the woman appears in the doorway.

Her eyes move from Nicole to the dead woman and back again. In an instant.

That's all it takes for Nicole to see who she is. She recognizes her from the photos she was provided beforehand. *This* is Allison Fitch. She's about the same size and height as the dead woman. Roughly same color hair.

Fitch screams, turns, runs.

Nicole knows she has to move quickly to shut the woman up. Forever.

Twice the work for the cleanup crew. They'll have to deal with it.

Nicole intends to take the same shortcut out of the room that she used to enter it. Straight across the bed. Sees the moves in her head without even having to think about them. Push off the floor with left foot, right foot hits the bed, left foot lands on other side.

Should save her a full second.

Fitch has just slipped from her sight, tearing through the kitchen for the door. Nicole leaps onto the bed, but her foot gets tangled in the rumpled bedspread. Nicole tumbles forward off the far side of the mattress, dragging the bedspread with her as she slams into the wall.

She untangles her foot from the spread, comes through the bedroom door like a sprinter charging out of the blocks. The door to the hall is open. She can hear frantic footsteps, at least a floor below.

Not good.

Nicole descends the two flights of stairs three steps at a time. Bursts onto the street. Stops, looks both ways.

No sign of Allison Fitch to the north.

No sign of Allison Fitch to the south.

Nicole takes out her cell and calls Lewis. "You're not going to like this," she says.

Lewis calls Howard. Tells him the wrong woman was killed. That Fitch got away. And that it's even worse than that.

The dead woman is Bridget.

"Mother of God," Howard says. "What are you telling me? *Bridget?* She killed *Bridget?*" He is saying all this in heated whispers so Agatha will not hear him on the other side of the office door.

"Goddamn it, Lewis, you said this was the

way to handle it! I *listened* to you! You said you knew someone who could handle this! Sweet Jesus, Bridget?"

"Howard, you can vent later. Right now, we have to think. Fast."

Howard wants to rant some more, but appreciates that time is not on their side here. Lewis is right. They have to move quickly. "She can't be found there," Howard says. "Bridget can't be found in that apartment."

"I agree."

"But she has to be found. She can't just . . . disappear. That'll drag on for months."

"I agree."

Howard is thinking. He doesn't know the condition of Bridget's body, and does not want to know any details, except for one. "Is it possible to make this look like an accident, or better, self-inflicted?"

Lewis is quiet for three seconds. "Yes. Maybe." Then, "Morris and Bridget have several residences in the city."

"Yes."

"We need the one that's easiest to get into. One without cameras, or a doorman. I have people who can do this. They'll be dressed as movers."

Howard forces himself to concentrate. "Bridget's apartment, the one she had before she met Morris. Off Columbus. No doorman, and I remember her saying the surveillance cameras were for show. They're not hooked up to anything. She hung on to the place for when friends came into town. The key should still be on her ring."

"Address."

Howard gives it to him.

"Okay," Lewis says. "I know how we can do this. I have her phone. You'll get a call within the hour. From Bridget's phone. You'll take this call in front of Agatha. When you answer it, you'll pretend to talk to her."

"I'm not an idiot, Lewis."

"Howard, just let me work this out. You take the call, you ask her what's wrong, she's upset. Then she's going to hang up, and when Agatha asks what's going on, you say, 'Bridget said, "Howard, I'm so sorry, but he's sucking the life out of me. I can't take it anymore." ' Does that work for you?"

"Yes."

"Then call Morris. Tell him you're worried about Bridget. You got this strange call from her."

"I've got it." Howard's thinking of loose ends. "A note," he says.

"Way ahead of you," Lewis says. "Found a sample of her handwriting in her purse. Piece of cake. Done it before."

There are things Howard still does not know about Lewis. But as angry as he is, he's also grateful at this moment for his skills.

"Go," Howard says.

Lewis ends the call.

Howard takes a moment to attempt to decompress. He places his palms on the desk, leans back in the chair, closes his eyes, hoping he can go to that place where he can just catch his breath, but that place is a hundred thousand miles away.

Dear God.

Agatha, he suddenly remembers, is planning to go out to lunch with friends. He needs her here. She's his witness.

"Agatha," he says, walking out to her desk, making sure he has his cell with him, "I need you to pull together all the polling numbers we've done on Morris in the last six months."

"All those reports are in the computer," she says. "I can show you."

"I know, but what I want you to do is summarize the lot of them into a one-page memo for me. A hard copy."

"I'll get to that right after lunch," Agatha says.

"I need it now. As soon as you can get it to me."

Agatha glances at the time in the corner of her computer screen. "Of course, Howard. I'll get right on it. I'll just — I'm just going to have to make a call and reschedule something."

"Thanks, that's great."

His cell rings and it's as though a grenade has gone off in his Armani suit jacket. He attempts to disguise his alarm, takes out the phone and puts it to his ear without looking to see who it is.

"Howard here."

He is waiting to hear nothing. He is getting ready to say something like, *Bridget? Are you okay? What's wrong?*

Morris says, "Hey, we still a go for tonight?"

"Morris. Hello."

"Did you forget?"

"No, of course not. We have to talk."

"The *Times* hasn't been able to advance the story, but they've got to be trying."

"Agreed." He pauses. "Will Bridget be joining us?"

"No. This whole thing, it's making her so anxious, the last thing she wants is to hear about it through dinner."

"She's not the only one," Howard says.

"I still think it was the right call," Morris says. "If I had to make the same decision again, I'd do it. And if it comes out, that's what I'll say. See you tonight."

Howard slips the phone into his jacket and looks at Agatha, who is printing something off her screen. "I'm sorry. You had a lunch planned, didn't you?"

"It's okay," she says.

He returns to his office but leaves the door open. Tries to look busy, in case Agatha walks in. But it is impossible to focus on anything. He is waiting for the call. And thinking about how this could have happened.

He should have told Bridget to stay away from that Fitch woman. He hadn't thought it necessary. Not for a minute did Howard think she was going to connect with her again.

That she would go to Fitch's apartment. At the same time as —

His cell rings.

Howard grabs the phone, looks at the call display: BRIDGET.

"Hello?" he says, getting up from behind his desk, strolling out past Agatha's desk. She is stapling some papers together.

"Bridget, Bridget, what's wrong?" he says, standing by Agatha's desk. She senses something is amiss and stops what she's doing.

"Bridget, are you okay?" he says. Pauses. "Where are you? Tell me where you are."

Agatha's expression becomes increasingly concerned. Howard exchanges a worried glance with her.

"Bridget?" He takes the phone from his ear and says, "She hung up."

"What's wrong?" Agatha asks.

"She wasn't making any sense. She said she was sorry, and then something about how Morris was sucking the life out of her, and she couldn't take it anymore."

"She said *what?*"

"It was — it made no sense. She didn't sound like herself." He fumbles with his phone. "I'm calling her back."

He enters the number. "She's not answering. Come on, come on. Goddamn it, Bridget, answer the phone."

"Did she say where she was?"

"No. She's not picking up." He taps the phone. "I have to call Morris. Maybe he knows where she is."

Of course, Morris does not. He tries to get her on her phone, too. He, Howard, and Agatha start calling Bridget's friends. They try her favorite shops to see whether she has been there. The restaurants where she lunches with friends and clients.

Morris can't imagine where she might be, or what she meant by what she told Howard.

It isn't until hours later that Howard comes up with the idea of checking her old apartment. He and Morris get there before the police.

It is determined to be a suicide.

Most people, when they make the decision to kill themselves, choose more traditional methods. An overdose of pills. A gun to the temple. A leap off a tall building.

Bridget Sawchuck, the police determine, chose a more unorthodox, although not unheard of, technique. (Several people close to the investigation say it is reminiscent of how the Ben Kingsley character in *House of Sand and Fog* takes his life; there is speculation that she got the idea from the film, but neither Morris Sawchuck nor any of her friends know whether she ever actually saw it.)

First, she writes a note to her husband. Four words: "Morris: Forgive me. Bridget." Investigators will conclude it looks like her handwriting. Maybe a little off in a couple of places, but the woman was about to end her life, after all. Penmanship was not uppermost in her mind.

Once she has completed the note and places it on the carpet just inside the apartment door, she takes a garment bag from the closet and pulls it over her head. She secures it around her neck with several turns of duct tape. Forensic investigators will find traces of tape adhesive on her fingers.

With what little air she has left, she lies on the bed and secures her wrists to the bedpost with a set of handcuffs, so that once she starts panicking about being unable to breathe, she won't instinctively try to stop what she has set in motion. Morris will say he has no idea where she got these. Police will conclude she purchased the cuffs at some point from a sex shop — with cash — for the express purpose of using them to help end her own life.

There is, admittedly, much about the death that is suspicious. A woman cuffed to a bed with a plastic bag secured around her head. But there are no other signs of violence or any kind of struggle. No indications that anyone else was there. There is the short note.

Most persuasive of all is the call from her cell to Howard's. The cellular provider is able to determine the call came from the area where Bridget was found. Agatha tells the police she was right there when Howard got the call. She heard his side of the conversation. Bridget was clearly in distress.

Howard tells the police it was definitely Bridget on the phone. He knew her voice. And she did not sound coerced in any way. The call sounded entirely genuine.

Everyone involved knows this is a sensitive case. As sensitive as they come. The dead woman is the wife of the attorney general. Morris Sawchuck, through Howard, exercises his influence. There will be a complete lid put on this, given that the evidence tips toward suicide and not foul play. After a couple of days, a statement is released to the press that Bridget Sawchuck "died suddenly."

Code for "suicide." No further details are released.

A totally distraught Morris Sawchuck puts his political ambitions on hold and attempts to put his life back together.

Meanwhile, police conduct a cursory investigation into the seemingly unrelated disappearance of Allison Fitch. Lots of people go missing, and she has, according to her mother, vanished for extended periods before, usually surfacing when she needed money.

Courtney Walmers, more annoyed than

freaked out by her roommate's disappearance — she assumes Fitch ran off to avoid paying off her debts — is approached by a man who identifies himself as an undercover policeman. He tells her Allison Fitch, during the day, had been selling crack out of this apartment — Courtney didn't think much of Allison, but is shocked beyond belief, and baffled that if Allison was dealing drugs, why was she always broke? — and that the place is still under surveillance. He wants to sublet her apartment, maintain the appearance that it is still a place where drugs are sold. He will pay her first and last months' rent in a new location, as well as make up any money Fitch owed her.

Courtney is horrified. Courtney wants out. Courtney takes the deal.

Lewis Blocker sets up the motion-activated camera in the apartment door.

Nicole goes to Dayton in her search for Allison.

Morris grieves.

Howard wonders every day whether he will have a heart attack.

And then, nine months later, a man comes knocking on the apartment door with a printout of a murder that the entire world can see if they only know where to look.

FORTY-ONE

Julie said, "Okay, so let's go through this again."

I had my clothes on now, sitting on Thomas's bed, and he was back in his chair in front of his three monitors. Julie and I sat like pupils in front of a teacher who was reviewing what was going to be on the final.

Julie said, "Thomas here sees this picture on the Net, manages to get you to go to this address in Manhattan to check it out, which you do, but not really, since your heart's not really in it, but you do talk to some lady who lives next door."

"Yeah," I said.

"And Thomas, who's totally unimpressed with your investigatory skills, calls the landlord and finds out two women used to live in this place, but they've both moved out, and the place has been sitting empty since then, but the rent's being paid by some guy named Blocker. How'm I doing so far?"

Thomas nodded. "Excellent." He looked at

405

me. "She's doing very well."

"Go on," I said.

"And within a couple of days of your little mission, the image on Whirl360 is altered," Julie said. "*That* kind of blows my mind."

"Yeah, mine, too," I said. "But it doesn't make any sense. I didn't say anything to the woman down the hall about seeing the image online. Thomas, did you say anything to the landlord about what you saw in the window, on your computer?"

He shook his head. "No."

"So then, what's the connection?" I asked.

Julie was thinking. "You didn't tell why you were at that address? Did you tell that guy you had lunch with? Your agent?"

"No. I didn't mention a word of it to him."

"Nobody followed you?"

I gave Julie an eye roll. "Really."

She grimaced. "Okay, maybe that's a bit out there. But think back to when you got to the place on Orchard Street."

I sighed. "After I finished the meeting I grabbed a cab and got out at Orchard, a few blocks north of where I needed to be. I headed down, slowly, with the printout in my hand, comparing the window patterns and the brick and everything until I was sure I had the right building. It had the same air-conditioning unit in the window and everything."

"How'd you get in?"

"Some guy was coming out and I slipped in. I went upstairs, knocked on the door, no one answered. Nothing else to tell."

Julie was thinking. "What were you going to say, if someone had opened the door?"

"I was going through several ideas in my head and finally decided to play it straight. That we'd seen this image on Whirl360 and were curious to find out what it was."

Thomas shook his head disappointingly.

"So you had the printout in your hand the whole time," Julie said.

"Yeah, I guess I did."

"So the person heading out of the building saw it, the neighbor lady saw it, and anyone else you walked past saw it."

"No . . . I don't think . . . Shit. I took it out at one point, and I know I put it back in my pocket eventually, but I'm not sure when."

"So that lady might have seen it," Julie said. "Or someone else you didn't even notice."

"Maybe there was a camera in the lobby," Thomas said. "Didn't you think of that?"

I looked angrily at him. "No, I did not think of that. Why the hell would I think of that?" But I supposed it was possible. Calming down, I said, "Okay, let's say somebody, somehow, saw that sheet of paper I was carrying. How do we make the leap from that to the image disappearing online now?"

Julie said, "For the sake of argument, why don't we say that what Thomas saw in the

407

window was . . . *something*. Something that someone —"

"Like who?" I asked.

"Work with me here. Okay? Let's say whatever's shown in the window is something someone wouldn't be pleased to find out was online. And once they found out it was, they had to have it removed. Think about it. Think of all the candid shots these Whirl360 cars have taken. Husbands cheating on wives, wives cheating on husbands."

"But they blur the faces," I said.

"Okay, but let's say, for example, just for fun, you're some guy in Hartford and you want to see if your house is on Whirl360, and you find it, there's a car in the driveway you recognize as your golfing buddy's Lincoln, except he's never been to your house. But your wife's home during the day, when the picture was taken. Or let's say you're that guy with the Lincoln, and you find out that picture's up there before your friend does. What do you do?"

"I get what you're saying."

Thomas chimed in, "It's like that car I saw that hit the other car in Boston." To Julie, he said, "Ray wouldn't do anything about that."

"There's all kinds of shit online that if you knew about it, you'd freak out," Julie said. "And maybe when you were waving around that piece of paper, you tipped somebody off about the head in the window."

"Maybe," I conceded. "So let's say you're right, and that my visit and the doctoring of the image are linked. How the hell would you go online and change it?"

"You'd hack in," Thomas said.

Julie nodded. "Sounds logical. How else would you do it, right?"

"I guess," I said.

"It'd be worth calling Whirl360, asking them if anyone has tried lately to break into their system," Julie said. "Get through their firewall or whatever they call it."

"Where would you begin?" I asked. "Who would you call?"

Julie smiled. "You may know how to draw pictures but you're clearly clueless when it comes to getting answers. I'll take that on."

Julie obviously had the smarts to find stuff out. What I was less sure was whether we should be trying. Was this something we needed to get involved in? Could nosing around backfire, get Thomas in trouble? We'd already had the FBI here. Did we want Whirl360's security people at our door, too?

But I kept those concerns to myself, at least for the moment, because I had more immediate questions. "Thomas, tell me again what the landlord said when you called him. About the women who used to live there?"

"He said the apartment got empty late last summer. I don't think they were sisters or related. They had different names."

"What were they again?"

"Courtney and Olsen."

"Those were their first names?"

"I think so. I had a hard time understanding him because of the accent. I told you that."

"Olsen doesn't sound like a woman's first name," Julie said. "Did he give you their full names?"

Thomas turned to his desk. "I wrote it down," he said. "Courtney Walmers and Olsen Fitch."

"Wait a second," I said. Something about the name rang a bell. "Olsen Fitch?" Hadn't I come across a name like that recently? "Thomas, let me sit there." I got him out of his computer chair, opened up a new browser, and conducted the same search I'd done on Dad's laptop of any news stories that had mentioned New York's Orchard Street.

"Hang on . . . hang on," I said. "Here we are. I knew that name rang a bell. Thomas, is it possible the landlord was saying 'Allison Fitch' instead of 'Olsen Fitch?' "

Thomas thought. "I guess."

"Okay, so here's a story about the police issuing a statement that they were trying to find an Allison Fitch. She lived on Orchard, and worked at some bar and didn't show up for work. There's just the one story here, no follow-up."

"That's probably the person in the window," Thomas said, standing close to me, like he wanted his chair back as soon as I was willing to surrender it. "It's a woman. She got smothered, and then they got rid of her body."

For a guy who didn't watch TV crime shows, Thomas was pretty fast with possible scenarios.

"Thomas," I said, "why don't you sit back down here while Julie and I talk about how to handle this."

"Are you going to go finish having sex?" Thomas asked.

I felt my own face flush, but Julie was very cool. "Maybe later," she said. "We're going to talk about this first. We can have sex any old time."

Thomas was already back at it, exploring some city that looked to be European. Sensing my curiosity, he said, "Prague."

Julie and I retreated into the map-covered upstairs hallway.

"What do you think?" I asked.

She raised her hands hopelessly. "Damned if I know."

"Same here."

We went down to the kitchen. Julie went looking for coffee and found a jar of instant. "Tell me this isn't all you have."

It was. As she filled a kettle she said, "Call me crazy, but I think there's something going on here."

411

"Yeah," I said reluctantly.

"Why the hell would someone erase that head from the window if there wasn't something funny about it?"

"Agreed."

"So what are you going to do?"

"Do?"

"I know you said you weren't really going to call the New York police like Thomas asked, but that was then. You gonna call them now?"

"None of the reasons that would have kept me from calling before have changed," I said.

Julie looked surprised. "Excuse me? That altered picture sort of changes things."

I reminded her about the FBI. "Thomas is already on their radar for sending e-mails to the CIA and Bill Clinton. Say we call the New York police, or even the Promise Falls cops. That'll probably trigger some sort of alarm, and the FBI'll be notified. And when the FBI brings everyone up to speed on my brother's activities, that he's been writing the CIA with all his street memorization updates, just how seriously do you think anyone's going to take him? Especially when what he claims to have seen is no longer on Whirl360?"

Julie's shoulders slumped. "Shit. But there's more than just what Thomas saw, and you still have the earlier printout. And there's that missing woman."

"Who may or may not still be missing," I said.

"Yeah, but that can be checked. Ray, I get your hesitation here, and being worried that the cops will think there's nothing to it, but I gotta tell ya, this makes the hairs on the back of my neck stand on end. I know what I'm going to do. Tomorrow I'm going to call Whirl360 and talk to whoever's in charge of muddying images on the site and ask if someone hacked into it. Or if they changed it themselves for some reason."

"And you think I should call the cops," I said.

"I think you should call the cops."

I raised my hands in defeat. "Fine, I'll call the cops. Which ones?"

"NYPD," Julie said.

"I don't even know what precinct that would be." Using Dad's laptop, we concluded it was the seventh. I entered a number on the Web site into my cell phone. "Here goes," I said to Julie while I waited for the connection.

"Yeah, hello," I said when someone picked up. "I need to talk to a . . . I guess I need to talk to a detective."

"Is that an emergency call, sir?"

"No, it's not. I mean, it's important, but it's not an emergency."

"Hold on."

A few seconds later, someone else picked

413

up. A man with a gruff voice. "Simpkins."

"Hi, my name is Ray Kilbride. I'm calling from Promise Falls."

"What can I do for you, Mr. Kilbride?"

"Okay, this is going to sound kind of crazy, but I just need you to hear me out. My brother may have witnessed a homicide. Or something."

"What's your brother's name?"

"Thomas Kilbride."

"And the reason you're calling and he isn't?"

"I think he's more comfortable if I do this."

"And that's because?"

"Look, that really doesn't matter, and the thing is, he's not really the only witness."

"Who else is a witness? Are you a witness, Mr. Kilbride?"

"Sort of. The thing is, there could be a great many witnesses. There's a record of the crime on the Internet. At least, there was."

A pause at the other end of the line. "I see. Who got killed, Mr. Kilbride?"

"Okay, I don't know for certain that *anyone* did, but it looks like someone being killed in a window. And it might be a woman named Allison Fitch."

"Is this something you saw posted on YouTube, sir?" the detective asked, his voice already filled with skepticism.

"No, it was on Whirl360, where you can —"

414

"I know what it is. You telling me your brother thinks he saw a homicide on that site?"

"That's right. Listen, at first I thought he was imagining it, but —"

"Why would you have thought he was imagining it, sir?"

"Because my brother has a history of psychiatric problems and —"

Click.

I looked at Julie.

"You don't have to tell me," she said. "I'd have hung up, too. Could you have laid it out for him any worse?"

"I told you it was a bad idea."

Julie threw her hands up. "Okay, you were right, I was wrong. You want to stay out of this, not get Thomas involved, I suppose that makes perfect sense. You've got no stake in this personally. And even if someone did see you with that printout, they've got no idea who you are."

"That's right. I didn't give anyone my name."

"Well, there you go," Julie said. "You've got nothing to worry about."

FORTY-TWO

"Let me have a look at the picture again?" the woman behind the counter said.

Lewis Blocker handed her the printout at the art store in Lower Manhattan. It was a screen-capture image from the surveillance video shot through the door of the Fitch apartment. It was the best image he'd been able to get of the man who'd come knocking with the Whirl360 image in hand. The face was slightly fish-eyed, but Lewis thought it was good enough for someone to make an identification.

She'd already glanced at it once and said she didn't know the guy, then decided she wanted to have another look at it.

"So what'd this guy do, exactly?"

"Credit card fraud," Lewis said. "Identity theft."

"Oh yeah," she said. "That's a big problem."

Lewis guessed the woman was around thirty. Jet black hair, skin like Morticia

Addams, ruby red lipstick. She had studs in her ears, one through her right nostril, and another just below her lip. Lewis wondered how many other piercings she had that weren't visible, where they might be.

She held the sheet in her hand and cocked her head to one side. "His face looks kind of puffy."

"That's just the way the camera makes it look," Lewis explained.

"I don't know. I thought maybe I recognized him, but now I'm not so sure."

"Let me tell you what this guy's been up to," Lewis said, hopeful that once she knew what a bad person he was she'd be more inclined to help. He hadn't actually told her he was a cop, but had flashed an open wallet at her, just long enough for her to get the idea. "He rips off real credit card numbers from real people, then makes new cards with all that personal data transferred onto it, goes on a wild buying spree for a couple of days, then ditches the card. Usually, by that time, the credit company has caught on to the fact that the usual spending for this card has changed, has alerted the owner, and shut the card down."

She shook her head in wonder. "Fuckin' amazing." There was a hint of admiration there, like maybe she was wishing she could figure out how to do this herself. "I thought, ever since everyone started using those chip

417

cards, this stuff didn't happen anymore."

"If only," Lewis said. "New technology just slows the bad guys a while until they figure out a new way around it."

He told her when he believed the man had been in the store. A couple of mornings ago.

"I was on, but I don't remember this guy," she said. She looked across the store, saw a tall, dark man restocking brushes. "Tarek, you got a second?"

Tarek came over and stood across the counter from the woman, next to Lewis.

"This cop here's trying to find this dude," she said. "I don't recognize him, but he says he was in and bought some shit couple mornings ago."

"What's he done?" Tarek asked, examining the printout.

Lewis went through it again.

"We still get paid, though," Tarek said. "If it's credit card fraud, the credit card company pays back the cardholder."

"I know," Lewis said. "But that doesn't mean it's not in your interest to try to help get this guy."

"Yeah, well, it won't make any difference with him," Tarek said.

"What do you mean?"

"I remember him. He paid cash."

"Cash?" Lewis said. Who the hell paid cash anymore?

"He bought some airbrush supplies, I think,

418

and some markers."

"Do you know who he is? Has he shopped here before?"

"I don't know who he is, but yeah, he's been here before. At least that's what he said. Said every time he's in the city, he pops in."

"He's from out of town?"

"Yeah."

"Did he say where?"

Tarek shook his head. "I don't think. I asked him if he was on our e-mail list, and he said he was."

"Can I have a look at that?"

"I don't think the manager'd want to just turn it over. Besides, there's hundreds and hundreds of people on it."

"What was he buying the airbrush equipment for? Specifically. What kind of work does he do?"

Tarek thought a moment, the studded woman looking at him expectantly. "He said he was an illustrator. But you know, there's only a few million of those. Oh, yeah, and he said he was going to be doing some stuff for a news Web site."

"What Web site?"

"Some new one. I don't know. Something political, like the HuffPo."

"The what?" Lewis asked. He knew his way around the Internet, but he still preferred a real newspaper to reading one online.

Tarek shrugged. "You know, the one with

the lady with the accent. She's on Bill Maher's show once in a while."

Lewis hated that guy's program. Left-wing dickhead.

"But not that site? A different one?"

Tarek shrugged. "That's all I know. Good luck."

Lewis got a booth at a cafe around the corner, ordered a corned beef on rye with a dill pickle and coffee, and called Howard Talliman.

"You know that HuffPo site?" he asked.

"Of course," Howard said. "Why?"

"You know about some new site that's coming out that's similar to it?"

"I could ask around," Howard said. "Why?"

"Just ask and get back to me quick as you can."

Lewis was finishing his coffee when his cell rang. "Kathleen Ford's starting one up," Howard said.

"Should I know who the hell she is?"

"Yes."

"Okay, so I think it's possible she may have hired our man to work for her."

"You got a name?"

"Not yet, but I will. You got some contacts for this Ford chick?" Lewis had out his pen and notepad, scribbled down a couple of numbers Howard gave him. "You know her?"

"We are familiar with each other," Howard said. "But I wouldn't drop my name. She thinks I'm a reptile."

Lewis ended the call, thinking maybe this Kathleen Ford was a pretty good judge of character, although he had no illusions that, if she were to meet him, she'd view him any differently.

FORTY-THREE

She so wanted to call her mother. It was like an ache.

It had been nine months. Allison Fitch couldn't believe she'd managed to hold off this long. Not that she hadn't considered it dozens of times. More than once she'd picked up a phone — not her own; she'd pitched it within minutes of fleeing her apartment building — and started dialing. Once, she'd discovered a cell on a stall floor in the ladies' room at the Lubbock restaurant where she was working briefly, and dialed every digit of her mother's phone number but the last before she'd thought better of it and dropped the phone back where she'd found it. It was entirely possible her mother's line was being tapped, her place being watched. Her mother didn't own a cell phone, and even if she did, Allison figured there was probably a way to bug those, too. Didn't they do it on that TV show about the drug trade in Baltimore?

She didn't know for certain, of course, that

anyone was listening to her mother's phone conversations. But assuming they were, was it likely they were still doing it now, all these months later? Sooner or later, wouldn't they just give up?

Allison could only imagine what her mother was going through. True, she had a history of putting Mom through this kind of anguish. When she was nineteen, hours before boarding her flight, Allison had informed her mother she'd be gone to Uruguay for a month with her boyfriend, the one who played electric piano in that band, and she'd been away for ten days before she even realized they'd actually gone to Paraguay. Then, at twenty-one she was given a car — an old rusted Neon, but who's complaining — by her uncle Bert, on her father's side, which prompted her to check out Malibu, which was only twenty-two hundred or so miles away. Threw some clothes in a bag and set off on her own. Five days into the trip she decided to drop in unannounced on her cousin Portia in Albuquerque, which was along the way, and when Portia opened the door and saw her she screamed, "Oh my God you have to call your mother she's called everyone in the family and thinks you're dead!"

But disappearing for nine months was, even by Allison's standards of irresponsibility, over the top.

There was no way to tell her mother it was different this time, that there was no safe way to let her know she hadn't called home not because she was a thoughtless, self-centered twit, but because she was afraid that if she did, she'd get herself killed.

Allison figured it was better to put her mother through hell and show up one day, alive, than put her mind at ease by calling and end up dead. In some ways, she thought, maybe her history of never considering how her actions affected others was a blessing. Perhaps it would make her mother worry less. If Allison were the kind of daughter who always let her parents know where she was every minute of the day, and then went missing, well, that'd be a real cause for concern.

Allison wanted to think that was the case, but knew in her heart it wasn't. Her mother had to be going out of her mind.

Occasionally, during her travels, she'd borrow someone's computer and do a search on herself, see if there were any news stories about her disappearance. There was one, not long after she'd gone missing, but very little after that. Not much comfort there. Knowing that you mattered so little. That you could vanish off the face of the earth and they weren't putting your face on the side of milk cartons. Maybe she was too old for that.

But there certainly were stories about the death of Bridget Sawchuck.

Whoa.

They were short on details, but what few details there were Allison knew to be total flights of fucking fantasy.

"Died suddenly." Yeah, well, that was sort of true. But not really.

If Allison hadn't been totally convinced before that running and hiding was the smartest thing to do, she certainly was after seeing the stories about Bridget. If the powers that be could cover up the murder of a woman like her, they could do anything.

Coming forward was not an option. Of course, to do so would mean she'd have to cop to a blackmail scheme, but she figured that to be the least of her problems. Allison feared that telling the authorities what she knew could get her killed.

So she kept moving. Starting with her flight from her apartment.

The second Allison Fitch saw what had happened in that bedroom, that someone had been sent — clearly — to kill her and had murdered Bridget Sawchuck by mistake, she just ran. She came out onto Orchard so fast, passersby could have been forgiven for thinking there'd been a gas explosion. She ran south for no particular reason except that if she'd gone north she'd have had to dodge a group of five middle-aged women blocking the sidewalk as they all tried to share one Fodor's book. She turned west at the first corner, then north at the next, west at the one after that, running flat out, going in a different direction at every cross street, her only goal to elude whoever that woman was who'd killed Bridget.

She turned, abruptly, into a coffee shop. She had no idea what street she was on. As she flew past the counter she shouted, "Latte, medium," so no one would give her a hard time about using the bathroom, looked desperately for a sign that would tell her where it was, and instinctively descended a set of narrow brick steps to the basement. Found it, tried the door. It was locked.

"Just a minute," someone called from inside.

Allison stood there at the bottom of the stairs, watching, waiting for that woman to come down after her.

A man emerged from the bathroom. She slipped into the tiny room with its one toilet and sink, dropped the lid, and sat down. She got out her phone as she struggled to get her breath.

Thought about who to call.

When your brilliant plan to blackmail the wife of an attorney general goes south, and people at the highest levels send someone to kill you, who do you call?

Good question.

Looking at the phone, she suddenly realized it might be used to track her. She powered it down, lifted the lid off the toilet tank, and dropped it in.

Think, think.

Okay, going to the police was too risky. And it was a safe bet they'd be watching her mother's place. She couldn't call any of her friends. She'd burned most of them, anyway, like Courtney. Borrowed money she'd never paid back. Taken tips meant for others. Slept with friends' boyfriends.

There wasn't a bridge she hadn't burned.

You are one stupid bitch, she thought.

She had a few hundred dollars in her purse. Enough to buy a bus ticket out of New York. Once she was out of the city, and felt reasonably safe, she'd have to figure out her next step.

Someone banged on the bathroom door. Allison's heart skipped a beat.

"Hey! You eatin' a pizza in there or what?"

She settled first in Pittsburgh, if one defined "settled" as a place you stay for more than one night. Her bus ticket took her as far as Philadelphia. From there she hitchhiked. Figured she'd just head west, but not in a direction that took her too close to Dayton. Slept in a park in Harrisburg her first night, then in the morning went into a McDonald's restroom and tried to make herself look like a human being with what she had in her purse, which amounted to little more than a comb, lipstick, eyeliner, and mascara. She needed work, no question about it. A shower, to start.

Allison didn't see that she had much choice but to find a homeless shelter. She was given something to eat and had a shower. She brought her purse in with her, hanging it just out of reach of the spray, so it wouldn't be stolen.

Her credit cards were useless to her. Most were maxed out, anyway, but she knew the moment she used one, they'd have her. She snapped all of them in two and tossed them in the trash.

One of the conditions of staying at the shelter was that she would have to help out. She opted for the kitchen detail. It was the closest thing they had to the work she'd normally done. She stuck it out there for the better part of a week, until one day when a pair of city cops came in asking questions. Not about her — they were looking for witnesses to the beating death of a homeless man three nights earlier — but they spoke face-to-face with Allison. She worried that if her face was on a missing persons file anywhere, and these two cops happened to see it, they'd remember where they'd run into her.

Time to put more distance between herself and New York.

Her plan had been to keep heading west, but that would take her right past Cincinnati, and that was a little too close for comfort to Dayton. What if someone she knew, who knew her mother, recognized her? She didn't want to take the chance, so she tacked in a southerly direction, hitching several rides that landed her in Charlottesville, a beautiful college town. She didn't find herself working in the halls of academia, however. She got another kitchen job, in a diner that had a "Help Wanted" sign in the window.

By this time, she'd spent all her cash, and the diner job wasn't enough to allow her to find a place to stay. Lester, who owned the diner, said she could sleep in his truck, a Ford pickup with a bench seat, and use the restaurant bathroom to clean up.

She lived that way for five weeks before moving on. Lester was starting to expect certain favors in return for the fine accommodation he was providing her. Allison wasn't interested, on any level, but it took a raw egg down the front of his pants to persuade Lester.

Time to hit the road, again.

She hitched to Raleigh. Then Athens. A couple of hungry weeks in Charleston. Then, farther south, to Jacksonville. It was a good plan, getting to Florida as winter started to settle in. She didn't have a coat or winter clothes, and had no money to buy any.

As she became more desperate, she occasionally suppressed her nature and found a way to say thank you to the men who gave her rides, provided they were willing to throw a few bucks her way. You did what you had to do.

In Tampa, she found work making up rooms at a motel called the Coconut Shade, a place where customers often rented by the hour. No references, no ID, no previous work experience required. She said her name was Adele Farmer. Octavio Famosa, the manager, of Cuban descent and in his midforties, offered her not a place to sleep in his truck, but a rollaway bed in a storage room.

Allison figured he'd be looking for something in return, like most of the men she'd encountered, but she was wrong. Octavio was a kind, decent man. His wife, Samira, had died the year before from liver disease. He was raising their seven-year-old daughter, but he did not like to bring her to his place of work because it was not a proper environment. A place where people came, almost exclusively, to have sex. So his sister looked after his daughter when he had to work.

"People have needs," he said, and shrugged. "And yours is for a safe place to stay. I have been where you are."

Some days, he'd share his lunch with her. Every once in a while, on the night shift, he'd give her ten dollars from the till and send her to the nearby Burger King for something they could split. They would talk. Octavio's par-

ents were still in Cuba, and he hoped someday to bring them to Florida. "Before they
are too old to come," he said. "I want them
to see their granddaughter. What about you?"

"There's just my mom," she said. "My dad
died a few years ago, and I don't have any
brothers or sisters."

"Where is your mother?" Octavio asked.

"Seattle," she lied. "I haven't talked to her
for a while."

"I bet she misses you," he said.

"Yeah, well," she said. "Not much I can do
about that."

"You remind me of my daughter," he said.

"How is that possible? She's just a little
girl."

"I know, but you both need your mothers.
You are both very sad."

This entire experience, from the moment
she'd fled her apartment to living now in
Tampa, had given Allison Fitch time to do a
lot of soul searching.

She was not, she concluded, a very good
person.

She had lived off others and offered nothing in return, starting with her parents. She'd
always thought of herself first. Her wants, her
needs. What kind of person, she'd started asking herself, lies to her mother so she'll send
money? What kind of person uses that money
to book a vacation when she owes rent to her
roommate? What kind of person turns a

sexual relationship into an opportunity for a huge financial payoff? What kind of person resorts to blackmail?

A bad person.

A very bad person.

A total shit.

That's what she was. Maybe, she kept telling herself, she had it coming. She'd brought this on herself. That much was clear. She wouldn't be here, after months on the run, changing stained sheets in a one-star hotel in a bad part of Tampa, sharing Whoppers with Octavio, if she hadn't always thought of herself first.

Karma was some bitch.

One night, talking to Octavio, she said, "Do you believe that if you do bad things, eventually you get punished?"

"In this world?" he asked.

"Yeah, I guess."

He shook his head regretfully. "Sometimes yes, sometimes no. I have known people who, their entire lives, deserved to be punished for the things they had done, but never were. All one can hope for is that they get what's coming to them after."

"If you get what you deserve while you're still alive, do you think, when you die, that things are already settled?"

"I don't believe you are a bad person," Octavio told her. "I believe you are a good person."

432

She cried. She cried for a very long time. She cried so long that she exhausted herself. Octavio tucked her into her rollaway bed in the storage room. He sat on the edge of the bed and patted her shoulder until she went to sleep.

He wanted to help her. He believed that whatever Adele Farmer had done, her mother would forgive her.

When he was sure Adele was sleeping soundly, he took her purse from beneath her bed. In it, he found identification that showed she was not Adele Farmer at all. She was Allison Fitch.

And her mother was not in Seattle, as Allison had said. There was a tattered letter in the purse, a letter from her mother dated more than a year ago, in which she told her daughter that she loved her very much, and hoped that she was happy in New York, but that she was always welcome to move back to Dayton.

Dayton?

Octavio checked the return address sticker on the back of the envelope, wrote down some information, then returned the letter and the ID to the purse and slid it back under the rollaway bed. He went online and found a phone number for Doris Fitch. It was late to be calling — it was past midnight — but Octavio was sure the woman would want to know where her daughter was, regardless of the hour.

When he got Doris Fitch on the phone, he spoke in a whisper, but she was nearly hysterical at the news.

"Oh my God," she said. "Oh my God, she's alive. I can't believe it. How is she? Is she hurt? Is she okay? Put her on! Put her on the phone. I have to hear her voice."

Octavio said he believed that if Allison knew he had been speaking to her mother, she would take off, that it would be better if Doris were to come down from Ohio and surprise her daughter.

Doris Fitch, who was thrilled by this news but still smart enough to be cautious, said that if Octavio was not going to put her daughter on the phone, she needed some sort of proof that it was really her daughter working at the motel.

Octavio said, "She told me that when she was little, around eight or nine, you would do finger puppet plays, that you would reenact entire scenes from *The Wizard of Oz* for her with your fingers, and that she loved it so much."

Doris Fitch thought she would die.

"I'll get a flight out tomorrow," she said. "Tell me where you are, exactly."

Octavio gave her the name of the motel, and the address. "When you get off the plane, just tell the cabdriver. He will find it."

When he got off the phone, Octavio felt

very good about himself. He had done a good thing.

Adele — Allison — was going to be so surprised.

FORTY-FOUR

I'd made an appointment for two, Monday afternoon, to meet with Darla Kurtz, who was the administrator of Glace House, a residence for psychiatric outpatients. I'd left Julie at the house. She'd already spent the entire morning on the phone trying, with very little success, to track down someone to talk to at Whirl360.

Glace House was actually a beautiful, celery green three-story Victorian home in an older part of Promise Falls, with gingerbread trim and a porch that wrapped around two sides. Most likely built in the 1920s, it sat on a corner, with an expansive front yard and hedges running along both sidewalks. I parked on the street and as I walked up the driveway spotted a wispy-haired, stick-thin man in jeans and a T-shirt putting a fresh coat of white paint on the front porch railing.

"Hello," he said to me.

"Hi," I said.

"You can't be too careful," he said.

436

"I'm sorry?"

"You can't be too careful," he repeated.

"About what?" I asked.

He smiled. "That's what they say." He gave me a wink and went back to his work.

I rang the front bell and a short woman in her fifties held the door open for me. "How are you?" she said.

"Ms. Kurtz?" I said.

She nodded.

"I'm Ray Kilbride. We were talking about my brother, Thomas? I think Laura Grigorin was in touch with you?"

Another nod. "Of course," she said, peering over a pair of reading glasses.

If she were a man, I'd say she had a brush cut, but maybe you don't call it that when it's a woman. She led me into her office, which was in a room just off the front foyer. Years ago, this must have been a very stately home, but a quick look showed that it had been made into apartments. A plump woman in a heavy winter coat was sitting on a set of steps that led to the second floor. It was as warm in the house as it was outside, and I couldn't understand why she was wearing it. She stared at me blankly as I slipped into the office.

"First, thanks for seeing me," I said. The wall of her office showed degrees in psychology and social work. "I've heard some good things about Glace House."

She smiled. "Well, we try."

I gave her a quick sketch on Thomas. "I guess he's what you'd call pretty high functioning in many ways. But not quite able to live on his own, at least that's my worry. Our father died recently, and he looked after all of Thomas's needs. Made his meals, did the laundry, cleaned the house, didn't really expect anything of Thomas, which in turn, I guess, made my brother pretty dependent. But I think, given the opportunity, he's perfectly capable. Dad just found it easier to do everything himself. But even if Thomas could look after himself and his meals and so forth, I don't think he's capable of looking after the house himself. Paying bills, making sure the property taxes are looked after, that type of thing. I'm not sure he'd be able to handle it. And the thing is, he does have some strange notions."

The woman smiled. "He'll fit in fine here, then. Did you meet Ziggy?"

"Ziggy?"

"He's painting out front."

"Yes, I did. He mentioned something about not being too careful."

"That's because any one of us might be an alien. In disguise."

"Oh," I said. "Good advice, I suppose. Listen, I don't know whether Laura mentioned that my brother is pretty attached to his computer."

"I believe she did say something about that."

"He's always on those sites where you can explore city streets. Would that be a problem if he lived here?"

She shook her head. "No. In fact, many of the residents have them. It keeps them in touch and connected and entertained." She rolled her eyes. "Not always the kind of entertainment I would prefer."

"Thomas has been known to fire off e-mails that have caused us a bit of grief later." I filled her in.

"Well," she said, "it happens. If someone were to do that here, we'd have to remove Internet privileges for a period of time. If it persisted, we'd have to cut them off. But most everyone here, they're eager to please."

She showed me around. The house was orderly and well maintained. In the kitchen, I found one resident loading a dishwasher while another sat at a table eating a jelly sandwich. There were two rooms sitting empty on the second floor, one that looked out to the street and the other overlooking the backyard.

"Views don't matter a lot to Thomas," I said. "You'd probably be best saving the better one for someone else."

Each of the rooms was roughly twelve by twelve feet. There was a bed, a couple of chairs, and a desk. There were two bathrooms on each floor.

"You'll want to bring him over," she said, "to check things out."

"Yeah," I nodded, feeling anxious.

Another woman approached. She was wearing a cardigan that looked a couple of sizes too big, a peasant skirt, and a pair of those neon purple plastic sandals, Crocs. Her hair was long and frizzy, and she looked pretty riled.

She stood in front of the two of us and said to me, "Are you Ray Kilbride?"

"Yes," I said, hesitantly.

She extended a hand. "I'm Darla Kurtz."

Slowly, I accepted her hand and gave it a shake, all the while looking at my tour guide. She smiled sheepishly at me.

The new Darla Kurtz said to me, "I'm sorry. I got held up at a city hall meeting." Then, to my guide, she said, "Barbara, you've been very naughty, again."

"I'm sorry, Mrs. Kurtz."

"I'll talk to you later."

"Okay." Barbara turned to me and said, "I hope Thomas gets to come and stay here. He sounds really interesting."

I got out of there about an hour later. The real Darla Kurtz was every bit as welcoming as the phony one, but she had more specific questions. She also wanted me to bring Thomas in for a visit.

I was getting into the car when my cell rang.

"Get this," Julie said.

"What?"

"So I've been getting bounced all over the place at Whirl360. The place is in absolute chaos."

I slammed the door and reached for the seat belt with my free hand. "So they have been hacked?"

"No, shit, not that. One of their top people got killed."

"What? When?"

"Yesterday. Him and his wife."

"Who are we talking about?"

"Hang on, I made some notes. Okay, the guy's name was Kyle Billings, and his wife's name was Rochelle. They live in Oak Park, in Chicago. That's where the company's head office is. The wife's sister was trying to get in touch with her last night, couldn't get her or her husband on the phone, no answer at the house but both cars were there. So they called the police, and they were both in the basement. Dead."

"Jesus."

"Yeah, no kidding," Julie said. "Guess what Billings did at Whirl360?"

"Tell me."

"He's the guy who wrote the program that automatically blurs faces and license plates and all that kind of thing."

I was about to put the key into the ignition

441

and stopped. "Jesus."

"And this other stuff, I just got this off the *Chicago Tribune* Web site. They're attributing this to unnamed sources in the police department. How they died."

"Go on."

"Okay, so Billings was stabbed. Something very long and pointed, like an ice pick, maybe. But the wife — are you sitting down?"

"Julie, for Christ's sake, just tell me."

"She was suffocated, Ray. Someone put a bag over her head."

FORTY-FIVE

Lewis Blocker went online and read everything he could find about Kathleen Ford and her new Web site. She had a lot of money to put behind it, and was said to be attracting big names to write for it. She'd lured a prominent columnist from the *New York Times*. Some well-known talking heads from Fox and MSNBC had agreed to be regular contributors. There'd be plenty of celebrity gossip. In these respects, it was much like the site it was taking on. But Kathleen Ford was going to offer a few new things, too. She'd attracted two or three novelists — Stephen King and John Grisham were among those rumored to have been approached — who would write serially for it. Every week, a new installment, just like in the old Victorian newspapers. There was even some mention of an animated political cartoon, but there was no hint as to who might produce it.

Lewis took special note of that.

He wrote down a few questions, thought

about how he was going to play this, and then found a contact number for the public relations department of Kathleen Ford's enterprise.

He was put in touch with a woman named Florence Highgold. Lewis couldn't believe it was a real name, but she did actually work there, so what the hell. Lewis explained that he was doing a freelance business piece on Ford's new Web site for the *Wall Street Journal.* He was particularly interested in the kind of talent pool Ford was intending to draw from.

"This whole serialized novel thing," Lewis said. "I'd heard that the guy who wrote *The Da Vinci Code* had been talked into writing something."

Florence laughed. "Even with the resources Ms. Ford has, I'm not sure she could afford him."

"Well, if she can afford King and Grisham —"

"We're not confirming that either of those men have in fact been commissioned to do anything for the Web site," Florence said.

Lewis asked her about the launch date for the site, how many visits they expected it to receive. Would it be a site you had to pay to read? And if not, would all their income be derived from advertising?

He made it sound like an afterthought

when he asked, "And what about artists? Does a site like that need a lot of illustrators?"

"Well, you certainly need Web artists to come up with a concept for the site," Florence said. "You need a distinctive graphic design. But once you have that up and running, it kind of runs itself."

"So it's not like you'd have contributing artists in the way you would contributing writers."

"That's not entirely true. We've already said we'd like to do animated political cartoons."

"You have someone for that?"

"We do," Florence said. "Are you familiar with Ray Kilbride's work?"

Even as she said the name, Lewis was tapping it into a search engine. When the results popped up, he hit Images.

The screen filled with dozens of postage-stamp-sized pictures.

"Yeah, I believe I have," Lewis said. He clicked on an illustration of Newt Gingrich that had appeared in a Chicago magazine, credited to Ray Kilbride. "He did that Gingrich drawing, didn't he?"

"He may have. He's done so many," Florence said.

Lewis clicked again and up came a caricature of noted New York crime boss Carlo Vachon, sticking up the Statue of Liberty. "And I remember one he did of that mob guy."

"Maybe," Florence said. "Like I said, he's got a pretty comprehensive portfolio."

"Uh-huh," Lewis said, clicking to a second full page of images.

One of them was not an illustration, but a photograph. He clicked on it. Up popped a photo of a man leaning over a drafting table, sleeves rolled up, an airbrush in his hand, smiling at the camera.

The photograph was from an art magazine's Web site, and accompanied a short article about Ray Kilbride, who lived in Burlington, Vermont.

"Are you there?" Florence said.

"Yeah, yeah, I'm here," Lewis said, holding alongside his computer monitor the printout he'd been showing around the art store, comparing the two faces.

"Was there anything else you needed to know?" she asked.

"No, I think I've found the answer to my question," Lewis said.

"Do you know when the article will be running in the *Journal*?" Florence asked. "Because Ms. Ford will want to —"

Lewis ended the call, then went to the online phone directories. He found a listing for an R Kilbride in Burlington.

He picked up the phone again, dialed Howard.

"Yes, Lewis," Howard said.

"Found him," Lewis said.

446

FORTY-SIX

Octavio Famosa couldn't decide what to do.

Should he tell Allison Fitch — and that was how he thought of her now, not as Adele Farmer — he had been in touch with her mother in Ohio? That Doris Fitch would be flying in today to be reunited with her? Or should he say nothing, and let her be surprised?

Even though he suspected she would be angry with him, he believed that, ultimately, she would be grateful. Yes, he had snooped about in her purse, and called her mother behind her back. But it was often stubbornness and pride that kept family members apart, even when they desperately wanted to be together. Pride was a terrible thing, Octavio mused. It stood in the way of so much happiness.

One reason he didn't want to tell her was that he wanted to see the look on Allison's face when her mother arrived at the hotel. Octavio had seen many shows on television, especially on *Oprah*, where people who had not seen one another in years were reunited. He loved to see the people's expressions when a long-lost son or daughter walked on-stage to embrace them.

Octavio had to admit that he was a bit of a sentimentalist.

As much as he wanted to keep what he had done a secret from Allison, he also felt that as her friend, he had to be honest with her. In the short time they had worked together they had developed a trusting relationship. They talked to each other. Octavio had bared his heart to her, and Allison had done the same with him, albeit changing a few of the details so as not to reveal who she really was.

She was a girl in trouble — he knew that. He'd sensed it from the moment he'd met her. And a girl in trouble needed her mother.

When Allison woke the next morning, and emerged from the back room into the office, still wiping the sleep from her eyes, he considered telling her right then. But he lost his nerve. As she did every morning, Allison used the bathroom adjoining the office to have a shower and get dressed. By eight thirty, she was ready for work.

It had not been that busy a night. Only eight units had been rented, and of those, only three had checked out so far. The people who stayed here, if they did happen to spend the entire night, were not generally inclined to vacate their rooms early. They drank and did drugs and had sex until the middle of the night, then slept in until ten or eleven or noon, which was check-out time. If they slept in past that, Octavio had to bang on their door to wake them because he knew, especially with repeat customers, that they did not want to have to pay for a second night.

"Where should I start?" Allison asked.

"Three, nine, and eleven are ready for you," Octavio said.

"Okay."

"Did you sleep well?"

"I guess."

"That's good," Octavio said. "It looks like it's going to be a very nice day. No rain in the forecast."

Allison didn't say anything. She never cared whether it rained or not. Octavio believed that for this child, it was raining every day, even when there were no clouds in the sky.

"Okay, so, I guess I'll get started," she said.

"Some breakfast? You are going to have some breakfast?"

"I'm not hungry," she said.

What a pitiful girl she was. Octavio wanted to tell her, to bring some sunshine into her life.

About an hour later, he worked up his nerve.

He found her cleaning the bathroom in unit nine. She was on her knees, cleaning the toilet, when he came into the room.

"Adele?" he said. He almost called her Allison.

"Yeah?" she said, looking at him through the bathroom door, blowing a stray lock of hair out of her eyes.

"I need to talk to you for a minute."

"Go ahead," she said, squirting some cleanser onto the floor.

"No, you must stop for a second."

She put down the cleanser and a sponge she had in her other hand and stood up. She came into the room and stood by the television.

"Am I fired?" she said. There was no sadness in her voice. Just resignation.

"No, you are not fired. You are a good employee. I would not fire you. Although . . ." he said, his voice trailing off. "It's possible you may not want to stay."

"What's going on?"

"I need to tell you, first of all, that anything I did was with your best interests at heart."

"What are you talking about?"

"I've been very concerned about . . . about how sad you are."

"Octavio, what have you done?"

He looked down at the stained and tattered carpet. "Last night, when you were sleeping, I went into your room."

"You what?" Allison's eyes were wide and accusing.

"It is not what you think!" Octavio said, holding up his hands defensively. "I was a total gentleman. But . . . but I looked in your purse and —"

"You were in my purse?"

"Just listen to me, okay? Let me tell you everything. I found the letter. A letter from your mother."

"Oh my God," Allison said.

"And I know that you are not really Adele Farmer, but that is okay with me. I am not judging you at —"

"How could you do that? How dare you go into my things?!" Her cheeks were flushed and her breathing had grown rapid.

"Wait, wait!" Octavio said, now thinking maybe this hadn't been such a good idea at all. But he had to tell her everything now. She had to know. "I called her."

Allison stared at him, blinked. "What?"

"I called your mother last night. I told her you were here, that you were okay. Allison, Allison, please, she was . . . she was ecstatic. She was so happy to know you are okay, that you are alive."

"No," Allison whispered, disbelieving.

"She is coming," Octavio said. "She is flying down here to see you. She loves you so much! She will help you! Whatever trouble you —"

Allison shoved him out of her way as she ran to the door.

451

Octavio shouted after her, "I'm so sorry! I am sorry!"

She didn't know how much time she had. Maybe, just maybe, they hadn't been tapping her mother's phone. But she had to assume that they were. And if they were, and if Octavio had spoken to her mother the night before, after she'd gone to sleep —

Plenty of time to send someone to Florida.

"No no no no no," she said under her breath as she ran for the office. She would grab what few clothes she had, stuff them into her backpack, and get the hell out of there. She didn't know where she'd go. It didn't really matter. All she knew was that she had to get away from this place.

Right now.

She ran into the office, threw open the door to the back room. She dropped to her knees to pull her purse and backpack out from under the rollaway bed.

Felt a sudden, very sharp pain in her side.

By the time Doris Fitch arrived that afternoon, the hotel parking lot was cordoned off with yellow police tape.

FORTY-SEVEN

Julie met me at the house. She was standing by her car as I was pulling into the driveway.

"Tell me again," I said as I got out.

She repeated what she had told me on the phone. That a Whirl360 employee named Kyle Billings, and his wife, had been murdered in their home. The woman had been suffocated with a bag, and I couldn't help but think of the similarity between that and what Thomas had found on the Internet.

I also couldn't stop thinking about the fact that Billings was the person who created the program that obscured faces on Whirl360.

"Someone like that could have changed that image," I said.

"Yeah," said Julie. "That's kind of what I was thinking."

"I don't know what the hell to do," I said. "You didn't tell Thomas any of this, did you?"

She shook her head. "Hell, no. I don't even know if he knows I'm out here. I think this news might get him pretty agitated."

"*I'm* pretty agitated," I said. "You find out anything else?"

"I'm going to make some calls about Allison Fitch. See if she's still missing."

"Okay." I put my hands on her shoulders. "You know you don't have to do this. You don't have to get mixed up in whatever the hell this is."

"Oh, okay," she deadpanned. "Guess I'll be off, then. Give me a call sometime."

I smiled. "Why are you doing this?"

"I don't know. 'Cause it's fun?"

I laughed. "Maybe for you. I don't need this. That your only reason?"

She shrugged. "I kinda like you. I figure, I keep helping out, shit keeps happening, it builds this sexual tension thing we have going."

"Really."

"Yeah. Maybe, one of these times we start getting hot and heavy, we'll actually consummate the event."

"Consummate," I said. "I always thought that sounded like soup."

She smiled. "I like you, Ray. And I like your brother, too. I like helping you out. And I have to tell ya, if Thomas really *has* seen something online, it's one hell of a story."

"So you're using me," I said.

"Yes, yes, I am," she said. "I'm trying to exploit you sexually, and professionally."

"Works for me, I guess. But I still don't

know what to do now. Calling the cops, that didn't go well."

Julie said, "I know, that went badly. But Jesus, *this*? What happened in Chicago? Someone's going to have to listen to this."

"The trick is trying to get someone to hear the whole story before they hang up."

I slipped an arm around her. As we started walking toward the house, my cell rang. It was Harry Peyton's office.

"Hi, Ray," Alice said. "I can't seem to find your father's life insurance documents. Would you have those?"

I really didn't need this now. "Can it wait?" I asked. "How's tomorrow?"

"Okay, normally, I'd say yes, but I'm taking tomorrow off and Harry's going to be in court."

I had a thought. "Is Harry there?" I asked.

"Yup."

"Okay, fine. I'll head in shortly." I ended the call and said to Julie, "I've got an idea. You want to hang out here till I get back?"

"What else would I do?" she said. "I've only got a job."

Ten minutes later, I was in Harry's office with my father's policy in hand. I'd found it in one of the kitchen drawers. I didn't really intend to, but, wound up as I was, I pretty much threw it onto his desk.

"Ray, what the hell's up with you?"

"That's what you wanted, right?"

"Yes, this is what I wanted. Ray, really, what's going on? It's about Thomas, isn't it?"

I forced myself to sit down. I felt as though I'd had coffee injected directly into my veins.

"Sort of. But not exactly. I mean, it started off with Thomas, but now it's something bigger. And I need to talk to you about it."

He closed his eyes for a moment, as if steeling himself. "Fire away."

I had to take a deep breath myself. "Thomas saw something. Online. He was going through various streets in New York and he spotted something in a third-floor window."

Harry listened while I told him the whole thing. Thomas's belief that what he'd seen was a murder. My trip to New York. His call to the landlord. The altered image, the murders in Chicago, and a missing woman.

"Good Lord," Harry said. "I've never heard anything like this in my life."

"I feel I've got to call the police, but I tried that once already, and it didn't go well."

"There's a shocker."

Everyone was a smart-ass today.

"Yeah, it went badly," I said. "But it's reached the point where I have to do something. I thought maybe you'd have some words of wisdom. God knows I could use a few."

"Well, I think your instincts are well intentioned. Calling the police does seem like the right thing to do. But let me ask you a few questions first." He sat forward in his chair. "First, how do you know Whirl360 doesn't periodically review the street scenes it's posted, and if the program finds something it overlooked before, it doesn't make a change?"

That had not occurred to me. "I don't know. If what you're suggesting were the case, I still think it's pretty amazing that the change got made within a couple of days of Thomas finding it, and my knocking on the door of that apartment."

"You may be right. But, Ray, is it possible the image was never there in the first place?"

"Harry, Thomas didn't imagine it. I saw it with my own eyes. I saw it the day Thomas found it."

"What I'm asking you is, is it possible Thomas *put* it there?"

That stopped me. "What?"

"Could Thomas have fiddled with the image that you saw on his computer, to make it look like the woman in that window was being smothered?"

I didn't have to give that much thought. "Thomas doesn't have the skills or know-how to hack into Whirl360 and fiddle with the images."

"Okay," Harry said, nodding. "But what if he were able to change the image on just his own computer? I don't know — manipulate it somehow and insert it. And then later, when you thought the image had been tampered with, it was actually back to the way it was before Thomas started messing about with it."

I shook my head slowly. "I don't . . . I don't think so."

"Did you ever see this image on any computer other than Thomas's?"

That stopped me. "No." I shook my head. "But the landlord did confirm that there used to be a couple of women living there, and that one of them was reported missing."

"What else did the landlord tell you?"

"He didn't tell *me* anything. It was Thomas who talked to him."

Harry Peyton didn't say anything.

"Oh, come on, Harry. Are you saying Thomas made up all that stuff from the landlord?"

"I didn't say that, Ray," he said. "But . . ."

"The name Thomas got from the landlord checked out, same as the one in the *Times* story."

"Thomas doesn't have access to the *Times* Web site? He couldn't have already read it, before he gave you that name? Ray, I'm only asking you the questions the police are going to."

I slumped in the chair. "No, no, that's not possible. The thing is, I believe Thomas. Maybe that makes me a fool, but I don't

458

think he doctored any images. I believe he talked to the landlord. And, Harry, Julie did *not* make up what she found out from the Whirl360 people. Two people were *murdered*. People who are linked to this image on the Web site."

"I hear you, Ray."

"Yeah, but I get what you're saying, too. Even if I tell the cops our suspicions, I'm probably not going to have much more luck than last time."

Harry shrugged and eyed me with sympathy. "Look, I'm not saying you are, but what if you're wrong about Thomas? What if — and please forgive me for this — but what if this thing he saw was something that was pointed out to him during one of his conversations with President Clinton?"

I ran my palm over my forehead. A major storm front of a headache was moving in. A migraine monsoon. "I appreciate your caution, Harry. But there's something going on. There has to be a way to get this information to the cops. They need to hear the whole story before they dismiss it."

Harry mulled that one over. "I have a friend. Barry Duckworth, a detective with the Promise Falls police. Maybe if I were to approach him, act as an intermediary. Barry knows and trusts me, so if, after I explain everything to him, he thinks there's anything worth checking out, he can follow it up with you. Or he can call the NYPD. He'll be able to get someone to listen to him."

I liked it. Harry had credibility. He was a trusted member of the community. I might not get far trying to tell this tale to Duckworth, but Harry'd be able to get the whole thing out before Duckworth hung up on him, or threw him out the door. And Duckworth, in turn, would have credibility with another police department.

"Yeah," I said. "Okay." I suddenly nodded with enthusiasm. A heavy weight began to lift from my shoulders. "I appreciate this, Harry. I do."

"No problem."

I stood, but something was holding me there.

"Something else on your mind?" Harry asked.

"I don't even know whether to mention it," I said. "But maybe Dad said something to you about this sometime."

"Go ahead."

"Thomas said to me — I'm trying to remember his exact words — but he said something like 'things happen in windows.' And then, when he was pissed with me, when he didn't think I'd done a very thorough investigation in New York, he said I was acting the same way I had before when someone in a window was in trouble."

Harry pressed his lips together. "Sounds

like he was talking about himself," he said.

"Yeah," I said. "And there's another thing. Something Len Prentice said."

"Yes?"

"Len came by the house when I was in the city. He got Thomas riled up. Tried to get him to leave the house for lunch and Thomas refused to go, and he kind of hit Len. Struck him."

Harry's eyes widened. "Oh my."

"Nothing really happened, and Len isn't pressing the point. But he said Dad told him Thomas had pushed him down the stairs, and when I talked to Thomas about it, he more or less admitted it."

"Your father never mentioned anything about that to me," Harry said.

"Thomas said Dad was trying to tell him he was sorry, about something that had happened to Thomas when he was thirteen, but Thomas said he didn't want to talk about it, and that's when he pushed Dad. He landed on his back."

"Dear God," Harry said.

"But Dad wasn't angry. Or so Thomas says. Dad supposedly said he'd understand if Thomas couldn't forgive him."

"Did you ask Thomas what it was?"

"I tried, but he's not saying," I said. "I'll try again, when the time seems right. What could Dad have done to Thomas that he'd

461

feel the need to apologize for, after all these years?"

I caught Harry looking at the clock.

"I'm sorry," I said. "I'm like an episode of *As the World Turns*. Thanks for everything, Harry."

I was walking to the car when my cell rang.

"Me," Julie said.

"You still at the house."

"Yeah."

"Thomas okay?"

"Yeah. I went upstairs, asked him to go on Whirl360 and show me my sister Candace's place. All I had to do was tell him the name of it and that it was in New York and he found it."

"What place?"

"She runs a bakery, specializing in cupcakes, in Greenwich Village. Lives over her shop."

"*That* cupcake place? The famous one everyone's always lined up for? The one that was in *Sex and the City*?"

"You watched *Sex and the City*?"

"Uh, maybe a couple of times."

"It's not that cupcake place. It's another one. Anyway, he found it on West Eighth just like that. It's called Candy's, in case you ever want to go there. So, how'd it go at the lawyer's?"

I told her how Harry Peyton was going to

462

act as an intermediary between the police and myself.

"Sounds good," Julie said. "I know Duckworth. I've gotten quotes from him a few times. Listen, Ray," and her voice went very serious, "I found out something else. I did a news search on Allison Fitch this morning and came up with nothing, and decided to try it again this afternoon, on your dad's laptop, and I got a hit."

"You did?"

"Yeah. Just a short story, out of Tampa. A woman with that name was found dead at a hotel there."

Not again. Every time Julie started looking for people attached to this mess . . .

"You there, Ray?"

"Yeah. Yeah, I'm here."

"Can I tell you something, Ray?"

"Sure."

"I think this whole thing is getting really fucking weird."

FORTY-EIGHT

"Hello?"

"Thomas, it's Bill Clinton."

"Hi."

"How are you?"

"I'm very good, sir."

"Thomas, I wanted to remind you how valuable you are to us. Do you know what the phrase 'black ops' means?"

"Those are secret missions?"

"That's right. Covert operations run by the CIA and other government agencies. Operations that the White House has to be able to deny any knowledge of should they somehow become public."

"Okay."

"When we have operatives in the field, conducting black ops — style missions, they can run into trouble, the kind where they have to slip away in a hurry. That's why you're so important. Not just if all the online maps disappear one day, or there's another earthquake or tornado. So you never know

464

when we'll call, asking for your suggestions on an escape route."

"I understand."

"The reason I'm calling is to tell you, again, that there are things in your past you shouldn't be talking about, or else the folks at the CIA are going to lose confidence in you. You'll look weak. Or worse, like a tattletale. You understand?"

"I do."

"Good. That's good to hear."

"Can I ask you something . . . Bill?"

"Go right ahead."

"My brother and I, well, mostly me, but we were talking about aliens the other day, and I wondered, when you were president, did you find out what really happened at Roswell? Do they have an alien spaceship there?"

"Thomas, you fulfill your mission successfully, and I'll tell you everything."

FORTY-NINE

Nicole called Lewis in the morning from Florida and told him it was done. Lewis told her to catch the first flight north that she could. She'd found Allison Fitch, and he'd found the man who'd paid a visit to her apartment. Together, they were going to retrieve him. A man named Ray Kilbride.

"Retrieve?" Nicole said.

"We have to know what he knows. We have to know why he was there. My employer wants to talk to him."

"Whatever."

"And you're not flying to New York," Lewis told her. He gave her another destination, closer to where they'd find Kilbride. "I'm heading up that way now."

"Fine," she said, and ended the call.

Then Lewis contacted Howard Talliman.

"She's been found. And she's no longer a problem," Lewis said. He felt safe discussing these things with Howard, knowing that the man had a security expert who swept his office every morning for listening devices.

"That's a great relief, Lewis."

"And I'm heading north to deal with our other problem."

"It's still too early to relax."

"I agree," Lewis said.

"We have to know why Kilbride had that printout. We have to know why he was there. Have you any reason to believe he's anything other than what he purports to be?"

"He's an illustrator. Plain and simple."

"Not everyone is who they appear to be, Lewis."

"I know. But I've torn his life apart since finding out he's our guy. I've got his Social Security number. He's got fifty-four bucks charged to his Visa card. He lives frugally. He's paid off his mortgage. Last year he reported an income of $73,675 to the IRS. He drives an Audi Q5. He's gotten four speeding tickets in the last ten years but other than that his record is clean. Never been married. Got a brother named Thomas who lives with their father in Promise Falls. That sound like some undercover CIA guy to you?"

"No, but it doesn't make any sense for someone who makes his living doing silly drawings to show up at a murder scene with that printout in hand. Did he stumble upon the image online and then come investigating, or did he already have an inkling of what had happened at that address before he went

467

looking for the image? Either scenario is troubling, but the latter particularly so. No illustrator would be doing that. A private detective might be. An FBI agent might be." Howard paused, as though steeling himself for his next thought. "As might someone from the CIA."

"Howard, I've told you what I know. When you've got the son of a bitch in front of you, you can ask him whatever you want. I'm gonna fly up, rent a van there."

"Keep me informed," Howard said, concluding the conversation.

Howard had always known the Goldsmith matter might still come back and bite them in the ass, even though the man was dead. But did it really make sense that the CIA might be sniffing around Orchard Street? There had to be people at Langley who already knew everything. For God's sake, the plan had originated there. It wasn't as if this whole thing had been Morris's idea from the outset.

Was it possible that those left behind after Goldsmith's death were covering their asses by finding a way to lay off more of their troubles on Morris? But even then, how had they connected Morris to Orchard Street? Had they also been keeping tabs on Bridget? Learned of her link to Allison Fitch? Which could have led them to the Web, and the image, and —

It did seem far-fetched.

And yet, some facts were not in dispute. This man Ray Kilbride had shown up at Allison Fitch's apartment, presumably led there by an online image of Bridget Sawchuck's murder.

Howard felt he needed to talk to Sawchuck. To sound him out on a few things, without actually telling him about Fitch, or Kilbride, or what had happened at Orchard Street, because Morris still had no idea how his wife had actually died.

That she had not killed herself. That she had been murdered as a direct result of an action taken by Morris's best friend.

Morris picked up on the third ring. "Just on my way to lunch with the mayor," he said. "What's up?"

"I've been thinking about what you said, Morris. About how you think it's time. I know you think I'm not listening to you, but I am. I know what you're feeling."

"Funny you should mention it, Howard. I've been wondering who you are lately. I've been wondering what happened to the Howard I used to know. The one who liked to takes chances and stir up some shit."

"I don't mind stirring up shit, but I don't want you stepping in it," Howard said. "Which is why I've been stepping very carefully of late. You're my friend, Morris. Any advice I give you, you need to know that I'm

469

giving it to you as a friend first."

Morris waited a moment before responding. "Okay."

"I've been thinking about how you want to move forward, and I think the only thing that's holding us back is our uncertainty with regard to the Goldsmith matter."

"Right."

"I need a certain comfort level, Morris, that we're done with that."

"I concur. The fact is, Howard, ever since Goldsmith — poor Barton, God bless his soul — took his own life, I've felt that the risks have been minimized. The scandal of it all, being branded as some kind of traitor to his own government, it was more than he could bear, and totally unfair. His number one concern was always for Americans, for their safety."

Howard paused, then said, "Morris, do you think it's conceivable that people within the agency would have any reason to be monitoring you in the wake of all this?"

"I'm not sure I follow you."

"Let's imagine a hypothetical. Let's suppose the CIA had people watching you. Just suppose. What would their motives be?"

"The only one I can think of is, those who were close to Goldsmith, those who know what he was doing, who were complicit in what he was doing, would be worried I might come forward. But they'd also know that such

470

an action on my part would be political suicide."

Howard concurred. "Do you think, in the early stages of this, before Barton took his own life, he might have had people watching you and, I don't know, maybe even Bridget?"

"Why the hell would they be watching me or Bridget? Is something going on I don't know about?"

"Of course not. You know I tell you everything."

"That's never been true, Howard. You tell me everything I need to know, and don't tell me the things it's better I not know."

Howard had to agree with that, too. "All I'm saying is, before you get back in the game, we have to imagine certain scenarios, as unlikely as they may be, and develop strategies for dealing with them."

"Agreed, but this is crazy talk. Look, forget about the business with Goldsmith. It's going to be okay. And the thing is, while we sit around waiting to be sure the problem's gone away, we're wasting valuable time. We need to sit down now and plot out our next move. We need to decide on key people, who we're going to use. We need to start studying our opponents' weaknesses. Jesus, Howard, I hardly need to be telling you this. You wrote the playbook."

"I know."

"Let's get together tonight."

Howard knew what that meant. It had been their routine, over the years, to get together after midnight and work through till dawn, drawing up battle plans. It was when they got their best work done, when there was no fear of interruptions.

"Yes," Howard said. "That's what we'll do."

"Good. Talk to you later, my friend. Lace up those boxing gloves."

Morris hung up.

Maybe, before tonight's meeting, Howard hoped, there'd be some answers from Ray Kilbride.

Lewis was about to board his short-haul flight north when his cell rang.

"Hello," he said.

"I understand you've been trying to reach me," a man said.

"Victor," Lewis said. "Thank you for calling."

"What can I do for you?"

"It's about a former employee of yours."

"Living or dead?"

"Living."

That narrowed it down for Victor. Very few people left his employ. "Okay," he said.

"I engaged her services, and she made a very big mistake."

"Really."

"It's reflected badly on me. She's rectifying the problem she created, but when the matter is resolved, I have to make this right. For my own reputation."

"I understand."

"But I felt I owed you the courtesy of letting you know about the course of action I want to pursue. If you object, I won't do it."

"I should have done the same thing myself, but I was weak," Victor said. "I took her in, treated her like a daughter. How does she thank me? She leaves. You won't get any trouble from me on this."

"Thank you. How are things in Vegas?"

"Too many people are bringing their children."

Lewis said good-bye, put his phone away, and got on the plane.

FIFTY

Back at the house, I said to Julie, "Let's take a walk."

We headed out the back of the house and down the hill, to the creek.

"I've got some calls in to the cops in Tampa," Julie said, tapping the cell phone bulge in the front pocket of her jeans. "See what else I can find out about Fitch."

I nodded.

"You're kind of quiet," she said.

"I'm thinking about some things Harry said. About Thomas." I told her about his speculation, that Thomas might be making some of this stuff up. Doctoring the image online, making up his chat with the landlord.

"You think that's what he's doing?" she asked.

I hesitated. "I don't know. I don't think so. I mean, he believes things we know are not true, but he really believes them. Like the online map meltdown, and talking to Clinton. But some things aren't made up at all. It was you who found out about what happened in Chicago, and now Florida."

"Would Thomas deliberately lie to you?"

I'd never really thought about that. "I guess it's possible. But when I asked him about this thing that happened with Dad, about pushing him on the stairs, he admitted it. Although it wasn't like he volunteered the information."

"He pushed your Dad down the stairs?"

I shook my head, like I didn't have the energy to get into it now. "When there's something Thomas doesn't want to tell you, or own up to, he just keeps quiet. He clams up." I stopped, watched the creek water trickling past. "Well, he lied to Dr. Grigorin. He told her he'd watched a movie with me when he hadn't, trying to get her off his back, I guess. God, I just don't know."

"Are you going to talk to him?"

"I'll try. In the meantime, like I told you, Harry knows a guy, a detective with the Promise Falls police. He'll bounce all this off him so I don't have to worry about making a fool of myself with another call to the cops."

"That's good," Julie said. "Duckworth is a good guy. He doesn't instinctively hate reporters."

I said, "Some other stuff's nagging at me."

"Like?"

I opened my arms, gesturing to where we were standing. "This is where it happened.

This is where my father died." I pointed to the hill. "That was where the tractor rolled. Stopped about here. This is where Thomas found him."

She looped her arm into mine. "I'm sorry."

"I've been thinking a lot about him. About Dad. And about Thomas. He told me when they had this incident on the stairs, it was about something that had happened to him when he was thirteen. Something he didn't want to talk about. And Dad, according to Thomas, was trying to tell him he was sorry, that he'd understand if Thomas didn't forgive him."

"He didn't say what it was about?"

"He wouldn't tell me. But" — and I hesitated — "there's something more."

Julie looked at me and waited.

"I haven't talked to anyone about this, but there was something kind of weird on Dad's laptop." I told her about what I'd found in the search history.

"Child prostitution?"

"Yeah."

"That's kinda strange."

"Yeah," I said.

Julie shook her head strongly. "I didn't know your dad, Ray. Why's this got you worried? You think he was into something weird?" Then the implications started to sink in further. "God, you don't think your dad assaulted Thomas when he was a kid, do you?

You think that's what he was talking about when he said he'd understand if Thomas didn't forgive him?"

"It's a huge leap, putting it together like that," I said, "but without any real facts, your mind starts going places it shouldn't."

"Did your father, with you, did he ever —"

"Never," I said. "Absolutely *never.*"

"Then that's not it," Julie said with finality. I liked it that she'd defend my father even without knowing him. "What else?" Julie asked. "I can tell there's something else on your mind."

"It's . . . it's nothing."

"Talk to me. You've got all these things weighing on you, and you haven't had anyone to talk them over with. What is it?"

I slowly shook my head, looked down. "I think there's something funny about how Dad died."

"Funny how?"

"It's just, okay, the way they say it happened, he rolled the tractor while he was on the side of the hill here. And that's probably what *did* happen."

"So what's the problem, then?" she asked.

"They never brought the tractor up. It was still down here by the creek. Not upside down, of course, because Thomas had managed to get it off him before the paramedics got here."

"Okay, I'm not getting this," Julie said.

477

"I came down here to see if it would start, to take it back up to the barn. And it did start. But the key was already in the OFF position, and that thing that goes around the lawnmower blades was raised, like he'd stopped cutting grass."

Julie thought about what I was saying. "So, you think he rolled the tractor after he'd turned it off."

I nodded. "That's right."

"Isn't that possible? That maybe the tractor was acting up, and he stopped it to see what was wrong? I don't know a lot about riding lawnmowers, but if something gets caught in the blades, wouldn't you have to turn every-thing off to see what was the matter? And wouldn't you have to lift up that thingie so you could look under there to see what it was?"

I felt like I'd been hit in the side of the head with a two-by-four. I laughed, put my hands on Julie's shoulders, and said, "You're a ge-nius."

"I am?"

"Here I was, driving myself crazy, thinking this was some goddamn locked-room mys-tery, and the answer's so fucking simple."

"Oh," Julie said, feigning umbrage. "So it took a simpleton to put it all together."

"No, no, but you're right. Okay, so he's go-ing along, maybe he hits a rock or a stick or something, and he figures it's jammed into

478

the blades. He has to stop the tractor, raise the housing, then get out and take a look. But as he's getting off, or maybe when he was getting back on, he leans just a little too much toward the bottom of the hill, and tips the tractor on top of himself."

If it still weren't so tragic, I'd have had some pleasure finally putting it together. Or having it put together for me.

"That makes perfect sense," I said, giving Julie a quick hug.

"What did you *think* had happened?"

"I was thinking he must have stopped because there was someone else there. Someone had walked down the side of the hill and waved to him or something, and he stopped, killed the ignition, and raised the housing. Like maybe he was going to stop and head back to the house. I'd been thinking, I don't know, that someone was actually there and saw it happen, but didn't tell anyone, or call the ambulance, or anything."

Julie said, quietly, "Someone like Thomas."

I sighed and briefly hung my head, feeling ashamed. "It had crossed my mind. That maybe he'd headed out of the house for some reason, wanted to talk to Dad, and there was an accident. God, I'm an idiot. Like there aren't enough things to worry about, I have to invent more."

"Maybe you've been doing the same thing with what you found on your father's laptop.

Lots of things have simple explanations. They just seem complicated when you don't know what they are."

I took Julie into my arms again and held on to her. "I know I keep saying this, but thanks."

"Wait till you get my bill." She put her head on my chest. "Listen, I should get back to the paper and write up a couple of things that have nothing to do with your and Thomas's big international conspiracy. And then I'll make those other calls, to Florida."

"What should I do?"

"You know, honestly? Right now? Probably nothing. See what luck your lawyer has with Duckworth, and I'll see what I find out, and you just stay here and make sure Thomas doesn't see someone getting pushed off the Eiffel Tower or anything."

"Don't even joke. What about later? You want to come back?"

"Not for dinner. Your dinners suck. Why don't I come out later, maybe around eleven? I've got to cover the evening session of the Promise Falls City Council. After I file my story, I'll bring over a bottle of wine. We can try messing around again."

"You really want to give that another shot?"

Julie smiled. "I thrive on danger."

I walked her back to her car, gave her a kiss through the open window, and watched until her car had disappeared down the road. When I got upstairs, Thomas was exploring

480

Stuttgart. I said, "I don't know what the hell to make for dinner. I was thinking maybe bacon, lettuce, and tomato sandwiches."

"I don't care," he said, his eyes focused on the monitor.

I got the bacon, lettuce, tomato, and some mayonnaise out of the fridge, and was just about to start frying up the bacon when I noticed we were down to one slice of bread and a heel.

"Nuts," I said, and wondered whether there was a pizza place in Promise Falls that would deliver this far out.

That was when someone started banging on the front door.

"God," I said under my breath. "Just don't let it be the FBI again."

FIFTY-ONE

Lewis's flight got in ahead of Nicole's, which gave him time to arrange the rental of a white panel van. Two seats up front with an empty cargo bay. When Nicole got off the plane she said she needed to hit a Home Depot on the way. She couldn't take ice picks on a plane, and had to buy them as she needed them. Lewis grabbed a roll of duct tape and some moving blankets.

They pulled up in front of the house. It was still daylight.

"So we're just bringing him back," Nicole said.

Lewis, behind the wheel, nodded at all the empty space behind them. "Yeah. My boss has some questions for him."

Nicole nodded. Neither of them spoke for a few seconds. Finally, she said, "I know you're not happy with how this went down."

"No shit," Lewis said.

"But once we bag this guy, take him back, that takes care of things," she said.

"Hope so," he said. "Depends on what kind of answers we get from him."

Nicole glanced across the road to the house. "Either way, I'm done at that point."

"Well, after he's been questioned, we're going to have to deal with him. This isn't like when you're fishing and do catch and release."

Nicole shot him a look. "But after that, we're square."

"Sure," Lewis said.

Nicole looked back at the house. "How you want to play this? You want to knock on the front, I'll come in around the back?"

"I don't see why we don't both go to the front door. Do we look threatening?" He grinned at her. "We look like a nice couple. We need directions. We need the phone. Listen, once he opens the door, we're walking right in."

Nicole reached down, gave the top of the ice pick that was tucked into her boot a reassuring tap. Lewis rooted around between the seats for a backpack that contained a few things he might need, including the tape.

"Let's go," he said.

They got out of the van, crossed the street, and walked up the drive. Lewis went up the porch steps first, but waited until Nicole was standing next to him before he knocked.

FIFTY-TWO

It wasn't the FBI.

It was Marie Prentice. She was standing there with a dark blue soft-sided bag the size of a picnic hamper. It looked insulated. I wondered whether she'd come alone, or if Len was in the car, waiting for her. I glanced out, saw that the car sitting next to mine was empty.

"If I can't get you boys over for dinner," she said, her body listing to the side that was holding the bag by a broad strap, "the least I can do is bring something over for you. I can't believe it's taken me this long, but sometimes I don't have as much energy as others." There was a warm aroma wafting upward. Spices, cheese.

"Marie," I said, "you really shouldn't have."

"It was no trouble at all," she said.

"Let me take that from you," I said. "It looks heavy." I took hold of the bag's strap and eased it out of Marie's hand. "It smells wonderful. Come on in."

While I didn't like Len much, I didn't have the same feelings of animosity toward his wife. I didn't want to offend her, and what the hell. I was hungry.

"I was just thinking about ordering a pizza," I told her.

"Oh, you don't want to do that," she said.

I put the bag on the kitchen table and unzipped it. "What is this, Marie?"

"It's my own recipe," she said, sounding slightly out of breath. "Well, not exactly. I mean, it sort of started off as a recipe from the *Barefoot Contessa*? But instead of using tuna steaks, I used tuna from the can, because that's the only kind Len will eat, and she threw in all kinds of things like lentils and wasabi powder and I put in some peas and noodles, and I guess when you get right down to it there's really nothing the same about them except both recipes have tuna in the title."

"It looks great," I said. "The pan's still hot. Did you just take it out of the oven?"

"I did. Where's Thomas? Is he upstairs?"

"He is, Marie," I said, but did not offer to get him. Given his run-in with Len, I was worried that finding out his wife was here might be troubling to Thomas.

"Do you think he'd like to come down and try the casserole?"

"If it's okay with you, I'm just going to leave him be for now," I said. "But I'll tell him you're the one to thank for dinner."

"There's some buns in the bag there, too," she said, but her voice was suddenly less cheery. "You see, part of the reason I came by is, I just wanted to apologize to him. And to you. For Len's behavior the other day."

"Len and I already spoke about this," I said. "It's okay."

"I heard the two of you talking in the basement and he really shouldn't have said those things to you, about your brother. Even if Thomas is a bit off, Len shouldn't have talked to you like that."

"And Thomas shouldn't have hit him," I said. "Lots of blame to go around."

Marie said, "Len was just trying to do a good thing. It was my idea. I was the one who suggested he try to get Thomas to go out, for lunch, or to come back to the house. Actually, he'd come here to invite you both, but you were gone for the day."

"That's right."

"Where'd you go? To the city?"

"Yes, Marie."

"Len just doesn't understand why Thomas has to be the way he is. You have to forgive him for that. Len thinks everyone should just buck up, you know? I don't think he gets that some people are different. That they can't help being the way they are. He figures if he can do something, everybody should be able to do it. Sometimes he's even that way with me. He says to me, 'Just stop being so tired. It's all in your head. Come with me when I go on a vacation.' But it's not in my head. I have a disease. You can look it up on the Mayo Clinic's Web site. Can I sit down? I get tired when I stand too long."

"I'm sorry," I said, and pulled out one of the kitchen chairs for her. She sat, letting her arms hang down straight at her sides.

"I'll be fine in a minute or two," she said. "In my kitchen at home I've got a chair right there by the stove. I can sit anytime I want, even stir things while sitting."

"I'm going to put this in the oven to keep it warm," I said, taking the casserole and putting it on the center rack.

"He doesn't even understand that I can't do everything he wants to do," Marie said, and then, realizing her comment might be taken any number of ways, blushed. "I mean, you know, like traveling. He's up to it, but I'm just not. But I tell him, if you want to go away, you go. You have a good time. The first time I said that, I didn't think he'd actually go, but off he went once he found somebody else to go. And he had such a wonderful time over there, I didn't see how I could say no when he wanted to go back."

"Well," I said, since I had no comment.

"And not for a second do I believe what Len's been saying about Thomas," she said.

"What would that be, Marie?"

487

"He can't hear us, can he?" she asked worriedly.

"No."

"Len's been saying if the police ever started to investigate what happened to your father, they'd probably be taking a pretty good look at Thomas."

"Why's that, Marie?"

"Len says your dad always took chances on cutting grass on the side of that hill, but even so, he was the kind of man who always knew what he was doing. He says if the police ever started thinking he got pushed, that someone was there and let that tractor fall on him, well, they'd have to look no further than Thomas. I'm just telling you what Len says. I was thinking he might have said as much to you when you were over, before I opened the basement door, and I wanted to tell you I'm very sorry if he did. I don't think Thomas would do that. He's a good boy, basically. How high you got that oven set? Don't put it up to 350 or anything. Just warm it a hundred degrees. Just for ten minutes or so."

I adjusted the oven.

I thought I'd put it behind me, this obsession I'd been having about the tractor key being in the OFF position, the raised housing. Julie's interpretation of things had made a lot of sense. But now I was wondering whether my earlier supposition, that someone had stopped to talk to my father, and might

488

have been there when he died, could still be true.

But I didn't hold Len in very high regard, especially lately, so the fact that he and I might be on the same wavelength also gave me pause. And why the hell was he doing this kind of speculating? What had kicked off this line of thinking? I'd only started letting my mind run a bit wild after I'd examined the tractor. Len, so far as I knew, had not been out here to inspect the accident scene before I moved the machine to the barn.

Was he basing his opinion on what my father had told him? If so, it seemed a stretch to draw a line from a push on the stairs to toppling a tractor onto someone. Especially when that someone was your own father.

Or was it possible Len was up to something else? Did he believe what he was saying, or was he trying to make trouble for Thomas? Why would he do that? Was he trying to plant an idea in Marie's head? And again, why?

"The thing is," Marie said, "Len's always judged people harshly. He's like that. You should hear him go on about the people in Thailand. They're nice and all, but he says they don't drive like Americans, their building standards aren't the same as here, and the place can be so politically unstable at times. He says they need to get over all their petty squabbles and just run their country. And Len has never had much patience for

489

monarchies. He doesn't get why someone should get to run a country just because they were born into the right family. But it doesn't stop him from going back, even if he has to go without me."

Thailand.

Over the years, I'd heard friends talk about what a wonderful place it was. Hot, lush, one of the most beautiful countries on the planet. Terrific nightlife, a rich culture, spectacular food. But every travel destination had its problems. Paris had its pickpockets and unpredictable strikes. London was expensive and, occasionally, subject to terrorist violence. There were those bombs on the buses, and in the tube, a few years back. Same with Moscow. Mexico had its drug wars. Some of America's greatest cities had to contend with vicious gang wars.

What was it I'd heard about Thailand? Certainly the political unrest Marie had mentioned. But there was something else.

Prostitution. *Child* prostitution.

I wondered whether Marie's inability to travel was the real reason Len went on these trips without her.

FIFTY-THREE

"This is the sort of thing I'd have thought you might have checked first," Nicole said, sitting in the passenger seat, her feet propped up on the dashboard, the ice pick poised between her two index fingers.

Lewis said nothing.

"I might have found out whether our guy was actually in Burlington, Vermont, before flying the hell up here. But that's just me."

"It was the right house," Lewis said through gritted teeth. The van, driving through the night, was doing close to eighty, and felt as though it might float off the highway. They were heading west. He figured it would take them about two hours, maybe a little more, to get to their new destination.

An elderly neighbor had spotted them standing on the porch of Ray Kilbride's house when no one answered. She said her name was Gwen, and that she was picking up Ray's mail and any flyers left at the door while he was away, in Promise Falls. His dad

491

had just died, she said, and he was staying there while he sorted things out. He was looking after his brother, too.

"Can I help you with something?" she'd asked.

"Wait a minute," Nicole'd said. "You say someone named Ray lives here?"

"That's right."

Nicole had turned to Lewis and said, "I told you this was the wrong house. We're on the wrong side of town."

Lewis had shrugged. "I'm an idiot," he'd conceded.

"So you're not looking for Ray?" the neighbor had asked.

They'd said no, got back in the van, and pointed it in the direction of Promise Falls.

Along the way, Nicole needled Lewis about his fuckup. She wanted to get under his skin. Push him. See how angry he'd get.

It would be a clue to his intentions.

She said, "If it was me, I wouldn't have gone up and knocked on the front door. You find a way inside the house, get the jump on them there."

Lewis tightened his grip on the steering wheel. "Yeah, I guess you're right. We'll try it your way."

Being nice.

That was when she knew he was going to kill her when this was over. He was being nice so she'd be off her guard.

It would be easy to take him out first. She could put the pick through his neck while he drove, then grab the wheel, get her foot on the brake. In a big van like this, it wasn't hard to shift over to the driver's side.

Nicole knew she could do it.

But she had to let this play out. She needed answers to what was going on as much as Lewis and his people did. Had to find out whether this Kilbride was as big a risk to her as he was to those who'd hired her in the first place. And then she'd have to decide how much of a risk her associates — not just Lewis — posed to her. Whether she'd have to do something about them. Because she was done with this. She was through. She'd had enough.

Something had happened to her in that basement in Chicago. When she'd killed that Whirl360 guy's wife. Nicole didn't want to take any more orders from any of these men.

She'd ride this one out to its conclusion, keeping a close eye on Lewis the whole time. She'd taken at least one major precaution in the event he got the jump on her.

Lewis said, "Maybe, if we get a second, we can run in somewhere, get some coffee. My treat."

Oh yeah, he was definitely going to kill her.

FIFTY-FOUR

"This is good," Thomas said, shoving another forkful of Marie's tuna medley into his mouth.

"Yeah, not bad," I said. But I'd found, once Marie had left, that I did not have much of an appetite. The things Len had said to her, that she'd repeated for me, were stuck in my head. I couldn't shake the feeling he was up to something. Trying to lay something on Thomas that he hadn't done.

"I'm going to have seconds," Thomas said.

"That's fine. And maybe you'd like to clean up after dinner."

"Is that fair?" he asked.

"What do you mean, is it fair? Sure, it's fair."

"But you didn't make dinner. I thought, if you make dinner, I clean up. Or if I make dinner, you clean up. But Marie made dinner." He shoveled some more in.

"So if I follow your logic," I said, "if someone other than us does some of the du-

494

ties, whatever's left is my job."

He chewed slowly, like he was formulating an argument. "Well," he said, "that was just how it struck me at the time."

"So maybe we should both clean up," I said. "What about that? You clear the table and load the dishwasher, and I'll scrub out that casserole dish. Judging by how you're going there's not going to be any left over."

"Okay," he said.

Ten minutes later, we were standing side by side at the kitchen counter. I was filling the sink with soapy water as Thomas put our glasses and cutlery into the KitchenAid. Our shoulders were brushing up against each other, and we actually had a kind of rhythm going. We weren't talking, but it was the closest I'd felt to him since coming back here.

But later, as he was wiping down the kitchen table, Thomas said, "You ever feel like someone who was your friend really isn't your friend anymore?"

He wasn't looking at me when he asked. He was focused on making the table as clean as possible.

"Yeah, that's happened to me a few times. Who are we talking about here?"

"I don't know if I should say."

"It's okay. If you can't tell me, who can you tell?"

He caught my eye. "The president."

"Clinton?"

Thomas nodded, walked over to the sink to rinse out the cloth, and draped it over the faucet. "He's always been nice to me, except the last couple of times we've talked, it's kind of different."

"What do you mean, different?"

"I don't know. He's been putting a lot of pressure on me."

"Maybe you shouldn't talk to him anymore."

"When the president calls, you kind of have to talk to him," Thomas said.

"Yeah, well, I guess that's true."

"But he's telling me I can't talk about certain things. Things that don't have anything to do with my mission."

I rested a hand on his shoulder. "You want to go in and talk to Dr. Grigorin tomorrow? I could see if I can set something up."

"That might be good," he said. "I don't like it when the president says I'm going to look weak."

"Weak?"

"Like, if I say certain things, I'll be in trouble. He doesn't even want me to tell you."

"Tell me what?"

"About when I was in the window. When I waved to you, and you didn't see me. Because you didn't look up."

I stood there with him, the two of us leaned up against the kitchen counter. "When was this, Thomas?"

"The day you tried to find me. When you found my bike in the alley. Do you remember that?"

"Yes," I said. "I rode all over downtown trying to find you. I even shouted out your name."

"I heard you," Thomas said quietly. "That was when I got away, and ran to the window. I wanted to call out but I knew he'd get mad. But if you'd seen me, then Dad would have believed my story."

"Got away? Thomas, what happened?"

"He hurt me," he said. He briefly tucked his hand under himself. "He hurt me back here."

I put both hands on his shoulders now, squeezed. "Tell me what happened. Someone did something to you? Who? Who did something to you?"

"Dad got so mad," he said. "He got so mad when I told him. He said I had to stop making things up. He said if I ever talked about it again, he didn't know what he'd do. But I knew it would be something awful. Maybe he and Mom would send me away. To a place. So I never talked about it."

I hugged him. "Thomas, I'm so sorry."

"And I think . . . I think I'm ready to talk about it. But the president says I can't. He says if I tell anyone, bad things will happen."

"Thomas, who hurt you?"

He looked down into his lap. "I need to

think about this. I don't want to go against the president's wishes."

"Would you tell Dr. Grigorin?"

"I've wanted to, but haven't. You know who I would be okay telling?"

"Who?"

"Julie."

"You'd tell Julie?"

He nodded. "She's nice to me. She talks to me like I'm a regular person."

"Okay, well, she's coming back tonight, kind of late, but I'm sure she'd talk to you."

"Is she coming back to have sex with you?" he asked.

"Probably not now," I said, and smiled. "I think it would be great if you talked to her. I do. Can I be there, or would you like to talk to her by yourself?"

He thought about that. "She'll tell you later, won't she?"

"If you asked her not to, no, I don't think she would."

He looked down, pondering. "It would be okay if you want to be there."

"Okay. But she's not going to be here for a while, so do you want to watch some TV or something?"

"No. I have to go back to work. Even if I don't like the president's attitude lately, I still have my work to do."

"Sure," I said.

"But before Julie comes, I want to get some

pictures to show her."

"What pictures?"

"Our photo albums. So she'll know what I looked like then. And what you looked like. They're in the basement."

"Whatever you want. You know where they are?"

He nodded, then left me for his room. I went out to the porch and sat down for the better part of half an hour, until it was dark enough that you could see the stars. I went in, plunked myself down in front of the TV, and flipped through the channels. Nothing held my interest. It wasn't likely that anything could. I was preoccupied. Thinking about Julie. About my father. About Len Prentice.

About a face in a window, and two dead people in Chicago, and the late Allison Fitch.

About how I wouldn't have to be thinking about a lot of these things if Thomas had a different hobby. Stamp collectors never saw possible homicides, so far as I knew. Same for jewelry makers and gardeners.

I wondered whether Harry Peyton had had a chance yet to talk to this Duckworth guy he'd mentioned. Barry Duckworth. Was that why I hadn't heard anything yet? Had Harry talked to him, and Duckworth was looking into things right now? Or did Duckworth listen, and say it was the biggest crock of shit he'd ever heard in his entire life?

I couldn't think of any good reason why I

shouldn't just find out myself.

I turned off the TV, grabbed the laptop, and looked up the Promise Falls Police Department. I found a nonemergency number and dialed.

"Promise Falls Police Service," a woman said.

"I'm trying to reach Detective Duckworth," I said.

"I think he's gone home," she said. "Who's calling?"

"Ray Kilbride."

"Let me check." She put me on hold. While I was waiting, Thomas came down the stairs.

"What are you doing?" I asked, putting my hand over the receiver.

"I'm going downstairs to look for the photo album," he said, and disappeared through the door to the basement.

"Hello?" the woman on the switchboard said. "Mr. Kilbride?"

"Yes?"

"I reached Detective Duckworth at home for you. Hold on and I'll connect you." There was a pause, and then, "Go ahead."

"Hello?" I said. "Detective Duckworth?"

"Who is this? You told the switchboard you're Mr. Kilbride?"

"That's right."

"This some sort of joke? Not Adam Kilbride."

"No, sir. This is his son."

"Which son?"

"I'm Ray Kilbride."

"Okay, right," Detective Duckworth said. "You're the one from, where is it? Vermont somewhere?"

"Burlington."

"And your brother, that's Thomas?"

"Yes." I was guessing Harry had filled him in pretty thoroughly.

"You'll have to forgive me there a second ago," he said. "It threw me, when the girl called, said it was Mr. Kilbride. I'm sorry about your dad."

"Well, thanks. And thanks for talking to me. I don't know where to turn. I'm in kind of a mess here, as you probably know."

"Yeah, your dad and I had spoken," Duckworth said.

I felt as though someone had put my head in a paint mixer for a second. "Excuse me?" I said. "When was this?"

"A couple of weeks back," Duckworth said.

From the basement, Thomas shouted, "Ray!"

"My father spoke to you a couple of weeks ago?" I asked.

"That's right. That isn't why you're calling?"

"No — I mean, *yes*. I was just following up," I said.

"I told your father, if he wanted to proceed, it wasn't going to be an easy thing to prove."

"Ray!" Thomas shouted again.

"Hang on!" I shouted back. "Sorry about that. My brother's trying to find something in the basement. You were saying, it wouldn't be easy to prove."

"Not considering all the time that has elapsed. And the fact that your brother's testimony is going to be problematic, as I'm sure you can appreciate. Your father did. Also, he wasn't sure he wanted to put your brother through all that. He was a good man, your father. Only spoke to him the once, but he seemed like a decent guy, a good father. With a lot on his plate."

"Detective Duckworth, you won't believe this, but only in the last minute have I gotten any kind of inkling what you're talking about," I said. "My brother was assaulted, wasn't he?"

"Your father didn't share this with you?"

"No. But since I've been back here, since Dad died, some things have come up that have made me wonder whether something was going on. Something my father was worried my brother would never forgive him for. And . . ." I hesitated about whether to get into it, but what the hell. "My father had looked up child prostitution on the computer, but I don't know what sites he actually went to. My brother erased the history before I could find out."

"Yes, well," Duckworth said, "that does

502

figure into it. I'm not sure how much to discuss this with you, Ray, and to tell you the truth, your father held back some pretty relevant information. Like exactly who —"

"Ray!"

"Jesus," I muttered. "Detective, have you got a number where I can get back to you? In a couple of minutes? I really need to talk to you."

"Sure."

I grabbed a pencil from a kitchen drawer and scribbled the number down on a scratch pad. "I'll get *right* back to you."

"I'll be here."

I ended the call and left the phone on the counter. As I approached the basement door, I shouted, "For Christ's sake, Thomas, I was on the phone." I didn't see him as I came down the stairs. The basement was L-shaped, and I figured he was around the corner, where Dad had kept the photo albums.

"Where the hell are you?"

"Over here," he said.

I came around the corner, and there was Thomas. His eyes wide with fear. His arms were pulled back, like he was clasping his hands together behind himself.

And he wasn't alone. There was a woman standing behind, and to his side. She was holding Thomas by the hair with her left hand. In her right, she had what appeared to be an ice pick, and she had the tip touching the soft part of my brother's neck, just below the jaw.

FIFTY-FIVE

The woman said, "So you're Ray."

"Yes," I said, unable to take my eyes off the ice pick.

She tugged on Thomas's hair. "And this one? Thomas? He's your brother?"

"Yes."

"Ray, no one has to get hurt here if you don't do anything stupid."

"Okay," I said. "Please don't hurt him."

Thomas looked like he was standing out in the cold. His body was trembling. I couldn't see his hands, but I bet they were shaking. In our life together, I had never seen him look more terrified.

"Ray, tell her to let me go!"

"It's okay, Thomas. I'm going to give her whatever she wants."

"That's good, Ray," the woman said. "So long as you cooperate, everything will be fine." I noticed she had one of those Bluetooth thingies in her ear that was mostly hidden by blond hair that fell to her shoulders.

"You're clear to come in," she said, like she was talking to her shoulder. "We're in the basement."

"Just tell me what you want," I said.

"Right now I want you to be quiet," she said, still holding Thomas by the hair, the ice pick dimpling his neck. "Things'll be moving along shortly."

Even from down in the basement, I thought I could hear a car pulling up to the house. A distant sound of crunching gravel, then a door opening and closing. About half a minute later, the front door opened, and seconds after that, I heard someone coming down the steps behind me. I turned my head around, and once the man had descended far enough for the bare bulb to cast light on his face, I got a look at him. Tall, bald, heavyset, a nose that had been broken at some point.

He looked at me. "So you're Ray Kilbride."

"Yes," I said.

"Who's that?"

"This is the brother," the woman said. "Thomas."

"Hello, Thomas," the man said, his voice even. "I'm Lewis. I see you've met Nicole." As he came up alongside me I noticed a bulge under his leather bomber jacket that was larger than an ice pick. Slung over his shoulder was a small backpack.

"There's not much here but you're welcome to it," I said.

506

"Not my computer!" Thomas blurted.

Lewis cocked his head slightly to look me in the eye. "You think this is a robbery? Is that what you think?"

"They can't have my computer," Thomas repeated. "You can have my dad's."

"What do you want, then?" I asked.

"I want you to put your hands behind your back," Lewis said. He unzipped the backpack and took out a set of plastic handcuffs, the kind you see riot police using on protesters.

"Please," I said. "This is some kind of mistake."

Lewis said, "If I have to ask you again to put your hands behind your back, my friend's going to let some air into your brother's neck."

His voice carried a calm sense of authority. Coplike. My guess was, if he'd ever been one, he wasn't now.

I put my hands behind me. He slipped the narrow plastic bands over both wrists and pulled them snug. They bit cruelly into my skin. I immediately wiggled my fingers, wondering how long it would be before I started losing feeling in them.

"You good, Lewis?" the woman asked.

It worried me that they didn't care if we knew their names. I tried to calm myself with the thought that maybe they were using assumed ones. But that struck me as unlikely.

"Yeah," he said, at which point the woman

507

took the pick away from Thomas's throat and released her grip on his hair. She gave him a small shove in my direction.

"I'm scared, Ray," he said. He turned enough that I could see his wrists were already cuffed similarly to mine.

"I know," I said. "Me, too."

"We take them both?" Nicole asked Lewis.

"Good question," he said. "Let me think on that. First, I'm gonna do a walk-through of the house. Make sure there isn't anyone else around."

He went back upstairs, leaving Thomas and me with Nicole.

"Listen," I said to her, "we're —"

"Shut up," she said.

Lewis was back in two minutes. He had a puzzled expression on his face as he descended the stairs.

"What's the story upstairs?" he asked.

"The maps?" I said.

"Yeah. And the computer."

"They're mine," Thomas said. "I hope you didn't touch any of them."

"I think we need to move this party upstairs," Lewis said.

I nodded. I nudged my shoulder up against Thomas. "Come on, man," I said. "We'll do what they say and then everything'll be okay." I didn't know what else to do but lie.

Thomas went up the stairs after Lewis, and Nicole followed me. Thomas and I both took

508

the steps cautiously since we couldn't grab the two-by-four banister. I thought about spinning around and giving the woman a good kick in the face, and maybe if it had just been her, I'd have tried. But that would leave Lewis up in the kitchen, and if that bulge in his jacket was a gun, as I suspected, he'd make quick work of the two of us.

We crossed the first floor and went up the stairs to second-floor hallway.

Nicole had not seen what Lewis had already found. A hallway with maps stuck to the walls everywhere. She cast her eyes everywhere, across maps of South America, Australia, India, as well as detailed street maps including San Francisco, Cape Town, Denver. And that was just in a two-foot stretch.

"It gets better in here," Lewis said, pushing open the door to Thomas's room.

Nicole went in first, seemingly mesmerized by the walls, done up just like the hall. She said nothing as her eyes roamed over the maps. At one point, she reached out toward a map of Australia and, almost dreamily, touched her index finger to Sydney.

"And look at this," Lewis said to her, pointing to the computer monitors. Each of the three screens offered a different vantage point of the same street. "Where is that?" he asked me.

"I have no idea."

Thomas said, "Lisbon."

"Lisbon," Lewis repeated. "This is Whirl360, right?"

Thomas nodded.

"Whose computer is this?"

"Mine," my brother said.

"Why are you looking at Lisbon?"

"I look at everything," he said.

"What do you mean, everything?"

"He means everything," I said. "He looks at cities all over the world."

"Why?"

"It's a hobby," I said.

Thomas shot me a look, obviously wondering why I was lying. Then, to Lewis he said, "You already know, don't you?"

"Excuse me?"

"About the maps disappearing, and how I'm going to help the black-ops people."

Nicole said, "What the fuck?"

"You're the bad guys," Thomas said, like we were all kids playing cops and robbers.

Lewis cracked a smile. "I guess we are. So, let me ask you boys this. Which one of you was looking up Orchard Street on here?" He looked at me. "I thought it was you, since you're the one who came knocking on the door."

I felt a chill. It was starting to become clear just how much trouble we were in.

"The neighbor," I said.

Lewis shook his head. "Motion-activated camera. Trained on the apartment door."

510

So now we knew. "Oh," I said.

"Got a picture of what you were holding in your hand."

"Oh," I said again.

"So who was it?"

"I found it," Thomas said, a hint of pride in his voice. "I saw the lady with the bag over her head. Ray went to check it out for me."

Lewis looked at Nicole and said, "Well, I guess that answers your question." When she raised a questioning eyebrow, he added, "About whether we're taking one of them or both."

FIFTY-SIX

"We should take that with us," Nicole said, pointing to the computer tower that was connected to Thomas's monitors.

"Good idea," Lewis said.

"No," Thomas protested. "No, no!"

"Thomas," I said, nudging him again with my shoulder. "There's bigger stuff at stake here than the computer."

"But it's mine!" he said. He was horrified, watching Lewis start to unplug the wires that ran out of the back of it. "Stop it!"

Calmly, Nicole said to me, "Are you going to be able to control him?"

"Yes. Just let me talk to him a second."

Nicole allowed us to move a couple of feet away. I faced Thomas, leaned my head in close enough that I was nearly touching his forehead.

"Listen. We're in a tough spot here. I can always get you another computer. A way more powerful one. But the only way I'm going to have a chance to do that is if we co-

512

operate with them. You hearing me?"

"It's mine," he said.

"I need you to hold it together, Thomas. Can you do that for me?"

He raised his head, looked into my eyes. "You'd have to get me one that's just as fast."

"I'll get you one that's even faster," I said, making a promise I knew I was never going to be able to keep.

Lewis pulled the disconnected tower to the edge of the desk and asked me, "So what were you doing there?"

"What?"

"You heard me."

"My brother asked me to check it out. He was on that site, he saw something funny in the window, and he asked me to check it out when I was in the city."

"Oh," Lewis said. "So, it was just a huge coinkydink."

I smiled nervously. "Pretty much."

"You're telling me your brother's just goofing around online, sees this thing, and you decide to go all the way into the city to check it out."

"Yes."

Lewis looked at Nicole. "That's all it is. Just a bit of innocent Web surfing."

"Great. I guess we can go home now."

"Yeah," Lewis said, and came over, putting his face to within an inch of mine. His breath was hot on my cheek. "When we get where we're going, you're going to need to come up with a better story than that. You'll have lots of time to think of something on the way."

"Where are we going?" I asked.

Nicole said, "Tape."

Lewis reached into the backpack and brought out a roll of gray duct tape. He tossed it to Nicole. "Be my guest."

"I'm telling you the truth," I said. "It's just like I said. We don't know anything."

Nicole tore off a six-inch strip and slapped it over my mouth.

"Don't do that to me," Thomas said as Nicole started tearing off another strip. "Don't do that to me!"

He was in midscream as she applied the tape. His mouth was half open, and one side of the tape was caught on his lower teeth, allowing Thomas to keep moving his jaw.

"Shit," she said, and tore off another strip to seal the bottom half of his mouth. "Okay, we're good."

Lewis zipped up the backpack, slipped the strap over one shoulder, then picked up the computer tower with two hands.

Just then, a very faint ringing.

"What's that?" Nicole said. "That your cell?"

"No," Lewis said. He was looking around the room and his eyes landed on the old landline phone on Thomas's desk, still there from the days when he used dial-up for the Inter-

514

net and had his own number.

It was flashing red with an incoming call. Thomas always kept the ring volume very low, and he hardly got any calls, anyway. I couldn't think of anyone who might be calling him. It could only be one of two things. A wrong number, or a telemarketer.

But Nicole and Lewis wouldn't know that.

"Answer it or not answer it?" Lewis asked Nicole.

She was thinking, watching the light flash. "If someone's expecting him to be here, and he isn't . . ."

Thomas's eyes looked like they were going to pop out of his head, looking at that flashing red light.

Lewis snatched up the receiver. The first thing he did was cough, then sniff. When he spoke, he adopted the tone of someone sick with a cold.

"Hello?"

After a short pause, he said, "It's Thomas." Another sniff. "I'm coming down with something. Who's this?"

Half a beat went by. Then Lewis said, "Bill who?"

His eyebrows popped up momentarily, and then he smiled. "Yeah, well, I'd love to chat, Bill, but it's my bowling night with Dubya."

He hung up the phone. Nicole was looking at him, waiting for an explanation.

"Crank call," he said. "Some asshole pretending to be Bill Clinton."

I glanced at Thomas. I'm sure I looked more surprised than he did, because he didn't look surprised at all. Annoyed, maybe, that he hadn't been able to speak to the former president.

FIFTY-SEVEN

If it hadn't been for the tape, I probably would have said something along the lines of *holy shit*.

But neither Nicole nor Lewis had given the call another thought. They had other things on their minds. Like hitting the road, with Thomas and me as baggage.

Lewis headed out of the room first, the computer tower in his arms. Nicole motioned with her ice pick for us to follow. As we reached the top of the stairs I caught a glimpse of the front door swinging shut, Lewis already outside. My hands still bound behind me, I wondered whether there was anything I could do now that Nicole was, briefly, without her partner.

But what could I hope to accomplish? She had a weapon, and I had no free hand. I thought about something as simple as running. Bolting past Thomas, heading out the back door and into the night. Down the hill, through the creek, and once I was into the fields beyond, keeping low and out of sight until I got to some nearby house, where I could call the police.

It would mean leaving Thomas on his own, but abandoning him — briefly — might be my best chance of saving him.

These thoughts were running through my head — when it was Thomas who bolted.

He jumped down the last couple of steps. I expected him to do what I'd been thinking, and run to the back of the house, but he managed to wedge his foot into the front door before it closed all the way and kicked it open so he could run out onto the porch.

It wasn't an escape attempt. Thomas was going after his computer tower.

"Lewis!" Nicole shouted from two steps above me. Before I could do anything, she reached down and grabbed my shirt collar. "Don't even think it," she said, and I felt the tip of the ice pick touch the soft skin just under my right ear.

Outside, I heard something crash, then some scuffling in the gravel.

We went down the rest of the stairs at a steady pace. By the time we got outside, Thomas was on his back, looking up at Lewis, his body arched awkwardly with his hands cuffed behind him. A couple of feet away, the computer tower was on its side by the back of a white, mostly windowless van.

Lewis dragged Thomas to his feet. Then he

and Nicole corralled us at the rear doors of the van, which were still closed.

Nicole held her hand out for Lewis's backpack. He tossed it over and she produced the tape again, looping it around my knees and ankles. She did the same with Thomas. "You're going to have to hop in," she said, opening the two doors at the rear of the van. It was wide open for cargo, with two seats up front. I saw what looked like a small pile of folded moving blankets.

From his backpack, Lewis took out what looked like winter ski masks, with holes for the eyes, mouth, and nose.

He pulled the ski mask down over my head, with the holes at the back. I heard Thomas grunting his objections as his ski mask went on. Someone took me by the shoulders — Nicole, I thought, since the hands felt smaller than a man's — and led me into a quarter turn. "Two hops and you're at the bumper," she said. "Sit down and shoogle yourself in."

It took three, and I nearly fell over on the third. I felt the bumper at my knee, turned around, sat on the edge, and leaned over carefully until my upper arm touched the floor. Then I slowly shifted my body forward into the vehicle.

"Okay, dumb-ass," Lewis said to Thomas. "Shuffle on over here." I felt the van shift as Thomas fell into it. "Move up."

Then Nicole's voice. "We'll be on the road

519

for a few hours. Not a sound out of you. We'll be making stops. Tolls, gas. Somebody might come up to the window, say something. Don't be stupid and make any noise. That will get you killed. It'll also get whoever hears you killed."

"We already need gas," Lewis said. "Went through a tank getting here from Burlington."

I heard some ruffling next to me. The moving blankets. Someone was unfolding them, shaking them out. They were draped over us, I supposed, in case anyone looked inside. I didn't think it could get any darker, at night, inside the ski mask, but I was wrong. The world went pitch-black, and the sounds around me became more muffled.

The rear doors slammed shut; then the driver's door opened and closed, followed by the passenger's. I didn't know which one of them was driving, not that it mattered. The key was turned and the van rumbled to life. Tires crunching on gravel as we rolled on down the driveway, away from my father's house, and then turning onto the road.

We're never coming back here, I thought.

I had a lot of time to think, in my lightless, smothering isolation.

I'd thought, when we first headed out, I'd be able to get some sense of where we were going by the turns the van made. Hadn't I

520

seen that in a movie somewhere, or a *Batman* cartoon, or a *Sherlock Holmes* episode? The hero concentrates on the vehicle's movements, estimates the speed by the sound of the tires, pictures the landmarks they're passing, and by the time they come to a stop, he knows exactly where they are.

After three turns I had no idea where we were.

Just after we left the house, we made a stop for gas. I guessed we were at the Exxon, where I'd filled up a couple of times since coming back to Promise Falls. But once we were on the road again, I soon lost my bearings. It wasn't long before I was certain we were on an interstate. We were doing probably sixty or seventy miles an hour, and we weren't stopping or slowing down at all. Occasionally, I could hear the roar of eighteen-wheelers passing us, which suggested interstate to me. Every five or six seconds there was a small *thunk* as the tires went over a pavement seam. The tires would hum, then *thunk*; hum, then *thunk*. If I'd been sitting in the driver's seat, I might not have noticed the repetition, but lying on the cold metal floor of the van, there wasn't much else to listen to. Every noise and bump was amplified.

And throughout all these various ruminations, one other thought kept surfacing.

Who the hell called Thomas's phone?

Who had identified himself as Bill Clinton?

Surely not *the* Bill Clinton.

I'd walked in on Thomas when he was having one of his imaginary chats with the former president, and the receiver had been sitting firmly in the cradle. He had *not* been on the phone talking to anyone.

But none of us had imagined that phone ringing. I hadn't imagined Lewis saying the caller had identified himself as Bill Clinton. Lewis handled the call the same way I might have, had I not been familiar with Thomas's fantasies.

Except now I wasn't sure what was fantasy and what was real. I couldn't explain that phone call. It made no sense to me at all.

It couldn't be Clinton.

Couldn't be.

But it was somebody.

As I was thinking that, another phone began to ring. We were about half an hour into our trip. At first I wondered whether it might be my cell, which Lewis had slipped from my jacket at one point and tossed into his backpack, but I was pretty sure I'd seen him power it off. Maybe Julie calling to find out what had happened to us, why we weren't at the house when she arrived. But it was a different ring. Mine sounded like a piano, but this one mimicked an old-fashioned phone. After two rings, I heard Lewis say, "Here."

I struggled to filter out all other sounds so I

could hear his side of the conversation.

"Yeah, we're on the way back . . . no problems . . . Yeah, he's got a brother, he's the one found the thing online . . . he's kind of weird, a mental case or something . . . I don't know, I'm leaving that for you to ask . . . And the place was freaky, the walls plastered with maps . . . No, no, like *everywhere* . . . Yeah, okay, and I'm bringing back a computer, the tower, they were using to surf that Web site . . . Yeah, and one other thing, kinda strange, but probably nothing. Phone rang, I answered it, pretended to be the brother with a cold. Anyway, caller said he was, and I'm not making this up, the caller said he was Bill Clinton . . . No, no real accent, but I only talked to him a second . . . I mean, yeah, s'what I figured, too, a crank call or something . . . Okay, see ya at the toy store."

The next few miles went along in silence. Finally, Lewis said, "You haven't got much to say."

"You want to play I Spy?" Nicole said.

"Fine." More silence. After another couple of miles, Nicole said, "Shit."

"What?"

"I got a cop in my side mirror." So Nicole was driving. "Coming up in the passing lane."

"He got his lights on?" Lewis asked. With all the blind spots a panel van offered, Lewis probably couldn't see the car.

"No, he doesn't, but — shit."

"What?"

"He's got them on now."

And then we all heard a couple of *whoops* of the siren. I could sense Thomas stirring close to me. He'd no doubt been listening to everything just as closely as I had, and this most recent development probably had him wondering whether this was cause for hope.

The van slowed.

"Just be cool," Lewis said.

"You still carry a shield?" Nicole asked. "He thinks you're NYPD, he might cut us some slack."

"No." Lewis called back to us, "Either of you make a sound, cop gets shot."

The van went off the edge of the shoulder, smooth pavement changing to crushed stone. It came to a stop and Nicole put it into park, left the motor running.

"Pulling in right behind us," she said. "The door's opening. Here he — it's a woman."

"Shit," Lewis said. "They're always worse."

I heard a window power down. Nicole said, "Officer."

"License and registration," she said.

"Sure. Hon, you want to check the glove box?" Nicole asked Lewis, who sounded like he was shuffling through some papers, looking.

"This your van?" the woman asked.

"No, it's a rental," Nicole said. "We're just

going to his sister's in White Plains, helping her move to Albany. Was I speeding?"

"You have a taillight out," the police officer said.

"Oh, nuts. Is that my fault?" Nicole asked. "Isn't it the rental agency's?"

"When the vehicle is in your control, ma'am, you're responsible for any problems."

"Okay, well, if that's the way it is. If I get fined for this, can I go after the rental people?"

Nicole was good. She wasn't trying to blow her off, get rid of her in a hurry, which would set off alarms.

"That'd be up to you. I'm not going to ticket you. But if you're going to have this truck for any length of time, you're going to have to get it fixed. And you can send that bill to your rental company."

"Appreciate that, Officer. Okay, here's the registration, and here's my license."

"I'm going to take these back to my vehicle, ma'am. Please wait here until I return."

"Of course."

I heard the officer's footsteps as she went back to her cruiser. Nicole said, softly, "Everyone's being very good."

A few seconds later, the cop was back at the window, saying, "Okay, here you go. Your license, registration. And like I said, you get that taillight fixed first opportunity."

"Of course," Nicole said.

"Thanks, Officer," Lewis chimed in.

And then the cop, asking, "What you got in there?"

I didn't know about Thomas, but my heart stopped. The world, at that moment, seemed to freeze, as though we'd drifted into some kind of suspended animation.

I was thinking, *Please get out your gun, lady. Get out your gun.*

But Nicole didn't miss a beat. It was like she'd been waiting for the question. She said, "We have a stack of moving blankets so the furniture doesn't get scratched."

"You mind opening up the back for me?" the woman said.

"Hmm?" said Nicole.

"Just open it up and then you folks can be on your way."

"Sure," Nicole said. I heard a seat belt unbuckle and retract. I wondered whether she was reaching for her ice pick, or if Lewis was getting out his gun.

A door opened and it sounded as though Nicole had gotten out. Two sets of footsteps came down the side of the van, came to a stop around the back.

She's going to die. The cop is going to die.

"Could you open it, ma'am?" she said.

"Sure thing."

I was expecting to hear the door unlatch, but instead, there was some kind of electronic squawking. Static. Then the cop saying

526

something unintelligible.

Then, "Good night, ma'am. You can go." Then footsteps running away, the roar of the police car, tires hitting asphalt and squealing.

A door opened again, and the van shifted slightly as Nicole got back in.

"What the hell happened?" Lewis asked.

"She got some kind of emergency call."

We got back on the road.

Over the next hour, there was the sound of more traffic. We weren't able to maintain a steady rate of speed. The humming of the tires sounded hollow as we crossed a bridge.

We were clearly in a more densely populated area. There were the sounds of other cars, radios, horns. We turned left and then right, and left again. More turns than I could count or remember.

Finally, the van lurched to a stop, then backed up, turning sharply. The sound of the engine echoed back at us, like we were in a garage, or an alley.

Nicole killed the engine and the two of them got out. Seconds later, the back doors opened.

"Okay, kids, we're here," Nicole said.

FIFTY-EIGHT

It can't mean anything, Howard thought, moments after he'd finished talking to Lewis. He paced the floor of his brownstone living room, trying to think it through.

That call to the Kilbride house from someone claiming to be Bill Clinton was no doubt what Lewis believed it to be. A crank call. Or it could even be that it *was* Bill Clinton, just not *the* Bill Clinton. Howard himself knew a Franklin Clinton, a Robert Clinton, an Eleanor Clinton. Promise Falls probably had half a dozen Bill Clintons. Every town in America probably did.

And as worried as Howard was about the CIA's possible involvement in his and Morris's troubles, it made no sense at all to him that a former president would in any way be involved. That seemed even more preposterous than a Vermont illustrator doing undercover investigative work.

Soon enough, he'd be able to sort it out, once he was able to ask Ray Kilbride and his brother questions face-to-face. He had every confidence that Lewis, and this woman who'd botched things in the first place, and whom Lewis had brought along for this assignment, would be able to persuade them to talk.

Howard wondered about that, about why Lewis had brought her in for this — Howard sincerely hoped — last step in tying up any loose ends in this unfortunate mess. But he had a feeling. Now that this matter was coming to a close, Lewis was going to settle things. The woman's error had caused them all a great deal of grief. Howard had known Lewis long enough to know that he couldn't let that go.

Lewis would do what he felt he had to do. And Howard didn't need to know about it.

Nearly three hours later, another call from Lewis. "We've arrived."

"I'll be there shortly," Howard said.

They'd gotten into the city late, behind schedule. Howard was not going to be able to have his meeting with Morris Sawchuck. He'd call him from the car to cancel.

Howard stepped out onto the front stoop of his Eighty-first Street brownstone. His black Mercedes was parked just up the street. He walked to it and, standing by the driver's door, got out his cell phone and called Morris.

"Hey," Morris said. "I'm on my way."

There were muffled driving sounds in the background. He'd be in his town car, with his driver, Heather, who was available to chauffeur him around whenever he needed her, 24-7.

"I'm sorry, Morris, but I'm afraid I'm going to have to reschedule."

"What's going on?"

"I'm a little under the weather. Might be the flu. Let's talk in the morning. Maybe we can do this tomorrow night. A hundred apologies."

"Sorry to hear that. I was looking forward to this, but if you're sick, you need to take care of yourself."

"Thank you. I'm grateful for your understanding." Howard forced a chuckle. "Our plans for world domination will hold until tomorrow." He opened the driver's door, slipped in behind the wheel, the phone pressed to his ear the whole time.

"Of course," Morris said. "We'll talk then."

Howard ended the call, tossed the phone onto the leather passenger seat, pulled his door shut. He keyed the ignition and took off down the street.

Heather was just turning the town car onto Eighty-first when Morris, in the backseat, was telling his friend to take care of himself, that they would talk the next day.

Heather said, "Isn't that Mr. Talliman up

530

ahead, sir?"

Morris shifted to the center of the seat and peered through the windshield, saw Howard's car pulling away from the curb.

"Yes," Morris said. "He certainly appears well enough to drive."

"Would you like me to pull up alongside him?"

Morris only had to think for a second. "No. No, we won't do that."

"Home, then?"

"No," he said. "Let's see where he goes."

Which they did. All the way downtown to East Fourth Street. Howard parked his Mercedes at the curb and walked up to the front door of a darkened shop. There was an alley to the left of it, and a white van parked there.

"What is that place?" Morris asked. His eyes weren't as sharp as they used to be, but Heather was an owl at night.

"Ferber's Antiques," she said. Even though the display window was unlit, she said she thought she could see a variety of children's toys. The kinds they didn't make anymore. Metal cars, old trains, what looked like a Meccano crane, a Rock 'em Sock 'em Robots boxing game.

"What the hell is he doing at a toy store in the middle of the night?" Morris said. "The place is closed."

"Yes," Heather said, "but someone's there. A light just came on in the back. More like just a flicker, really."

Morris watched as someone unlocked the door, opened it wide enough to allow Howard to slip inside, then closed it after him. A moment later, another flicker of light, like a curtain was moving from side to side, and then the shop went dark.

"We'll wait," Morris said.

FIFTY-NINE

Earlier that evening, the Promise Falls City
Council was in a heated debate about
whether to sell advertising on city land. The
way it would work was, businesses could
purchase a small sign that said This Garden
Supported By, followed by the company's
name. The sign would be stuck into the
ground wherever the city maintained gardens.
So residents might see one by the tulip
garden at the south end of the common, or
along the median on Saratoga, or in the small
park in the west end of town where dog owners could let their pets run off the leash.
Some council members thought the signs
would be a blot on the landscape. Others
thought the plan was a great way to bring in
revenues without raising taxes. Someone
asked, "What are we going to do when a sex
shop wants to sponsor a garden across from
a church? Has anyone thought about that?"

Julie McGill, sitting at the press table, taking notes and giving a very good impression

of someone who gave a shit, was wondering whether she'd bought the right kind of wine to take when she went back out to see Ray.

She didn't really know if he was a red wine guy or a white wine guy. Maybe he wasn't a wine guy at all. She hadn't known him long enough to really know. So before she'd come to cover this council meeting, she'd bought two bottles of California red, one California white, and one French white, and a six-pack of Amstel. That way, she had all bases covered.

The problem was, she'd left all of it in her car when she got to city hall. It wasn't like you could walk into the mayor's office and say, *Hey, can you put these in the fridge while I write down all the stupid shit you and the rest of the council say over the next couple of hours?* Okay, maybe it wasn't such a big deal with the red, which supposedly you didn't serve chilled, although Julie still liked it that way. But maybe, once she got to Ray's place, they could start with the red and put the two bottles of white into the freezer for half an hour or so.

God, all this planning around drinking, it was like being back in high school. Although, she had to admit, her attitude on the subject had not changed much since then. What did it matter what they drank so long as they got a good buzz on? And then, maybe, with any luck, they could finish what they'd started the other night.

She wouldn't have to go back to the office to write this. The *Standard* had an office at city hall. Julie would pop in there, write a story on one of the computers about this ridiculous debate, file the damn thing, and get the hell out of here. These bozos actually had to think about this? It amazed her that even one person thought putting up tacky advertisements alongside roses, tulips, and azaleas was a good idea. You didn't need brains to hold office; you only needed votes.

Sitting there, taking notes, Julie thought she'd rather be making calls about Allison Fitch. Who she was, why she'd disappeared, how she'd ended up dead in Florida months after vanishing from her New York apartment. She believed there was a story there, but she knew that when and if she got it, it'd be a hard sell with her own editors. "What's this got to do with Promise Falls?" they'd want to know. She'd have to sell them on a local angle. That'd be Thomas, who'd inadvertently uncovered whatever it was that had happened by exploring the planet on Whirl360.

That gave her pause.

Would Thomas be okay being part of the story? How would Ray feel about it? She'd written plenty of stories without giving any thought to the embarrassment it might cause the principals, but she didn't want to do that this time.

She'd find a way around it.

The ads-in-gardens debate ended with a courageous vote to defer any decision at all, and instead refer the matter to a committee for further consideration. Everything left on the agenda was of even less consequence, so Julie grabbed her notepad and her purse and filed her story from the *Standard* office on the premises. Then she got in her car, reached around to the floor behind the passenger seat to make sure her beverage purchases were still there, and headed out of town to the Kilbride place.

She was about two hundred yards from her destination when she saw a white panel van pulling out of the driveway, heading her way. The van's headlights flashed past. She couldn't see who was driving, and didn't really even try to catch a look. It didn't strike her as a big deal. At first, she wasn't sure the van had come from Ray's driveway.

She did catch a glance in her side mirror of the van retreating, enough to notice that it had one burned-out taillight.

Julie hit her blinker and turned into the drive, rolled the car up to the house. Ray's car was there, as was his father's old Chrysler van, and the house was lit up like there was a party going on. The living room lights were blazing, and she could see the lights were on in Thomas's room.

She grabbed the booze from the backseat,

got out of the car, climbed the steps to the porch, and rapped on the door. When no one came after ten seconds, she opened it and shouted, "Hello?"

She waited a moment. When she heard nothing, she called out, "Ray? I can't drink all this wine alone! Well, maybe."

Still no response.

She went into the house, set the bag of bottles on the closest chair, and gazed into the kitchen. No one there, so she went to the bottom of the stairs and called up, "Anybody home?"

Julie went up the steps two at a time, poking her head first in Thomas's room, then the spare room and what used to be Ray's father's bedroom. The door to the bathroom was open.

Something about Thomas's room.

Julie returned to his room, stepped in, and immediately saw what had caught her attention at an unconscious level a moment earlier. A jumble of disconnected wires on the desktop. All three monitors were blank.

The computer tower was gone.

"What the . . ." Julie said under her breath.

She went back downstairs, and as she was going through the kitchen she noticed light spilling up from behind the open basement door. "Anyone down there?" she called.

She went down the stairs even though no one responded. Something on the floor caught her attention. Something even more worrying than the missing computer tower.

A white plastic wrist restraint.

"No," she whispered.

She ran back up the stairs and out the rear door. She ran to the top of the hill that overlooked the creek and shouted for Ray and Thomas. Then she ran over to the barn and did it again.

"Fuck me," she said, and ran back to her car.

She'd been here, what, maybe four minutes? Not a long time, but a van could cover four or more miles in that time. What kind of chance did she have of catching up with it?

That didn't stop her from spinning the car around and hitting fifty miles per hour before she'd reached the end of the drive. The car skittered and nearly went onto two wheels as she turned onto the road, then floored it in the direction the van had gone.

Once she hit the first intersection, which direction would she go? Left? Right? Straight? She didn't have a clue where the van was headed. On top of that, she didn't know with any certainty that Ray and Thomas were in it.

"Shit!" she shouted. Why the hell hadn't she just phoned his cell?

She fumbled blindly through her purse on the seat next to her until she'd found her phone. She held it in front of her, one eye on the road and one on the phone, and called up Ray's number, tapped it.

She put the phone to her ear, her left hand gripping the wheel. It rang once, twice —

"Come on! Answer your fucking phone, you asshole!"

After the seventh ring, it went to voice mail. "Hi, this is Ray. I can't —"

"Fuck!" Julie screamed, but not because Ray had not picked up. She slammed on the brakes, let her phone fly so she could get both hands on the wheel, and steered the car over onto the shoulder.

Up ahead, at the Exxon station, was the van.

A man was standing at the side, using the self-serve pump to fill the vehicle. From where she sat at the edge of the road, she couldn't see the front of the van, although she thought she could see an elbow resting on the sill of the driver's window.

What to do? She wasn't even sure it was the same van that had pulled out of Ray's place. It sure looked like the same van. A commercial type, no windows on the side. Should she drive in, pull up to the pump right alongside? See whose elbow that was? Whether there was anyone else in the van?

All she could think of was Allison Fitch, the dead couple in Chicago. If the people who'd killed them had figured out Ray had been to the apartment, then —

The man replaced the cap on the van's gas tank, replaced the pump, and went into the Exxon to pay. So he was using cash, since you could use your card at the pump if you wanted to.

Lots of people paid cash.

But if you didn't want a record of where you've been, you sure wouldn't use credit.

Before Julie could decide what to do, the decision was made for her. The man returned to the van, getting in on the passenger side. The taillight came on — just *one*, so this was the right van — and the truck pulled out of the station and got back on the road.

Julie took her foot off the brake, and followed. She kept well back. There weren't that many cars on the road this time of night, and the van was big and boxy, and white, so it wasn't hard to keep it in sight.

The van slowed a couple of times at intersections, like the driver didn't know where they were, or which way to go. But soon the van found its way onto the interstate, and got on the southbound.

Which, if you followed it for a couple of hours, would take you into New York City.

Julie glanced down at her fuel gauge. About half a tank. She hoped to God that wherever this van was going, it got there before she ran out of gas.

Once they were on the highway, Julie stayed

540

well back so as not to make the driver of the van suspicious. Her phone was somewhere on the floor in front of the passenger seat. She unbuckled her seat belt, and through some precarious contortions managed to reach the phone with her right hand, her head dipping below the dashboard, while still keeping the car going in a straight line.

Glancing back and forth between her phone and the road, she called the Promise Falls police, identified herself as a reporter for the *Standard*, and asked to speak to Detective Barry Duckworth.

"He's off duty," the dispatcher said.

"Well then fucking get him at home and tell him to call me!" Julie said.

"Excuse me?" the dispatcher said.

Julie rattled off her cell phone number. "Just have him call me, okay? It's about the Kilbrides."

"We'll see," the dispatcher said frostily, and hung up.

Shit, Julie thought. She'd come on too strong. She didn't like her chances that the dispatcher would pass on her message.

Seconds after the dispatcher ended the call, a police car screamed past Julie in the passing lane, giving her a momentary heart attack. At first, illogically, she thought it had something to do with her call to the Promise Falls cops, but this was a New York State police car, the kind that regularly patrolled the interstate.

Julie watched as it continued to speed away from her, but as it got closer to the van it slipped into the lane behind it, rode there for a minute or so, and then the flashing lights came on.

"Yes!" Julie said as the van pulled over to the shoulder.

Julie did the same, killing her lights, but she kept driving along the shoulder, closing the distance between herself and the patrol car, so she could get a better look at what was going on. She figured if Ray and Thomas were actually being held against their will in that van, as she suspected, this would be the end of it. This would be their rescue.

The cop — it looked like a woman from here — approached the van. She shared some words with the driver, probably asking for license and registration. Then she went back to the cop car, got in, and sat there while the van waited.

"Come on, come on," Julie said aloud.

A good three minutes went by before the cop got back out of her car and returned the paperwork to the driver. Then — hello, what was this? The driver — it was a woman, a blonde — was getting out, coming around to the back of the van with the cop.

She wants her to open up the back.

"Open the door open the door open the door."

But just as the blonde had her hand on the lever, the cop turned and ran back to her cruiser, hopped in, and sped away.

"No!"

Julie could guess what had happened. Another, more urgent call had taken priority.

Maybe, when the trooper was talking to the driver, she'd noticed something in the back that raised her suspicions. Not actual bodies. If she'd thought she'd seen bodies — living or dead — she wouldn't have headed off to another call. A large box, maybe? Some kind of container big enough to contain a body?

She had to have seen *something*.

"Shit," Julie said as the flashing lights of the police car faded away in the distance. The woman got back into the van, and seconds later it continued on its way.

So did Julie.

Almost twenty minutes later, Julie's cell rang. She answered without looking to see who it was.

"Hello."

"Detective Duckworth here. What's so important you have to get abusive with our dispatcher, Ms. McGill?"

"I think — okay, I don't know for sure — but I think someone may have snatched Ray Kilbride and his brother."

"What are you talking about?"

She told him about getting to the Kilbride house seconds after the van pulled out of the

543

driveway. The fact that no one was home. The missing computer, the set of plastic cuffs.

"He was supposed to call me back," Duckworth said.

"What?"

"Ray Kilbride called me. Then he was interrupted, said he was going to call me back soon, and he hasn't."

"I'm right," Julie said. "They've been taken."

"Who the hell would do that?" Duckworth asked. "Listen, I'm gonna go out to the Kilbride house, see what's going on. You got the license plate on the van?"

"I'm not close enough to read it. When I had the chance, I wasn't thinking."

"Okay, look, anything happens with the van, call me at this number. This is my cell. Got that?"

"I got it."

She stayed with the van.

There was an accident at the far end of the Lincoln Tunnel. Traffic was getting through a car at a time by the mouth. The white van was about five car lengths ahead. Once it was past the accident, it took off.

By the time Julie's car was past the fender bender, and she drove onto the island of Manhattan, the van was nowhere to be seen.

"Motherfucker!" she shouted, banging her fist against the steering wheel.

SIXTY

After pulling off the moving blankets and dragging me from the van, Nicole or Lewis tore off the tape that was binding my legs. But the ski mask stayed on. They led me through a door and guided me no more than half a dozen feet down what I supposed was a short hallway. My shoulder brushed up against a wall at one point, and wooden boards creaked below my feet. Hands from behind held both my shoulders, as though guiding me through a doorway.

Then the hands stopped me, and turned me 180 degrees.

"Sit," Lewis said, working my bound arms over the back of what felt like a standard wooden chair, then shoving me down into it. Then he ran a couple loops of duct tape about my waist, securing me to the chair. He didn't tape my ankles to the legs, so I moved them around in small circles, getting my blood circulating wherever I could. Suddenly, someone grabbed a fistful of ski mask at the top of my head and yanked, grabbing some of my hair in the process.

I blinked several times as my eyes adjusted to the light, although there wasn't all that much of it. Lewis was standing directly in front of me, then moved out of the way as Nicole brought Thomas into the room. He was pushed down onto a second chair a couple of feet away from me, taped in, and then Nicole pulled his ski mask off. He blinked a couple of times, as I had, then exchanged a frightened glance with me.

"I'll get the computer," Lewis said. "And let Howard know we're here."

We were in a windowless room, about twelve by twelve, that had the feel of being the back of a shop. In one corner was a heavy, antique rolltop desk, the sliding door in the up position to allow for a computer. The various cubbyholes were jammed with paperwork, what looked like bills, receipts, newspaper clippings. The walls were almost entirely covered in shelves, made from the same kind of planks that made up the worn, wood floor. The shelves were crammed with old, musty books, antique clocks, Royal Doulton figurines, old-fashioned cameras with bellows that could be stretched out, accordion-style. But most of all, there were toys. Decades-old tinplate cars and trucks, the paint worn off by children who were very likely dead now. Pewter toy soldiers. Dinky

Toys, like the ones I had when I was a kid. I spotted an Esso tanker truck my father had given me around the time I was three. An assortment of Batmobile models, in metal and plastic and in various scales. A set of lawn darts and hoops, like we once had and played with in the backyard until Thomas nearly speared the neighbor's dog. A child-sized plastic fireman's helmet in red with the word "Texaco" emblazoned across the front. Cardboard boxes of old board games based on long since canceled television shows, like *Columbo*, *The Six Million Dollar Man*, *The Brady Bunch*, and *The Man from U.N.C.L.E.* And, of course, countless dolls. Barbies, Raggedy Anns, Cabbage Patch Kids, and life-sized plastic babies whose eyes would shut when you laid them flat. Some were minus limbs; others, heads. One shelf contained a collection of old metal robots; another a pile of tinplate trains that looked as though they'd been in a catastrophic wreck. Three black balls, each about the size of a squash ball, which I recognized as sixties-era Wham-O Super Balls, the kind that could bounce over a house.

But I didn't feel nostalgic, looking at these treasures from yesterday. What I felt was scared. Scared shitless.

Lewis returned with the computer tower and set it on the desk. He detached various cables from the computer that was there, then attached them to Thomas's.

Nicole, expressionless, addressed Thomas and me. "Someone's going to be asking you some questions, so the tape's coming off. If either one of you starts yelling, I hurt the other one. Fast and hard. Are we clear?"

We both nodded. Nicole ripped the tape off me with one short, cruel, backhanded stroke. I winced, licked my lips, and tasted blood. When she did it to Thomas, he yelped. "That hurt!" he said, like he'd been kicked in the schoolyard. But then he immediately apologized to Nicole. "Sorry. I'll be quiet. Don't hurt Ray."

I said to him, "You okay?"

He shook his head. "No. My arms hurt, my lips hurt, and I can't feel my hands."

I couldn't feel mine, either. The plastic cuffs had cut off most of the circulation. I appealed to Nicole. "My brother's hands, they're probably turning blue. Mine, too. Can you help us out here?"

Lewis went into his backpack for a pair of orange-handled snippers. "Don't do anything stupid," he said as he cut my cuffs, then secured my wrists to the chair with duct tape. The blood rushed back into my fingers, and I closed and opened my hands a dozen times to get the tingling out of them. Lewis did the same thing for Thomas, then went back to work on the computer tower, hooking up the last of the cables and pressing the start but-

548

ton. The machine began to whir and the monitor he'd commandeered started lighting up.

Thomas said, "Anything that's on there is confidential."

The home screen, powder blue with only a couple of icons on it, cast a soft light across the room. There was one to open up an Internet browser, one for mail, one down in the corner for trash.

Lewis went on the Net and checked the computer's Internet history. Thomas hadn't had an opportunity to clear it, as was his custom at the end of the day, but there wasn't much to look at. Just plenty of locations from Whirl360.

Lewis said, "Don't you ever look at porn or anything?"

Thomas didn't appear to understand whether this was a serious question. He said, "I don't have time."

Lewis was clicking from image to image, city to city. All the different places Thomas had been exploring today — well, yesterday now. It had to be after midnight. "Why do you — no, I'll let Howard ask you. No sense going over it twice."

He got out of Whirl360 and opened up the mail program.

Thomas said to me, "He shouldn't be reading those." Then he started in with questions. "What city are we in? What street are we on?

What's the address?"

I'd been wondering the same thing, although maybe not with the same level of detail. We'd been driving long enough to be in New York or Boston or Buffalo and probably half a dozen other urban centers. We could be in Philadelphia, for all I knew.

Nicole ignored him, as did Lewis.

Thomas looked at me. "I want to go home."

"I know. I know. Just try to hang in."

Lewis was opening one e-mail after another, shaking his head slowly, no doubt trying to puzzle out what the hell Thomas was up to with all his updates to the CIA.

"What the fuck . . ."

He continued to read updates while Nicole looked around the room. She'd pull out a book, check the cover, put it back. She took a doll off the shelf and examined it like it was a souvenir from another planet. "My mother didn't let me play with dolls," she said to no one in particular.

Everyone looked up when we heard a knock. It came from a different direction than the way we'd come in. We'd entered this room, it seemed to me, from a side door, but the knock sounded as though it was coming from the front. Lewis left the computer, pulled aside a green curtain that served as a door between this room and the front of the shop. As light spilled into the front room I could make out more, and more orderly,

550

displays of antique toys.

"It's him," Lewis said to no one in particular as he slipped out of the room.

Who was *him*? It had been mentioned more than once that someone wanted to talk to us. Someone Lewis and Nicole reported to.

I was no less scared than I'd been since we left the house, but I was also curious. When you're pretty sure you're going to end up dead, wondering who you'll meet next provides some distraction.

I heard a small bell jingle as Lewis opened a door. There was some muffled conversation, then two sets of footsteps working their way to the back of the store. I heard a man ask Lewis, "What is this place?"

Lewis said, "One of the guys who helped me move Bridget's body owns it. He's a toy nut."

Bridget?

Then Lewis appeared, holding back the curtain to allow a stout, short, balding man in his fifties to come in. He was wearing a topcoat that looked like it was made of camel hair or cashmere, and an expensive suit under that.

He ran his eyes over Thomas and me. It struck me that he looked more dumbfounded than menacing.

"So, these are our guys," he said to Lewis.

"Yup," he said.

Then the man's eyes landed on Nicole.

She'd put away the doll and was leaning against one of the shelves stuffed with books, her arms crossed over her breasts.

"You," he said contemptuously. "You're the one who fucked this up."

"Nice to meet you at last, too, Howard," she said, meeting his gaze, staring him down.

Thomas and I gave Howard an excuse to break eye contact with her. He said to me, "Which one are you?"

"Ray Kilbride. That's Thomas. My brother."

Thomas said, "Tell that man — Lewis — tell him to leave my computer alone."

Howard turned to Lewis and said, "You have it hooked up?"

"Yeah. There's some weird shit on here. All these e-mails."

Howard reached into his jacket for a slender case, from which he extracted a pair of reading glasses. "Open a few."

Lewis did some clicking. Howard read quickly through the e-mails. "Are they all like this?"

"Yup."

"All addressed to Bill Clinton, care of the CIA?"

"Yeah."

Howard looked at us, then back at Lewis. "Tell me about the phone call again."

"Someone called the house, asked for that one, said it was Bill Clinton. Like I said."

"But you also said it didn't sound like him."

552

Lewis shrugged. "I mean, I've never talked to the man, but no, I don't think it sounded like him."

"People sound different on the phone," Thomas said.

Howard was still looking at the screen. "These e-mails, they're all in the sent file?"

"That's right," Lewis said.

"What about in the in-box, or the deleted messages. Are there actually any messages *from* Bill Clinton or anyone at the CIA?"

Lewis did some clicking. "Nothing."

Howard said, "Hmm." He went back through the curtain and returned with another chair. He sat it in front of Thomas and me. He looked first at me.

"Ray, I have a number of questions I need straight answers to. I suppose you understand what will happen if you don't provide them."

"I have a pretty good idea," I said.

He nodded slowly, like we were on the same wavelength. "We'll get back to the Clinton thing. But it makes sense to start from the beginning. Who do you work for?"

"I'm self-employed. I'm an illustrator. I work freelance."

"I see. You don't do any freelance work that's not related to illustration?"

"No."

"And how about you?" he asked Thomas. "For whom do *you* work?"

"I'm sort of self-employed, too," he said.

"But I work for the CIA."

"That's not true," I said. "Thomas —"

Howard held up a hand to shush me. "Thomas, tell me what you do for the CIA."

"I shouldn't be telling you," he said. "It's black ops."

Howard's eyebrows shot up. "Black ops?"

"That's what President Clinton said. But that's just part of it."

"If you don't tell me, Thomas, I'm going to have them start by breaking one of your brother's fingers."

"Don't hurt him," Thomas said. But I could see him struggling with whether to sacrifice me to protect the mission.

"It's okay," I said. "Tell them. I'm not saying this because I don't want them to hurt me, Thomas." I decided to play into his worldview. "I would imagine they already know most of it, anyway."

He nodded slowly. I wasn't sure whether he actually believed me, or was relieved to have found a way to tell Howard what he wanted to know without feeling too guilty about it.

"Well," Thomas said, "I'm helping them for when all the online maps disappear, because that's going to happen sooner or later, and also I'm going to be on call, if there's an agent in trouble. Like, if he's on the run in Mumbai or something and doesn't know which way to go, he'll call me and I can tell him." He said this all very matter-of-factly, like a kid discussing his paper route.

"Explain that a little more," Howard said.

"Which part?"

"Any of it."

"I memorize maps. I memorize cities. I memorize the streets. So when all the maps disappear, I can help."

Lewis said, "The computer history's all Whirl360."

"You memorize streets on Whirl360?" Howard asked.

Thomas nodded. "That's right."

Howard smiled and tapped his own head with an index finger. "And you keep it all up here?"

Again: "That's right."

"So how does this work? If I give you an address, you can describe it for me?"

Thomas nodded.

Howard gave him a skeptical look. "Okay," he said, playing along. "My mother lives on Atlantic Avenue, in Boston. She has an apartment there."

Thomas closed his eyes. "Near Beach Street? That's nice along there. Is she in that building with the real estate office on the first floor? All the sidewalks there are made of red brick. They look really nice." He opened his eyes.

Howard appeared slightly unnerved. He looked my way and I said, "He's never been to Boston."

"Okay, I got one," Lewis said. "The twenty-seven-hundred block of California Street in Denver. Between Twenty-seventh and Twenty-eighth." He said to Howard, "I grew up there."

Thomas closed his eyes again. "Was it in one of the one-story blue houses, or the six-story apartment building across the street with the walls that are kind of white, then go to brick color, then back to white, and —"

"Jesus Christ," Lewis said. "It's like he's got a fucking computer in his head."

Howard said, "Which was it, Lewis? One of the little blue houses, or the apartment?"

"The apartment," he said quietly.

Howard took a very long breath, laced his fingers together, and rested his forearms on his thighs. "How many cities are you memorizing, Thomas?"

"All of them," he said.

Howard's head retreated a little in surprise. "All of them in the United States?"

"In the world," Thomas said. "I'm not done. The world's very big. If you asked me about, say, Gomez Palacio, in Mexico, I haven't gotten there yet. There's probably more places I haven't gotten to than I have gotten to, like smaller cities and towns, because I'm trying to finish the big cities first."

"Okay," Howard said, glancing over at Nicole, who hadn't moved a muscle since he'd last spoken to her. "So, Thomas, let's say we've established that you really do have some kind of gift. I have to admit, I am impressed."

"Thank you," Thomas said. Despite our current situation, the praise pleased him.

"So this is what you do, you memorize these streets," Howard said, a statement, not a question. "And what are all those e-mails about?"

"Updates," Thomas said, with a tone that suggested that was a pretty dumb question. Like, *What the hell else would they be?*

"Updates on?"

"On how the project is going. When I memorize new cities, or parts of them, I let the president know."

"And what's this other thing you mentioned, about all the online maps disappearing?"

Thomas gave Howard a wary look. "I bet you know all about that."

"Well, if I do, then it won't hurt if you tell me."

"There's going to be some kind of catastrophic event that destroys all the online maps. A virus or something. Maybe caused by some enemy of the United States. This will happen after everyone's gotten rid of their paper maps, because we all rely on the computer now. It's kind of like photos. Everyone used to have their pictures developed on paper, but now they post them on-line. When everything crashes, everyone will lose all their photos. It'll be like that with maps."

Now Howard looked at me. "Is he for real?"

"Yes," I said.

"Does this freakish ability of his have something to do with why you showed up at Allison Fitch's apartment on Orchard Street?"

I nodded. "Thomas was memorizing that street, and he saw the woman in the window. With the bag over her head." My mouth was dry, and I licked my lips. "He wanted me to check it out."

"How did he know to look for it?"

"He didn't. He just found it."

"No," Howard said. "I don't believe that. The odds of that, they're a billion to one."

"No," Thomas said. "The odds are that eventually I will see everything."

Howard turned to Lewis. "What do you think?"

"I don't know. Seems kind of unlikely to me. Maybe someone asked him to look for it."

"Is that what happened, Thomas? Someone asked you to look for it?"

"No," he said. "Nobody did."

"Not even Bill Clinton?" Howard followed the question with a nervous laugh.

"No, I just send him the progress reports.

He's my liaison with the agency."

"But he never e-mails you back. There aren't any e-mails in your in-box, or in the trash."

"He communicates with me, but not through e-mail."

"Communicates how?"

"He talks to me. Lately, he's been using the phone."

"What, his voice just comes to you?"

Thomas nodded.

I'd been so preoccupied with everything that had happened to Thomas and me the last few hours, I hadn't had much time to think about that phone call. I still had no idea what it meant, and was wondering whether I had to understand it to somehow use it to my advantage. This bunch was clearly in the dark as much as I was.

Howard gave his head a shake and said to Lewis, "There's no goddamn way this freak has chats with a former president."

"I agree," Lewis said. "Can't be."

"Thomas," Howard continued, "do you see a doctor? A psychiatrist?"

"Yes. Dr. Grigorin."

"And does he have you on medication?"

"It's a she," Thomas said. "Yes. It makes the voices go away. For the most part. But I can still hear the president sometimes."

"With a phone, and without a phone," Howard said.

"The phone's clearer," Thomas said.

"No way," Howard said again. "There's just no way."

"You're right," I said tentatively, making Howard turn and look at me. "It makes no sense that a former president of the United States would be phoning someone like Thomas and using him for the CIA. It's ridiculous. You're absolutely right."

Howard could tell I was going someplace with this, so he waited.

"I mean, you've seen what Thomas can do. He has an extraordinary talent. But at the same time, his view of reality is sometimes at odds with what the rest of us believe. He was diagnosed with schizophrenia when he was much younger."

Thomas gave me a disdainful look that said, *That doesn't mean I'm not right.*

I continued, "I mean, this whole thing about all the maps disappearing, and black ops. It's kind of over the top. But let's say you have someone with a tremendous gift, but who also tends to believe in grandiose conspiracies, who believes that very powerful people are interested in what he has to offer. Do you call him up and say, 'Hi, this is Joe Blow. I wonder if you could do a little snooping around for me?' Or do you call him up and say, 'Hi, I used to be president of the United States, and I need your help.' "

Howard studied me for several seconds.

"What are you saying?"

"Okay, I'm gonna come clean here. I'm saying that my brother's not doing work for the CIA, or the FBI, or Bill Clinton, or Franklin Delano Roosevelt. But he is, unknowingly," and at this point I looked apologetically at Thomas, "helping Carlo Vachon."

"Who?" Thomas asked.

"Vachon?" Lewis said. "The mob guy?"

Even Nicole, who had been doing her best to look disinterested in the proceedings, perked up at that.

"A mob guy?" Thomas said.

"And," I continued, "they value Thomas so much, and keep such close tabs on him, there's a very good chance his people are watching this place right now."

SIXTY-ONE

"Preposterous," Howard said. "That's simply preposterous."

"Hang on, hang on, hang on," Lewis said, shaking his hand at Howard. "When I was checking this guy out" — and he nodded at me — "I came across one of his drawings, his illustrations, you call them. Of Carlo Vachon."

"That's right," I said. "I did it for a magazine, and he liked it so much, he wanted to buy it."

"It wasn't a flattering portrait," Lewis said. "You had him sticking up the Statue of Liberty."

"Mob guys love that kind of thing," I said. "It's like politicians. Even when you do a cartoon savaging them, they want the original framed on their wall. Better that kind of attention than none at all."

"I still don't believe it," Howard said.

"I didn't want to take any money for it — not that he offered, since I think he was

562

expecting it for nothing. But when we said he could have it, he invited me to lunch."

"You had lunch with Carlo Vachon," Howard said.

"Yeah."

"Where?"

Think fast. "The Tribeca Grand." Where Jeremy and I had met with Kathleen Ford.

"What did you have?" Howard asked.

Don't try to lie any more than you have to.

"I have no idea. I was scared shitless and remember almost nothing." I paused. "I drank a lot. But he asked me about my family, and I got to talking about my brother, and what he does, and Vachon became very, very interested."

Howard didn't say anything this time. He waited.

But Thomas jumped in. "You never told me about this. When did this happen?"

"Just hang on." To Howard, I said, "Vachon didn't care all that much about the rest of the world, but having a guy who knew New York City with his eyes closed, who could remember every street detail, he said he could use someone like that. For some of the same reasons Thomas mentioned, like if you have an agent on the run. Except it's not agents. It's people working for Vachon."

"I'm not happy about this, Ray," Thomas said. "You should have told me about this."

"He's not an easy guy to say no to," I said.

563

"You know how many murders are tied to the Vachon family? You think I was going to tell a guy like that to get stuffed?"

Howard and Lewis were exchanging looks, wondering whether to believe this crock of shit. The good thing was, it seemed to be buying me some time. Time for what, I didn't know. But we weren't dead yet, and that was definitely a plus. I wondered what efforts, if any, were being made to find us. Julie had been intending to come back to the house. What would she have done when she found the house empty, no sign of us, the car still in the driveway?

Howard was about to say something, when his cell phone rang. He took it out, saw who it was, and grimaced.

He put the phone to his ear. "Hi, Morris . . . No, no, don't worry. You didn't wake me . . . Yes, I'm in bed, but I can't seem to settle down . . . Yes, sure, I could call him tomorrow . . . Uh-huh . . . he did do good work on that campaign . . . No, I don't mind, and again, I'm sorry about having to cancel tonight. I just wasn't up to it . . . Uh-huh . . . Okay, then . . . You, too, take care."

He ended the call, put the phone away, glanced at Lewis, and said, "He wanted to meet tonight."

The phone call done with, Howard returned his attention to me. "Now, where we were?

564

Oh yes, your story. I find it implausible at best."

"What part of everything you've heard so far *does* strike you as plausible?" I asked. "My brother found, online, a murder you folks carried out. Does that sound plausible? Does it sound plausible that a bunch of professional killers like you would leave yourselves so vulnerable and exposed?"

I had him there.

"If you don't believe me," I said, "why don't you call him?"

"Excuse me?" Howard said.

"Vachon. Give him a call."

Howard laughed. "Now, there's an idea. I'll give the head of one of New York's most powerful crime families a call in the middle of the night. I'm sure that would go over well." Then he got serious. "Why would they be keeping an eye on Thomas? Why should I believe they might be watching him now?"

I swallowed. "If you had a resource like Thomas, wouldn't you want to keep him safe?"

I could see the slightest hint of worry in Howard's eyes. I don't think he believed it, but he was afraid to dismiss what I'd said altogether.

"Let's say this story of yours is true," he said. "Carlo Vachon is Thomas's guardian angel. Was it Vachon who had him looking for the window?"

Which was the better answer? Yes, Vachon was on to them, or no, he didn't know a damn thing about it? Maybe, if I'd had some idea of who'd actually died in the apartment, I'd know which answer to give. At one point we'd thought Allison Fitch had been murdered there, but she'd only died in the last day. Lewis had said the words "Bridget's body" to Howard when he had arrived. I had no idea who Bridget was, but wondered if she'd been the Orchard Street victim.

While I was thinking, Thomas said, "I found it on my own. I told you."

Howard leaned back in his chair and took a long breath. "I swear, I don't know what to make of this." He turned so he could look directly at Lewis. "If this is some random event, if this *Rain Man* freak here really stumbled upon that image on the Web site by chance, then our problems end here."

"Yeah," Lewis said.

"The Clinton thing, the e-mails to the CIA . . . debunking those details eases my mind in ways I will not bother to elaborate on." He rubbed his chin contemplatively. "But this other matter, of Vachon . . ."

"I'm not buying it," Lewis said.

Howard spun his butt around on the seat so he could address Nicole. "You've been rather quiet."

She didn't respond.

"Have you any thoughts on this matter?"

566

She thought a moment. "I think, if they were keeping tabs on Thomas, they'd have rescued him by now. If you feel your other concerns have been addressed, then all you have left to do is get rid of these two."

"Yes," Howard said. "You may be —"

I think it's fair to say all of us just about jumped out of our skin at that moment. Someone was banging on the front door of the shop.

"Jesus," Lewis said.

Howard looked at me. "Is that them?" When he found me speechless, he asked the same question of Thomas.

Thomas said, "Maybe."

The banging continued. Then, shouting: "Howard! Howard, I know you're in there!"

Howard's eyes went wide. In that instant, he looked truly rattled, more than any other time since he'd arrived.

"Dear God," he said. "It's Morris."

SIXTY-TWO

Shortly after putting his phone away, Morris Sawchuck said to his driver, Heather, "I'm not waiting any longer. I'm gonna find out what the son of a bitch is up to."

"I'll be here," she said.

Morris got out of the town car, stormed across the street, and banged on the door of the toy shop. "Howard! Howard, I know you're in there!"

Morris put his eyes up to the glass and cupped his hands around his head. There was a light on in the back of the shop. Then a curtain was pulled back and Howard strode toward the door. He turned back the dead bolt and opened the door six inches.

"You're up and around," Sawchuck said.

"Morris, Jesus, what are you doing here?"

"Open the door," Morris said.

"Morris, you can't —"

Morris threw his shoulder into the door and knocked it wide open, tossing Howard back and causing him to trip on a child's pedal car

568

from the 1950s. Sprawled out on the floor, he found himself looking up at Morris.

"What's going on here?" Morris demanded.

"You have to leave. You don't want to be here. You have to —"

"I'm not going anywhere! You lied to me, Howard. You lied to me about being sick, about what you've been doing tonight. And I've got a feeling you've been lying to me for a long time. I swear to God, if you don't tell me what's going on, I'll —"

He looked to the back of the store, and the light coming through the curtain. He could see shadows moving behind it.

"What's going on in there?"

Howard, pleading, said, "You have to leave. This is what I do for you, Morris. I keep things from you. I get things done. I make the sausages. Nobody likes to know how they're made, but I do it for you, to protect —"

"Oh, fuck off," he said. "This is different."

Morris took a step toward the curtain and Howard clutched his leg. "No!" he said.

Morris stumbled and kicked, catching Howard under the chin with the toe of his Florsheims.

"Shit!" he shouted, releasing his grasp. Morris made it to the curtain in under two seconds, threw it back, and stared.

A man he recognized — Lewis, who had done work for Howard for years — and a woman, standing at the back of the room, he did not.

And two men bound into chairs.

"Hello, Morris," Lewis said as the attorney general stared, openmouthed, at the scene before him.

Howard, out of breath, his chin bloodied, stepped through the curtain.

"Morris, I told you —"

"Who are these men?" Morris asked.

"I'm Ray Kilbride," said one. "And this is my brother, Thomas."

"Who are you?" Morris asked the woman.

"The fuckup," she said.

"Untie these men," Morris ordered. He wasn't giving the order to anyone in particular, but it was clear he expected Lewis or Howard to respond.

Howard said, "It's not that simple."

"Oh, I think it is," Morris spluttered. "I don't know what the hell is going on here, but this is kidnapping. You can't hold these men here against their will."

"There are things you don't know," Howard said.

"Then tell me," he said.

"It's . . . complicated."

Morris's eyes narrowed as he looked at Howard. "Maybe if you talk really slow I'll be able to understand."

"It's about the murder," the one named Thomas said. "On Orchard Street."

570

"What murder? What are you talking about?"

"Shut up!" Howard said. "Morris, we're leaving right —"

From behind, Howard grabbed him by the arms and tried to steer him out of the room, but Morris shook free.

"What murder?" he asked again.

The one named Ray said, "We don't know, but it might be someone named Bridget."

SIXTY-THREE

The moment I uttered the words, it was like the air had suddenly been sucked out of the room. Something palpable happened to Howard, Lewis, and Nicole at that moment. Their breath was taken away and they didn't know what to do about it.

And this man they were calling Morris, it was like he'd been hit by lightning. He seemed frozen and electrified simultaneously. Stunned by what I'd said, too shocked to react in any way but to look stupefied. And yet, I could see that wheels were turning. There was something about his eyes, like they were moving around at a hundred miles an hour, processing this latest bit of information.

In that instant, it was as though everything had changed. Some kind of balance had shifted. We were now in a very different situation from the one of five minutes earlier. Whether it meant things were better for Thomas and me, I didn't know, although I hadn't thought our situation could get any worse.

And about Morris. The moment he'd walked into the room, I recognized him.

I couldn't place him at first, maybe because I wasn't seeing him in the proper context. If I'd been watching the news, I'd have known instantly. But seeing him here, in the back of this toy store, with three very bad people, I couldn't figure out who he was. It was like when, every morning, the same person hands you your coffee at Dunkin' Donuts, and then you see that person at the mall. You know you know them, but can't figure out from where.

So it took a minute or so before I realized this man was the attorney general for the State of New York.

Morris Sawchuck.

I'd read about him. I'd seen him on the news. In fact, hadn't there been a lot going on with him a few months back . . .

In the midst of everything that was happening in that room, my mind was racing. Why had he been on the news so much? Why had I seen his picture so often? And in all those pictures, wasn't he usually shown with a beautiful —

Oh fuck.

I didn't actually put it together until after I'd said what I'd said.

About Bridget.

Now I remembered the stories. The sudden, unexplained death of Bridget Sawchuck, the wife of New York's attorney general. You had to read between the lines to guess what had happened. She'd killed herself.

Except Lewis had said this shop was owned by someone who'd helped him move Bridget's body.

Oh God, Thomas, what did you get us into?

The silence that followed my comment felt as though it lasted minutes, if not hours, but in reality it was probably no more than four or five seconds.

Morris was the first to speak. And he spoke to me.

"What did you say?"

"The person who got killed. It might have been Bridget." Now I realized the significance of what I was saying. I was talking about this man's wife. What I didn't know yet was whether Morris Sawchuck looked shocked because he didn't know, or because I did. For all I knew, the man had had his wife killed.

All that was about to become clear. Or clearer.

Morris said to Howard, so calmly that it was frightening, "What's he talking about?"

"I don't know," Howard said, rattling the words off too quickly. "He's some kind of crazy person, him and his brother. They're a couple of nutcases, going around spreading

574

stories that could damage you. That's what they're doing."

"No," I said. "My brother found out what they did. They brought us here to kill us and —"

"Shut the fuck up," Lewis said.

"No, let him talk," Morris said. "I want to hear what this nutcase has to say."

"Thomas was surfing the Net," I said. "Whirl360. He saw someone being murdered in the window of an apartment on Orchard Street. I think it was your wife. Bridget, right?"

He nodded slowly. His face was becoming flushed.

"Really, you shouldn't listen to —"

"Howard," Lewis interrupted. "Enough."

"What? Lewis, let me —"

"No, we have to bring him into it," Lewis said. "He's either on board, or we'll have to kill him, too."

"What?" Morris said, turning on Lewis. "Who the hell do you think you are?"

"I'm a survivor," he said. "So's Howard, and so are you. There's only one way everyone survives this, and that's to get on board."

"What happened to Bridget?" Morris demanded. "I want the truth."

The room went quiet for another few seconds. It was Howard who spoke first. "It was an accident. A horrible mistake."

"Dear God," Morris said. "You didn't."

575

Howard continued. "There was a woman, Allison Fitch. She was blackmailing Bridget. She was trying to damage her, to ruin you. We — I was afraid there were things she knew that could hurt you very badly."

"Howard."

"Politically fatal, Morris. I was going to pay her at first, I was, but it became clear that wasn't going to solve our problem. Lewis and I talked and we decided we had to deal with the Fitch woman more . . . permanently."

"I can't believe I'm hearing this." Morris couldn't take his eyes off Howard.

"But when it came time to do it, to take care of the problem, something no one could have foreseen came up. She wasn't there. Fitch wasn't in the apartment." He paused, swallowed. "But Bridget was. She was mistaken for Fitch."

"But . . . but we found her. In her old apartment," Morris said. "You and I, we found her there."

"She . . . was moved."

"But you talked to her!" Morris said. "You spoke to her on the phone! She told you I was sucking the life out of her! She was going to kill herself!"

Howard had to look away. "I . . . it was faked. There was no call. I made that up."

Morris grabbed Howard by the lapels and threw him up against the shelves, knocking that Esso tanker truck and a Batmobile to the floor with a loud clatter. "You son of a bitch!" he shouted, shaking the man. He let go of a lapel, made a fist, and drove it straight into Howard's face. Howard yelped and fell to the floor. Morris pounced on him and was about to punch him again when Lewis locked arms around him and dragged him off.

"Stop!" Lewis said. "You can sort this out later, but right now we have to figure out what to do."

"I'm gonna kill you," Morris said, still in Lewis's grasp, staring down at Howard. "You bastard! You son of a bitch!"

"It wasn't my mistake!" Howard said. "It wasn't my fault!" He pointed across the room. "It was hers!"

Now all eyes were on Nicole.

Morris said, "You?"

"Like they said, it was a mistake," she said coolly.

"You killed Bridget?"

"They told me Fitch would be there. And someone *was* there. But it wasn't Fitch." Nicole shrugged. "Sorry."

Morris said, "Excuse me?"

"I said, sorry. Not much else I can say at this point, really."

Morris, aghast, looked at Howard, then Lewis.

Lewis said, "She's kind of right." Noticing that Morris was speechless with rage, he continued, "Howard, I think there's a good-faith gesture we can make with Morris as a way of moving forward."

"What are you talking about?" Howard said.

"We can't bring Bridget back, but we can help make things right," Lewis said, reaching into his jacket and taking out his gun.

He spun around, pointed it at Nicole, and pulled the trigger. I was expecting a louder bang, but the gun was equipped with one of those silencer things on the end of the barrel.

What made noise was Nicole being thrown up against the shelves, the back of her head banging into them, then dropping facedown onto the floor. Two shelves gave way and an avalanche of toys crashed to the floor. A Super Ball bounced in tall arcs across the room.

"I was going to get around to it sooner or later, anyway," Lewis said.

Sixty-Four

The room was as still now as it had been when I'd first mentioned Bridget. Morris Sawchuck looked disbelievingly at Lewis, at Nicole on the floor.

"What in God's name have you done?" he asked him.

"What I always do," Lewis said. "Take care of problems for you and Howard."

Suddenly, Morris reached into his jacket and now there was a gun in his hand, too. I guessed, when you were the attorney general, you packed heat. Lewis seemed to know instinctively what Morris was going for, so by the time Morris had his weapon pointed at Lewis's head, Lewis had his pointed right back at Morris's.

They stood there, frozen, guns pointed at each other.

"Let's all try to calm down," Howard said.

Morris, not taking his eyes off Lewis, said, "No one kills for me. No one does this kind of thing on my behalf."

"It's already been done," Howard said softly, standing behind Morris. "This isn't going to get better if you shoot Lewis. We need him."

"Jesus, Howard, just shut up."

Lewis had his arms locked, his finger on the trigger, the gun still pointed straight at Morris's head. His stance, his posture, suggested he was more used to doing this than Morris, but the attorney general looked equally committed, ready to shoot if he had to.

"No," Howard said. "You have to listen. Things have already been done on your behalf. Bad things. *Ugly* things. Things that, if they come out, you'll never be able to distance yourself from, never be able to convince people you didn't order yourself. Morris, *listen* to me. They'll put you away forever. Not just me, not just Lewis, but all of us. You may not be able to see it, but there's blood on your hands."

Morris and Lewis kept their guns trained on each other.

Howard continued, "It gets worse. The whole world will believe you killed Bridget. They're going to think you had her killed, Morris. I know you want to do the right thing here, but we're too far past that. And things will come out about her. About Bridget. Although . . ." His voice trailed off. "They hardly matter now."

580

Morris was breathing through his nose. In and out, in and out, his nostrils flaring with each agitated breath. Then, as suddenly as he'd raised his weapon, he lowered it and looked down at the floor, an admission of defeat. He tucked the gun back into his jacket.

Lewis slowly put his arm down, but kept the gun firmly gripped in his hand.

Even though Morris shooting Lewis might have been in my interest, I breathed a sigh of relief along with everyone else. I looked over at Thomas, expecting him to be a nervous wreck, but he had his eyes closed. I was guessing he'd had them closed through most of this.

"Thomas," I said. "You can open your eyes."

He did, looked briefly at Nicole's body, then at me. He said nothing, but his eyes were pleading. They were asking me to get us out of here. My eyes didn't have a reassuring answer.

Morris was shaking his head. Lewis and Howard watched him warily, unsure of what he'd do next.

Morris turned, brushed past Howard, threw back the curtain, and started walking toward the front door.

"Morris?" Howard said.

"What the hell's he going to do?" Lewis said. "Goddamn it."

Howard went after him. I could see that Lewis wanted to, as well. He gave Thomas and me a quick look, figured we weren't going anywhere, and followed the two other men.

I heard the door open, but it closed almost immediately, suggesting to me that Morris had tried to leave but one of the other men had slammed the door shut before he could. The three of them began arguing, talking at once. I didn't know what they were saying, and right now, I didn't care.

I figured if Thomas and I were ever going to have a chance, this was it.

I leaned forward in the chair so that my feet were planted firmly on the wood floor. They hadn't taped my legs to the chair so I actually had limited mobility.

"What are you doing?" Thomas asked.

"Shh," I said.

I waddled myself backward, with the chair attached, so that I was back to back with Thomas. I set the chair down gently, careful not to make any scraping sounds, although it's unlikely the others would have heard anything with the kind of heated discussion they were having. The curtain had fallen back into place, and they'd have to actually come back in here to see us.

I placed my chair close enough so that my fingers could reach the tape securing Thomas's wrists to his chair.

582

"We're getting out of here," I said, struggling to get fingers from both my hands onto the tape so I could tear it. There were several layers, and it was going to be tough to rip through them with only the tips of my fingers. If I could just start a small tear . . .

"Hurry," Thomas whispered.

"Just hang on."

"Ray, you should have told me you had me working for a mobster person."

"It was all bullshit," I whispered, manipulating the tape with my fingers. "I made it up to buy us some time."

"Oh," he said. "That was very smart."

"— Christ's sake, no, you wouldn't dare!" Morris shouted, the first distinct sentence fragment I'd heard since they'd left the room.

I could feel the rip I'd started growing. "It feels looser," Thomas said.

"When you're free, you untie me, and we're out of here."

"Okay," he said. "Ray, I don't even know where we are."

"Soon as we hit the street I'm sure you'll know."

I tore the tape another half an inch, felt it come apart.

"That's it," Thomas said. "I can get my wrists free, but there's still tape around me."

"Just get out of it as fast as you can."

I could hear Thomas struggling with the tape. I twisted around, saw him trying to shake off bits of tape from his wrist; then he attacked the strips around his waist.

"Almost done," I said.

The men weren't arguing quite as loudly, but they were still talking.

"Faster," I whispered.

"Okay, okay," Thomas said, and he stood up from the chair, liberated from it. "Now you."

Lewis said, clear as a bell: "I'll go check on them."

"Go," I whispered.

"It'll only take a second," my brother said, starting to pick at the tape around my wrists.

Lewis's footsteps were approaching.

"There's not time!" I whispered urgently. "Go! Run! Get help!"

I could sense Thomas's panic. He didn't want to leave me.

"But —"

"Get the fuck out of here!"

So he did. He headed into the short hallway off the side of the room that led to an outside door. He ran, pushed open the door, and was gone.

"Yeah, yeah," Lewis said, stopping midway to the back room. "Don't worry."

Just before he came through the curtain, I glanced down at Nicole and wondered, *Why isn't there any blood under her?*

SIXTY-FIVE

Thomas burst into the narrow alley, the white van right there in front of him, filling the space between buildings. He had to blink a couple of times until his eyes adjusted to the darkness, then looked in both directions, figuring out instantly which was the way to the street. He ran for it.

He came out of the alley, turned right for no other reason than that was what his instinct told him to do, and kept on running, past a bike shop, a tailor's, other businesses. But he wasn't paying much attention to them. All he could think was that he had to get away, he had to get away as fast as he could, and he had to get help.

Ordinarily, he would have known instantly where he was, but there were two things working against him. First, he was in a state of panic. And second, it was night. Whirl360's images of the world were all taken during the day.

The first couple of blocks he was running

585

almost flat out, but for someone who'd spent years and years sitting in his bedroom at the computer without ever going outside for exercise, it was pretty impossible to keep up the pace.

So Thomas eased back from a gallop to a brisk walk. He made a number of random turns along the way. A left turn at this cross street. A right turn at the next.

Get away get away get away.

He reached a point where he had to stop. He leaned over, put his palms on his knees, and caught his breath. He was wheezing and his chest hurt.

He straightened up, wandered around in a couple of wind-down circles, and then, once he had his wind back, looked around. Even though it was dark, there were enough street-lights to focus in on things, see storefronts, read street signs.

On one corner, Stromboli Pizza, with some words written on the wall: "This moment is more precious than you think." Next to it, some place offering vegetarian food. Across the street, a shoe store with all kinds of different sneakers in the window.

Without looking up at the street signs, Thomas said, "St. Marks Place and First Avenue."

Then he allowed himself to look at the sign, saw that he was right.

"I know where I am," he said aloud. "I

know where this is."

A short man with shoulder-length hair was strolling past at the time and said, "Good for you."

Thomas, too mesmerized by his surroundings, took no notice of the man.

"This is New York," Thomas said. "This is Manhattan. I know where I am."

He walked over to the pizza restaurant, went right up to the glass, and touched it with the tips of his fingers.

He could feel it.

Thomas could feel the glass beneath his fingers.

He saw something in that window, something he had never seen before, not in any of the world's cities that he had explored.

He saw his *reflection*.

Whirl360 had never been like this. He'd been able to see the homes and storefronts and signs and benches and mailboxes. He could even zero in on them, enlarge them for close examination. But he could only imagine what these items felt like to the touch.

He smelled something.

Bread cooking. Dough. Pizza dough. It was too late for the restaurant to be open, but there were lingering aromas.

It smelled so good. So delicious. Thomas realized it had been a long time since he'd had anything to eat. He'd never been able to smell the things he saw when he was on the computer.

Behind him, a truck rumbled past. Thomas spun around, watched it head up First Avenue. Here, the trucks moved, made noises. The people walked. And their faces weren't blurred.

His Whirl360 world was noiseless. Odorless. Nothing to touch.

Thomas marveled at everything around him. Standing here, at the corner of First and St. Marks Place, was like being inside his computer monitor, but even *more* real. This was *amazing*.

For the first time, he thought of all the other places he had been. All around the world. Tokyo. Paris. London. Mumbai. San Francisco. Rio de Janeiro. Sydney. Auckland. Cape Town.

What would it be like to be in those places, to physically be there? To actually feel the streets beneath your feet? To smell these places? To hear their sounds?

It filled him with a sense of wonder.

It was almost enough to make him forget what he had to do. But not quite.

"Ray," he said under his breath. "I have to help Ray."

But how was he going to do that?

He didn't see any police cars around, and he didn't see any phone booths. And even if he did see one, he had no money on him. No change, no bills, no wallet full of credit cards.

Thomas didn't even own a credit card. Wouldn't know the first thing about using one.

"Taxi!"

Thomas looked up the street, at a man who'd raised his arm in the air to attract the attention of someone driving one of those yellow cars. The man hopped in and the yellow car took off.

Thomas didn't have a cell phone, either. If he did, he could call the police, he supposed. But Ray always carried a cell phone, and their father had had one, and Julie had one, so it seemed safe to assume that most people carried them. Any number of these people walking by on the street probably carried them.

Two teenage girls, their arms linked as if to support one another as they teetered along on their high heels, were coming from the south.

"Excuse me," Thomas said, putting himself directly in their path. "I bet you have cell phones. Could I borrow one to call 911?"

The girls stopped abruptly, blinked. Thomas thought they seemed frightened about something. They unlinked arms and went quickly around him on each side, one muttering, "Creep."

Thomas guessed they must not have had phones, so he tried stopping two other people. The first was an old man in tattered clothes who was intensely interested in the contents of a trash can. He seemed more interested in the half cup of coffee he'd found than in helping Thomas. The other person was a middle-aged woman who clutched her purse more tightly to her bosom and quickened her step when Thomas asked for her phone.

Maybe no one in New York had cell phones. Thomas wished Julie were here to help him. He liked Julie. Julie would know what to do.

But how could he get in touch with her? Even if he had a phone, he didn't know her number. So what could —

Wait a second.

Julie had a sister who lived in the city. She had a place that sold cupcakes. What did Julie say her name was? Candace? That was it. And her store was called Candy's Cupcakes. Julie had said Candace lived above her shop.

On West Eighth.

Thomas closed his eyes for a second. He could see it. The window filled with baked goods. The red-and-white-striped awning. The couple of wrought-iron table and chair sets out front on the sidewalk.

Thomas bet if he could find Candace, she'd know how to get in touch with Julie.

Now he just had to get to West Eighth.

Thomas looked up the street, saw another one of those yellow cars approaching. So he walked out into the street, right into the middle of the lane, put both hands into the air, and shouted, "Taxi!"

The driver hit the brakes and the car screeched to a halt.

"You some kind of fucking nut?" the cabbie shouted.

Thomas walked up to the driver's window. "Sir, I need you to take me to Candy's Cupcake shop on West Eighth Street in New York City."

"Where the hell do you think we are now?"

"We're at St. Marks Place and First Avenue," Thomas said, thinking a man who drives a cab should know that kind of thing.

"Get in," he said.

Thomas ran around the car to get into the front passenger seat. "The back!" the driver shouted, shaking his head. Thomas got into the backseat and, although it had been a long time since he'd seen a movie, said what he thought was the logical thing to say at a time like this. "Step on it."

The driver stepped on it.

"I have to get help for my brother who's being held prisoner," Thomas said.

"Uh-huh," said the driver.

"That's why I'm in such a hurry. It's all because of the woman who was murdered in the window."

"Listen, pal, we all got problems, you know?"

Thomas, observing street signs as they passed them, said, "I think there's a better way you could go."

"Never heard that before," the cabbie said.

There was so little traffic it wasn't long before the taxi pulled up in front of the cupcake store. "Looks closed," the driver said. "If you need a cupcake real bad I know a few all-night diners could help you out."

Thomas looked at the second-floor windows, figuring that was where Candace lived, but he didn't know how to get up there. Maybe the apartment entrance was through the shop. If he banged hard enough on the door, maybe she would wake up and come down.

Thomas pulled on the door handle, putting one foot down on the pavement. "Thank you very much."

"Whoa!" the cabbie said. "There's five-eighty on the meter."

"What?"

"You owe me five-eighty."

"I don't have any money," Thomas said. "I don't need it because I'm home all the time."

"Five-eighty!"

Thomas said, "My brother has money. When he's not abducted anymore, he could pay you."

"Get the fuck out of my cab," the driver said, and floored it the moment Thomas had closed the door.

He walked to the door of Candy's Cupcakes and banged on the glass. The shop was dark, but he thought he could see light in the back.

"Hello!" he shouted. "Candace?"

He banged the door continuously, the glass rattling relentlessly. Finally, a small black man came striding through the store, unlocked the door, and opened it a foot.

"Knock it off!" he shouted.

"I need Candace to call Julie," Thomas said. He could smell baking aromas, and this man had what looked like cake batter splattered on his shirt. Was he working in the middle of the night?

"What?" the man said.

"I have to talk to Julie. It's about Ray. They've got him tied to a chair."

"Piss off!" the man said, and started to close the door, but Thomas was pushing back.

"I have to talk to Candace!" he shouted. "Does she know Julie's phone number?"

The man yelled to the back of the store: "Boss! Hey, boss!"

Seconds later a woman in a full white apron, her hair in a net, appeared and came to the door.

"What's going on?" she asked.

"This nut bar's screaming for you, something about a sister? Julie?"

The woman shunted the man aside and opened the door wider. "Who are you?"

"Thomas."

"Thomas who?"

"Thomas Kilbride. Are you Julie's sister?"

"Yeah."

"Do you have to work in the middle of the night?"

"What the hell do you want? What's this about Julie?"

"Do you know her cell phone number?"

"Why?"

"I want her to help me save Ray."

Candace shook her head in exasperation, stuck her hand into her pocket, and pulled out a cell phone. She called up a number, hit the button, and put the phone to her ear.

She looked surprised that someone picked up so quickly.

"Hey, listen, it's me. I'm *really* sorry to call you but there's this crazy guy here, says he has to talk to — uh, Thomas. He says his name is Thomas. Okay." She handed the phone to him. "She wants to talk to you."

Thomas took the phone and said, "Hi, Julie, they kidnapped me and Ray and took us here and I got away and they've still got Ray and he helped untie me but there wasn't time for me to untie him and —"

"Are you at the cupcake shop?" Julie asked incredulously.

"Yeah."

"I can be there in two minutes. Stay there!"

Thomas handed the phone back to Candace. "She'll be right here."

Candace, looking perplexed and bewildered, said, "How come, if my sister's in New York, she doesn't call me?"

SIXTY-SIX

Morris Sawchuck had slipped his gun, the one he'd started carrying back in the days when he was receiving death threats, back into its holster and had his hand on the inside of the front door to Ferber's Antiques, but before he could open it Howard threw up a hand and slammed it shut.

"What are your intentions, Morris?" Howard said.

"Get out of my way."

Lewis had caught up to them. "It's a good question," he said. "What are you planning to do when you walk out of here?"

"I don't care what happens," Morris said. "Nothing's worth this. I'm going to tell them what I know. They'll believe me or they won't."

Morris felt something cold and hard touching his temple. He shifted his eyes left and saw that Lewis was holding the barrel of his gun to the attorney general's temple.

"You think that'll make it easier, Lewis?

Blowing my brains out? You think you're in a mess now? Think that'll make your problems go away?"

"Maybe," he said. "Howard, get his gun."

Howard reached under Morris's coat and removed the weapon and handed it to Lewis, who tucked it into the waistband of his pants.

Howard said, "I know this has all been a terrible shock, a hell of a lot to take in. I get that. But you need to think before you do anything rash. The thing is, Morris, while all of this was done to help you, things are kind of turned around now. You have to help us continue to help you, or there won't be a you anymore."

"I don't know why I didn't cut you loose years ago."

"You didn't because I've always done my job so well. You know it and I know it. But understand what happens if you don't play ball. Lewis here will put a bullet through your brain. And then you know what he's going to have to do?"

Howard tilted his head in the direction of the street. It took Morris a moment to figure out what Howard was getting at.

Then he knew.

"Dear God, for Christ's sake, no."

Howard nodded. "Tell him, Lewis."

"We kill you, then we have to kill Heather," Lewis said. "Because sooner or later, she's going to come in here looking for you."

597

Howard said, "I've been where you are now, Morris. When this all started, when I gave Lewis the okay to take drastic action where Allison Fitch was concerned, I couldn't believe I was doing it. I'd never taken that kind of step before. Never, believe me. All the things I may have done for you in the past, they've never included murder. And then . . . then it went horribly wrong, and I felt even sicker. But you know what? You reach a point where you realize there's no going back. You've made your decisions and you have to live with them. That's what you're going to have to do, Morris. You're going to have to make a decision and live with it."

Morris placed an arm against the door, leaned his head into it. "I need a minute."

"Of course you do."

"Tell me about that woman," he said to Lewis, who had taken the barrel away from his temple. "The one you killed."

"A killer for hire," Lewis said. "She had it coming. She's done a lot of bad things, and the worst of all was screwing up, killing Bridget. You have to know, I was never going to let her get away with that."

Morris felt as though he might collapse. He threw a hand onto Howard's shoulder for support. The three men stood there that way for a while, Lewis and Howard apparently willing to wait for Morris to come around.

What choice did he have, really?

"I don't want you to hurt Heather," he said.

"I can't believe you haven't been putting it to her," Lewis said, trying to break the mood.

"She has two kids," Morris said. "Two little girls."

"Yeah, well."

Howard said some consoling words to Morris, made some of the arguments he'd already made all over again.

Finally, Lewis glanced back toward the curtain and said, "I'll go check on them."

Howard said, "This Vachon business, I want to know more about that. Do what you have to do to find out if Ray's feeding us a line of shit."

"Vachon?" Morris said.

"Long story," Howard said. Then, to Lewis, "Once we're sure we have nothing to worry about there, then, well, I want them dealt with as mercifully as we can."

"Yeah, yeah. Don't worry."

Lewis headed for the back room.

"Howard," Morris said, "for the love of God, you can't just —"

"Shit!" It was Lewis. He'd pulled back the curtain, then called to Howard, "We got a problem."

SIXTY-SEVEN

Nicole is doing her dismounts from the uneven bars. A double salto backward tucked with full twist. A double salto backward piked. An underswing with a half turn to salto backward, tucked with a full turn.

She can't get them right.

She keeps landing on her head.

Time after time. Her head plunges like a missile. Pounds into the mat. She feels her will snap. The pain's tremendous. Her skull throbs.

It gets worse. An ice pick is sticking up through the mat. After her head hits the mat, her body topples over and the pick plunges into her chest.

It keeps happening over and over again. Letting go of the bar, spinning through the air, twisting and turning, but nothing is going as it should. She tells her body to spin one way and it does the opposite.

This is not happening, she tells herself. *This cannot be happening.*

600

Nicole was right. It was not happening. Although it was true that her head was injured, that she had taken a blow to the chest.

Realization was slowly returning to her. Before she had opened her eyes, things began to make sense.

Lewis had shot her.

Yeah.

Just like that. Wanting to make an impression on Morris. She'd figured it was coming, that Lewis would try this sooner or later. She just hadn't expected it at that moment.

But she'd also known that could happen. That you could be on your guard, and still slip up.

The bullet hit her, hit her hard. Lying there, before she opened her eyes, she wondered whether it had pierced the Kevlar, made it all the way through the formfitting vest, but she did not think so. It felt more like she had been kicked than shot.

It wasn't the bullet that knocked her out. It was being thrown back, hitting her head on the edge of that goddamn shelf. She was seeing stars before she hit the floor.

But now she was waking up. And she was listening.

Probably best to just stay put for a while.

Sixty-Eight

"Where is he?" Lewis barked at me. "Where the hell is he?"

"Gone," I said.

Howard showed up, fixed his eyes on the empty chair littered with duct tape scraps. What little color there was in his face seemed to drain away instantly. "Dear God." Then he glared at Lewis. "You let him get away."

Lewis tore out of the room using the side door, no doubt hoping Thomas had only just left, that he could catch up with him and drag him back. Thomas had only been gone a few seconds, half a minute tops, but if he was running flat out, it would give him enough time to get a healthy head start.

I just hoped that, having gotten away, Thomas would have the sense to go to the police, even if that wasn't exactly what I'd asked. I'd only told him to get help. I'd assumed he'd know what that meant, but he was no sooner out the door than I wished I'd been more specific.

At the moment, he was my only hope.

"How did — how the hell did he get free?" Howard asked.

"I told you he was talented," I said, perhaps with just a touch of smugness. "Maybe he's gone for Vachon. Maybe his people were out there waiting for him. I wonder what they'll do when he tells them what you —"

Howard snapped. He swung his arm back and hit me across the face with the back of his hand. He put more into it than I would have thought possible for the short little fucker.

"Enough bullshit!" he said.

My cheek burned, my brains rattled.

The curtain opened and it was Morris. "What the hell's happened now?"

"One of them got away," Howard said. "The one with the atlas in his head."

"Atlas?" Morris had a long way to go to get up to speed.

"Lewis has gone looking for him. God help us, he better find him."

"You can't keep this up," Morris said. "You can't. It's unraveling. You're unraveling. You have been for months." He took out his phone and held it up. "You took my gun but you didn't take this. I told Heather to take the rest of the night off. In fact, I told her to take the next couple days off. To get out of town. I didn't want to take any chances. She's gone. I think that was the last straw for me,

Howard. Threatening Heather. A total innocent. You're a man with no lines left to cross."

Howard looked at him, no doubt assessing the implications.

"What else did you tell her?"

"I told her you were going to give me a lift home. You and Lewis."

"So if anything happens to you, she'll know."

Morris nodded. His voice was strangely calm. "Let this man go. And you and Lewis would be smart to turn yourselves in. Either that, or you better be on a jet to Bolivia by noon with a couple of new identities. You know the best lawyers in the city, Howard. Pick one out for yourself and one for Lewis. Then the clock'll start ticking, see who can cut the best deal by ratting out the other. No one knows better than us how the game is played. I guess that's basically what I'm going to do, too. Howard, let this man go."

I was already working on it. I'd been straining at the tape around my wrists since the moment Thomas had left. I'd been picking at the edges with my fingernails, trying to create even a tiny bit of slack.

Howard said, "I wish it were that simple, Morris."

Lewis reappeared, winded. "No sign of him," he said.

"Morris says we should get lawyers," Howard said.

"What?"

"He's not going to play."

Lewis sneered. "Morris, I thought we had an understanding. What about —"

"Heather's gone," he said. "And I'm leaving, too. Don't worry. I'll get a cab."

Morris swept the curtain aside and headed for the front door. Lewis, gun in hand, followed him. "Morris," he called out.

I heard the same swift sound I'd heard when Lewis shot Nicole. Then a body hitting the floor.

Howard didn't even look. Didn't pull back the curtain. He knew what had to have happened. When Lewis reappeared, he walked straight past Howard and came up on my right side.

"Where would your brother go?" he asked me. "Has he got the sense to go to the cops or will he just run and hide somewhere?"

I had to admit the latter was a possibility. "I don't know," I said. "If I were you, I'd assume the worst."

Lewis evidently felt a need to let off some steam just as Howard had, so he hit me, too. Not a slap across the face, but a gun to the side of head. A pistol whip. My right ear exploded in pain, and my left nearly touched my shoulder. I shouted out and watched the room spin around for several seconds.

It was during that period of disorientation I

thought I saw Nicole's arm move, bump ever so slightly into a Dinky Toy tow truck that had fallen from the shelf and landed on its wheels, making it roll forward a quarter of an inch. But then, pretty much everything had seemed to be moving in the seconds after that blow to the head, so I figured I'd imagined it.

"We have to assume we don't have much time," Lewis said.

"Great," Howard said. "Just great. The police may be coming and now we've got three bodies to get rid of."

I wasn't dead yet, but I figured that time was coming. I continued twisting my wrists back and forth.

"There's no time for that," Lewis said. "We just have to get out of here."

"Where the hell are we going to go?" Howard asked.

"I know people," Lewis said. "I know people who can hide us until we get the paperwork we need."

"God, you fucked this whole thing up from the very beginning," Howard said. "From the moment you decided to kill Fitch, to hiring her" — he pointed to Nicole — "to letting that freak get away."

"I can go alone," Lewis said, walking around me, standing between Nicole's body and me. "If that's what you'd prefer."

"Christ," Howard said, shaking his head in

defeat. "Let's finish this and get the hell out of here."

I kept twisting and twisting, thinking, if I could manage to get my wrists free, I could propel myself, with the chair attached, at Lewis, somehow grab him by the throat. Anything. Because the gun was in his hand, and I knew his intention was to use it on me in the next few seconds.

But I just wasn't there yet.

"Okay," Lewis said, bending his elbow so that the gun was pointing at my head.

And then he screamed. A horrific, gut-wrenching scream.

When he cast his eyes down at the source of his pain, I did as well.

There was an ice pick right through his calf.

SIXTY-NINE

"Where's Ray?" Julie asked Thomas. "Think, okay? Think."

They were sitting in her car, the engine running, out front of her sister's cupcake shop. Candace stood on the sidewalk, watching the two of them, obviously wondering what the hell was going on.

"It was dark, and I was running," Thomas said. His body was trembling, and his clothes were soaked with sweat. "I was running so fast I wasn't paying attention, not until I got to St. Marks and First Avenue." He looked at Julie. "It was just like on Whirl360, but you could touch things and smell them."

"Focus," Julie said. "You say you ran out into the alley and out to the sidewalk. Which way did you go then?"

"Right."

"So you didn't run across the front of the shop where you were being held?"

"No, the other way."

"What were the first things you passed?"

608

Thomas thought. "There was a tailor's, and a bike shop, and . . ."

"What?"

"I think it was called Mike's Bikes," he said.

"Okay." Julie grabbed her phone from the top of the dashboard. "I'll see if I can find it."

"Wait," Thomas said. Now he had his eyes closed. "Mike's Bikes. It's next to the tailor shop." He jerked his head slightly to one side, paused, jerked again, paused.

"What are you doing?" Julie asked.

"I'm working my way up the street," Thomas said. He was clicking his mouse, in his head. Advancing through the Whirl360 images.

"What street?"

"East Fourth," he said. "It's on East Fourth."

Julie already had the car in drive and, without even a wave good-bye to her sister, slammed on the accelerator and tore up the street, pitching Thomas's head back against the headrest. He opened his eyes.

"I can tell you how to get to Fourth," he said.

"I can figure out that part. Just tell me *where* on Fourth."

Thomas closed his eyes again. His head kept jerking. "I'm at an antiques store," he said. "Ferber's Antiques. It looks like it has toys in the window."

"What's the address?"

He gave her a number. "I think that's the place. That's where Ray is."

Julie ran a light, turned at a cross street, floored it.

"Do you have a gun?" Thomas asked, eyes open again.

"What?"

"Do you have a gun? The man had a gun, and the woman had an ice pick."

"I don't have a fucking gun," she said. Julie knew she couldn't go storming into this place on her own.

She needed the NYPD and the FDNY. What she didn't have was time to explain. Julie pointed to the cell phone. "Hit 911, then give it to me."

Thomas picked up the phone. "Do you hit the talk button first and then the number?"

She grabbed it from his hand, glanced from the phone to the windshield and back again a couple of times, then put the phone to her ear.

When the 911 operator came on, Julie adopted a panicked tone and said, "There's a fire! It looks like it's started in the back of Ferber's! The antiques store on East Fourth! And I think I heard shots, too!" She provided a street number, then ended the call before the operator could ask her anything else, and tossed the phone into Thomas's lap.

Worked when she was back in school and didn't want to take her exams.

SEVENTY

The ice pick had entered the side of Lewis's right leg about five inches below the knee. Nicole had driven it straight in, through his jeans, and the tip had come out the other side, poking through his pants, the tip crimson.

It had the effect of pulling that leg out from under him, because he dropped right there, to both knees, crushing one of the board game boxes, screaming the whole time. He let go of his gun and twisted around so he could get hold of the handle of the ice pick to pull it back out.

That wasn't something I wanted to see, but I was transfixed, as was Howard. What we both ended up seeing was even worse. Nicole sat up and got her hand on the pick before Lewis could, and instead of pulling it out and using it on him again in a new spot, or shoving it in even farther, she yanked on it *sideways*. The steel within his leg made new paths through his flesh, causing him to cry out again. He jerked his leg furiously, the heel of his boot catching Nicole, who was up on one arm and on her side, square in the chest.

It knocked her onto her back, but she was up in a second.

Lewis was scrambling, looking for his gun. It was on the floor in a rapidly growing puddle of his blood. He went to grab it, but Nicole had her hands on it first.

She wrapped her hand around the wet, bloodied grip and pointed it at Lewis's head. He had rolled onto his back, had raised himself half up with his arms, and was scrambling backward, crablike, dragging the wounded leg after him.

Nicole was on her knees now, both hands on the gun, her arms out straight and steady. "I hate guns," she said. Her blouse was torn open, revealing something else, dark and padded.

A vest.

"Nicole," Lewis said. "Listen, listen to —"

She pulled the trigger and blew a corner of his head off. His body went flat, the floor a mass of blood and skull and brain matter.

Howard threw his hand to his mouth, like he was going to vomit. He turned, flung back the curtain, and started to run. Nicole scrambled after him.

In the distance, I heard sirens.

I pulled my left hand free of the tape, which now hung loose from my right hand and

613

started tearing into the tape around my stomach that held me to the chair.

The sirens grew louder.

But even closer, the sounds of a car screeching to a stop in the alley. Someone shouting. A woman.

"Thomas!"

Shit.

I broke free of the chair and dived to the floor, scattering toys before me. I wanted to get over to Lewis, to his body.

There was a gun, tucked into the front of his pants. Morris's gun, maybe.

In the front room, I heard a *pfft, pfft* and then the sound of another body dropping.

From outside: "Ray!"

"Thomas, stop!"

Julie.

I was on my knees, reaching for the gun, my fingers just touching the grip, when the curtain flung back. I glanced up, just in time to see Nicole's boot catch my jaw.

It was one hell of a kick.

I saw stars as my body was catapulted backward. My arms went out instinctively to brace my fall, but it still hurt like hell when I landed. Something sharp dug into my back, then skittered out from under me. A toy dump truck.

My right hand had landed on one of the other items that had tumbled off the shelves. Even before I looked at it I could feel that it was part plastic, part metal.

Nicole pointed her gun at me. But before she could squeeze the trigger, there was a loud bang from the short hallway that led to the alley.

A door being thrown open.

"I got help!" Thomas screamed. "I got Julie!"

"No!" Julie, sounding as though she was a step behind him, screamed.

Nicole's eyes turned toward the voices, and the gun followed. The second Thomas appeared he'd be dead.

I glanced over at my right hand, which was draped across the blue plastic fins of a foot-long, metal-pointed lawn dart.

It wasn't exactly a javelin. But I wasn't just good at throwing one of those in high school. I was pretty damn good at regular old darts.

In the milliseconds I had before Thomas ran in, I hoped throwing darts was like riding a bike. *You never forget how.*

Despite the throbbing in the side of my head, the pain in my jaw and my back, I moved with lightning speed, grabbing the dart by the tail end, swinging it back over my shoulder, then pitching it forward with everything I had.

"Ray!"

Thomas burst into the room.

The dart went into Nicole's neck. It went

in far enough, an inch or two, that it hung there.

Her mouth opened but no scream came out. Her right hand held on to the gun as her left flew up. She grasped the dart, and yanked it out.

It was like water from a tap.

Blood spurting everywhere.

Nicole dropped the dart and clamped her left hand over the wound. She dropped the gun from her right, turned, stumbled over to the desk.

She coughed and blood spilled from her mouth as well as her throat. She used the desk to briefly support herself, but only for a few seconds. She dropped to the floor as the sirens became almost deafening.

Now Julie was in the room, and she hit the brakes as soon as she saw the carnage. A firefighter, running in behind her, nearly knocked her over when she stopped so abruptly.

"Ray?" she said.

Thomas was already helping me to my feet. "Look who I found," he said. "I brought Julie." He smiled. "I'm back."

SEVENTY-ONE

Over the next twenty-four hours, Thomas and I, and Julie, had to answer a lot of questions from a lot of different agencies. We were questioned separately, and together, by New York City cops, state police, FBI, even the Port Authority, for all I knew. One guy, I was told later, was from Homeland Security, but there were so many who wanted to pick our brains that I couldn't figure out which one he was.

Thomas, when we had a moment together, expressed some concern that there was no one from the CIA. "You'd think they'd be here, wanting to see how I'm doing," he whispered. I could see the disappointment in his eyes. He was hurt.

The benefit of all these hours of interrogation was that they had a way of informing us about what had happened. The blanks started to get filled in, in large part because the fire department and paramedics had arrived in time to save Howard Talliman and Morris

Sawchuck, both found bleeding on the floor of the toy shop.

Talliman, whose condition was critical, had not been all that forthcoming so far, but Sawchuck, who'd been shot in the lung and was listed in serious condition, was telling prosecutors everything he knew. Because he was hooked up to various machines to assist with his breathing, he was answering questions as quickly as he could type them on the laptop they'd brought into the ICU.

A lot of what had happened became clear during our kidnapping. Fitch's blackmail attempt — what she knew or claimed to have known was still not entirely clear to us — led to a decision to kill her. Bridget Sawchuck was killed by mistake. Nicole killed that couple in Chicago as part of her mission to get the image of the smothered woman off the Internet.

That was kind of it, in a nutshell.

Lewis Blocker, of course, was dead.

And the paramedics were not able to save Nicole. Turned out that wasn't her real name. There was talk that in another life she was some kind of Olympic athlete — that explained the power in that kick — but the cops were still trying to piece a lot of things together.

I didn't feel good about killing the woman. I knew I'd had no choice, but I took no pleasure in it. I was going to be having nightmares about this for a very long time.

Bottom line was, I'd rather it was her being put in the ground than me. Or Thomas.

Many of the questions that were put to me, when I was being questioned alone, were about Thomas, and his bizarre preoccupation. I know they were in touch with Dr. Grigorin, and our good friends Agents Parker and Driscoll of the FBI made an appearance. They confirmed much of what I'd been saying: that while Thomas was certainly unique, he was not a threat to anyone or himself. By the end, it appeared the various law enforcement agencies were not only persuaded that Thomas was harmless, but that he was a hero. Bridget Sawchuck's murder would never have come to light without his explorations on Whirl360.

What was left unspoken was that it was these same explorations that led, ultimately, to the deaths of Kyle and Rochelle Billings. Whether this crossed Thomas's mind I don't know, and I certainly didn't point it out to him. Maybe because their deaths were as much my fault as his. I was the idiot who'd waved that printout around when I'd knocked on Allison Fitch's apartment door, which, evidently, had been picked up on a surveillance camera.

The one thing that never came up was the call Lewis took in Thomas's bedroom. Thomas told me he'd never mentioned it, and neither had I.

Thomas was more withdrawn than usual in the wake of everything that had happened. What we'd been through would be traumatic for anyone. Yet I wondered whether Thomas's idiosyncrasies actually made him better prepared to cope. He generally shut the world out, except those parts he could access on-line. With that kind of wall around him, maybe he'd taken in less of the horror.

I just didn't know.

He had been brooding, though, and I wondered whether it might have less to do with our recent experience and more to do with what he had seemed ready to tell me just before Nicole and Lewis invaded the house. This thing that had happened to him, when he was thirteen, that had sparked trouble between Dad and him.

He'd said, back then, that he might be willing to talk about it with Julie, but the time wasn't right yet. We needed to decompress before we tackled anything else.

Besides, I had a couple of things on my mind, too.

I'd been debating whether to stay at my father's house, live there with Thomas, at least for the foreseeable future. But to my surprise, when I proposed the idea to Thomas, he was reluctant.

"I don't think I want to live with you," he

said. "Look at all the trouble you got me into." He said he wanted to live at the place I had gone to visit, so long as he could keep his computer.

Which still left me the option of selling my place in Burlington and moving into Dad's house permanently. Then I'd be close to Thomas, could check in on him as often as I wanted. Over breakfast, our last morning in New York City, we talked about traveling. Thomas said he wanted to touch the window of a particular pastry shop in Paris.

"I think," I said, "if we go all that way, we might want to go inside and eat the pastry."

"I guess that would be okay," he said.

Our future plans weren't the only thing on my mind. I couldn't stop thinking about the phone call.

We went home with Julie, in her car.

I shouldn't have been surprised to find a police car blocking the end of the driveway at my father's house when we got back. The press — reporters other than Julie — had gotten wind of the story and been trying to find Thomas and me. So far, we had managed to avoid them. Not just because we didn't need the aggravation, but because I wanted Julie to have a chance to break the whole story before anyone else got the details. Our — well, mostly my — firsthand accounts of what had happened were going to give her a hell of an exclusive.

The uniformed officer sitting behind the wheel got out to see who we were. Once we'd identified ourselves, he pulled his car out of the way. Julie drove up to the house and stopped. Thomas got out first. Although he was never very demonstrative, I could tell he was excited to be home.

As he was approaching the house, I called to him, "Do not touch the phone in your room."

"Why?"

"Just don't," I said. "Don't even go near it."

He didn't argue. He didn't care that much about phones. It was the fact he had no computer to return to that most upset him. If he asked me once he asked me ten times on the way home when we would be going out to get him a new one.

I came around to the driver's door. Julie powered down her window.

"Thanks," I said, bending over, my head half in the window.

"You say that a lot."

"It's 'cause you're so damned nice."

"I'm going to the office. I've got a story to write up. Did I tell you about it?"

"A little," I said.

"Maybe I'll give you a call later."

"Look forward to it," I said, then leaned in and kissed her.

I watched her drive off, then went into the house. I was going to head up to Thomas's room first thing, but I saw the light flashing on the phone in the kitchen, and thought I'd better check the messages.

There were five.

"Hey, Ray. Alice here. Harry needs you to come in and sign a couple more things. Let me know."

Beep. I hit 7 to delete.

"Ray? Hey, it's Harry. Alice left a message for you yesterday. Right? Give me a shout."

Beep. I hit 7 again.

"Ray, Jesus, Harry here, I saw the news. God, I hope you guys are okay. Look, when you get back, call me."

Beep. 7 again.

"Hi, I'm trying to reach Thomas or Ray Kilbride. My name is Tricia, and I'm a producer for the *Today* show and we'd very much like to get in touch with you. It's very important that —"

Didn't have to wait for the beep this time. Hit 7.

"Hello, this is Angus Fried, from the *New York Times*, and —"

7.

I was parched, so I ran water from the tap until it was cold, filled a glass, and drank it all without taking a breath.

It was time.

I didn't know what I was going to learn

when I checked the call history on Thomas's phone, on his separate line. Maybe nothing. Maybe the ID had been blocked, and the identity of whoever called the house would remain a mystery forever.

I put my empty glass in the sink and started heading for the stairs.

There was a rapping at the front door.

Standing there was an overweight, middle-aged man in a rumpled suit, his shirt collar open and black tie yanked down, holding up a badge for my inspection.

"Mr. Kilbride?" he said. "Our man at the end of the drive there told me you were back. I understand you've had quite the few days. You and I, we really didn't get a chance to finish our chat the other night, on the phone. I'm Detective Barry Duckworth, with the Promise Falls police. It's a hell of a thing you've been through. I've heard all about it. But I was wondering if we could still have a word about your father."

SEVENTY-TWO

"Come in," I said.

Detective Duckworth and I took seats in the living room. "I can understand that you've got a lot to deal with, all that's happened to you in the last couple of days. How are you doing?"

"Okay, I guess. It was . . . harrowing."

"Yeah, that would be the word. Are you up to finishing the conversation we were having the other night?"

"I am," I said. "It seems like a long time ago." I rubbed my forehead. "You had been speaking to my father."

"That's correct."

"He'd gotten in touch with you," I said.

"He had."

"Tell me about it."

Duckworth settled in the chair, relaxing his arms at his sides. "Your father contacted me about something that happened to your brother, Thomas, when he was in his teens. But for years, your father didn't believe it had happened — he didn't believe your brother. Because he, well, how should I put this . . . ?"

"My brother is not what you'd call a credible witness," I said.

"There you go."

"Because he hears voices when there are none to be heard, sees conspiracies where there are none to be seen." I hesitated. "Most of the time."

"So when Thomas came to your father many years ago, alleging an assault, your father was reluctant to believe it. In fact, he refused to believe it, because Thomas was pointing the finger at one of your father's friends. He accused your brother of making it all up, and told him to never talk about it, never to bring it up again."

"An assault," I said. "Thomas managed to tell me just a bit about this, before we were kidnapped."

"A sexual assault," Duckworth said. "At the very least, an attempted one. An attempted rape."

I felt anger welling up within me. "Who did Thomas tell my father it was?"

Duckworth held up a hand. "I'm getting to that. Your dad, he did talk to the man, this friend of his, and the man was stunned, shocked by the accusation, denied it completely, and your dad, he believed him. Because he couldn't believe Thomas. Thomas had lots of crazy tales back then, I gather."

"It's always been that way."

"But then something happened to change your dad's mind," Duckworth said.

"What was that?"

Duckworth looked around the room, saw the new TV, the Blu-ray player. "Your dad, he liked the high-tech stuff, didn't he?"

"Yes," I said. "He did. He liked his toys, his gadgets. A lot of men, they get to his age, they resist the new technologies, but he thought they were pretty cool. He loved to watch sports on that TV."

"Your dad was thinking of getting a new phone," Duckworth said.

That hit me. "How did you know that?"

"He told me. That's how it happened."

I gripped the arms of my chair, like I was strapping myself in for a rough ride. "Go on."

"Your dad wanted a cell phone that would do lots of fancy things, instead of just being a phone. Me, I got a phone that does a lot of things but I don't know how to do hardly any of them. Had it a year before I could figure out how to take a picture with it. But that was the very thing your dad was interested in having a phone for. To take pictures."

I nodded. "Okay."

"He told me he'd been looking at a few of them, but getting recommendations from store people, you don't know whether to trust them. Maybe they're just trying to sell you the most expensive kind. You want to know what your friends got, what they have to say. Word of mouth, you know?"

"Sure."

"So your dad happened to be with one of his friends, he told me — this would be the same friend your brother had accused way back when — and he picked up his phone to have a look at it. Just curious. This friend wasn't in the room at the time, but your dad didn't think anything of it. Didn't think he'd mind. He wanted to see how the camera worked on this phone, so he pressed the whaddyacallit, the camera app, and up it came. And then he tapped again, so it brought up the pictures that had already been taken." Duckworth paused to catch his breath.

"What?" I said.

"He didn't like what he saw."

I swallowed. "What were the pictures of?"

"Boys," Duckworth said. "Pictures of young boys. These weren't friendly family pictures, if you get my drift. These were young boys — ten, twelve, thirteen years old — in provocative poses and positions. Your dad, he could barely describe them to me, they upset him so."

"These were pictures his friend had taken."

Duckworth nodded. "Seems he'd just come back from some trip. A place where a person with those kinds of tastes can find just what he's looking for. And in that instant, when he saw those pictures, he realized that what your brother had said years ago was the truth. He hadn't been making it up. A man who would take these kinds of pictures was the sort of man who would have assaulted your brother."

"Who?" I asked, but I believed I already had the answer.

Duckworth held up his hand again. "Let me tell this. So when this friend of your dad's came back into the room, your dad confronted him with it. Asked him what the hell it was. Said he now realized it had to be true, what Thomas had told him."

"What did the man say?"

"Denied it to hell and back, of course."

"What'd my dad do?" One thing I was pretty sure he must have done was a search on his laptop for child prostitution.

"I guess he stewed about it for a while. Finally, he called me. He said he was just sick about it, that he'd tried to apologize to your brother about it, that they'd had a fight over it. He wanted to know whether the man could still be charged, for what he did to Thomas. I told him it was pretty unlikely. It happened so long ago, and given your brother's tendencies, it would be pretty hard to get a conviction."

"What about the pictures on the man's phone?"

"Your dad knew he'd probably deleted them right away, soon as he left, but even so, he was asking me, could someone go after him, for paying to have sex with kids in some foreign country."

"Thailand," I said.

"Excuse me?"

"I think we're probably talking about Thailand. I know it's not the only country in the world where that sort of thing is available — hell, I'm sure it goes on in this country — but one of Dad's friends has traveled to Thailand."

"I haven't answered your question about who the friend is," Duckworth said, "because I don't know. Your dad never told me, because he hadn't decided what to do about this man." He sighed. "And then he had that accident. And died."

"Yeah," I said. "He had that accident."

SEVENTY-THREE

"Len Prentice," I said.

"Say again?" Duckworth said, getting out his notebook.

"Dad worked for him for years. They'd been friends a very long time. Thomas has never liked him. Len came by here the other day, tried to force Thomas to have lunch with him. Maybe he was trying to find out what Dad might have told him before he died." I thought a moment. "And he takes trips without his wife, to Thailand."

"Well," Duckworth said. "That's pretty interesting, isn't it?"

I felt exhaustion wash over me. All that had happened in the last few days, and now this. "The son of a bitch. The fucking pervert. He forces himself on Thomas, and knows he can get away with it, because if Thomas ever says anything, Len can just say, 'Hey, you know that kid — he's nuts.' "

"It's part of the pattern," Duckworth said. "They target the vulnerable, people they can control."

Blood pulsed in my temples. I wanted to get in the car, go over to Len Prentice's house, and throttle him. Strangle the bastard with my bare hands.

"Thomas went years without ever talking about this," I said.

"Because he got into so much trouble before, when he told his father about it," Duckworth said. "He just wanted it to go away."

"And when my father brought it all up again, when he tried to tell my brother that he now believed him, how must that have made Thomas feel?" I wondered aloud. "It must have made him angry. That now, finally, Dad was prepared to do something about it. When the damage was already done."

Duckworth nodded solemnly. "Maybe so."

I clasped my head with my hands. "I'm on overload."

"I don't doubt it."

We were both quiet for a moment. I was the one who finally spoke. "There's something that's been troubling me from the moment I came home, after I got word that my father was dead."

Duckworth waited.

"The circumstances. They've always bothered me."

"How so?"

"I know it looked like an accident. He was

riding the tractor along the side of a steep hill, and rolled it. But he'd been mowing like that, safely, for years."

"A lot of people do the same foolish thing for years, and one day it catches up with them," Duckworth offered.

"I know, I know. But when I went down to bring the tractor back to the barn — it hadn't been moved since the accident, other than when Thomas pushed it off Dad — I noticed that the key was in the OFF position. And the housing for the blades? It was raised. It was what he'd have done if someone had come down the hill and wanted to talk to him. He would've had to turn off the engine, and he would have lifted the blades up, because he wasn't cutting grass anymore."

"No one ever came forward to say they'd talked to your father before the accident. That they were there when it happened."

"Who would?" I asked. "If they'd pushed him over."

Duckworth thought about that. "I don't know, but that's an interesting theory."

"While Dad was debating what to do about Len Prentice, Len Prentice must have been going out of his mind. Would Dad go to the police — well, he did, but he never gave you a name. Or would Dad tell Len's wife, his friends? If he couldn't actually bring him up on any kind of charges, maybe he'd try to ruin his reputation. Let everyone know just what kind of man Len Prentice was."

"It's possible."

"Len gets so worried, he comes out to the house one day, trying to talk Dad out of doing anything, maybe coming up with some cockamamie explanation for why there are pictures of naked boys on his cell phone. Finds Dad cutting grass on the side of the hill. Dad stops the tractor, they get into an argument, Len gives Dad a shove, and he goes back, taking the tractor with him, and it kills him. Len might have had time to get help, or get the tractor off Dad, but he chooses not to. Len's known, for years, that my Dad took chances on that hill. Mom used to beg Len to tell him not to do it."

Detective Duckworth pursed his lips while he thought about all this.

"You think a guy's going to keep those kinds of pictures on his phone?" he asked. "His wife might find them."

I put up my hands. "I don't know. Marie, she's not much of a gadget person. Look, I don't have all the answers, but there's something wrong with that man. I can just feel it."

"I suppose," he said, "that at the very least it might be worth going over to talk to him about it. See what he has to say."

"Yeah, let's do that," I said.

"Whoa," he said, putting up his hand.

"I'm coming. I have some things I want to ask him. If you don't let me come with you,

I'm going to be banging on his door two seconds after you leave."

Duckworth considered this. "You let me do the talking."

I said nothing.

"Okay, let's take a ride over there. You can direct me?"

"I can," I said. "First, I want to tell my brother I'm heading out for a little while. And there's just one other thing I have to do."

"I'll be waiting for you out on the porch."

Duckworth got up and was heading outside as I went up the stairs.

Maps still hanging everywhere. They had, for the first time, a comforting effect on me. I went into Thomas's room.

He was sitting in his computer chair, staring at his computer monitor and keyboard. Without the tower, they were a car with no engine.

"Are we going to get a computer now?" he asked.

"Not right this second," I said. "You be okay here for a while, on your own? There'll still be a cop out by the road."

"I guess. Where are you going?"

"I'm going over to see Len Prentice."

Thomas frowned. "I don't like him."

I considered asking Thomas, right then, to tell me what had happened to him, who had done it, but decided not to. He'd been through enough in the last few days without

635

me forcing him to talk about that event.

"I don't like him, either," I said.

I turned my attention to the phone on his desk. "Have you touched this?" I asked.

"You told me not to."

"I was just asking."

"I haven't touched it."

I reached across the desk, pulled the phone closer to me. I hit the button that would give me the call history.

There had been no calls to this phone since the night we'd been abducted.

There was a call at 10:13 p.m. that night. It was the only number in the call history.

It was, I was pretty sure, a local number.

"Thomas," I said, "this is showing only one call to this phone, ever. You've never gotten any other calls up here? Not even telemarketers?"

"I always delete the history after every call," he said. "That's what President Clinton started telling me to do."

But Thomas hadn't been able to erase the history that night, when Lewis Blocker answered the phone.

I didn't think it was smart to dial this number directly from Thomas's phone. I used my cell. I entered the number, put the phone to my ear, and listened.

"Who are you calling?" Thomas asked. "Are you calling the president? He told me never to call him myself. And if that's his number it

636

should have been deleted."

I held up a hand to silence him. The phone at the other end rang once.

Then a second time.

A third.

Then a pickup. Some fumbling, and finally, a voice.

"Hello, Harry Peyton here."

SEVENTY-FOUR

"Hello?" Harry said again. "Someone there?"

"It's Ray," I said, when I'd found my voice.

"Ray!" Harry exclaimed, his voice full of exuberance. "Jesus Christ! You're back!"

"We're back," I said.

"My God, what happened to you? The details coming out on the news are sketchy, but you found out Morris Sawchuck's wife had been murdered? Good God, man, how on earth did you get all mixed up in *that*? Well, okay, I know Thomas had something to do with it, but Christ almighty, you could have ended up dead."

"Came close to it," I said, thinking. Trying to put it together.

"We called your place a few times, couldn't reach you. At first we figured maybe you'd gone back to Burlington for a couple of days and took your brother with you."

"No."

Harry laughed. "Yeah, well, we know that now, don't we? Are you okay? I mean, physically? You guys all right?"

"Wrists a bit sore," I said. "Kind of hurt all over."

"Hell of a thing," Harry said. "Listen, these things I need you to sign, we can do that anytime. You get your life back to normal and then —"

"No," I said. "Let's do it now."

"Well, sure, let me just check my book —"

"I'll be there in a few minutes."

"Ray, wait. Ray? You know you called me on my personal cell. Why didn't you call on the office line? Where'd you get this number?"

"See you soon," I said, and ended the call.

Thomas looked at me. "How's the president?" he asked.

I walked down the hall to my father's room, closed the door, and sat on the edge of the bed. I set the phone on the bedspread, ran my hands across the fabric, feeling the texture of its ridges on my palms.

What the hell was going on?

Harry Peyton had phoned the house pretending to be former president Clinton. The only person he could have hoped would have believed it was my brother. Harry knew about my brother's fantasies.

He was playing into them.

The call Lewis took couldn't have been the first one. No, there had to have been others before that. Calls my brother took. Conversations my brother believed he was having with

Bill Clinton.

But I also knew, from my own observations, that Thomas had had these conversations when there really was no one on the other end of the line. I'd seen him conducting imaginary chats without the aid of a telephone.

Harry Peyton knew about those chats.

And had decided to make them real.

I grabbed my phone, came out of Dad's room, and went back in to see Thomas, who was still sitting, dejectedly, in his computer chair.

"When you'd get a call, on that phone, from . . . you know, what would he tell you?"

Thomas blinked. "You remember I told you, how he hadn't been as nice lately?"

"Yeah."

"He said something bad would happen to us if I talked to you about things. About things that had happened to me, and things that the president was telling me now. He'd say everything was just between us, and he wanted to know about me personally, about you, and Dad. He didn't used to ask those kinds of questions, when he would talk to me without the phone. When I would just hear him."

"What did he ask about Dad?"

"He wanted to know if he talked about his friends, whether Dad had told me anything bad about them. Because Mr. Clinton had to be sure that no one in my circle was an enemy or a spy or anything."

"What did you tell him?"

Thomas shrugged. "Not that much. I told him I didn't like Len Prentice, and that I really didn't like Mr. Peyton, which was why I didn't go to Dad's funeral, because I figured he would be there."

"Thomas," I said gently, "the thing that happened to you, a long time ago, in the window, it was Mr. Peyton who did that, wasn't it?"

His eyes looked distant. "Dad said I wasn't supposed to talk about that. Ever. Even after he said he was sorry, after he knew it was true. He said I couldn't talk about it until he knew what to do about it. But then, eventually, I might have to." He looked away. "I didn't want to ever do that. Dad made me try to forget about it for so long, I didn't think I could do that. Tell the police, or talk about it in a courtroom. No, never."

I went to my phone, went looking for a number that turned out not to be in its memory. I needed a phone book.

"We'll talk later, okay, Thomas?" I said. "And go get you a computer?"

"Okay," he said. "Do you want me to make dinner?" It was such an unexpected offer I thought I might cry.

"I don't even know if we have anything," I said. "We'll sort it all out when I get back."

I came down the stairs, glanced outside, saw Detective Duckworth standing out on the porch, waiting for me. I found the phone book in a drawer in the kitchen, opened it, looked up a home number for Len Prentice.

"Hello?" It was Marie.

"Hi, Marie. It's Ray."

"Oh Ray, oh my, Len and I, we heard about you and Thomas on —"

"I have a quick question for you. I just need you to answer this for me."

"What? What do you want to know?"

"When Len went to Thailand, I know you didn't go with him, but did anyone else?"

"Yes, of course. Harry went with him. Harry Peyton. Although Len was a bit disappointed because Harry was always off doing his own thing. Tell me how you and Thomas are —"

I hung up, went out on the porch to join Duckworth.

"Change of plan," I said.

On the way into town in Duckworth's car, I tried my best to explain what I believed had happened. That when Harry Peyton found out Dad knew about his Thailand adventures, and that Dad now believed Thomas's tale of what Harry had done to him when he was a boy, Peyton panicked.

"I think he killed my father," I said. "Or at the very least, did nothing to save him. And maybe even before Dad died, and certainly after, Harry started calling my brother on his line, played into his delusion. He was trying to make sure Thomas didn't talk about what Harry had done to him, I think. Figured Thomas would keep quiet about it if it was a presidential order."

"This is the damnedest thing I've ever come across," Duckworth said. "And believe me, I've come across some things."

"What did Harry say when he called you?" I asked. "About Thomas, and what he'd seen on the Whirl360 site?"

"What's that?" Duckworth said, his wrist resting atop the steering wheel.

"I went to see Harry, told him about what Thomas had seen online, that maybe it really did mean something, that I needed to talk to the police but was going to have a hard time convincing them. Harry said he knew you, that he'd give you a call on my behalf."

Duckworth shook his head slowly. "I've known Harry Peyton a long time, but he never called me about that."

"Son of a bitch," I said. "The goddamn son of a bitch."

Duckworth glanced over at me. "You think he knows that you know?"

"Last thing he asked me was, why did I call him on his cell? Wanted to know how I got the number."

Duckworth ran his tongue over his upper

lip. "I'd say he knows."

"Yeah," I said. "I think he does."

We walked into Harry Peyton's law office. Duckworth had insisted on taking the lead, and went through the door ahead of me.

Peyton's secretary, Alice, looked up from her desk. She smiled at the two of us.

"Hi, Barry," she said to Detective Duckworth. Then, "Ray, my God, I can't believe what you've been going through."

"We need to talk to Harry," Duckworth said.

"The two of you are together?" Alice said.

"We need to talk to Harry, Alice," Duckworth repeated with a sternness he hadn't used before.

Alice's smile faded. She picked up her phone. "Some folks here to see you," she said.

The heavy wood door ten feet beyond her desk opened a couple of seconds later. Harry kept hold of the knob on his side as his eyes landed on us. First me, then Barry.

It was seeing me there, with a police detective, that did it. I could see it in his eyes. He knew it was over.

"Harry," Duckworth said, starting to walk toward the door, "I need to ask you a few questions."

Harry stepped back and slammed the door closed.

Duckworth bolted forward, turned the

644

knob, and pushed, but the door wouldn't budge. I got up next to him and, like an idiot, tried the door myself.

"Harry!" Duckworth shouted. "Open the door!"

Harry said nothing.

Duckworth snapped at Alice, "Is there another way out of that office?"

"No," she said. "The windows don't open."

"You got a key?"

While Alice rooted through her desk drawer, I put my mouth up to the door and shouted, "I know, Harry! I know what you did! To my dad, and to my brother!" I banged on it with my fist. "Come out here! Come out here, goddamn it! We know! Dad found those pictures on your phone and —"

"Get the fuck out of here!" he shouted from inside his office.

"He found those pictures on your phone and he knew! He knew Thomas had been telling the truth!"

"Find that damn key," Duckworth told Alice.

"You're finished, Harry!" I shouted. "Even if they don't convict you for what you did to Thomas, or my father, you're ruined in this town." I brought my voice down, but loud enough that he could still hear me. "Everyone's going to know what you are, Harry. I'm going to make damn sure of that. That you're a pervert, and a murderer."

"Here it is," Alice said.

"Give it," Duckworth said, taking the key from her.

"There's something you need to know," Alice said.

"You hear me, Harry?" I said, raising my voice again. "Do you hear me?"

Duckworth nudged me aside, getting ready to slip the key into the lock. "What's that?" he said to Alice.

"He keeps a —"

That was when we heard the shot.

"Down!" Duckworth said and instantly put his arms around me and carried the both of us to the floor.

Alice, still behind her desk, screamed. And kept screaming.

"Stay down," Duckworth said, pressing his hand on my back as he got to his feet. He took a gun from his jacket and called out, "Harry!"

No answer.

"Harry!"

Duckworth slipped the key into the lock, turned it, then put his hand on the knob and turned, pushing slowly on the door at the same time.

"Oh, man," he said.

SEVENTY-FIVE

"I've only been here once before," Thomas said as we turned off the main road and into the well-manicured grounds of the Promise Falls cemetery. "When Mom died, remember?"

"I remember," I said, taking the Audi down to a crawl as we meandered along the narrow, paved roadway, stones and memorials gliding past our windows. Thomas, who did not think much of the navigation skills of Maria, my in-dash GPS lady, didn't touch the system on the way over.

The events of the last week had changed him. Changed us all.

But Thomas wasn't like the rest of us. He'd always seemed, certainly to me, incapable of change. He was a prisoner of his illness. And yet, he was not the same person he used to be.

A couple of days after Harry Peyton had taken his own life, I bought Thomas a new computer. We got it all set up at home, and he was right back onto Whirl360 as I went downstairs to open a beer.

Twenty minutes later, he was down in the kitchen. It wasn't time for lunch, or dinner. He just needed a break. He took a Coke out of the fridge, sat at the table and drank it, and then went back upstairs. When I peeked in on him later, he was reading the *Times* online.

Wonders never ceased.

He'd been to see Dr. Grigorin, and when she spoke to me after his appointment, she said she'd noticed a change, too.

"Let's just see," she said, careful not to raise any expectations. "But I think he's going to make the adjustment well. It's possible, and I don't want to read too much into this, but Harry Peyton's death may have been, in some way, liberating. Maybe Harry was one of the reasons Thomas didn't want to come out of the house."

Thomas claimed to be looking forward to his new accommodations. "Staying in this house," he'd said to me that morning, "reminds me too much of Mom and Dad. When it was me and Dad, that was okay, but with both of them gone, the place feels kind of strange." He'd paused. "And I know you don't want to live here with me."

"Thomas, that's —"

"You want to live with Julie. So you can have sex with her."

648

"Yeah, well," I'd said.

"I don't want you to get me into any more trouble," he'd said. A familiar refrain these days. Like I'd knocked over the first domino. Like it was me who saw Bridget Sawchuck online.

After breakfast, he'd asked to be driven to our father's grave, so that he could finally pay his respects.

I'd told him what had happened at Peyton's office, that I had figured out a few things. That Peyton had assaulted him back when he lived above a shop on Saratoga. That Dad, having seen the pictures on Peyton's phone, had finally come to believe Thomas. Everyone was a believer now. The police, as part of the investigation into Peyton's suicide, seized all his computers and found plenty of the kinds of images that made my stomach turn just to think of them.

I did not tell Thomas my belief that Harry Peyton was responsible for our father's death. It was mostly conjecture on my part, but it made sense. I could imagine Harry coming out, trying to get my father to back off. The two of them arguing, the tractor flipping over.

I chose not to tell Thomas because I felt he'd been through enough. And since there weren't going to be any charges leveled against Harry, this was never going to go to court. None of it would ever come out.

"They're in the same plot, right?" Thomas

said as I brought the car to a stop. "Mom and Dad?"

"That's right."

"Did you know you can see this cemetery on the computer? There's a really good satellite view of it. I've looked at it lots of times. I know exactly where to go."

And he did. He hopped out of the car with enthusiasm and strode off across the lawn. I came around the car and caught up with him.

As he approached the gravestone, he slowed, stood a respectful six feet away directly in front of it, and bowed his head ever so slightly, his hands clasped together in front of him.

I came up behind my brother and rested a hand on his shoulder.

"Hi, Dad," he said. "I would have gone to the funeral but I didn't want to see Mr. Peyton. But I thought I should finally come and see you. Mr. Peyton is dead now, and I think that's a good thing, even though you're probably not supposed to say something like that."

I squeezed his shoulder.

"Anyway, I miss you. Ray is teaching me to do more things. I'm making meals and learning how to look after myself more, which is another good thing, because I'm moving to this place where you have to help out."

He stopped talking, but he showed no sign of wanting to walk away. I had the sense there was something else he wanted to tell our father. I gave his shoulder another squeeze.

"So, I also wanted to say I'm sorry. Not just about not going to the funeral, and not helping out more." He swallowed. "I wanted to say I'm sorry about pushing you, on the stairs." He paused. "And on the hill."

My hand froze.

"I'm sorry I got so upset about maybe having to tell the police things about Mr. Peyton. I just had to come out and talk to you about it. I never meant to shove you. And I'm real sorry I didn't call for help right away." Another pause. "I was really scared."

I took my hand off Thomas's shoulder.

"So, I guess that's all," he said to our father. "I'll come up and see you again soon."

Then he turned to me and said, "Can we go see my new place now? I'd like to figure out where all my stuff is going to go."

He stepped around me and started walking. I stood there, numb, and watched as Thomas made his way back to the car.

ACKNOWLEDGMENTS

I had help.

Thank you to Susan Lamb, Eva Kolcze, Danielle Perez, Juliet Ewers, Nick Storring, Kristin Cochrane, Spencer Barclay, Mark Rusher, Helen Heller, Bill Massey, Jeff Winch, Kara Welsh, Cathy Paine, Sophie Mitchell, Alex Kingsmill, Paige Barclay, Ali Karim, Brad Martin, Mark Streatfield and Elia Morrison.

And, of course, Neetha.